THE

PEACE

KEEPER

THE

PEACE

KEEPER

a novel

B.L. BLANCHARD

47N⬤RTH

Text copyright © 2022 by Brooke Blanchard Tabshouri
All rights reserved.

Published by 47North, Seattle

www.apub.com

Amazon, the Amazon logo, and 47North are trademarks of Amazon.com, Inc., or its affiliates.

ISBN-13: 9781542036511
ISBN-10: 1542036518

Cover design by Faceout Studio, Molly von Borstel

Printed in the United States of America

For Toufic.
You were right.
Don't tell anyone I said that.

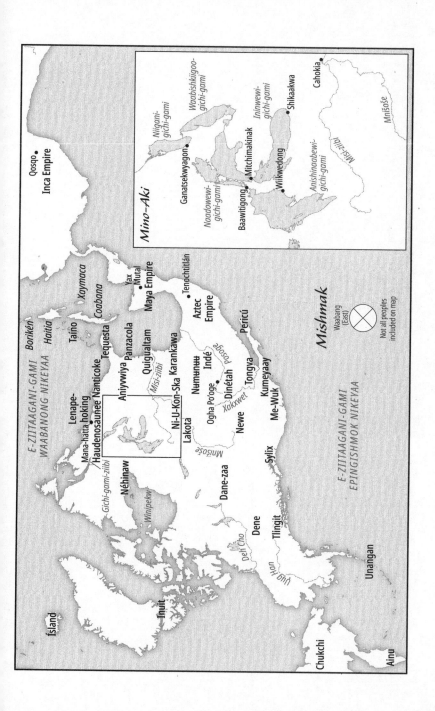

An Urban Indian belongs to the city, and cities belong to the earth. Everything here is formed in relation to every other living and nonliving thing from the earth. All our relations. The process that brings anything to its current form—chemical, synthetic, technological, or otherwise—doesn't make the product not a product of the living earth. Buildings, freeways, cars—are these not of the earth? Were they shipped in from Mars, the moon? Is it because they're processed, manufactured, or that we handle them? Are we so different? Were we at one time not something else entirely, Homo sapiens, single-celled organisms, space dust, unidentifiable pre-bang quantum theory? Cities form in the same way as galaxies . . . We ride buses, trains, and cars across, over, and under concrete plains. Being Indian has never been about returning to the land. The land is everywhere or nowhere.

—*Tommy Orange, There There*

Grandfather,
Look at our brokenness.
We know that in all creation
Only the human family
Has strayed from the Sacred Way.

We know that we are the ones
Who are divided
And we are the ones
Who must come back together
To walk in the Sacred Way.

Grandfather,
Sacred One,
Teach us love, compassion, and honour
That we may heal the earth
And heal each other.

—*Dr. Art Solomon, "Grandfather Story"*

Chapter One

Anishinaabe Moon: Manoomin Giizis (Ricing Moon)
Islamic Calendar: 13 Dhu al-Hijjah 1441
Chinese Calendar: Cycle 78, year 37, month 6, day 14 (Year of the Rat)
Hebrew Calendar: 13 Av 5780
Mayan Calendar: 13.0.7.13.2
Gregorian Calendar: Monday, 3 August 2020
Ethiopian Calendar: 27 Hamle 2012

Everyone in Baawitigong remembered where they were the night Neebin was murdered.

Except for her son.

It happened the night of the ceremony celebrating the beginning of the traditional Manoomin harvest. A full Ricing Moon had bathed the village in silver light, and the sound of drums, dancing, and laughter had filled the crisp and cloudless sky. Like many other seventeen-year-old boys, Chibenashi had left the harvest festival early with his friends, partied a little too hard, and passed out. When he woke up, his mother was gone, and so was his memory of the night.

His sister, who had been only twelve when it happened, never recovered from the trauma of losing her mother so young. Their father confessed to the murder and had disappeared from their lives as suddenly as their mother had. Taking care of his sister for the last twenty years had been both his privilege and his penance.

"Ashwiyaa?"

This morning, she lay on the floor in the living room of their wigwam, neither seeing nor hearing, wrapped in a blanket with Binesi, the thunderbird, stitched in beads with its wings spread protectively across her back and around her arms as the gray morning light peeked through the windows. The fireplace—large, open, and framed by river rocks—was empty and cold, ashes from fires past layered one on top of another in a dull heap. Ashwiyaa withdrew deeper into herself, spinning the blanket into a cocoon around her. Chibenashi envied her. She was like this most mornings, especially now. Tomorrow was Manoomin.

Chibenashi gently shook Ashwiyaa's shoulder.

"Miine!" she yelped with a start. She began hyperventilating. He wrapped his arms around her and shushed her, desperate to calm her before she spun out of control and he was trapped at home with her for the rest of the day. He rocked her back and forth as if she were a baby. Ashwiyaa's breathing slowed in time with her big brother's hand stroking down her long hair. She shivered like a new fawn, afraid of every snapped twig, hoping that if she lay still, she would disappear. Outside the window, they could hear the tinkle of the wind chimes from their neighbor's home. Ashwiyaa's gaze was fixed on the unblinking eye of the dream catcher in the window. Their mother had twisted the branch and woven intertwining helixes from blue sinew, then strung it with white and yellow beads and shells so it looked like a galaxy. It was like she still watched over them, catching some but not all of the nightmares before they reached her children.

It did nothing for guilt.

"Did you dream about anything last night?" he asked.

She did not respond. Which usually meant that she could not remember her dream. Not a bad sign but not a great one either. *Not bad* was about as good as things got in their family, so he let himself smile just a bit.

The smartwatch on his wrist dinged. Ashwiyaa knew what this meant. She gave him a pained look and grabbed his wrist. Her grip was strong and her nails long and ragged. They dug into the flesh of his arm like talons.

"Meoquanee will be here in a little bit to check on you," he said. Ashwiyaa stared at him, silently, shaking her head. "I promise."

A staring contest ensued. If Ashwiyaa won, he was staying home. Slowly, painfully, she released him. Victory was fleeting. Clearly, it was going to be one of *those* days.

He quickly showered and dressed; he had a small window of opportunity to get out the door before this turned into an ordeal. He made for the door and walked straight into his mother's best friend, Meoquanee. What she lacked in height and girth she made up for in stubbornness and confidence. "Tall on the inside," she called it. Chibenashi had once told her that that should have been her name.

Meoquanee bore a basket full of frybread and venison covered with a towel to keep it warm—comfort food for what was one of the hardest days of the year for him and Ashwiyaa. "Better than that garbage you find down at the port," she said in greeting, as if frybread were healthy. Chibenashi met her morning smile with a scowl, and she patted him on the cheek in return and brushed past him into the wigwam. He grunted and shut the door.

Meoquanee greeted Ashwiyaa in a singsong voice as she waved a sprig of cedar to purify the wigwam. In response, Ashwiyaa curled up further. Chibenashi wanted to join her. It was too early, and Meoquanee was too happy. Meoquanee hummed to herself as she put away the food and began tidying the kitchen.

Meoquanee had once confessed to him that she had always felt responsible for his mother's murder, that she should have recognized the signs of a problem in the marriage, and yet she hadn't intervened.

3

Meoquanee had been making up for her perceived failure by caring for Chibenashi and Ashwiyaa as if they were her own. No amount of protest could make her stop. Everyone else had stopped long ago. Not her. Even though they were now in their thirties, she came every day as if they were still children in need of a mother. Chibenashi supposed they still were.

Chibenashi and Ashwiyaa had not been blessed with a large clan or the endless parade of aunts, uncles, grandparents, cousins, cousins of cousins, great-aunts, and great-uncles common to most other families in the village. While everyone in the community was "family" to a certain degree, it wasn't the same. So Chibenashi, Ashwiyaa, and Meoquanee had stitched one together—imperfect and mismatched but somehow a more cohesive whole. Meoquanee's marriage had ended long ago, and her son and husband had disappeared to Shikaakwa shortly thereafter. As far as Chibenashi knew, Meoquanee had not spoken with either of them since the day they left. He never asked, and she never told. They were two motherless children and a childless mother, connected through the double-carbon bond of grief. Each filled an empty hole for the other.

Meoquanee had finished the kitchen and moved to the living room with a small bowl of frybread. She sat next to Ashwiyaa on the floor and propped her up next to her, stroking her hair the way Chibenashi had earlier. Meoquanee offered Ashwiyaa a piece of frybread, but she shook her head. Meoquanee looked around the room and swept her eyes up to the ceiling, where the sanded-birch walls sloped until they kissed at the top in a pointed arch. "You know," she said, "this wigwam is too big for the two of you."

It was, probably: multiroomed and multileveled yet cozy during the long, harsh, and unforgiving winters when the sun seemed to hibernate along with the animals. Its roof of tapered arches kept the heavy snows from accumulating. There were unused and empty spaces. But that didn't matter. These empty spaces were a memorial to the family that their father had destroyed. They were never leaving. *Chibenashi* was never leaving.

"Maybe," Chibenashi muttered. He knew where this was going.

"It can be hard, you know. Living where such a terrible crime occurred."

And there it was.

"We can handle it here," he said, trying to sand the defensive edge off his voice.

"No one is suggesting you can't," she agreed a little too readily. She stared at him carefully as she spoke. Meoquanee was a counselor, and she had that piercing look that made you feel like she could see through you to your thoughts. Her insight was sharp and usually right. It felt like ants crawling over his skin.

"Think about what's best for you, is all I'm asking." She glanced back at the birchbark boxes now stacked neatly on the shelf. "You and Ashwiyaa."

"I've got her," he said, his voice dropping an octave.

"I know. But you know, taking care of someone else means that you need to take care of yourself."

He had no interest in retreading this ground. "I'm off," he said. He craned his neck to see his sister, but she was still motionless, maybe even asleep. Good. Best for him to sneak out.

"Wait!" Meoquanee whisper-shouted and brought him a piece of venison wrapped in frybread. "You know you won't eat until lunchtime otherwise." Chibenashi smiled ruefully as he accepted the food and the feeling behind it, and made his way out.

◆ ◆ ◆

The beauty of living in a small village was that Chibenashi knew everyone. The downside was that everyone knew him.

Baawitigong, a port town where ships from one great sea passed through on their way to the other, covered both sides of the river connecting Anishinaabewi-gichigami and Naadowewi-gichigami. In the summer, the port was full of cruise ships with tourists from all over the world: Europe, the Islamic Empire, Aztec and Mayan nations far to the south, not to mention the other nations of Mishimak. Walking down by the port, you could hear a plethora of languages, not just the Anishinaabemowin spoken by the various tribes that had come together to form the multicultural nation of Mino-Aki: the Anishinaabe, Odawaa, Neshnabé, Hocągara, Myaamia, Memoceqtaw, Maskoutench, Meshkwahkihaki, Othâkîwa, Giiwigaabaw, Shawanwaki, and Wyandot.

He made his way down the main road past the communal farms that the locals shared: a sugar bush grove for maple syrup, where bucket after bucket was hung from the trees; a grove of raspberry and blackberry bushes, where families dropped berries into jars tied around their waists; and seemingly endless rows of various types of squash. These led into another cluster of wigwams, including the one where Dakaasin had grown up. The pang as he passed it was as fresh now as it had been the first day after she left. He crossed the center of the village, where the memorial to the Great World War stood, commemorating those who had died fighting overseas to protect Baawitigong's freedom nearly eighty years earlier. Chibenashi's grandfather's name was on it. He inhaled the sweet smell from a spiral of smoke from the tobacco burning at its base.

Despite its location at the center of a major river that connected the two largest gichigamiin, Baawitigong remained small and true to its roots as the ancestral home of the Anishinaabe. The world still came to it in droves, for there was nothing like the beauty of Baawitigong in the summer; Chibenashi did not have to leave the town in order to know that. In the winter, giant icebreakers cut through the sheets of ice to deliver timber and iron ore from the end of one lake to the tip of the other. All these ships stopped in Baawitigong, but none of them stayed. In the summer months, the village grew large with both tourists and seasonal workers to cater to those tourists. Outside of those magical few weeks, however, Baawitigong was much like the rest of his corner of Mino-Aki: full of farmers, fishers, loggers, and ranchers. Small enough to know everyone and everything that happened. There were no secrets here, and nowhere to hide from the prying eyes of one's friends, family, or neighbors.

"Boozhoo, Chibenashi."

Or colleagues.

Chibenashi raised his hand slightly in greeting at his two fellow Peacekeepers as he entered the dakoniwewigamig for the day's work. They were the only three in the village.

"Boozhoo, Ziigwan," he said around a mouthful of apple he'd picked off one of the trees that lined the road between his wigwam and the dakoniwewigamig. It was one of his favorite things about summer, and particularly the Ricing Moon: it was as if the trees would never stop giving.

Ziigwan was a couple of years younger than Chibenashi and, like him, had grown up in Baawitigong. Her head was shaved on one side and gelled into spikes on the other, with the tips dyed pink. He handed her an apple, and she gave him a small smile.

The head of the dakoniwewigamig, Peezhickee, sat snoring at his table in the corner, his makizin-covered feet crisscrossed on the table. His hair, long and gray, fell past his shoulders. His creased, leathery face scrunched up with every deep inhale and exhale.

"Slow day," Ziigwan said, as if it weren't slow here every day.

Chibenashi fixed himself an espresso from the machine in the corner. "Mmm," he said in reply.

"You could take the day off, you know. Peezhickee and I have things covered."

Peezhickee made a particularly loud snore as if to punctuate the point. One foot slid off the table but did not wake the old man.

"I'm sure," Chibenashi said with a chuckle. He sat next to her and made himself comfortable. Their role in Baawitigong primarily entailed walking from one end of the village to the other, chatting with people, and waiting for something to happen. And Chibenashi did not like chatting.

"Big celebration tomorrow for Manoomin," she said, changing the subject—but not really—as she scrolled through her phone. Without looking at it, Chibenashi knew she was reading the community events page for Baawitigong. He knew it had likely been linked from the local news site, which had a feature story on it about his mother's murder that he'd refused to read. "I hear tell there's going to be a pretty good turnout."

"Mmm."

"You planning on being there?"

Chibenashi nodded. He sipped his coffee with deliberate care.

Ziigwan looked at him from the corner of her eye. She always thought she was so subtle. "You planning to say anything?"

Chibenashi set his cup down on the table a bit harder than he meant to. The clang of copper on wood echoed through the room and startled them both out of their politeness. That was all the response he was prepared to give her, and all she apparently needed to hear. She went back to her careful review of the phone in her hand. Peezhickee continued to snore his way through the exchange.

After her death, the sacred fire had been lit, and their mother's spirit had traveled for four days and nights to join her ancestors. One day, Ashwiyaa's and Chibenashi's spirits would follow her there. There was no cause to continue to grieve—not really. She had moved on long ago. But tradition also held that children were vulnerable when the spirits left the body. Precautions were taken; Chibenashi still remembered the scrape of charcoal across his forehead after his mother's death but before her burial. It had replaced the stickiness of her blood. But the hurt still lingered, particularly on the anniversary. He appreciated that there would be no formal commemoration today. But everyone still remembered.

Chibenashi was not going to speak at the sacred fire. Why would he do so? To accept the hollow condolences from people who knew him but did not really know him, to shrug off the people who simply wanted to be close to notoriety, no matter what it was about? For people to take his picture and stream his words live on their phones in a perverse form of "I was here"? To have to stand away from his sister in order to say the words while exposing her to torment she was not equipped to cope with?

Words were meaningless on the best of days, and this day was among the worst.

◆ ◆ ◆

"Have you eaten yet?"

Chibenashi shook his head as his best friend, Kichewaishke, stepped aside to welcome him into his wigwam. Kichewaishke lived just down the road from Chibenashi and Ashwiyaa, yet Chibenashi's visits were rare. He always needed to get back to his sister, but tonight he had too much on his mind to sort through before he was prepared to handle someone else.

Kichewaishke was a mashkikiwinini, tending mostly to emergency and urgent-care illnesses and injuries. During the heavy tourist season, he primarily treated alcohol poisoning or severe sunburns. In winter, when just the locals remained in Baawitigong, he also acted as the general healer, often with people simply popping by his wigwam seeking advice. More than once, he had stitched up a cut at his kitchen table while also sharing a cup of coffee and gossip. He always said that between himself and Chibenashi, they knew all of Baawitigong's secrets. Chibenashi never bothered to tell him that he had none.

"Boozhoo," said Kichewaishke's wife, Okimaskew. "Have you eaten yet?"

She had one hand on her very pregnant stomach and held the hand of their four-year-old daughter, Biidaaban, in the other. Biidaaban was small for her age, with wide eyes like black holes. Nothing escaped them.

"Do you like my dress?" Biidaaban asked in greeting. She was wearing her regalia for Manoomin: a dress in deep jewel tones of purples, greens, and splashes of yellow, with flowers embroidered in undulating designs. It was covered in small bells, as were her makizinan. She let go of her mother's hand to demonstrate a twirl and a few dance moves for him. "I'm making jingling music."

"It's very nice," he said.

"It's pretty," she corrected him, still spinning.

"It's very pretty."

Suddenly, Biidaaban stopped. "Why are you sad?"

Chibenashi couldn't help but chuckle at that, ignoring his friend's tutting at his daughter's bluntness. He'd always appreciated that about Biidaaban. She scared him a little.

Biidaaban scowled at his reaction, which made Chibenashi only want to laugh harder. "Why are you laughing at me? You are sad," she said with authority. "You haven't been this sad since your uncle died." That had been two years ago.

"I was."

"But you're not always sad."

She didn't need to know the truth. "No, thankfully."

"I remember earlier in the summer, when you brought the blackberries over, and we ate them by the fire. You were happy. You laughed a lot. But you haven't come over since then."

"Chibenashi has to look after his little sister, remember?" Kichewaishke said. "Just like you'll have to look after yours once she comes."

"That doesn't make any sense. His sister is a grown-up."

As if Ashwiyaa's ears were burning, Chibenashi's phone buzzed with what he knew was a text from her.

Chibenashi touched the phone in his pocket by habit, then took the little girl's hand. "You're right," he said. "She is a grown-up. But that doesn't mean that I stop taking care of her."

"Well, I'm not doing it when I'm old like you."

The adults all laughed, which made Biidaaban scowl. Okimaskew led her daughter toward her room while Chibenashi and Kichewaishke went back outside to the front of the wigwam by way of the kitchen, where Kichewaishke grabbed two bottles of baakwaanaatig lemonade on the way out. This was the good imported stuff, sweetened with honey instead of maple syrup, which everyone in the village used when they made it at home. They settled themselves on two chairs. It was late, but at that time of year, the sun would not set until well after most people would have gone to bed. Kichewaishke animoshan, Waabigwan, perked up at the sight of Chibenashi and followed them outside to lie down between them, tail wagging eagerly.

Chibenashi's phone buzzed again. This time he checked it. Ashwiyaa wanted to know where he was and when he would be home. He briefly tapped the answers to her questions, then stuffed the phone back in his pocket. He could feel Kichewaishke's eyes on him as he did so. Kichewaishke didn't say that Chibenashi didn't have to answer every single one of his sister's texts. He'd said it enough in the past.

Neither man spoke nor looked at the other as the sky slowly turned as pink as the drinks they nursed. They both knew what was coming, and why Chibenashi was there, and there was no point in talking about it.

Ashwiyaa texted a few more times, and Chibenashi dutifully responded to each one. He could feel her anxiety radiating from the phone. It made sense; he rarely deviated from his routine and was usually home by now. But he only wanted a few moments, just a few moments, free from responsibility, to sit with his friend in peace.

"You take on too much, you know," Kichewaishke said eventually. "You'll flame out if you don't let some of it go."

Chibenashi did not respond.

"I know tomorrow's going to be hard on you. But we're all here for you. All of us."

Chibenashi gripped the neck of the bottle tighter. It felt weird, the sweating glass in his hand. Only imported products were packaged in something as indestructible and impractical as glass.

"If you want, I can send something with you for Ashwiyaa?" Kichewaishke offered. Chibenashi shook his head.

Kichewaishke waited a few moments, then spoke again. "It wasn't your fault, you know. No one thinks that. No one has ever thought that."

Chibenashi bolted out of the chair as if it were on fire. He did not speak or move once he was on his feet, but he could feel the night closing in on him, though the sun still shone. Flocks of omiimiiwag traversed the sky, blotting out the sun like fast-moving clouds, the distant chittering filling the silence between the two friends. Their shadows crossed his face.

His phone buzzed with another text. He didn't even have to look to know it was Ashwiyaa. It was always her. No one else ever texted anymore.

Kichewaishke was wrong. Of course it had been his fault. If he hadn't gotten drunk and stupid at Manoomin—if he had just been there for his sister, she wouldn't be so dependent on him now. It didn't matter that he'd been told for twenty years that it hadn't been his fault. He knew better.

"Thank you for the drink," he said, not facing his friend. Without releasing the grip on the bottle, he turned and staggered home, anxiety all but gluing his feet to the ground.

"I mean it," Kichewaishke called after him. But Chibenashi was far enough away that he could ignore him without being rude.

◆　◆　◆

Ashwiyaa had mercifully gone to bed early that night, which was the closest Chibenashi ever got to a vacation. He sat in his living room, alone, in the dark, sipping some iced tea from the fridge, and flipped through the channels of the TV. It was like having company. The news was all about Manoomin, interviewing families for their plans. Not what he wanted to hear. He briefly landed on a show set in Shikaakwa and changed the channel as fast as he could. He saw an old movie, a love story, he'd once watched in a theater—a period piece involving an arranged marriage that had led to the two leads falling in love. It was the wedding scene, and the blanket was being draped over the nervous couple. He remembered when he'd first seen the film, and whom he'd seen it with. The reminder that once upon a time he hadn't been so alone led him to mash the buttons on the remote in hopes of quashing the memory. He knew it was pathetic to let a twenty-year-old film dredge up memories of a relationship that had been over almost as long, and that awareness made it even worse. He didn't often miss alcohol, but in this moment, it might have helped.

He flipped to a documentary; a European man was speaking, and the subtitles revealed he was discussing wars fought between kings who all claimed absolute power over the same patch of beach. They had been fighting this battle for hundreds of years. Chibenashi snorted, shook his head, and changed the channel. As if any person could actually claim to "own" the earth or any part of it. He knew about the attitudes that other backward cultures had—they drew invisible lines around the land, claiming it for their own, and those lines were worth both living and dying for. Mino-Aki had no defined borders like that. No nation in Mishmak did. Such lines were not theirs to draw. You lived on the land; you didn't own it. You knew where lands roughly changed hands, but that was it. If you traveled internationally within Mishmak, your passport wasn't checked until you arrived at your destination, if it was checked at all.

The next channel stopped him short. It was a travel show, talking about the lush beaches of Abyssinia on the east coast of Africa. He paused with the cup of tea halfway to his lips as his eyes drank in the scenery. He gulped without swallowing anything. Abyssinia was so far away in every sense; it might as well be on another planet. Chibenashi knew of people who had traveled so far away, some even on a regular basis, and Baawitigong had a large influx of tourists, especially at this time of year. But the idea of being the one to go, to experience the sights and smells and tastes of another nation, walk on a different patch of the earth and truly appreciate how vast and diverse it was . . . he didn't dare dream he could actually do it. It was impossible. Ashwiyaa could never go. So he could never go. And watching it through the screen only made that feel more real.

He shut off the TV and stalked off to bed, downing the rest of the tea as he did. He was crashing. He figured he might as well go to sleep and get the misery of Manoomin over with.

Chapter Two

According to the stories the elders told to children in school, at bedtime, and around fires, it was prophesied, back when the Anishinaabe lived along the great ocean, that they should head westward. They would stop when they saw the food growing on the water. That food was manoomin, wild rice growing in thick paddies on the lakes—bountiful enough to feed entire tribes, healthy enough to be the staple of nearly every meal. So the Anishinaabe stopped, and they'd stayed ever since.

Many tourists came to Baawitigong specifically to view the harvest and celebration to follow. They were kept at a respectful distance, with a sea of smartphones and cameras capturing the odyssey of canoes that entered the lake at the same time.

The families of Baawitigong piled into the village's traditional birchbark canoes, waiting for them in the reeds. Kichewaishke stepped into his behind his wife and daughter. He took hold of a long birch pole and pushed the canoe forward into the small lake. In front of him, Okimaskew held two long cedar sticks. The canoe made its way into the thicket of manoomin stalks, which grew as thick as a virgin forest. Okimaskew bent the stalks and whacked them with her sticks. All the other families in their canoes did the same. Husk-covered grains began raining down into the canoes, creating a loud *swish-swish*. It could be heard across the lake amid the hum of traditional songs from the locals along the shore and in the canoes.

Chibenashi stood along the side—one eye on the locals, the other on the tourists, taking it all in. Officially he was on patrol, working security at this event rather than attending it. Not that it ever needed protection from anything.

Chibenashi had not participated in the harvest since the night of his mother's murder. He remembered her soft hands and gentle voice instructing them how to tap the stalks—not too hard, not too soft—to get the greatest yield of rice. It was a tradition handed down to her by her parents and grandparents, going back hundreds of years to when the ancient prophecy was first fulfilled. So much was automated these days, as the world grew smaller and technology eased the workload. But harvesting manoomin had been untouched by so-called progress and likely always would be.

Even if he'd wanted to participate, it wasn't like he could. People were kind to his face but not behind his back, making comments among themselves when they thought he couldn't hear. Or maybe when they just did not care about whether he could. "The prisoner's son," they'd mutter. "His father was locked away," they'd explain to their visiting relatives, who would be sure to keep their distance from Chibenashi after that. In the beginning, after it had happened, people were supportive—at least outwardly. They wanted to help, tried to help. But Ashwiyaa had responded badly to it, and eventually they all stopped coming. Then they stopped sending food. Stopped asking after his sister, after him. His father's stain had been tattooed on him, the mark so indelible that nothing could ever wash it off. Going to prison meant the system had failed all involved, that the person was beyond saving, and nothing could be done to make the family of his victims whole. No one else in Baawitigong had been locked away in recent memory. Chibenashi and Ashwiyaa were part of the community but only to the extent basic politeness required. Outside of that, he was the black fly on their otherwise idyllic bouquet.

"No Ashwiyaa today?" Meoquanee's voice was quiet but still managed to jar Chibenashi out of his thoughts. He hadn't even heard her approach.

He shook his head. "No, and if I weren't on duty . . ."

"She's stronger than you think, you know," she said.

Meoquanee knew better than most how bad things had gotten, and even she didn't have a full appreciation for how bad it was.

"No harvest for you this year?" he asked instead.

She snorted with laughter. "Of course not," she said. "And I am completely fine with that."

In Shikaakwa, where her husband and son had settled, such community harvests weren't likely to happen. People left the big cities to go home to their families for the first day of Manoomin, one of the largest holiday migrations in the world, rivaled only by the Lunar New Year in China in terms of the sheer proportion of people traveling. Meoquanee's family, however, never came to be with her. Her ex-husband's absence was to be expected, but Chibenashi knew that their son's refusal cut her like a knife. Baawitigong was the home of her son's ancestors on both sides; turning his back on her had been the same as turning his back on his heritage. It was unthinkable.

Others had not returned for the harvest, though they likely had their own nonfamily reasons for doing so. Chibenashi had not gone out of his way to notice absences, but it was apparent all the same.

Chibenashi's phone pinged. Officially, he wasn't supposed to check his phone while on duty, but like many rules in the Baawitigong dakoniwewigamig, this was loosely followed at best. He glanced around, saw that no one was watching him. All were watching the canoes return to the shore with their spoils. He could look.

Ashwiyaa. Of course.

Where are you?

Working.

Ashwiyaa replied almost immediately. He pictured her staring at the screen, her knuckles white as she held her phone in a vise grip, so desperate for his response that she was hardly blinking.

How much longer?

Chibenashi worried his lip a bit between his teeth.

It's Manoomin. Probably will be late.

I need you to come home.

He sighed, typed quickly, barely looking at his phone as muscle memory took over.

You know I can't.

He thought for a moment, then added:

I can ask Meoquanee to come by.

Chibenashi almost smiled at his own cleverness. Meoquanee would have a surrogate child to attend to during this large family-oriented holiday, and Ashwiyaa could be with someone she knew and trusted during a difficult day. Meanwhile, he could finish out his shift in peace, maybe even be able to take his mind off the heaviness of the day. A win all around.

His phone remained silent for what felt like a long time. He'd almost begun to worry when the response came.

No.

You.

And then, after a moment's hesitation:

Please.

Chibenashi felt the pull. He wanted nothing more than to give his little sister what she wanted. But today, he couldn't.

I'm sorry.

Then he stuffed the phone in his pocket. It vibrated once, twice, three times. Then three more in quick succession as his sister was no doubt pleading with him to cut his shift short. He understood. He should have been home with her—today of all days.

The phone buzzed, longer this time, meaning that Ashwiyaa was now calling him. He silenced it without removing it from his pocket. He felt it vibrate a moment later with a voice mail, which he ignored.

It killed him to do it.

◆ ◆ ◆

People were now dancing the rice.

It was one of those beautiful summer nights where the land and the people and the feeling in the air were just so beautiful that the sky itself would fight off the darkness longer and longer each day. *Just a few more moments to enjoy this splendor,* it beseeched like a child trying to avoid bedtime. *One more peek. I don't want to miss a thing.*

Everyone had migrated from the lakeshore to the wide field near the medicine lodge. Around a large sacred fire, huge iron pots had been filled with rice and heated up, just until the seeds began to pop open. After the rice had been parched, removed, and left to cool, it was ready to be danced.

All over, large tarps were laid out with two long cedar or birch logs, one end on the ground, the other elevated and leaning against a bench or another tree or even held up by people. The dancers, ranging from elders to children to mothers to young men, tied soft deerskin makizinan on their feet. The newly harvested rice was poured onto the tarps under the logs, and the dancers stepped in between them. When the music began, people sang as the dancers held on to the logs and began stepping in a slow heel-to-toe motion, twisting from side to side as they did. This ancient tradition was how their ancestors separated the pale husk from the dark edible grain inside. The piles of manoomin grew darker as the pointy black grains began to emerge from the husks. Alcohol had been flowing for many all day, and as the evening progressed, the dances became more and more clumsy and less and less rhythmic.

Once the rice had been danced, it was scooped up into traditional shallow birchbark baskets to be winnowed, further purifying the edible seed. This task was always handled by the oldest, most experienced person in each family. Toss the manoomin too high, and it would scatter on the ground; toss it too low, and the husks would not separate. It took a steady hand, trained eye, and years of experience to master it. The dust from the remaining husks flew out of the basket, catching the dying light of the evening. From the viewpoint of someone standing overhead, it would look like the entire event had been enveloped by a golden cloud. Eventually, enough of the husks were gone that the rice could be considered pure, and all would bring the first basketful to the sacred fire, where as a community they would cook and eat the first manoomin of the season together. Puffed in maple sugar, boiled in duck broth, fried in lard, and sopped up with frybread, all the traditional recipes were out in force tonight.

◆　◆　◆

The full Ricing Moon smiled over the scene.

Chibenashi and Meoquanee stood alone on the edge of the event, in the shadows of celebrating families, together in their isolation. If anyone saw them, they didn't acknowledge it. The laughter and music sounded louder than they should, like they were shouting in his face. Chibenashi watched young couples kissing in stolen dark corners, middle-aged couples reveling as if they were kids, and families dancing together. These were all things he'd once assumed he would have in his own life because why wouldn't he have the things that everyone wanted? This was back before *it* happened and his life changed from one of possibilities to one of resignation.

"Manoomin used to be my favorite night of the year," Meoquanee murmured.

Chibenashi nodded. "Mine too."

As they stood on the sidelines of the revelry, both silently mourned for the lost holiday they had once loved. Chibenashi ached for someone to notice them. No one did.

They watched the dancers around the sacred fire. Everyone wore their best festival regalia—buckskin and feathers and painted faces, jingling bells on skirts and jackets and makizinan. Beads decorated their clothing in shapes of their doodemag, their clans, which were represented by animals like beavers and adikameg and snapping turtles and cranes and deer, as well as other animals, real and mythical, including the Binesi. One waved the Anishinaabe flag: a medicine wheel divided into fourths to represent the four winds, four seasons, four stages of life, and four sacred medicines, each in a different color (white for north, yellow for east, red for south, and black for west) all against a white background. The firelight flickered off the glass beads, making the animals' eyes flash at the revelers. Old women handed out the manoomin that had been puffed and cooked in maple sugar, a treat for kids and adults alike. It was free for Anishinaabe, but tourists were charged.

"Will you have a drink?"

"Absolutely not." Chibenashi's response was out before Meoquanee had even finished her question. But what kind of question had that been? He was on duty, and he had learned the hard way what happened when he mixed alcohol with Manoomin.

He saw a hand waving at him from the other side of the crowd. Finally, an invitation. Kichewaishke was holding his daughter's hand, beckoning Chibenashi to come over. Little Biidaaban shook her hips to show off her new outfit again. The beads of the muskrat doodem stitched on her back reflected the flames, winking at him.

Meoquanee saw them, too, and smiled at the little girl. "Go," she said. "I've had about all I can handle of tonight anyway."

Chibenashi gave her a hug and kissed her cheek. "Can I ask a favor?"

"Always."

"Ashwiyaa is . . . well, would you mind looking in on her? Just for a few moments on your way home? I'll be off duty in a little while anyway, but she's having difficulty and . . . well, this year is particularly bad. I didn't expect to be out this late, and I should have taken the night off." He looked down. This was as much shame as he was willing to admit out loud.

Meoquanee nodded, gave Chibenashi another hug.

"Of course," she said. "I'll go now."

"I appreciate it."

"I'll see you again."

After giving him a kiss on the cheek, Meoquanee began weaving her way out through the throngs of people, quickly disappearing into the crowd.

Chibenashi pulled out his phone to text Ashwiyaa that Meoquanee was coming over after all, but before he could, Biidaaban rushed over and grabbed his hand.

"Miimishin!"

With surprising strength, she pulled him over to her father. Kichewaishke laughed and held up his hands as if to say, *I had nothing to do with this.*

As much as Chibenashi craved inclusion, he didn't want to dance. But Biidaaban was insistent, and even he was not resistant to her charms, much less a direct order. So he grabbed her hands, and her little makiz-in-clad feet stood atop his, and he decided one dance couldn't hurt.

The half-written text to Ashwiyaa remained unsent.

Chibenashi stumbled home much later, not from intoxication but exhaustion. Biidaaban had insisted on dancing for several long songs; then some drunken teenagers had gotten rowdy and decided to light a second, larger bonfire away from the sacred fire, near a large pile of brush that could have sparked an uncontrolled wildfire. Then three tourists from Europe had come to him, two of them in tears, because their wallets and passports had gone missing. A woman and her friends ran up to him to report that someone had slipped something called White Teeth, the street name for a drug often used in sexual assaults, into her drink, causing her to pass out and make her memory spotty. Nothing had happened, and the description of who had bought the woman her drinks—foreign, European, likely from a cruise ship—would make it nearly impossible to track him down. Still, Chibenashi took the information just the same. It was the closest that Baawitigong had come to a crime wave in all the years he'd lived here.

The wigwam was dark, and he fumbled for the light switch. The house was cleaner than he'd expected—Meoquanee's doing, no doubt. He helped himself to the jug of bark tea in the fridge. There was just enough left for one cup, so he didn't bother dirtying one—he drank deeply straight from the container. No one was there to nag him. There was no sign of Ashwiyaa, so he tiptoed to her room, where he found her lying in bed, on her side and with her back turned to him. He knew from the familiar sound of her deep, even breaths that she was asleep. Meoquanee had come through for him again, taken care of his family. With a tired smile, he padded to his room, toed off his makizinan, and face-planted into a deep and dreamless sleep.

Chapter Three

Chibenashi cracked an eye open, then realized it was brighter than it should have been at this time of day. He fumbled for his phone. Looked at the time. Cursed audibly. He had slept far longer than he had intended. He sat up and immediately doubled over as he cradled his throbbing head in his hands. He must have needed the sleep, but it was unlike him to overdo it like this, much less fail to set an alarm.

Today would be the cleanup—literally and figuratively—from the night before. Volunteer crews from all over Baawitigong would tidy up the site of the festival. No one was assigned or conscripted; it was just something they all did. Respect for the land was so woven into the fabric of their society that people spontaneously showed up to help. Chibenashi and Ashwiyaa would go too—a good distraction from what would otherwise be occupying their minds today—but at this time in the late morning, the cleanup would be well underway. He wondered if Ashwiyaa had gone without him. Unlikely, but perhaps Meoquanee had stopped by the wigwam this morning as well, though it was hard to believe she would have done so without dragging him out of bed by the ear, scolding him for failing to fulfill his basic responsibility of waking up in the morning.

Though today, of course, was not any morning. Twenty Ricing Moons ago today, he'd woken up with an even more debilitating head-ache and an even worse surprise and feeling of failure over his own actions. Life had never been the same. He'd been irritated at his mother for telling him not to drink the night before; he'd waved her off and gone with his friends, ignoring her as she yelled after him to be careful. He hadn't responded. And that morning, he'd had to face the cold, harsh reality that he would never get the opportunity to do so. The things he would say to her if he'd had the chance, any chance at all . . .

A meme began hammering at the birch outside, and the sound echoed in Chibenashi's head. He summoned his strength and vaulted out of bed.

Ashwiyaa was already up. She seemed startled to see him.

"Oh!" She nearly dropped her mug. "You're still here. I thought you would have left for work already." Her hand shook.

Chibenashi rushed over to her, sorry to have surprised her. Deviations from the routine were hard for her. "I overslept," he explained. "Late night with Manoomin, as you know."

She nodded. "You weren't here. I was scared."

He pulled his little sister into a hug. "I know," he whispered into her hair, rubbing his hands up and down her tense back. "I'm sorry."

"I didn't know when you would be back, and I was worried, and you know what today is . . ."

He nodded, feeling a knot form in his chest. He repeated his apology with each breath, like a prayer.

"It was longer than I thought," he said eventually. "Got busy."

Ashwiyaa did not respond.

"I did my best to make up for it."

His sister raised her head, looked at him quizzically. "How?"

"I asked Meoquanee to stop by to keep you company."

Ashwiyaa pulled away and gave him a puzzled look. "When?"

"I asked her pretty early in the night, just as the sacred fire was lit and dancing was starting."

"Meoquanee never came over."

Chibenashi's look now mirrored his sister's.

"What do you mean?"

"I mean I was here alone all night."

Chibenashi shook his head. This wasn't possible. "Maybe you were already asleep when she came by." Though that would have been unusual since Meoquanee had said she was going straight over. No reason to go back to her home first before going to theirs. While Meoquanee usually cooked her own food for them, she would have brought festival food with her from Manoomin.

"Weird," he said. "Something must have come up."

Ashwiyaa huffed.

"I'll call her today when I get a chance. But for now, I've got to go." He needed to shower and dress but didn't want to leave his sister in this state, especially after she'd been left alone all evening. He cursed himself for his stupidity. He should have arranged for someone to stay with her both last night and today.

Ashwiyaa turned around and went to her room, slamming the door behind her.

Chibenashi chased after her. He gently rapped on her door, which he discovered was locked. "Ashwiyaa," he said. "Please don't be like this."

"Just go," she said.

"I'll come check on you midday," he promised.

Ashwiyaa did not respond, but as he took a shower, he could hear her sobs over the sound of the spray.

◆ ◆ ◆

The field where the sacred fire had taken place was peppered with people cleaning up. This late in the morning, no trash could be found on the ground; large bags were piled up together neatly. The sacred fire had burned itself out, and the ashes had been swept away. People were chatting and raking up manoomin husks, stalks, leaves, and other bits of detritus. By the end of the day, it would be as if nothing had ever happened.

As he had done the night before, Chibenashi stood off on the side-lines, alone—observing but not participating. He scanned the crowd, expecting Meoquanee to be here, spearheading the effort and leading a team the way she always did; despite her short stature, Meoquanee always said that she felt she was the tallest person in any group. But he did not see her petite frame bossing others around or giving orders.

An old woman shuffled up to him, her back hunched with a load of bags that would collapse a man half her age. She refused his attempt to take them from her, swatting his hand away. He asked if she had seen Meoquanee that day. She replied that she had been there since first light—those young things were still sleeping off their hangovers, but she was able to rise early in the morning even after drinking half the village under the table—and had not seen her. "Now that you mention it," she said, "it is unusual."

On his way to the dakoniwewigamig, Chibenashi pulled out his phone.

Everything okay? he texted Meoquanee. **Ashwiyaa says you never made it last night.**

Ziigwan greeted Chibenashi with a scroll bearing a long list of names. Its length surprised him.

"This is all from last night?" He squinted through his headache to read the names.

Ziigwan nodded. "I see you're recovering about as well as I am," she said, pointedly not mentioning the significance of this anniversary. She picked up a cup of what smelled like strong coffee and sipped from it.

"Unexpectedly," he said.

"Drinking on duty isn't a good look for you," she said. "Not like you."

"You know I don't drink. I'm not sure why I'm feeling like this."

Ziigwan looked at him, and he looked at her. Neither needed to mention that the day would be hard on him no matter what had happened the night before.

Chibenashi walked over to the table and set down the list of people who would be coming in to make formal reports of minor infractions from the night before. He recognized some of the names as those he had assisted. There were usually a dozen or so on the list after Manoomin. Last night's numbered nearly thirty.

The Baawitigong dakoniwewigamig, like all others, emphasized oral reports. Chibenashi therefore set up both a video and voice recorder to capture everything. What they said would be distilled down to short summaries to provide reminders of what was said and how it was said, but these verbal reports were more important. The written word, for all its benefits, could not capture everything about a person making a report—their tone of voice, hand gestures, the rise and fall of volume, the dilation of their pupils, sheens of sweat on their brows, nervous twitches that could give away more involvement in an incident, looks of surprise and confusion. The spoken word could sear itself into your brain in the way the written word so often could not. All of this was relevant in investigations.

Just before the first interviewee was to arrive, Chibenashi pulled out his phone. No response from Meoquanee. He immediately called her. Straight to voice mail. He tried again. No answer.

He stood up. More than two dozen people were awaiting him, but Meoquanee's uncharacteristic silence outweighed their inconvenience. Without a word, he stalked toward the door.

"Chibenashi," Ziigwan called after him.

"Not now," he said, waving her off with his hand.

"You need to hear this."

"It's Meoquanee—"

"I know."

He stopped, turned. Ziigwan was ashen and grim. Peezhickee was awake, his face carved in granite.

An icy hand reached up inside Chibenashi's stomach, gripped his guts, and twisted with a sharp jerk.

"What happened?"

Chapter Four

The call had come in from Giiwedin, the old woman who lived in the wigwam next to Meoquanee's. Assuming Meoquanee would be at the cleanup, she'd come over to leave her neighbor some cool tea to relax her upon her return; it was their own sort of Manoomin tradition. Like Meoquanee, Giiwedin lived alone. Unlike Meoquanee, Giiwedin was alone because her husband had died and they had been childless, though not by choice, but she still felt like she and Meoquanee understood each other. With her long gray hair braided in two thick ropes down her back and a blanket over her shoulders, Giiwedin had shuffled over with the container of freshly brewed tea. She made it from the flowers and herbs that grew naturally in the small garden just outside her own wigwam. They would slowly cool over the course of the morning and allow the flavors to diffuse into the water, giving it a deeper taste that would quench any thirst in the heat of the afternoon. Giiwedin's tea was the best, she made a point of emphasizing several times during her conversation with the Peacekeepers.

The door was ajar, which was unusual, but Giiwedin had not given it much thought. Nobody locked their doors here. Most doors didn't even have locks, the occupants not wanting to dishonor their neighbors with any sort of mistrust. Moreover, Meoquanee was always headed somewhere, helping someone with something. An open door was a not-unheard-of casualty in such instances. Humming an old song,

Giiwedin let herself in past the post upon which Meoquanee's doodem, a loon, was carved and made her way to the kitchen.

When she saw Meoquanee, the jug shattered on the floor, spilling her carefully brewed tea everywhere.

◆　◆　◆

Chibenashi stood over the shards of Giiwedin's jug and the sticky remains of the tea. He carefully maneuvered around it, not quite registering the sight of Meoquanee's body surrounded by a pool of blood that had gelled on the floor.

She'd been murdered.

Stabbed.

In her own home.

Not again.

He bolted out the door and ran into the woods. He ducked behind the first large tree he found, leaned forward, pressed his hands to his thighs, and vomited uncontrollably. Gasping for air, he tried to take control of himself, but it was all too overwhelming.

Baawitigong had not seen a murder in twenty years. To the day.

He bent forward and retched again.

Ziigwan was kind enough to not mention Chibenashi's quick departure when he returned to the wigwam a short while later. Being a Peacekeeper first and foremost, she had, of course, confirmed whether Chibenashi was able to handle this.

"I can do this," he snapped. He couldn't face his failure to protect another woman in his life. He'd let his guard down, gotten lazy after his father had been locked away. He wondered what he had done to deserve tragedy not only coming into his life but also burrowing in so deep it could not be extricated, like the head of a tick draining the life from him.

"You knew her."

He had known her—but more importantly, she had known *him*. And Ashwiyaa.

"Name me one person in Baawitigong who I haven't known since my own birth or theirs," he pointed out. "You know Meoquanee too." He caught himself. "*Knew* her."

"Not the way you did."

"I'm fine." He wasn't fine, but he had to get through this. If he couldn't have prevented Meoquanee's death, he was going to solve it—and dealing with whatever unwelcome feelings might try to plague him would only hold him back.

Ziigwan gave him a long, hard look. He gave her one back. Neither was willing to forfeit the staring contest, which continued until they were interrupted.

A forensics team had come in from Wiikwedong, a larger town about one hundred kilometers to the west by the Arrow Train. Baawitigong had not the expertise, equipment, nor capacity for such work. While they waited for the team to complete their work, Ziigwan and Chibenashi interviewed Giiwedin, then canvassed the surrounding homes in the community. Many had been out at Manoomin all night; some answered the door still half-asleep, their eyes trying to blink away the harsh morning. They asked their questions anyway. Had they seen or heard anything? No one had. Had they noticed whether the door was open or closed when they returned home? They had not paid attention one way or the other, though one old man thought it may have been closed. His wife immediately contradicted him, saying it had been open. The man insisted that it had been closed, and she snapped that they couldn't even see the door from their wigwam. The husband said he could have sworn that he'd heard a man yelling, while his wife snapped back at him that there had been no noise and he was confusing the noise from the television *again*. The wife said that she thought she'd seen Meoquanee's son—you know, the one who wouldn't even call his own mother—wandering around Shikaakwa that day, and the husband had told her that she also thought that there had been a skunk loose in the wigwam when really it had just been a pillow, so her eyes couldn't be trusted, and besides, how would she even know what that boy looked like anymore, he'd be all grown-up now. Their bickering had continued long after Ziigwan and Chibenashi gave up on getting any useful information and left them. What time had they come home? No one was entirely sure. They hadn't been focused on time, and time was not typically top of anyone's mind in Baawitigong, let alone on Manoomin.

No one had ever been seen leaving or entering her wigwam over the years, except for Meoquanee herself and occasionally Giiwedin, Chibenashi, and Ashwiyaa.

What about any other friends—maybe even a boyfriend? That had provoked actual laughter. Meoquanee was as radioactive as Chibenashi.

"We should talk to Ashwiyaa," Ziigwan said, reviewing her notes and checking her voice recorder to see how much space she had left on it.

Chibenashi shook his head. "No need."

"What do you mean?"

"I mean she already told me that she didn't see or hear anything last night."

"Did you tell her about what happened?"

"No. I just know what she was doing last night. She told me."

Ziigwan gave him a look. "We have to be thorough."

"Does it not count when I interview her?"

"Was it an interview?"

"You know what I mean."

Ziigwan sighed. "It shouldn't, no."

"Please don't put her through this," he implored her. "She won't handle it well, especially today. I know her. She trusts me. She didn't see anything."

Ziigwan looked uneasy at the idea, but Chibenashi wouldn't let this go. He knew he was asking a lot of Ziigwan, who cared about him when so few others did. Ashwiyaa was hanging on by a thread, and this might make her snap altogether. And if she broke, the dam of grief and guilt in his heart would finally burst, and he'd be of use to no one.

Dejected, Ziigwan and Chibenashi sat on the ground outside Meoquanee's front door while the team from Wiikwedong did their work. They shared tea that Giiwedin served them. The old woman made good on her boast—it quenched a thirst. They sipped in silence, watching the birds overhead. Word was out already about what had happened, and a crowd started to gather on the other side of the crime scene tape. Aware they were being watched, Ziigwan and Chibenashi were careful to keep their expressions neutral, their demeanors calm. Chibenashi in particular knew he was being watched especially closely, given his history.

"Doesn't seem possible, does it?" Ziigwan asked, breaking the silence.

Chibenashi shook his head. He longed to check his phone, to see how Ashwiyaa was doing, but he did not dare do so with so many people around. It had not buzzed since his arrival. He hoped he could count on Kichewaishke to check on her. Normally, Meoquanee would have done it for him, without even asking.

"What about you?" Ziigwan asked suddenly.

"What about me?"

"Did you see or hear anything? I know you saw her at Manoomin."

"She was leaving early, was going to check on Ashwiyaa. I told you, Ashwiyaa said she never arrived."

Ziigwan's face fell. "She must have come home first and been surprised," she said.

The hand twisted his insides again. This time, it burned. If Ziigwan's theory was right, then only moments before her death, he'd been with her at Manoomin, asking her to once again do him a favor. He'd taken and taken and taken from her. What had he ever given her? What had either of them ever given her except for part of their load to carry?

35

"Yeah."

Chibenashi was interrupted from his thoughts by the sound of their names being called from within the wigwam. "We've found some things."

Ziigwan led the way. Leading the forensic team was a veteran investigator named Makade. He'd never been sent to Baawitigong before, but his reputation preceded him all the way out here. He was experienced in crime scene analysis as well as pathology. He was a thin man of about forty-five. His head was shaved, and his narrow eyes were framed by round-rimmed glasses, which reflected the summer sunlight. He was tall and spindly, like a heron, and his Adam's apple bobbed when he spoke. He fired up his own recorder and began speaking, both to it and to Ziigwan and Chibenashi.

"We estimate that she has been dead since late last night," he said. "Cause of death is stabbing following an attempted strangulation. You can see here"—he bent down and gently lifted some of Meoquanee's hair from where it covered her face and neck—"some bruising, which indicates that she was strangled before her death. However, whoever did strangle her could not finish the job. Likely not strong enough. This woman was small but tough. She fought back—we found some skin under her fingernails. She didn't go quietly. So the killer resorted to stabbing." Makade pointed to the knives on the kitchen counter; all were neatly placed in their holder, save for one missing. "We believe that the killer used one of the victim's own kitchen knives, as we have not been able to find the one that is missing."

Ziigwan nodded. "So it may not have been planned," she mused. "The killer first strangled and then looked for a weapon of opportunity."

"Precisely," Makade agreed. "She may have argued with someone, and the argument turned heated and violent at some point."

"Given the time you estimate, most of the neighbors were still out at the Manoomin festival," Ziigwan said. "We've spoken with everyone who lives nearby. No one saw anything."

"It might be worth checking on who was missing from Manoomin at that time," Makade said. "A major holiday and the victim is not in attendance. Who else was missing? Surely in this village, an absence would be noticed."

"Maybe," Chibenashi said, his voice hollow. "Maybe not."

"What do you mean?" Ziigwan added.

"It could have been someone from out of town, someone whose presence was not expected here."

"A tourist?"

"No," Chibenashi said pointedly.

"Her family," Ziigwan said.

Chibenashi's throat caught. Shikaakwa was a short Arrow Train ride away. And it was hard to fathom anyone else who would dislike Meoquanee to the point of arguing with her and then killing her.

Makade continued speaking. "We found knife marks in the floor here." He knelt down and pointed to a gash in the wood; the light inside the floorboard and thin shavings around it confirmed this was a new mark. Some bits of wood flaked off at his touch and into the thick, sticky blood pooled around it. "There are enough that we believe the victim was stabbed while lying down on the floor, likely with the attacker pinning her down. That makes it difficult to ascertain how tall the killer was, though given the victim's short stature, just about anyone would be taller than her."

Chibenashi thought back to how Meoquanee always felt she was the tallest in the room, and he swallowed the tears before they could reach his eyes.

Ziigwan looked around the room. "Anything missing from the house?" She was all business, as if this wasn't her first murder.

"No way of knowing," Makade said.

"I would know."

Ziigwan and Makade turned in unison toward Chibenashi. "I've been in and out of this wigwam my whole life. I know what possessions were important to her. It won't be perfect, but if something was gone, I'd probably be able to tell."

Makade nodded, but Ziigwan hesitated. She gently took Chibenashi by the elbow and led him outside.

"I'm fine," he said, pulling his arm out of his partner's grasp once they were out of Makade's ear- and eyeshot.

"It's not about that."

"Then what?"

She stared at him for a moment, apparently willing him to read her mind. "Well?" he snapped.

"You've been in the house your whole life."

"So?"

"And you spoke to her last night."

"So?"

"So that makes you a witness!" Ziigwan said. "It's bad enough that you've been involved this far, but you have personal knowledge of her whereabouts for at least part of the night."

"And I'll give a statement like any other witness. I'll give you one now if you want."

"Which could have been colored by what you've seen already." Ziigwan threw up her hands in a "stop" motion. "We need to pause this. You shouldn't be investigating."

"Of course I should."

"What time did you see Meoquanee last night, when you talked to her?"

Chibenashi sighed, looked up to the sky, half wishing Sky Woman would strike him down then and there. "I don't know; it wasn't dark yet, and it was obviously before she left. Certainly before she was killed, so it must have been fairly early in the evening, given the time Makade estimates."

"Aha!" Ziigwan jabbed her finger in his chest. "You see? Your memory is already being colored by what you've seen and heard here."

He pushed her finger away. "None of that is inconsistent with what I saw and heard. If anything, it helped pin down a time. If we were interviewing a witness, we'd give the outside time of death if they were unsure of a time."

"Chibe—"

"Please."

He stared at Ziigwan for a long time through watering eyes.

"With the day, and everything, and her relationship with my mother . . ." He shuddered. "I failed her like I failed my mother and my sister. Let me do this for her."

Ziigwan put her hands on her hips, bent her head down. "I get it," she said.

"Do you?"

"Yes. I really do."

Chibenashi wanted to scoff. There was no way she could. She hadn't experienced the murder of a family member, let alone two.

"But you will have done Meoquanee no favors by messing up the investigation into her murder. You're so close to this, emotionally and otherwise. You carry so much on your back. When your sister finds out about this . . ."

Chibenashi went light-headed at the thought. Ashwiyaa had never recovered from their mother's murder. And now to lose the next thing they'd had to a mother ever since . . .

"I owe it to Meoquanee." He dropped his hands to his knees, waited for the rush to stop. "After all she's done for me. This is the least I can do."

Ziigwan considered. They had no protocol for how to handle this; no training had covered it. "But you be careful," she said. "Don't touch a thing. You don't want your involvement in this case to compromise it."

"I would never let that happen," Chibenashi said.

◆ ◆ ◆

Chibenashi snapped on a pair of gloves and tucked his hair under a paper cap. Makade and Ziigwan and the rest of the forensic team had cleared out. In part it was to allow him to confirm whether anything was missing, and in part it was to give him space to grieve. He would have his chance over the next four days and at the burial, like everyone else in Baawitigong, but this was private. This was his.

Meoquanee's wigwam was smaller than Chibenashi and Ashwiyaa's. Birch-paneled walls, smooth as pearls to the touch, ran up to a tapered arch ceiling. Only one level. A small kitchen connected to a living area, and then branched off into rooms. If one stood facing the kitchen window, to the left was a hallway leading to two bedrooms and a bathroom, and to the right was Meoquanee's bedroom and bath. Through the window, Chibenashi could see the gathered crowd and the woods beyond.

The living area was spotless and sparse: an upholstered sofa and chairs with lacquered wooden legs arranged around a wooden table with two coasters and a half-empty glass of water. A flat-screen television was built into the wall. Shelves with some round birchbark boxes decorated with porcupine quills. He recognized Ashwiyaa's handiwork in a few of them. Meoquanee lived alone and did not use much of the house. She rarely ventured into the two bedrooms. One had belonged to her son, Sakima; Chibenashi remembered spending a lot of time in it during his childhood, playing video games with him. They hadn't spoken in years. Same with Meoquanee's ex-husband, Wiishkobak. They had all once been great friends, but Sakima and Wiishkobak had vanished as fully and completely from Chibenashi's life as his parents had. He remembered the last time they had all been together, and the corners of his eyes pricked. He shoved the memory down—*hard*.

It would be weird coming by this wigwam and not finding Meoquanee here. Chibenashi wondered who would live here now that she was gone. As far as he knew, everyone in Baawitigong who needed housing had it. Maybe multiple generations of a family living together would appreciate more space. Homes were lived in and passed on to those who needed them, not owned and bequeathed to heirs, but this particular home was so entwined with his memory of her that it would be difficult to imagine anyone else's life fitting into it. Sakima might claim it, as was his prerogative, but he hadn't been to Baawitigong in years.

After a moment's debate, he chose the two bedrooms over Meoquanee's. One had a bed for guests that Chibenashi could not remember anyone ever staying in, and one was empty except for a rolled yoga mat leaning against the wall and Meoquanee's winter coats hanging in the closet, all of which appeared to be accounted for. Both rooms seemed undisturbed from his previous visits, though he'd never been so thorough in inspecting them before. The connecting bathroom had that untouched look of a room that was unused—the very air felt stale.

The search of the other rooms revealed the same: undisturbed, at least from what little he had seen from his usual visits. He peeked in the bathroom; nothing unusual in there either.

It looked like Meoquanee had been here alone, as usual.

Chibenashi got on his knees, checked under the furniture. Not even dust. He went back to the shelves in the living room and began opening the round birchbark boxes that neatly lined the shelves as if they were on display. They were stitched together with sinew and embroidered with colorful porcupine quills to create pictures: flowers, a sunset, animals. One was empty; one was filled with sewing gear (thread, needles, mismatched buttons, porcupine quills); one was subdivided into small compartments, into which a variety of beads had been sorted by color; and one contained a stack of printed photographs.

Chibenashi stilled at this. He stood back from the shelf and removed the photographs from the box. He unconsciously sat on the couch as he reviewed them. On top was a stack of photos of Meoquanee and her son, along with some of his letters and school projects. Underneath were formal black-and-white pictures of Meoquanee's ancestors that had yellowed with age. A few looked familiar to Chibenashi, little bits of genetic resemblance winking at him from generations ago. They were stiff and serious, like most photos taken back then.

Then came the faded and out-of-focus pictures from Meoquanee's adolescence, before digital cameras. The colors were too bright, the lines fuzzy. He stared for a long time at one in particular, taken along the shores of Anishinaabewi-gichigami at the height of summer. The lake's crystal clear water sparkled in the sunlight, and two young women—arms around each other, long hair fanning out behind them in the wind, wide smiles on their faces—beamed into the camera. No, not into the camera. Just past it, as if they were looking ahead to the future spread out wide and inviting before them—a future that would be cut violently short for both of them. Meoquanee on the left, and his mother, Neebin, on the right. Her face. He couldn't help but trace it ever so lightly with his gloved hand. He sat there still as a tree, drinking in her features. Her face always faded in his mind until he saw it again in a picture, sharpening the haziness of his memory. His mother had been brushing some hair out of her eyes at the moment the photo was taken. Meoquanee only came up as high as Neebin's shoulder.

Ashwiyaa looked so much like Neebin, if Ashwiyaa would ever smile.

Chibenashi gazed back at his mother through time.

Meoquanee had hardly aged a day from when this photograph was taken. Chibenashi flipped it over to see if anyone had scrawled a date or other information on the back, but it was blank. It must have been before either had married or had children. Both could have been teenagers—or at least, they looked like teenagers to him. At thirty-seven, the line between children and young adults was beginning to blur. Each year, a greater share of the world looked like children to him. Regardless, they were young and full of life, with no idea of how badly it would end for them both.

Chibenashi scrubbed the tear running down his cheek. He pocketed the photo before he could stop himself. He didn't want to think of her family refusing it or, even worse, destroying it. He smoothed it down, protecting it from damage.

Then he saw a stack of papers beneath the photographs—some carefully folded, others brittle with age. He picked them up carefully and opened them. Reports from Meoquanee's school years. A picture of a makwa and her cubs that her son had drawn when he was small; he'd signed it in the messy-yet-deliberate handwriting of small children. He guessed that Sakima would have been about Biidaaban's age at the time he drew it. Another picture fell out of the stack: a man and woman being wrapped in a blanket by their parents at the end of a wedding ceremony. The picture was old, so Chibenashi figured it may have been Meoquanee's parents. He had never met them but had heard her speak of them with great love. And down at the very bottom of the box, with paper worn soft by repeated handling, was a folder filled with pictures and documents.

Chibenashi opened it carefully. It was full of his mother—Neebin's name was on documents and in photographs. He drank it all in: poetry cowritten by Meoquanee and Neebin when they were girls, in awkward language trying to sound profound; a notice that Neebin had won an award for a drawing at school, with Meoquanee finishing a close second. He read with a pang the invitation to his parents' wedding, and beneath it a virtually identical one to Meoquanee and Wiishkobak's a moon or two later. A painting done by Meoquanee featuring the silhouette of two girls along the bank of a gichigami in the summer sunset, not unlike the sunset everyone had enjoyed the night she was killed. He recognized it as similar to one his mother had painted, which hung on the wall of their wigwam; Neebin's version of the painting was more refined than Meoquanee's comparatively amateur attempt. Chibenashi had never known Meoquanee to paint, but judging by its placement in the box, it had been here for years. For whatever reason, she had apparently never wanted to display it. More and more documents and pictures—a testament to the life and friendship that had existed long before he was born. And with his Peacekeeper's eye, he saw a darker, deeper vein running through it all. Maybe love, or envy? The pile was the story of Meoquanee, always a step or two behind Neebin, following in her footsteps, and he could not tell whether she had been chasing or following her.

That gave him pause. Was that what he and Ashwiyaa had been to Meoquanee—a prize to be won? Something of his mother's that she'd always craved for herself? A stone formed in his stomach. He knew better than most that a person's true nature could be hidden from those who thought they knew them best. But the idea that Meoquanee, who'd been there to pick up the shards of his life, might have been someone he hadn't known as well as he'd thought was an extra blow.

Overwhelmed with grief, he ran to the bathroom and threw up in the toilet. Over and over he retched, not stopping until he had eliminated the feelings within him. He knew he was compromising the crime scene, but he couldn't hold it in. And nothing had seemed out of sorts when he'd checked it.

He breathed deeply, willing himself to regain control. He was a professional. He had to act like one. Even now. Especially now.

Chibenashi pulled himself up, stood at the sink. He leaned over it and breathed deeply in and out. In and out. He cupped water in his hands and rinsed his mouth, splashed his face.

That's when he noticed it: Meoquanee's toothbrush was gone. So was her toothpaste. This was unusual. She was scrupulous about her hygiene and health.

He opened the drawers and cabinets. No hairbrushes. No dental floss or sticks. No makeup. No contact lenses or solution. No nasal rinse. No creams or lotions.

He went to the shower. The soap, razor, shampoo, and conditioner were gone. No loofahs or washcloths.

No towels hanging on the railing.

He inspected the trash can. Empty. Wiped clean.

He returned to the room, searched for Meoquanee's dirty clothes hamper. There was none.

This meant something. Chibenashi stood there, processing it, until it clicked.

"There's no DNA," Chibenashi announced as he exited the wigwam.

Makade and Ziigwan stopped their conversation and turned to him at the same time. "What do you mean?" Ziigwan asked.

"There's blood, but to run DNA testing, you'd have to have a known sample of her DNA to compare it to, correct?"

Makade nodded.

"How do you usually get that?"

"We usually take it from something belonging to the victim, such as a toothbrush or a hairbrush."

"Can you take DNA from the . . . from a victim's body?"

"It's not ideal," Makade said. "Samples can become contaminated, and the victim's blood is often mixed with that of the perpetrator, or even just others who are in the home or have touched the victim. Better to have it from more than one source."

"You can't just swab her cheek or something like that?"

Makade shook his head. "Samples taken after death are not reliable. The DNA becomes fragmented. Decomposition begins shortly after death, and this affects DNA as much as the rest of the tissue. It does not provide a reliable sample. It must be taken from a living cell—or, at least, one that was alive at the time it was collected."

Chibenashi's head spun. "The killer took all the DNA with him."

Ziigwan looked at her partner with a mixture of curiosity and concern. "How could he do that?"

"It's all missing," Chibenashi said. "All personal things that would have Meoquanee's DNA. Her toothbrush, her hairbrush, dirty laundry, garbage, soap, razors. Whoever did this knew to collect everything that she would have left recoverable DNA on. To the point of even wiping the garbage can clean." Chibenashi brought them inside and led them through a reenactment of his search.

"Well, this makes things harder," Ziigwan said, stating the obvious. "Crimes without witnesses are difficult enough as it is. If all we have to go on is forensic evidence, Mediators will have to hold an initial hearing to assess responsibility, and that can be a challenge. To not even have reliable DNA . . ." She sighed. "It does not bode well for reaching a resolution." She looked at Chibenashi. "I'm sorry."

Makade stood stone-still, considering something. "Did the victim have any children?"

Chibenashi and Ziigwan nodded. "Yes, a son," Chibenashi said.

"Mitochondrial DNA," Makade said.

"What's that?" Ziigwan asked.

"Not all DNA is the same," he said. He launched into his explanation in a professorial tone. Chibenashi wondered if Makade had ever done any teaching; he was good at it. "Mitochondrial DNA is taken from the mitochondria of the cell—hence its name. What is unique about mitochondrial DNA is that it comes only from the mother; yours has the same profile as your mother's, and her mother before her, and so on.

"Mitochondrial DNA carries characteristics inherited from a mother in both male and female offspring. Thus, siblings from the same mother have the same mitochondrial DNA. In fact, any two people will have an identical mitochondrial DNA sequence if they are related by an unbroken maternal lineage."

"So what you're saying," Ziigwan said, "is that Meoquanee and her son will have the same mitochondrial DNA?"

"Correct. If you can get a DNA sample from him, you will have a DNA sample from her, and that can be used to create a profile against which we can test the blood found on the victim."

Chibenashi blew out a sigh. "Well, that will be easier said than done."

Chapter Five

Chibenashi took the long way home, avoiding people, avoiding his usual places—just walking until he was at the door to his wigwam. He breathed heavily, willing himself to go inside but finding it difficult to do so. He had no choice. There was no one but him left to do this now.

He entered.

Ashwiyaa stood there. Her face was haunted, her eyes hollow, and he knew that she could see the same expression on his face.

"So it's true," she whispered. He couldn't even nod.

She collapsed to the floor in a heap of sobs. This time, he wasn't there to catch her.

◆ ◆ ◆

No one from Meoquanee's family claimed her body or arranged her burial.

They knew she had died; Chibenashi had called them himself, all the way in Shikaakwa.

First her son, Sakima. For the length of three full breaths, he had not said a word in response to what Chibenashi told him. Then, in a flat voice, he said, "Oh," and hung up the phone.

Next, Chibenashi had called Meoquanee's ex-husband, Wiishkobak. His wife, Kishkedee, answered the phone. When Wiishkobak had finally taken the phone, and Chibenashi said Meoquanee's name, he had cut him off.

"I thought I could not have been more clear," Wiishkobak had said, his voice like an ice pick piercing the phone. "I want nothing to do with that woman ever again. Ever." He and Kishkedee had been married for over a decade. Or at least that's what Chibenashi had heard.

"Please don't hang up!" Chibenashi had cried. "Please."

Once Chibenashi had finally choked out the words, Wiishkobak went silent.

"Will you come?" Chibenashi had asked.

Three breaths, just like his son, before answering.

"No."

So Chibenashi arranged everything. He lit the fires all four nights, offering food and tobacco to her spirit. Because someone who had known and loved Meoquanee as family had what she needed for her journey to the next life. Westward, where the sun sets, toward the place of happiness. Meoquanee had been there for them in life; the least they could do was be there for her in death.

Chibenashi had gone back to Meoquanee's house and searched it again, this time for the possessions that Meoquanee would need in the land of the dead, which would be given away to those she had loved in life. He had chosen the items with care, particularly for what he would give Ashwiyaa. He had decided on a multistrand string of glass beads in white, red, black, and blue that he had seen Meoquanee often wear. It would be nice to see it around his sister's neck.

The Baawitigong cemetery was in a wide clearing deep in the woods, away from the prying eyes of the tourists. Hovering around the edges, several hundred meters in either direction, were the birches, pines, spruce, and maples, with just a hint of autumn colors beginning to peek through the green. Summer never lasted long. Everyone in the village had a relative, or several dozen, buried here. Small jiibeyg-amigoonsan, spirit houses, dotted the landscape in varying states of aging—some were painted, and some had long since been stripped gray by the weather. A few burial tipis hovered protectively over them, their long branches balanced and stacked into a large cone.

Wakwi, the medicine woman, performed the Bagidinigewin service on the fifth day. It was far better attended than his mother's. The chanting and drums soothed the sadness. Wakwi led everyone in a chant as she handed out blessed tobacco. Chibenashi was careful not to crunch the dry leaves in his hand. He murmured prayers with everyone else, the low words calling for Meoquanee's spirit to journey on and for her ancestors to lead her. Ashwiyaa prayed, too, which surprised Chibenashi, but he was grateful she was well enough to do so. Meoquanee had suffered horribly; she would need everyone's prayers to guide her.

Ashwiyaa was her nervous, borderline-catatonic self, particularly when others were around. She was wrapped in a blanket, and a single tear streaked down her round face. Thirty-two years old and she still had all her baby fat. Where the time was already etched in Chibenashi's face, hers was smooth as it had been twenty years earlier. A testament to the life and family they had once shared.

He and Ashwiyaa joined the line to drop the tobacco in Meoquanee's grave while Wakwi burned sage. Chibenashi looked into the cool earth below that was ready to swallow up his offering. With a gulp, he opened his hand and let the leaves flutter to the pile, his blessing mixed with those of the others. Once the sage was burned, Wakwi used a whistle to call the spirit of Eagle to the grave to accompany the ancestors and Meoquanee. Silence fell over the group as everyone waited with bated breath for an eagle to appear. Chibenashi scanned the sky; no eagle appeared. Not even a single omiimii. An empty, silent sky in a blue that was entirely too beautiful and too happy gazed down on them. It wasn't unusual for Eagle to fail to appear at a burial, but it was always disappointing when he did not come.

The mourners filed out, and the grave was filled in. Chibenashi watched layers of earth cover Meoquanee's body until two meters of dirt separated her from him. Once the burial was complete, Chibenashi retrieved the jiibegamig—a small house with an angled and slatted roof, only half a meter high and a meter long—and placed it over her grave. Inside, through the small hole on its entrance, he placed the items that would nourish her on her journey to the spirit life: her teapot; more sage and tobacco, blessed by Wakwi; a blanket. He knelt down and placed his hand on the jiibegamig. He heard movement beside him. Ashwiyaa. She was holding Meoquanee's beaded necklace in her hand. Chibenashi jumped up to comfort her, but she pulled away. She knelt down and placed it inside the jiibegamig. Chibenashi began to protest, but Ashwiyaa shook her head. He decided not to press the issue.

Before they could leave, Ashwiyaa pulled a pair of scissors from her pocket. She trembled as she took her hair and, one braid at a time, cut it to her chin, in a traditional Anishinaabe form of grief for those who are loved and lost. Chibenashi was surprised that she would do this, as she'd never once shown an interest in traditions. She hadn't even cut her hair when their mother was murdered, nor had she smudged by wafting smoke across her face from burning one of the four sacred medicines. The shorn hair joined the necklace in the jiibegamig.

After a long time, she stood up and faced her brother. She looped her arm through his as they walked through the cemetery. The trees cast purple shadows, and the faintest bit of pink colored the clouds as the sky began to blink its way asleep for the day. Neebin's jiibegamig still sat upon her grave; the spirit house had been battered by twenty unyielding Baawitigong winters but still stood in one piece after all these years. The siblings walked east, away from the direction they had sent Meoquanee on her final journey. Chibenashi hoped she would make it.

The return home felt longer than it usually was. Each step was deliberate, like they were trying to remember it.

With their backs to Meoquanee's final resting place, Chibenashi and Ashwiyaa exited the burial ground, unaware that an eagle had landed on her jiibegamig.

When they arrived home, Ashwiyaa and Chibenashi built a fire and sat together on the couch. They shared stories of Meoquanee—some funny, some sad, all heartwarming. Ashwiyaa even laughed once when recalling the fun they'd had with Meoquanee and her family back before their mother died. It had been so long since he'd heard her laugh that he almost mistook it for a meme's call. Had she always crinkled her nose like that? She looked so much like the woman in the picture that Chibenashi had seen in Meoquanee's wigwam. He drank it all in, not knowing when or if he would ever see or hear it again. When they went quiet once more, she rested her head on his shoulder companionably.

Moments like this were why it was all worth it to him: the stress, the heartache, everything and everyone he had sacrificed for her sake. He would give it all up again for these rare flashes of the girl she had once been, which reminded him briefly of the life and relationship they could have had together, had their father not taken it all away. Between the age difference and their parents' hovering, they had never had many moments like this as children.

For a second, he was grateful to Meoquanee for this moment, and then he immediately felt shame wash over him.

But after Ashwiyaa climbed into bed, Chibenashi could not sleep. He made coffee, wrapped himself in a blanket, and sat out in front of the wigwam. He watched the stars and the long, smudged arm of the Milky Way slowly sweep across the sky from east to west, studying him with unblinking eyes. He heard the animals and birds announce the coming sunrise. He watched Baawitigong wake up. Wakwi shuffled down the road and nodded at him in greeting. He thought about Meoquanee's journey to the happy lands of the dead and hoped her soul had made it. And he thought about what it meant that he, not Meoquanee's own son, had seen her off.

The Anishinaabe do not speak ill of the dead. If you had nothing good to say, it was best not to say anything at all. Their silence spoke volumes about just what her ex-husband and son thought of her in both life and death. Chibenashi did not know what had made their blood run so cold toward Meoquanee, who had been nothing but a source of warmth and strength. How her family could have been destroyed while she had been the force that had kept his together.

◆ ◆ ◆

There was not much demand for the work of the midewiwin on such a fine day as today, leaving the medicine woman with time to tend to Chibenashi one-on-one. The aroma of the wiigwaasi-mashkikigamig's cedar-lined walls and low ceilings mixed with the scent of the other three sacred medicines: sage, sweetgrass, and tobacco. Combined, they gave the lodge a rich, earthy, woodsy smell that made Chibenashi feel both warm and safe. It always had. It was a few days after the burial, and he needed it.

"I thought I might see you today," Wakwi said. "Your sister did not want to join you?"

Chibenashi shook his head. It had been years since Ashwiyaa had been here, but Wakwi always asked anyway.

"Remember to turn off your phone and leave it on the shelf." He dutifully wrapped it in a soft piece of leather before placing it on the shelf below a sign that reminded people to leave their phones behind. He didn't turn it off, though; Ashwiyaa might need him.

Wakwi led Chibenashi into the center of the wiigwaasi-mashkikiga-mig, shuffling with a bit of a limp as she did. He followed her to a spot in the middle of the floor next to a pile of hot stones. Dimly, he could hear the sounds of life outside, but they felt so far away. The stillness gave the already peaceful surrounding the air of otherworldliness, the way only a holy place can.

Wakwi sat cross-legged, her long gray hair wrapped in two braids bound with porcupine quills and deer sinew. In part it was a uniform, and in part it was personal choice—Wakwi was very vocal about how important it was to keep the old traditions alive, including the traditional dress of generations past. People today, she always said, didn't care about the old ways. Only about the next gadget from Japan, the next film from France, the next outfit from Gujaratra. Only what was new, before moving on to the next new thing without appreciating what they currently had.

Once they were comfortable, she looked at him, knowing what he would seek. But unlike most, Chibenashi wasn't here for ceremony. With his mother gone, and with Meoquanee gone, Wakwi was all he had left when he needed advice or comfort.

"Dreams are the most important thing governing your life and choices," Wakwi said. She ladled water onto the stones. The steam snaked up toward the ceiling, fogging the old woman's face in front of him. "Tell me what you dreamed last night."

Chibenashi rubbed his hand across his face. "Not a dream," he said. The steam was already making sweat bead on his forehead. "A memory."

◆　◆　◆

Wakwi considered carefully the broken man before her: late thirties, unshaven, his hair uneven and ragged like he'd tried to cut it himself but gave up halfway through. Shaggy, falling just to his chin, framing his anguished face. It was so rare for young people to come here outside of ceremony. The world was becoming more and more secular. But Chibenashi, he was special. Given all he had been through, and given his line of work, he came often.

"If a memory makes its way into your dreams, then it is worth paying attention to."

When Chibenashi didn't respond, she prompted him again. "The same?"

Chibenashi breathed out a long sigh and closed his eyes. Nodded. "Every night."

"Tell me what you see," Wakwi said.

Chibenashi shook his head.

"Every time you come here with this same dream, and every time you refuse to speak of it. Give words to what you see. Your dreams are trying to tell you something."

Chibenashi opened his mouth. Closed it. Opened it again.

"Would the pipe help?"

Chibenashi nodded. Wakwi handed him the pipe, full of the blessed tobacco with mint that would both relax him and allow him to access the memories that tormented him. Wakwi knew that the mind could not open while the body was pulled tight as a snare. He had come to her, which meant he needed help uncoiling himself so he could breathe. Without dreams, his connection to the spirit world was severed. It was no wonder that he was so tortured. Without dreams, he could only access part of the knowledge he needed to make good decisions for himself and his sister. It was like part of his soul had been amputated, and what remained was bloody and exposed. She could practically hear it crying out in pain, begging to be healed.

Chibenashi took a long drag and blew a smoke ring that dissipated into the steam. Such a trick took concentration, and Wakwi was pleased; it meant he was calming down. She watched as he closed his eyes and let the sweet smoke course through his veins, unspooling the tension within him. She could see him slowly relax, tendon by tendon. In the low beat of recorded drums that echoed through the wiigwaasi-mashkikigamig, he uncurled the fists he'd been making. When he opened his mouth to speak, his voice was lower by an octave.

"My brain is a tangle of thorns: confusing and painful. People are talking. It wakes me up. Think I may have been hit in the head. I don't feel pain. But I'm confused. I'm slow. I can't quite open my eyes yet. I feel around. Damp grass and dirt. I'm outside. There's sunshine on my face. I can already tell it's going to be a beautiful day. But something isn't right. I hear women crying. A commotion. Someone comes to me.

A woman. Meoquanee. She's worried I've been hurt. She helps me up. I open my eyes, briefly. Just a squint. The light is too bright. I sit up. Meoquanee's shadow blocks the sunlight. I'm on the ground outside my wigwam. I don't remember getting here. But that doesn't matter. What matters is what others are saying. They're telling me not to look."

Wakwi sat silently. Chibenashi was not really here anymore. He had burrowed deep into his memories, his dreams, and he had to stand tall and walk back out. Maybe he wouldn't be able to do it today, maybe not for many years—but he had to eventually. Otherwise he would remain trapped.

"I look anyway. It's so bright and beautiful. The breeze is whispering over my face. I can smell the flowers. Over the sound of the commotion around me, I can even hear the geese in the distance, eating bits of manoomin. It seems like everyone in Baawitigong is there. Too many voices, too many faces. I recognize everyone and no one. I feel someone trying to grab me, to pull me back in, but I won't let them. I see Sakima, trembling. His father, Wiishkobak, has his arms around him. Sakima is looking at me and shaking his head. He doesn't say a word to me. He hasn't said a word to me since.

"I'm asking where my sister is. Meoquanee is walking with me. She's telling me that they found her in the woods, huddled under a tree. She told them that she ran there when the fight started. What fight? No one will tell me. She won't go outside again after this. Not if she can help it. She remembers being alone all night, how cold it was. How afraid. My sister is screaming. She's screaming.

"I feel them in all of my nerve endings, her screams. The sound slices through me like an arrow. I take a step and collapse. I still can't quite make out what's around me. But I know Ashwiyaa is out there, and she needs me. She's so small and scared. I see a huddle of people walking from the woods. They're sheltering someone in the middle. No, carrying someone. I run to them. The group parts, and Ashwiyaa reaches for me. I pull her into my arms. She's still screaming and crying and sobbing. I hold her. She's trembling, shaking, and she can't stop; no matter what I say, no matter how tightly I hold her, she won't stop. Her tears become my tears. I don't even know why I'm crying. I only need to know that she is."

Chibenashi shuddered, put the pipe to his lips again. A deep inhale. He sat with it for a moment. He exhaled shakily.

"She's asking me what happened, and I'm telling her that I don't know. And it doesn't stop. It doesn't help.

"Now that I have her," he whispered, his voice thready, "I can finally take in everything around me properly. I see everyone. All of our neighbors and friends. My parents' friends. They look at us like they're waiting for us to shatter. A group of the men have formed a block to my right. I still see movement behind them. I understand what they're doing: they are trying to hide it from me. Whatever that commotion is, they don't want me to see.

"I keep hold of Ashwiyaa. People try to lift her from me, but I don't need them. It's no burden. It's protection. They tell me to stay back—one person even tries to stop me—but I won't let them. The men must all see the look in my eyes, and it must have done something to them, because they part ways to clear a path for me. When I see what's behind them, I fall to my knees. I barely hold on to Ashwiyaa. I scream as loudly as she does. I cling to her as tightly as she does me. I pull her closer because I don't want her to see. It's my mother. Lying in a pool of blood. Her eyes are open and gazing up directly at the sun. But she doesn't feel it burning her retinas. She's d—"

Chibenashi choked on the word.

"She's dead," he spat out. Tears squeezed through his clenched eyes and fell down his cheeks, mixed with the sweat. "She's dead. Stabbed in the stomach. I see a fly crawl across her cheek, and she doesn't do anything to swat it away. But that's not even the worst part. The worst part is the person sitting silently, stone-faced, next to her body, surrounded by men. He has blood on him. His bloody knife lays next to him.

"My father."

Chibenashi gulped a few breaths.

"He looks at me, and as soon as his eyes meet mine, everything goes black." He blew out a breath. "And I wake up."

Wakwi sat quietly, patiently, as she let Chibenashi feel the pain. After a long while, his breaths became deeper, slower. Eventually, he sat up again, furiously wiping the tears away.

In the twenty years since that day, Chibenashi had come to Wakwi for guidance. How to handle his anger with his father. How to best raise his sister. How to cope with the absence of a mother's love as he faced the brave new world of adulthood. Wakwi offered him the two things he had needed at every stage: a sympathetic ear and tough advice.

"It is always hardest this time of year," she said.

Chibenashi nodded.

"Think of all that you have accomplished since then," Wakwi replied. "You have so much to be proud of."

"Ashwiyaa," Chibenashi said, smiling sadly. "I should have done so much better by her."

"You did the best you could."

Chibenashi shrugged. "It wasn't enough."

"Not just her," Wakwi reminded him. "You as well."

He shook his head. "I need something to help me sleep," he said.

"If I give you something, you won't dream."

"Exactly."

"You must dream," she said. Without dreams, his spirit would be rooted to the physical world. Spirits needed to be free to communicate between this world and the next, and dreams were the conduit. She stood and went to the shelves behind her. She dangled a branch wrapped in a circle with deer sinew threaded around it like a spiderweb. Three feathers dangled from the bottom. "But if you do need assistance . . ."

Chibenashi swatted the dream catcher away. "I am not a child." He sighed. "And besides, I already have one. It does nothing."

"So you agree," Wakwi said, "that it is better to face the dreams than to block them?"

"Please," he croaked out.

"If you try to keep it out, it will only appear to you more forcefully than before. You must confront it. Learn to let it not hold you hostage." She took a few padded footsteps toward him and knelt down.

"Remember the cycle of life."

Wakwi raised her hand up and pointed a finger straight between his eyes.

"Creation." She drew her hand down in a half circle. Stopped at the bottom.

"Destruction."

She drew the other half of the circle and stopped her finger between his eyes again.

"Re-creation."

She drew the circle again, this time without pause. "Your mind and heart want to be here," she said, pointing to the top of the invisible circle. She dropped her finger to the bottom. "But it is stuck here. It wants to rise. But it cannot because your guilt weighs you down. To get from here"—she pointed at the bottom—"to here"—she drew her finger to the top—"is the journey of life. It is a circle that repeats over and over. Destruction is meant to be recovered from. Re-creation of something more beautiful and stronger than what existed before awaits. But you have to be willing to make that climb.

"Recall the story of Gichi-manidoo. He created the most beautiful world—the sky and the earth, the light and the dark, the land and the sea, the animals and plants, and man himself—all from the vision he had. And then the great flood destroyed it all. So he created, from that destruction, the Sky Woman, who rebuilt the world more beautifully, with even more plants, even more animals, even more land and sea than had ever been before. Where the world would have been confined to a small island, it grew to many continents, many nations, and people of all colors. The vibrancy and the diversity of it all were so far beyond what Gichi-manidoo could have imagined. And the Sky Woman could never have imagined anything so great had she not seen what used to be. The greater the destruction, the more beautiful the re-creation." Wakwi drew the circle one more time.

"And remember the Sky Woman's children! She first bore two children, the body and the spirit, but they destroyed each other. Losing both children is the worst thing that can happen to a woman—the creation of life, followed by its destruction. But following that, she bore two more children: man and woman, both physical and soul-spirit. And these would be the basis for all the humans in the world. From the destruction came re-creation—far more beautiful and complex than what came before.

"You have a beautiful future to build, Chibenashi," Wakwi said, handing him some sprigs of cedar to take home to his sister, a silent invitation for her to join him next time. "I hope one day you will allow yourself to move past the destruction and have a vision of a new life, and that you will live to see that life created before you."

Chapter Six

The Ricing Moon waned into nothing and was replaced first by the Changing Leaves Moon and then the Falling Leaves Moon. The summer tourists thinned out, only to be replaced shortly after by those who came to view the fall colors, pick apples, hike in the woods, and photograph the cranes before they flew south for the winter. Baawitigong would belong to its people again for the next few months. Many residents, like Peezhickee, migrated south with the birds, leaving only those who could not or would not travel. Like all those who show unconditional love, the people of Baawitigong embraced the place when it was at its least beautiful and most harsh. With the absence of tourists and reduced number of locals, the village could breathe a bit.

Those who would be staying prepared for the long winter ahead. They canned raspberries, strawberries, blackberries, and peaches. They chopped, split, hauled, and stacked firewood. They dried out and smoked fish, cured venison; stockpiled the sugarbush syrup that had flowed freely; placed orders for cornmeal, flour, and other supplies. Mail would still come as usual, but when the snow piled up, it could often be delayed. Baawitigong, like the animals in the surrounding woods, would go into hibernation.

All the while, Chibenashi sat in the dakoniwewigamig, staring at the scant amount of evidence that had been compiled in Meoquanee's case.

Still unsolved.

They had questioned everyone in the village. No one had seen anything. No one had heard anything. Apparently, the first night of Manoomin was the perfect time to kill someone without being caught: everyone was both out and accounted for, everyone was in sight of everyone else, and tourists roamed among them.

It must have been someone from Baawitigong. Tourists never went to the homes of locals, and even if they had, someone would have noticed and stopped them long before they reached the wigwams. The river, the port, the woods, the animals, the trees—that's what people came to see, not neighborhoods they could easily find in their own corners of the world. Moreover, according to Makade, the condition of the wigwam and Meoquanee's injuries suggested she had known her attacker. She had let him in. The crime was one of passion, of emotion. Someone who was letting go of something that had bottled up over time.

Meoquanee's wigwam had been emptied; the recycling crew had arrived to take the remaining possessions that had not been distributed to her friends and loved ones: her television, furniture, baskets, dishes—all things that would serve someone else here on earth far better than her. The men from the recycling crew took everything away, cleaned it, repaired it, wasting nothing and throwing nothing away unless it was beyond repair or refurbishment. Furniture would eventually be distributed to those in the community who had need of any of the items—a bed to one family, a table to another, and so on until everything was parceled out. There were few needy in Baawitigong. They lived by the principle of mino-bimaadiziwin—the good life: be good to one another, be good to nature, and live healthy in both mind and spirit. They took care of each other and, in doing so, took care of themselves.

To take care of Meoquanee, in death as in life, Chibenashi knew what he needed to do. But he was going to exhaust every other option first.

◆ ◆ ◆

Peezhickee, who spent every winter in Panzacola, sat down next to Chibenashi a few days before leaving.

"Have you consulted the files from twenty years ago?" he asked.

Chibenashi nearly dropped the bowl of toasted okosimaan seeds he had been nibbling on. Without Meoquanee, the quality of his diet had nose-dived. He set the bowl gently and deliberately down on the table.

"No."

"We could send for them. It will be difficult; resolved cases are filed away and access is restricted. We would have to go through layers of bureaucracy and file long statements of need since it's a closed case. But we could begin the process."

Chibenashi shrugged. What good would it do to exhume the past?

"It may present you with information and guidance as to how to approach this investigation," Peezhickee said, as if hearing Chibenashi's thoughts.

He shook his head. "I have guidance from Makade. We have the dakoniwewigamig protocols. Ziigwan and I are following everything."

Peezhickee gave Chibenashi a long, steady look. "You believe there is nothing to be gained from looking in the old files?"

Chibenashi gave Peezhickee a pointed look of his own, showing him a level of disrespect that was otherwise unthinkable. "Is there?"

Neither man spoke for a long time.

Just as Chibenashi formed an apology on his lips and looked down to summon the courage to deliver it, Peezhickee broke the silence.

"Then you know what you have to do," he said.

Chibenashi looked at him quizzically.

"You have been stalling."

Chibenashi bristled. "I have not."

"Yes, you have. You know where you need to go and what you have to do. The leaves have turned. The summer has gone. Winter is almost here. And yet you have done nothing."

Chibenashi looked away from Peezhickee. Focused on counting the crumbs from his okosimaan seeds that had fallen onto the floor. Seven.

"Do not mistake my meaning. I know you do not do it out of disregard. Far from it." He leaned in closer. The capillaries on his nose were visible, practically tattooed into his skin. "You are looking too much at who you have spoken to and who you have seen. You have not spent any time on who you have not spoken to or seen." The old man watched and waited for Chibenashi to connect the dots. With visible disappointment, he spelled it out. "Who did not claim her body? Who did not light the fires for her? Who did not attend the burial? That is who you need to talk to. Those who would have let Meoquanee's soul wander aimlessly. Their absence speaks louder than words ever could."

Chibenashi's throat turned itchy at the idea. He could handle calling them—barely. But this? Seeing them? That was a step he was not equipped to take. He could only handle so much grief in a single year.

Chibenashi shook his head. "I can't."

"You must."

"But . . ." Chibenashi swallowed. "But they are in Shikaakwa."

"So they are," said Peezhickee. "As are our files and the forensic equipment that we need and cannot access unless we accompany the materials to the laboratory."

Chibenashi cursed the chain of custody rules. They were ironclad and, if violated, made all the difference in the world in terms of what a Mediator would consider. Testimony could get you far, but in a case like this with no witnesses, it was all he had to hope for.

"I can call Makade," he said.

"You could," Peezhickee said. "But that's not his job. This is our case. We handle it."

"I am not going to Shikaakwa."

"No one else can."

"Ziigwan can go. She's worked the case, same as I have."

"I need Ziigwan here, supervising things while I'm away this winter. It's a full-time job. I can't spare her for the time it will take."

Chibenashi nearly scoffed out loud at that statement. So far as he could tell, Peezhickee's full-time job had been catching up on decades of lost sleep.

"But you can spare me?"

"No, but I'm sending you anyway. You know that the winter is too cold for anyone to think about committing any crimes. Not that we see many, as you know. If you want to continue to grow your skill set, you should go to the city. See how they handle things there. The experience will teach you much. Then you can return and teach us. You'll be back well in advance of the spring thaw, when everybody is itching to go outside and get their crimes out of their system."

Chibenashi shook his head. "I can't go to Shikaakwa."

"Why not?" Peezhickee, like any good Peacekeeper, asked the question to which he already knew the answer.

"I have . . . I have my sister, to start. She can't be left alone, and I can't take her with me. Baawitigong is too much for her most days; Shikaakwa would overwhelm her."

"What other reasons do you have for not accepting this assignment? You want to find Meoquanee's killer, do you not?"

"More than anything," Chibenashi said. "Truly. But besides my sister, there are other reasons. I have a home here. If I'm gone and you're gone, it's just Ziigwan handling everything by herself. I don't know where to go in Shikaakwa, what sorts of tests to ask for; I don't even know how long it takes to get results. I don't know where her family live or how welcome I'll be. Wiishkobak nearly hung up on me just when I mentioned her name." He was making excuses, but they were good ones. It's not like murder happened often in Baawitigong.

"All very interesting avenues for you to explore," Peezhickee said, as if responding to a completely different list of reasons than the ones Chibenashi had given him.

"I know," Chibenashi finally said.

"You know that oral testimony must be observed as well as listened to," Peezhickee said. "And if they would hardly let you speak to them over the phone to even inform them of Meoquanee's death, then they need to observe you as well as hear you. They left Baawitigong so long ago. They know you as a little boy, a child, a teenager. They need to see you as a man, a Peacekeeper who is solving a very serious crime. Perhaps they have something to hide, perhaps they do not, but you will never learn what it is until you go and meet them eye-to-eye, like any other challenge in life that is worth overcoming. And it must be you to do it. They do not know Ziigwan the way they know you. They would not open up to her."

There was no reason to believe they would open up to Chibenashi, either, judging by their last phone calls.

"And my sister?" he said finally, knowing the battle was lost.

"You have friends in this town," Peezhickee said. "They can look after Ashwiyaa as well as if you were here. I know Ziigwan would also look in on her from time to time. You have a mobile phone. And you would be gone only a few days. See where the evidence takes you. We'll arrange for a Peacekeeper in Shikaakwa to assist you so that you can finish your tasks as quickly as possible. I'll handle the request personally, make sure that you have everything you will need. I have worked in Shikaakwa before; it is very different from Baawitigong, but with the right help, you can navigate your way as you would here. You'll keep in touch with me. Go in with an open mind. See what you can learn."

Chibenashi sat for a long time, staring at the table, tracing the path of the grain in the wood with his eyes. It reminded him of trails in the woods—rivers of brown lines showing the passage of time. Physical proof that the past had once existed. The table had been sanded down so that when he ran his finger over the grain, it felt smooth as a stone, indistinguishable from the rest of the wood.

"I'll talk it over with Ashwiyaa," he said finally.

"No, you will not. She does not have a say in this. You will tell her that you are leaving."

There was no way that Peezhickee could understand that he was asking for the impossible. He couldn't just leave Ashwiyaa. She needed a constant in her life, and her one constant was him. Chibenashi's existence as a single person who could make decisions only with regard to himself had ended the night his mother died. Ever since, it had been him and Ashwiyaa against the world. He'd never left her and never would. He'd given up so much in the interest of not leaving her. Peezhickee was asking not just for the impossible—he was asking for the inconceivable.

But how could he possibly explain that? He couldn't. So he didn't try.

"I have to ease into it gently. I've never left her before. This will be hard."

Peezhickee sighed, got up. "You do realize, of course, that without knowing who did this to Meoquanee, your sister is potentially at risk?"

Chibenashi's head snapped to Peezhickee's. "What do you mean? There's nothing indicating that she or anyone else is at risk. It's been more than two moons."

"Until you know who did it, you can't rule it out."

Peezhickee knew his weakness. If there was any chance of Ashwiyaa being at risk, Chibenashi would move the stars and sky and very earth beneath his feet to protect her. And Peezhickee was right: further risk could not be categorically ruled out.

"But if I leave, I can't protect her," Chibenashi said weakly.

"Your presence could not save your mother or Meoquanee," Peezhickee said. "Your physical presence cannot stop bad things from happening. But solving this can. And solving it means you must leave Baawitigong."

Burning with shame, Chibenashi found that he could not argue with Peezhickee. So he didn't. With a curt nod, he agreed to the unthinkable: to protect Ashwiyaa, he would leave her.

"I will make the arrangements today," Peezhickee said. He patted Chibenashi on the shoulder. The gesture was fatherly. Chibenashi flinched. "I leave for Panzacola in three days. I will accompany you to the train; we will leave Baawitigong together. Shikaakwa will be ready for your arrival."

Shikaakwa might only need a couple of days to prepare for him, but Chibenashi doubted that he would be ready for Shikaakwa in the same amount of time.

Chapter Seven

To say that Ashwiyaa reacted poorly was an understatement.

"You can't leave me!" she had screeched through tears, grabbing on to him around the waist and crushing the air from him. They were in the living room of their wigwam, before the fireplace. She repeated this over and over even as her pleas were overcome with hiccups and chokes and sobs. "Please don't leave me!"

Please don't leave me.

That's what she had said to him the morning their mother was found dead and their father was taken away. Both parents gone in an instant; one heartbeat separating one life from the next. Ashwiyaa had crawled into her big brother's lap that night as they sat staring at the fire, beseeching him as she trembled. "Please don't leave me."

He had sworn that he wouldn't, and for twenty years he had made good on that promise. Today, he was breaking it. So he'd used the one argument he thought would work: that he was doing this for Meoquanee's sake.

"I have to do this," he had pleaded with her, both embracing her and pulling out of her grip. She was a mass of trembling blankets and clothes. "For Meoquanee. We've gone as far as we can here with what we have."

But even that hadn't worked.

"You'll figure it out," she had said. "You'll stay here and figure it out."

"I really, really wish I could," he'd replied.

"Have Ziigwan go. Or Peezhickee. Or anyone else. Just not you. Please not you."

"Ashwiyaa . . ."

"It can't be you. I can't lose you too."

She'd lost so many, and it was all his fault.

"Take me with you," she'd said suddenly. "I won't be in your way. Just let me come along. So I won't be here, all alone."

"I can't," he had told her. He would be staying near the dakoni-wewigamig in Shikaakwa. If he had it his way, he'd be working straight from sunup to sunup, no sleeping. Whatever would get him home the fastest. As much as he liked the idea of Ashwiyaa accompanying him so that he wouldn't worry about her, he knew that if she were there, he'd get no work done. He never brought work home with him because he had learned long ago that he would never be able to turn to it while she was around, and after she'd gone to sleep, he was often too tired. Her needs were too great. While Ashwiyaa could sleep like the dead or withdraw into herself for days or weeks on end, catatonic and not speaking, it never seemed to happen when he was working on something important. For this case, the most important one in his life? He couldn't risk it.

"I won't be long," he'd argued. "Just a few days. Just long enough to get a few things done. Enough to get back on track and help find who did this to Meoquanee. Then I'll be back, and I won't ever leave you again. I promise."

"You 'promise'?" Ashwiyaa pulled back. "You '*promise*'? Your promises are useless. You promised me once before, and now you're breaking it. What good is another promise from you?"

"I've kept my promise . . ."

"No you haven't! You promised that you would never leave me. Ever."

"Nishime—"

"Zhaan!"

With that, she'd turned and rushed away. Her hair was beginning to grow back, and it swished behind her. He had reached out to grab her, but she was too quick and vanished into her bedroom.

Chibenashi walked out the front door, where Kichewaishke had kindly excused himself when Ashwiyaa had begun her tantrum.

"You handled that as well as you could have," Kichewaishke said. They began walking toward his wigwam.

Chibenashi shook his head, looked straight ahead down the road and all the way to the woods far beyond. The trees were dusted with a very light snow. "I don't think I could have handled it worse."

"You always were your own harshest critic. Change is hard on the best of days, and given what the two of you are going through again . . ." Kichewaishke sighed. "No one deserves to go through this even once, let alone twice."

Creation. Destruction. Re-creation. The wheel would turn.

"We'll give her some space," Kichewaishke said. "Once she's calmed down a bit, we'll bring her over to our wigwam. Biidaaban will love having her, and Okimaskew will take good care of her."

"As will you," Chibenashi said. "I can't thank you enough for agreeing to take her in. I know it's a lot to ask of you."

"Nothing is too great of an ask," Kichewaishke said, clasping his best friend on the shoulder. "We're family; you know that."

They reached the wigwam and entered. Biidaaban ran up to her father, who caught her in his arms and used the momentum to spin her around. "Noos!" she cried happily. She regarded Chibenashi once they stopped spinning. "Why are you going on a trip?"

"I already told you why," her father said, putting her down with an *oof*. "You're getting heavy."

Biidaaban rounded on Chibenashi. "You haven't taken a trip before. Not ever. And you've never left your sister behind."

Goodness but this child observed everything and forgot nothing.

"Chibenashi is going to find out who hurt Meoquanee," her father said. "He's going to find out who did it, and has to go to the city to do it."

"Was it a Wendigo?" Biidaaban whispered, her eyes as wide as the full moon. She was referring to the man-eating creature that haunted the dreams and legends of the Anishinaabe. The Wendigo was still believed by many to be a force that inhabited the bodies of ordinary people, turning them evil. When people told stories of the Wendigo around fires late at night, they were large monsters who cannibalized others, growing larger and larger with each meal eaten. In the old days, people had blamed the Wendigo for any sort of violence perpetuated against others. It was the only way they had to explain the madness that makes one person attack or kill another. It explained why so few acts of violence occurred and how inexplicable it could often be. No need to seek out a root cause if someone could just be possessed by a monster.

Given what they had so far, Chibenashi did not think that a Wendigo could be ruled out entirely at this point. Keep all options open until they've been definitively disproven.

"Yes," her father said, baring his teeth and raising his hands like claws. "And the Wendigo will get you if you don't stop asking questions!" He darted forward, snarling at her. With a half-fearful, half-playful shriek, Biidaaban ran away from him to her mother, begging her to save her from the Wendigo. "Ngashi, help!"

"Kichewaishke!" Okimaskew admonished him from the kitchen. She came out with a glare on her face. One hand held Biidaaban's, the other cradled the baby, Megis, who was wrapped against her mother's chest, with a tiny hand lying limp as she slept. Okimaskew and the baby wore matching leather wristbands, tying themselves to both each other and the earth.

"I'll hear about that later," Kichewaishke said, a bit of concern edging his eyes. When she was upset, his wife could be scarier than a Wendigo. He gave Chibenashi a sheepish grin. "Don't you worry about us. We'll handle Ashwiyaa and Biidaaban and any Wendigos that cross our paths. You focus on what you need for Meoquanee."

As promised, Peezhickee walked Chibenashi to the train depot. He no doubt wanted to make sure that Chibenashi would not change his mind.

The Baawitigong train depot was small, as befit a small rural town, but had a large number of direct trains to all major parts of Mishmak, as befit a major tourist destination. A lot of seasonal destinations, though at this time of year, only the main thoroughfares still ran. The building was tall by local standards—about six meters high—and made of the same sanded, smooth logs that formed the walls of most wigwams. There were no fewer than twenty platforms lined up in a row, glistening steel leading to all four directions. Chibenashi and Peezhickee looked up at the digital departures board to confirm when they were leaving. Chibenashi's express train to Shikaakwa was due to leave in a short while, on one of the tracks pointed east—the direction of rebirth. Peezhickee's to Panzacola, on a track going south—the direction of maturation—was not due to leave until much later in the day. "No sense in waiting for my winter to begin," he explained. "My favorite café is in here anyway."

There was no café in the station.

So Chibenashi was to be babysat until he was in his seat and buckled in, the doors sealed shut, and the train on its way.

"How long has it been since you've taken the Arrow Train?" Peezhickee asked. He was already dressed for the subtropical weather of Panzacola, despite the chill in the air in Baawitigong. Winter came sooner and stayed longer up here, always overstaying its welcome.

Chibenashi shook his head. "It's been a long time."

"I go every year, and it impresses me every time. Over eight hundred kilometers covered in a short period of time, yet you don't feel the thing move. And even though you're going so fast, you will get some of the most breathtaking views of nature. It's like the trees keep up with the train's speed. You'll be in Shikaakwa well before late afternoon. And I'll be in Panzacola by sunrise. Got a lie-flat bed; I plan to sleep the whole way." He smiled. "What a time to be alive, eh?"

Chibenashi shrugged. He had no desire to be darting ahead toward Shikaakwa when he'd rather root his feet in Baawitigong and never leave. That had been the plan, after all. And if the last few months had taught him nothing else, it was that the place still held secrets, still had the ability to surprise him.

"I guess," he said finally.

"Now, you listen," Peezhickee said. "I've arranged for a Peacekeeper from Shikaakwa to work with you. He also has your lodging information; he'll deliver you to and from all meetings, appointments, and locations. Be your shadow."

"Do you really not trust me? I agreed to go."

"When you get to Shikaakwa," Peezhickee said, ignoring Chibenashi's accusation, "I want you to take a breath and take in everything. It can be very overwhelming, especially after living in Baawitigong your whole life. This is a different world. It's larger, louder, faster. Cities do not naturally breed community; you must carve your place out. They are crowded, but you will feel more alone than you ever have in your life. Mino-bimaadiziwin does not mean the same thing there as it does here. Confer with those who are with you. Trust their opinions and truly listen to them. You will not know their ways, so you will miss things. Follow their lead. But be discerning in what you hear and discriminating in what you believe. People go to cities to disappear and reinvent themselves. They are fresh, untouched snow—the ground beneath is hidden, and the surface above untouched. Anonymity is a precious gift that we do not have here. People move to cities to obtain it. They will cherish it above nearly all else and go to great lengths to protect it. That can mean denying everything about themselves—their reasons, their beliefs, and their past deeds. You must keep that in mind the entire time you are among them: people are not born in Shikaakwa; they are invented."

Chibenashi stood silent, absorbing what Peezhickee said.

"And finally," Peezhickee continued, his tone dropping an octave and lowering in volume, "I understand that this will be a difficult visit for you. There is much in Shikaakwa you have wanted to run from. Think of this as something you are running toward—a problem that only you can resolve. If you feel lost, simply remember who you are and where you are from. You are talented and smart; you will find what you are looking for. We are all counting on you."

Chibenashi nodded. It didn't make sense that Peezhickee would put this much faith in him now. He certainly didn't have it in himself. His life was one long, unbroken chain of failures, each one leaving death and destruction in its wake.

"I have my mobile phone with me. I want you to reach out to me as soon as you have received new information, or ruled something out, or have a question, no matter how stupid or meaningless you think it might be. This is our first murder in twenty years and the second one to affect you directly. Do not carry this burden on your shoulders alone."

They had reached Chibenashi's platform. The doors to the Arrow Train were open, and a tall, thin stewardess stood next to them, her eyes wide with welcome.

"Here." Peezhickee handed him a small parcel. Chibenashi didn't even need to open it to know it was tobacco. A gift for the Peacekeeper who would be helping him.

"Any last questions?" Peezhickee asked.

Chibenashi shook his head. Peezhickee could not answer his questions. He did not know whether what he would find in Shikaakwa could, either, but he had run out of other options. He had to try. He just hoped that he could handle the ghosts from his own past that lurked in Shikaakwa.

Like Dakaasin.

Or his own father.

The Anishinaabe never say goodbye. They do not even have a word for it. So Chibenashi and Peezhickee said all there was left to say.

"Minawaa giga-waabamin."

"Minawaa giga-waabamin."

Chibenashi loaded himself into his compartment, then put his bag in the overhead bin and took his seat next to the window. In his lap he kept the satchel with the case file and blood samples. Chain of custody rules required that he personally keep them in eyeshot the entire time, from when it was collected at the scene and then deposited at the station under lock and key to when he removed it and physically handed it off to the lab in Shikaakwa for testing. He may as well handcuff it to himself. He wouldn't be the first to do so in order to keep key evidence admissible. He'd considered it.

The seat next to him was empty, though it probably wouldn't be for long. Across from him, a teenager had his nose glued to his phone. Chibenashi could hear the muffled rhythm of whatever music he was listening to. Based on what little he could hear, music had only gotten worse since he was young.

He pulled out his own phone and texted Ziigwan.

Peezhickee had a lot of parting advice.

The response arrived just as the train pulled out of the station.

I don't think he's had a challenge in some time.

He settled into the seat. It was comfortable enough. The train picked up speed as he watched the landscape rush by at faster and faster rates. The train bisected the peninsula. Fields of trees, farms, and solar panels blurred past him, the glint of the sun off the solar panels winking at him as they sped past. When the train crossed the bridge bisecting Ininwewi-gichigami and Naadowewi-gichigami, he saw the large turbines that harnessed their great energy and powered cities and towns as far afield as Baawitigong and Shikaakwa. The lakes hadn't frozen over yet, so the turbines were still spinning furiously, storing energy in great batteries to power the towns and cities through the winter. As the train continued, he saw large mirrors that had been built to capture energy from the sunlight in the summer and the reflection off the snow in the winter. Shikaakwa would take the greatest share of it, as it always did with resources. The people of Baawitigong would use electricity but heat their wigwams with wood stockpiled over the course of the summer and early fall.

As the distance from Baawitigong grew and the distance to Shikaakwa shrank, he steeled himself. The unknown awaited him in Shikaakwa. Even more frightening was the known. It was true what was said among the Anishinaabe in parting. The same words he and Peezhickee had exchanged had been the same ones he'd exchanged with Dakaasin and his father before each of them had exited his life in favor of Shikaakwa. Words that now turned out to be true.

I'll see you again.

Chapter Eight

Shikaakwa didn't approach you gently from the horizon—it slapped you in the face in welcome. One moment, you were staring into the vast forests of trees, communal farms, and deer ranches interspersed with fields; and the next thing you knew, you were staring at a forest of buildings that had sprouted up out of nowhere. No villages or towns to warm you up to it. *Bam!* You were here now.

Chibenashi had brought his tablet, hoping to watch or listen to something, but even though he'd pulled it out of his bag, he hadn't bothered to switch it on. He'd been counting on—hoping for—a smooth transition into Shikaakwa. To gather his thoughts, steel himself against the past, and tamp down any anxiety. Maybe even practice some of the breathing exercises that Wakwi had once taught him. Instead, there it was, confronting him from the outset. Demanding to be seen. Refusing to give him space.

People from all over the world were drawn to Shikaakwa, and had his life gone differently, Chibenashi might have been drawn there as well. It wasn't Mino-Aki's oldest city. Mitchimakinak and Baawitigong, located at the straits between two gichigamiin, had historically been larger and more important. But after the Wyandot, Myaamia, and Meshkwahkihaki people had stopped fighting the Anishinaabe and been absorbed into the nation that had been called Anishinaabewaki—and then renamed Mino-Aki to appease them—those choke points on waterways had become less important. Shikaakwa, once a small farming community of Myaamia at the southernmost tip of the southernmost gichigami, had the advantage of being closer to large cities of other nations, like Cahokia. With the infighting of Mino-Aki over, it had looked outward, and Shikaakwa was the main gateway for that. It became the arrival point for international visitors, and with its access to all the gichigamiin, it had grown both outward and upward.

Chibenashi swallowed and squared his shoulders. Clutching the simple leather satchel containing the evidence, he retrieved his travel bag from the overhead compartment. Maybe he could do this.

The doors of the train opened. If the sight of Shikaakwa had slapped him in the face, its sounds punched him in the gut.

Baawitigong was named for the rushing rapids where the two lakes met each other. The noise of the rapids, plus the din of tourists that ebbed and flowed with the season, could make what had always seemed to Chibenashi as a lot of noise. This was particularly true when Baawitigong in summer was contrasted with Baawitigong in winter: In the summer, the town hummed. In winter, it held its breath.

Here he was, at the cusp of the Freezing Moon, and while Baawitigong was silently huddling for warmth, Shikaakwa screamed.

He exited the train and walked into an ant colony. Entire cruise ships' worth of people passed him in an instant. Loud, blaring announcements from overhead were repeated in several languages. It was the gateway for foreigners and Anishinaabe from every corner of Mino-Aki who wished for something they didn't have at home, like Dakaasin had—something more than what their towns or villages could offer them. Or who wished to run away from their homes and hide anonymously in this beehive, just one drone among others, like Meoquanee's family had. So they'd said.

And sometimes they were sent there against their will, pursuant to an act of justice following a Mediator's orders. Like Chibenashi's father.

He stood there, paralyzed, while the people moved around him at breakneck speed.

Shikaakwa was too much for him. And he hadn't even left the train station yet.

The walls around him crested skyward before tapering off—rounded ceilings with pointed peaks. Perfect for ensuring that heavy snowfall, for which Shikaakwa was famous, would simply slide down from the roof. At least that was familiar.

"Chibenashi!"

He swiveled his head around at the noise. Approaching him was a Myaamia man, about Chibenashi's age, with shoulder-length hair parted down the middle and a red, black, and white beaded headband. His jacket had a beaded fringe that swung back and forth in time with the swift movement of his body. He smiled at Chibenashi as if they were old friends. His eyes crinkled at the corners, the memory of a thousand prior smiles etched into them. His entire face was open and inviting, as if he considered any stranger to be a friend whom he hadn't met yet.

"I'm Takumwah," he said. "A Peacekeeper from the Shikaakwa Dakoniwewigamigong. I'm so glad to meet you."

Chibenashi looked his fellow Peacekeeper over. He carried no weapon, like the Peacekeepers in Baawitigong, but his belt was clipped with what presumably were other tools of their trade: a recorder, a notepad. There was nothing on his clothing identifying him as a Peacekeeper. He didn't even have the handcuffs that Chibenashi always carried but never used.

His accent was Anishinaabemowin, but his clothing was Myaamia. They were a minority in the country, albeit an influential one. Shikaakwa had been their ancestral homeland, but as time had passed, Anishinaabe culture and language had slowly seeped in. Still, they had their beads. The Myaamia always had their beads.

Chibenashi nodded at him. "Boozhoo." He fished into his pocket and removed Peezhickee's parcel. He thrust it at his host.

Takumwah somehow smiled even wider and brought it to his nose. "Good stuff," he said. "We'll smoke it together."

Chibenashi forced out a polite nod. He hoped it would be a quick smoke.

"First visit to Shikaakwa?"

Chibenashi paused. "Yes," he lied.

"You're going to love it, but it can be a bit much at first! At least, that's what people say. Me, I was born and raised here. Can't imagine living anywhere else. There's always something happening. Full of interesting people always coming and going.

"I'm glad I found you quickly; it's rush hour. Peezhickee mentioned that you would probably be a little lost when you first arrived. That all your luggage there? Need any help with that? No? Great, let's head out. That train ride can be killer. Though Baawitigong is pretty close. Never been there myself, but I have heard that it's just gorgeous, especially in the fall. All those colors on the trees. Maybe I'll make it up there this summer, before Manoomin. I hope you brought the evidence with you?"

Chibenashi nodded and indicated the satchel slung over his right shoulder, his dominant hand cradling it.

"Have you eaten?"

Chibenashi hadn't, but he nodded anyway.

"Great, we'll stop by the lab first. Chain of custody and all that. Plus if you bring it in before nightfall, you won't have to deal with the overnight staff. They can be a real pain. But the daytime crew is nice. We go out for drinks sometimes and make fun of the night staff. Hah! They will immediately stamp it and log it—no issues with admissibility on their end. The lab does good work, but it does take a few days. Usually more than a few, actually. Depending on the types of tests you want run. I got a brief rundown from Peezhickee, but we should probably discuss the particulars of the case to see what you might need. Also arranged for you to meet with one of the Advocates who has been assigned to this case. She's great, a really strong performer in front of a Mediator. Excellent at advocating for the Victim's point of view. Will tell you what she'll need in order to make a strong case. But we first need to talk to the family; Peezhickee mentioned that you hadn't done that yet. He sent me the list of names, so we can start on those whenever you want. I suggest tomorrow morning. Get a good night's rest and all that. You've been traveling all day; you'll be tired. We can stop for something to eat on the way to your lodging." By now they'd reached the door that led out of the terminal to the city, and Takumwah pushed it open without pausing for breath. "Brace yourself; it's cold out there."

The wind rushed into Chibenashi, chilling him to the bone. The city continued its primal howl. People seemed to multiply and appear out of nowhere. And Takumwah would not stop talking.

He didn't believe in the hell of other cultures—but if it did exist, Shikaakwa might as well be it.

◆ ◆ ◆

Shikaakwa sat at the southernmost end of Ininwewi-gichigami, spread out against the endless lake before it. Chibenashi caught sight of the lake as he joined Takumwah outside the station. It seemed to stretch on and on until, way far at the other end, it hit the tip of the peninsula. At the other end of that peninsula was Baawitigong. He was far from home. The gichigamiin sometimes froze over in the winter in Baawitigong. He wondered if that happened here as well.

Upon exiting the terminal, Chibenashi was confronted by a tall skyscraper. His gaze followed it all the way up to the top, so high he had to crane his neck to the point of hurting it. The lidless eyes of the windows looked down at him, judging him. He had slight paranoia that it would fall down. It reminded him of the way many of the tourists in Baawitigong would express fear that the tall trees in the woods would fall on them, which Chibenashi had always found ridiculous. He felt a wry solidarity with them at this moment. Then, noticing that no one else was staring up in wonderment, he ducked his head down. He shifted his eyes back and forth, trying to take in as much of the city as possible without advertising that he was from the village.

As they weaved through the hordes of people, Chibenashi stopped short at something he'd never seen before, could not even imagine: beggars on the street, hands out, heads bowed. Some people stopped to give them things—tobacco, food, whatever they had in their pockets. They sat on unrolled blankets with bags containing all their earthly possessions around them. He stood there, gaping, like the fish out of water he was.

"What's wrong?" Takumwah asked, backtracking a few steps.

"What are they doing out here? It's cold."

Takumwah shifted uncomfortably. "Well . . ."

Chibenashi stared at him. "Do they not have homes to go to?"

Takumwah shook his head and gestured for him to follow. Chibenashi took one last look at the line of beggars, wishing he had something to give them. Takumwah had the only tobacco on him. Chibenashi wished he could snatch it back.

"Why aren't they being taken care of?" he finally asked.

Takumwah shrugged. "Can't help everyone," he muttered. He led Chibenashi to another train, this one elevated three flights of stairs above the ground. The Shikaakwa monorail, known as the Sky Snake, arrived in perfect silence, just the barest whoosh of engine as it settled near them. It was rush hour, as Takumwah had said, and the monorail was crowded.

The Sky Snake slithered through the city. It seemed to Chibenashi that at each stop, the car completely emptied, then refilled itself with people. They took the wonder that was their city for granted, Chibenashi thought.

He was pressed into unfamiliar bodies. He had never been so close to so many people at once. He couldn't breathe in here, so tightly packed. And where was he supposed to look? At the ground? Out the window? He tried not to stare. He was used to foreigners who visited Baawitigong, though he'd never been in such close quarters with so many of them before. He accidentally met the eye of a man who looked like he was Lakota, judging by his clothing. He stared longer than he meant to, and the man did the same. After all this time, there was still awkwardness between the two cultures—too many centuries of war between them for feelings to completely be erased. After an uncomfortable long moment, Chibenashi looked away. A group of three young men with black skin spoke rapidly and loudly, punctuating whatever they were saying with hearty laughs. He had encountered enough tourists over the years to recognize the language as from somewhere on Africa's west coast—the Kingdom of Dagbon, or maybe the Fante Confederacy or Asante Empire. Gold jewelry glittered on them like stars in the night sky; probably Asante. Behind them was a Chinese couple snuggled up close together, with eyes only for each other. Next to them, he saw a Mayan woman reading something on a tablet, and Chibenashi wondered how she, presumably from the tropics, seemed to be handling the cold better than he was. A wiry European man with skin the same blue-white of a boiled egg huddled under a thick coat and fur cap.

Halfway down the car, an Anishinaabe teenager was drumming against the wall. One person shouted at him to stop, and the kid drummed louder in response. Takumwah droned on and on, pointing out various landmarks and going on about whatever it was he was going on about; Chibenashi had long since stopped listening in favor of people watching. Despite this discomfort, the large glass windows and doors extended up into the ceiling, affording Chibenashi a spectacular view of the city.

It was a forest of skyscrapers creating a canopy of life high above the ground. Many of these were Shikaakwa's famous "living skyscrapers." Most Anishinaabe, like Chibenashi, came from rural areas or small towns that were just as entwined with the land as their ancestors had been. All aspects of life had sprung from their relationship with the land and wildlife. It was therefore necessary, when Shikaakwa began to grow into the metropolis that it was, to ground it in the natural world. As apartments reached the sky, so did nature. Takumwah pointed out various high-rise apartment buildings that had level upon level of trees growing in them. Each floor had a platform jutting out, each at a different angle, that contained a number of trees sprouting up, bringing nature with them as the building climbed to the sky. The entire building was dotted with trees to the point that one could hardly see the structure within. Birds flew in and out of the trees just as they did back in the woods of Baawitigong; Chibenashi could see memeg, apichiwag, and misko-bineshiinhyag flying in and out. Each building was completely sustainable; the roofs of most were ponds surrounded by a thick crop of trees and solar panels. The glint of the sun flashed on their frozen surfaces, and Chibenashi was sure that during summer, each one would be as full of migrating birds as the ones in Baawitigong.

Interspersed among the living skyscrapers were centuries-old trees that seemed to be touching the sky themselves. Among them, buildings representing the various cultures from far and wide, whom Chibenashi had only been exposed to in passing by tourists, dotted the landscape. Christian churches, Islamic mosques, Shinto shrines, Buddhist temples all coexisted among various wiigwaasi-mashkikigamig of the Mide, the medicine society. He saw Shikaakwa's most famous building, the Tower of Resolution, which was built to partially resemble a large tree trunk standing upon a stylized turtle shell. Windows of colored glass in the shapes of giant dream catchers were carved into the tall stone walls. Peeking up between the buildings, flying proudly in the frigid sky, was the Mino-Aki flag.

As much as a modern city could be integrated into the environment, and complementing it rather than paving over it, Shikaakwa had managed it. It wasn't like the foreign cities that Chibenashi had seen, concrete jungles engaged in a never-ending battle to prevent nature from literally breaking through and swallowing it up. Most cities fought nature; Shikaakwa embraced it. Supposedly, most of the building materials had been recycled so that very little had been mined out of the ground.

The ground beneath them was thick with various trees along the roads and small parks in the medians that would be green and vibrant in the summer. Chibenashi spotted a few makeshift wigwams made out of logs and birchbark—like the wigwams of his ancestors—and frowned. The paved roads were narrow, and the sidewalks, made of packed dirt, were wide, lined with trees and bushes that, in spring and summer, would bear apples, cherries, berries, and various nuts that were ripe for plucking. A few hydrogen-powered vehicles that emitted water vapor from their exhaust pipes hummed quietly past. Gas-powered vehicles were prohibited in Shikaakwa, as they were in most of Mino-Aki. Other nations derived their wealth from hollowing out the earth for oil only to douse the surface in gasoline and light it on fire. Not this one.

Artwork was everywhere, depicting an idealized version of the rural lifestyle of places like Baawitigong (Chibenashi counted at least six errors and anachronisms), as well as the modern marvels of the city. On one building, a large photograph of a woman—the current leader—proudly advertised that Shikaakwa was the world's largest carbon-negative city. Someone had defaced it by painting fangs over her mouth—a Wendigo, growing larger with each life leeched, bleeding the people dry. Chibenashi heard a few muttered curses around him as her photograph filled the window.

Eventually, following a broken and garbled announcement from the speaker overhead, Takumwah indicated that this was their stop. Miskwaadesi: home of the central dakoniwewigamig, forensic science labs, Chibenashi's lodging, and the Tower of Resolution. Where the Mediation for Meoquanee's murderer—if he was ever caught—would take place.

Chibenashi swallowed and braced himself for the second time that day. He'd known this would be a possibility but had not expected it so soon.

"We're going in here?" he asked with what he hoped was nonchalance. "I thought we were . . . you know." He held up the bag containing the blood evidence.

Takumwah laughed. "Where do you think we're going? You want your lab results expedited, you need an Advocate to fill out a request and attach it to the sample. I've got one lined up. Comes from Baawitigong; that should give you even greater priority. Maybe you know her? Dakaasin."

Chibenashi dropped the bag.

Chapter Nine

Mediations were not resolved based on an Advocate's appearance, but Dakaasin always figured it couldn't hurt to look her best. Anything to make her client whole. She gave herself a final appraisal in the mirror in the bathroom on the fourteenth floor of the Tower of Resolution: hair cascading down her back with beads and feathers woven into some of the strands, long beaded earrings framing her face, copper bracelets on her wrists, and intricate makeup around her eyes. Nice and conservative. She smoothed down her ribbon skirt.

The offices of Victims' Advocates were on this floor, and Accuseds' Advocates were on the floor above. She would probably run into her counterpart on the elevator ride down. Today it would be Niimi on behalf of the Accused. Dakaasin liked Niimi; she always kept the Accuseds' humanity front and center. She had a few more years' experience as an Advocate than Dakaasin, and Dakaasin had learned much from her. At the same time, Dakaasin still didn't understand how Niimi could represent the interests of the Accused. Her heart bled too much for every Victim.

Once in the Mediation room, she took her seat at the Victim's table. The curved tables of the Victims, Accused, and Mediators all formed a circle around the center of the room, allowing everyone to see and be seen and heard equally.

Today's Mediation involved a young man who had abused and threatened his ex-lover. He'd found a way to hack into her phone, her tablet, her computer—recorded every keystroke, every phone call, every text message. He'd even made himself an authorized user on her devices so that he could log in as her; they recognized his fingerprint, his face, and his voice. The Victim had never known about any of this and had blissfully continued to move on with her life without any suspicion that she was being tracked. The Accused, who was angry following a day of watching her spend time with a new boyfriend, had approached the Victim and her new lover and started a fight. He'd beaten the Victim and threatened to kill her if he saw her out with another man again. The new boyfriend had tried to fight him off, but the Accused had been relentless and had easily subdued the new boyfriend. No one died, but the young woman had required hospitalization for her injuries.

Because the altercation had been witnessed by multiple people and the Victim could identify her attacker, there had been no need to have a prehearing to establish whether the Accused should stand responsible, which would have been required prior to this. He had conceded his part, which always made things run much more smoothly. Victims' families were often far more generous during Mediations if the Accused was willing to accept the responsibility. When the Accused fought, it generally soured both sides. Victims felt they were being victimized again, while the Accused dug in further and further, convinced of their own innocence. It made it harder to reach a final resolution that satisfied all parties.

Today was just about what would make the Victims—the woman and her boyfriend—and their families whole. Niimi sat at the table across so that the Accused and Victim could meet each other eye to eye as equals in the process. Dakaasin's client would be sitting behind her, in the first row of seats that surrounded the tables in concentric circles. She was already there, sitting between her parents, face calm. Victims generally were at this stage. Mediators tended to defer to what they wanted and what would satisfy them, within reason. Advocates on both sides usually discussed and negotiated before the final Mediation. In fact, it was not uncommon for all sides to show up to a hearing with a resolution already agreed on between them, and all the Mediator had to do was formalize it. This was not going to be one of those mediations. But it would be close. Niimi had already clued her in that, for the sake of his family, the Accused was not interested in a fight. Neither was the Victim Dakaasin represented; all she wanted—all she had wanted to do—was move on with her life. The new boyfriend's Advocate had said something similar.

Parties and Advocates in place, the Mediator arrived. Everyone stood; Dakaasin and the other Advocate put on their beaded leather headbands with three feathers in the back, part of the formal dress for Mediations. The Mediator, Waawaatesi, was not Dakaasin's favorite to work with but usually could be counted on to not set terms too favorable to the Accused. Unlike some Mediators, she would actually hear out both sides in full. She was an older lady, with gray hair that was short, wiry, and defied gravity. She was small and bony, like a bird. She wore a headdress that was more ornate than the Advocates' but not by much; such over-the-top formality was becoming less and less common in the Mediator courts. All parties sat once she did.

Dakaasin, as the Victim's Advocate, was invited to speak first.

"Thank you," she said. She stood tall and confident, her eyes scanning the room. She made sure to lock eyes with the Accused whenever her eyes passed over him to show that his power over the Victim was gone now. "Our system of Peacekeeping is one of restitution, of making people whole. That is all we come here today to do. This isn't about assigning blame or punishing the Accused. Rather, this is about restoring the past. All my client wants is to get back to where she was: happily involved with a new lover, having moved on from a past relationship. Now, we cannot change the past. What happened is what happened, and she is not asking us to change that. She simply wants what is fair, what will best approximate this rewind of the clock."

With the Advocates having given their arguments, the Victims were now afforded an opportunity to speak to the Mediator directly about the impact the crime had on them, and the Accused was afforded an opportunity to respond. Dakaasin looked over at the Victim, knowing that no matter what they did here today, they would never make her completely whole. But she was going to get her as close as possible.

The Victim stood from her chair. Her mother took her hand in support. All eyes turned to watch her. "I used to love him," she said. "And for a long time, we were happy. Then we weren't." She shifted, cast her eyes momentarily at the Accused. "The tracking wasn't about tracking. It was the control. That level of control from afar . . . it's hurt my ability to trust. We had broken up; I was free. And so was he. But then several moons later, I'm out with someone else, and I just . . . he hurt me. How do I know I'm safe to walk down the street again? That's the thing I really want back, I guess. Happiness is hard to promise and impossible to guarantee, but I do want to feel safe. And so whatever would make it so that when I walk down the street—either with a boyfriend or by myself or with a friend—I won't be afraid that he'll be watching me or that he'll act violent if he doesn't like what he sees. That's what I want again. To feel safe to be myself. I've lost that."

Then the Accused had his turn. He, too, sat between his parents as well as his two brothers. That was good for him, Dakaasin knew. Family being present showed support, that he had community around him to keep him from hurting someone again.

"I'm not a bad person," he said. "I just did a bad thing. And I did it out of love.

"I've never hurt anyone before. I never meant to hurt anyone that day. I loved her so much. I still do. That's why I did what I did. Love. When you love someone, you can justify anything.

"I don't mean that I don't take responsibility. I do. And if that means she can't be around me, I can accept that. I don't want to." He looked at the Victim. "But I'll do it for her. It'll kill me to do it, but beyond anything else, I want her to be happy. So for her, I will do it."

Dakaasin wanted to believe him. Maybe he wanted to believe it too.

After some closing statements, Waawaatesi issued her recommendation. The parties' desires seemed best resolved by the Accused agreeing to avoid all contact with the Victim; stay at least five hundred meters away from her home, place of work, and the boyfriend's home and place of work; and, if he were to run into her in the city, immediately remove himself to a new location. The Accused was to remain living with his parents and brothers, who would bear responsibility for ensuring he stayed out of trouble. The Accused would go to counseling and anger management courses to get the venom out of his blood and learn to control his temper. And, finally, the Accused and his family would pay the families of the Victim and her boyfriend for all out-of-pocket expenses paid toward their care, which was minimal since everyone was covered by nationalized health care. But it was ordered nonetheless; the point was to put them back in the position they had been in.

"I recognize that this does not turn back time," said Waawaatesi, "but may we agree that this best approximates that, and provides for nearly all of what the Victim has requested and the Accused has agreed to do?"

Dakaasin cleared her throat. She'd gotten everything she'd requested. So she decided to ask for even more.

"Respectfully," she asked, "I would like to be heard." Waawaatesi nodded. "Thank you. The Victim appreciates this resolution. However, to truly make her whole, more must be done. I would like to ask that the Accused's movements be tracked electronically until the start of the next moon to make sure that he does stay away. I would also like to ask that he be prohibited from using any electronic devices himself. He has abused them before and might do so again. It would be too easy for him

91

to continue to track the Victim and then sneak out to find her again. His family cannot watch him every moment."

The Accused made a noise of protest, which Niimi silenced. "This is too harsh," Niimi said. "The goal is to make the Victim whole, not to punish the Accused. The level of surveillance that is being requested is no better than imprisonment, and cutting him off from all communication devices is even harsher. Imprisonment is a last resort, not a first choice."

"It is the only way to ensure the Victim's safety," Dakaasin countered.

Waawaatesi raised her hand, and the two Advocates stood silent.

"I have heard enough," she said. "You are asking for punishment, not restitution. That is not what we are here to do. The Accused is willing to take responsibility for his actions. He has a good family and community who will keep him from further trouble. If they keep their commitment to him and his well-being, then the Victim will remain safe. I have spoken."

And with that, the Mediation ended.

"Wow," Chibenashi breathed. He hadn't been prepared to be at a Mediation, the supposedly Victim-centric process that would make one whole. No one was made whole after a crime. Their wounds were stitched shut, but that didn't make them whole.

"Yeah," Takumwah said. "Love can justify anything? That's some moose shit. Anyway. These things can get a little intense. Glad they reached a resolution fairly quickly, though. Sometimes it takes longer. You ever been to one before?"

Chibenashi nodded. "A long time ago." His father's Mediation had been perfunctory. He'd already confessed, and with responsibility accepted, there was only a discussion of what to do next to make his children whole. His father had requested imprisonment, and no one had argued against it. Chibenashi hadn't spoken at the Mediation, the way the Victim had here. He couldn't. When you'd lost everything, you couldn't actually ask for anything. It was impossible to know where to start.

"Come on. Let's try to catch Dakaasin before she gets too far."

Chibenashi reluctantly followed Takumwah toward the center of the room. The Accused had already departed, in keeping with the Mediator's order to avoid further contact with the Victim. He hadn't said goodbye, just been led out by his family, stealing one last longing look at the Victim. Dakaasin and her fellow Advocate representing the new boyfriend were speaking with their clients. She hugged the Victim and spoke with the family with a sad smile on her face. Chibenashi and Takumwah hovered awkwardly until the families left and Dakaasin was gathering her belongings.

"Dakaasin!" Takumwah called out with a wave.

Dakaasin turned her head and flashed a smile that turned into shock once she saw who was with Takumwah. She paused, frozen on the spot, as if time itself had stopped.

Chibenashi was sure that it had. His very heart seemed to have stopped beating.

Takumwah looked from Dakaasin to Chibenashi and back again.

"You two know each other?"

Dakaasin and Chibenashi remained frozen, as if each were daring the other to respond first.

"I'll take that as a yes."

Dakaasin, always the brave one, spoke first.

"You look well," she said to Chibenashi. The polite smile was just that—polite.

Chibenashi somehow found his voice. "You too." An awkward pause. "You're really good at this. Always knew you would be."

"Took a lot of practice," she said. "Years of it. Lots of mistakes along the way."

"No doubt."

Another long pause. Takumwah mercifully killed it this time. "We are looking to do some forensic testing. Would you mind signing off on the DNA request so that we can get it expedited? Time is of the essence on this one. We want to avoid asking the night crew, after all!"

Dakaasin gave a surprised look, blinking rapidly as if coming back to herself after being lost in thought. "Of course," she said. "This your case, Chibenashi?"

"Yes."

"Meoquanee?"

He nodded.

Dakaasin shook her head. "I heard about it. I'm so sorry. I know she was close to you." She considered Chibenashi for a long moment. "You're okay to work on this?"

He stared back at her, trying to keep his discomfort out of his expression. "Yes."

Dakaasin looked skeptical but shrugged. There was a lot in that shrug, but his defensiveness prohibited Chibenashi from reading into it. She signed the proffered form and returned it to Takumwah, who also signed it.

"That all?"

Chibenashi and Dakaasin stared at each other for a long time, to the point that Takumwah began to shift uncomfortably. He looked from one to the other and back again.

"Well," Takumwah finally said, breaking the painful silence, "we'll be in touch if we need anything further from you, yeah?" He took Chibenashi's elbow, which Chibenashi instinctively pulled away. "Always good to see you."

"You too," Dakaasin said, still locking eyes with Chibenashi, sounding distant.

◆　◆　◆

Dakaasin remembered how broken Chibenashi had been following his mother's murder and father's confession. He'd been happy before, care-free—just like any teenager should be. And then *it* had happened. The Chibenashi she had known and loved had died along with his mother, had been locked away like his father. He'd clung to her like a life raft, nearly drowning her as he fought to stay afloat. She'd kept them both going, with Chibenashi never realizing just how much effort it took her to do so. She wasn't just carrying him—she was carrying Chibenashi who was carrying Ashwiyaa. The weight of that sort of thing could snap you in half after enough time had passed. No one was strong enough to do that.

The opportunity to come to Shikaakwa had presented itself like her own life raft. She could become an Advocate and represent people like Chibenashi and Ashwiyaa, helping everyone find a resolution that could make victims whole again. She could make a difference. And the city itself offered endless possibilities. Baawitigong was both idyllic and stifling. It was isolated, remote, rural, and small. Very few opportunities for a career, if you wanted one. It was a beautiful cage, but your wings were clipped, and the sky was beyond your reach. There was a reason the cruise ships usually docked in the morning and left before dark; you could see the whole place in less than a day. The familiar was enough for many people. But Dakaasin had wanted more. The university beckoned, and she answered its call.

Still, moving from a small village like Baawitigong to a metropolis like Shikaakwa was a tall order for anybody. Though she had cousins and relatives of friends who had relocated to Shikaakwa, she knew that missing the close-knit community of support would be both liberating and frightening. It took a lot of courage to take that step, courage that she knew she had in her but that she also knew could abandon her unexpectedly. So she'd asked Chibenashi to come with her. Start a new life with her there, away from all of this—the bad memories, the pain, the hurt.

He'd refused.

How could she ask that of him, he'd said. Ashwiyaa needed him, and he couldn't leave her. And he obviously couldn't bring her to Shikaakwa— Baawitigong was too overwhelming to her; how could she possibly handle a place like Shikaakwa? She would be not only in a new place but also with all new people. He could help her, as could Meoquanee. And Dakaasin. How could Dakaasin even think of leaving Ashwiyaa, after all she had lost? And not to mention Baawitigong was the most beautiful place in the world. Who in their right mind could ever leave it?

In the end, it turned out that Dakaasin could.

And she had not looked back.

◆ ◆ ◆

"What was that all about?" Takumwah asked Chibenashi after he had marched him out the door of the hearing room.

Chibenashi gave Takumwah a look. He didn't like talking about this with anyone. With a near stranger? It was like having his skin peeled off. He had only been in Shikaakwa a short while, and it was already worse than he'd expected.

"Let's go talk to Sakima," Chibenashi said. No sense in spending any more time here than he had to.

"The Victim's son? You don't want to go and get settled first? We could talk to him tomorrow."

"No. Today."

Takumwah shrugged. "Well, then, come on. We pulled his address. He's across town, along the gichigami with the other fishermen. I'll show you the fastest way there."

Chibenashi nodded. The faster they talked to Meoquanee's son, the faster the test could be run and the faster they could move on to other witnesses and be out of there. Fast was good.

The sooner he got through this investigation, the sooner Ashwiyaa would be safe.

Chapter Ten

Shikaakwa's waterfront was famous around the world for the way the land and the lake, the buildings and the trees, all came together in the seamless harmony of nature and architecture. Against a backdrop peppered with living skyscrapers, tall buildings of glass, religious temples, and trees, the glassy, clear surface of Ininwewi-gichigami reflected the city back like a large mirror. It was the picture on almost every postcard of the city, and by far the most recognizable view for those who didn't actually live there. The water itself was so clean and clear that one could famously go out on the fifty-meter-long pier and stare down straight to the bottom. While it appeared to be only a couple of meters deep, it was actually over one hundred. Walking trails allowed people to meander along the water, and the gentle symphony of talking, laughter, and street music floated over the lake and into the sky above.

That was the Shikaakwa waterfront that the tourists saw.

A couple of kilometers north of this frontage, however, was the fishing district. It was the kind of place you smelled long before you saw it.

The housing units here were "living" buildings only in the sense that you could see and hear the bugs, rats, bats, and other vermin skittering in and behind the walls. They were "living" in that mold grew on the walls and in the corners of flickering light fixtures, and weeds sprouted in the packed dirt of the sidewalk and out of the gutters. They were "living" in that stray animals that might have been pets in other neighborhoods roamed the halls and the streets outside. They were "living" in that the smell of newly dead fish permeated everything.

The Anishinaabe valued fishermen, as they did anyone whose work served to feed the people. In Baawitigong, fishermen were given far better places to live. Chibenashi suspected that Sakima had done something to warrant such subpar housing—or at least something that kept him out of a home he would have otherwise been entitled to. Maybe something about Sakima made people want to give him less.

Chibenashi and Takumwah, still carrying Chibenashi's baggage with them, knocked on the door of a third-floor apartment. The door was old, with chipped blue paint peeling off in greasy curls. Music or a TV blared from another apartment down the hall. On a wood panel next to the door was a carved doodem. Chibenashi thought they must have the wrong apartment. Meoquanee's doodem was a loon, which should also be her son's. A bear was carved into this one. Maybe it was old, from a prior tenant. Nothing in this building looked like it was regularly maintained.

Way back in the olden days, doodemag were how the Anishinaabe had organized their society. Certain doodemag had been responsible for tasks such as healing, defense, hunting/gathering, communications, and teaching. No one did that anymore, though the old prejudices about certain doodemag still existed. Once upon a time, it would have been unthinkable to have anything but your true doodem affixed to a post outside your door. It was how you and everyone else knew your place in society. Now, the way the old folks told it, everything was confusing. No one knew anything anymore. You might as well pick your favorite animal to be your doodem, they said.

Chibenashi suspected this change had meaning.

For as long as anyone could remember, women had taken the doodem of the men they married, and that's what Meoquanee and Chibenashi's mother had both done. Such a practice was starting to fall out of favor, but the change hadn't reached the older generations yet.

The door swung open to reveal an overweight man in his thirties, with long uneven hair falling to his shoulders and a face that was unshaven, apparently due to neglect rather than design. He wore a stained shirt that he looked to have been wearing for several days. He was tearing into a piece of deer jerky with yellowed teeth. His eyes were bloodshot. His expression said, "I don't care."

Chibenashi swallowed. Sakima had really let himself go.

"You've let yourself go," Sakima said to Chibenashi in greeting, words struggling to escape around the wad of food in his mouth. Chibenashi almost laughed. He and Sakima had often had similar thoughts at the same time. He supposed it was a bit comforting that after years of tragedy and distance, some things never changed.

Sakima wasn't wrong; Chibenashi cared little for his appearance or health, beyond keeping himself alive and available to care for Ashwiyaa. He'd let himself go physically, mentally, and spiritually. He'd given up on his own well-being long ago.

Chibenashi introduced Takumwah and asked if they might come in. Sakima reluctantly led them into his small apartment. It was a single room, with a kitchen and living space dominated entirely by a narrow bed that Chibenashi doubted Sakima could fit in comfortably. The smell of fish was overwhelming. Chibenashi deposited his luggage next to the front door but was careful not to let it actually touch the wall.

"I'm so sorry for your loss," Chibenashi said to Sakima.

Sakima grunted some sort of acknowledgment at Chibenashi without even turning to look at him.

"What are you doing for work these days?" Chibenashi asked.

"Fishing."

"You fish for Adikameg?"

Sakima nodded.

"You like it?"

Sakima shrugged.

Chibenashi looked around the meager dwelling. "Not quite the same standard of living as if you were fishing in Baawitigong, is it?"

"No," Sakima said in a tone implying that had been the point.

"How long you been at it?"

"Since I left school."

"You finish?" Takumwah asked.

"No."

No surprise there.

Chibenashi noted that Sakima had no photographs of anyone on his walls or furniture. The blanket on his bed was so old and faded that it was impossible to tell what color it had been originally or what design had been on it. The furniture looked as if it had been recycled through generations of users without much refurbishment, and there was little evidence of cooking or other food preparation in the kitchen. Small wooden utensils from takeout orders were scattered across the small kitchen counter and on the table next to the bed. Chibenashi's fingers itched to collect them and put them in the sink, if not compost them altogether, but he managed to stop himself.

"How long have you lived in this place?" he asked.

"Since I left school."

Sakima was a couple of years younger than Chibenashi, so that meant he'd been here over fifteen years. No trace of himself anywhere; only garbage and filth.

There was no place for them to sit, so they corralled themselves around the counter—Sakima in the kitchen, Takumwah on the other side, Chibenashi in the middle, straddling both worlds. Sakima took a beer from the refrigerator but did not offer the others anything to eat or drink. It was a bottle of Emikwaan, the cheapest beer out there, widely reviled for both its taste and low alcohol content. "Turtle piss" is what most people called it.

"Do you mind if we speak with you a bit about your mother?" Chibenashi asked gently.

Sakima visibly stiffened. "What's there to talk about anymore? She's gone."

"Murdered," Takumwah corrected him. "And we're trying to figure out by whom."

"I know," Sakima said, bristling. "So why talk about her?"

"Why not talk about her?" Takumwah asked.

Sakima narrowed his eyes. "You assume I have something positive to say about her. Since I do not, I will say nothing."

"You didn't come back for Manoomin, did you?" Chibenashi asked. "I didn't think I saw you there."

Sakima took a drink before answering. "No, I didn't."

"Why not?"

Sakima shrugged. "Not really my thing. Besides, my family is here."

"Did you spend it with them?"

Sakima took another swig of beer.

"Why didn't you go to the burial?" Chibenashi asked. This was the real question he'd been wanting to pose to Sakima since it happened. "Or light the fires for her spirit?"

Sakima shrugged. "I said my goodbyes years ago."

"When was that?" Takumwah asked. "Was it when you left school?"

Sakima shook his head. "No. Before."

"When you moved to Shikaakwa?"

"Yeah."

"How old were you?"

"Fourteen."

"And how old are you now?"

"Thirty-four."

Takumwah's composure faltered for a moment. "What happened to make you cut off contact with your mother when you were only fourteen?"

Sakima took a long swig of his beer, seemingly considering what he wanted to say very carefully before he said it.

"We needed to start a new life," he said finally. "Me and my father."

"Why?"

Sakima slammed his beer down, sloshing some of it on the counter, making some of the wooden utensils rattle with the force of it. "Because we couldn't stay with her."

"Why not?" Takumwah was pushing Sakima to speak ill of his dead mother, and it was making Chibenashi nervous and physically uncomfortable. Maybe breaching such taboos was common here in the city. But back in Baawitigong? Chibenashi felt his blood pressure rise at the very thought of it. He could tell that despite living the balance of his life in Shikaakwa, Sakima felt similarly uncomfortable.

"The affair."

"Whose affair?"

"Hers."

That brought Chibenashi up short. Meoquanee, having an affair? Unfaithful to her husband? That wasn't the woman he knew.

"With whom?" Chibenashi rasped.

Sakima stared at Chibenashi for a long time. "I couldn't say," he said finally.

"Who could?"

"No one," Sakima replied. "Given the circumstances."

This was all going in the wrong direction.

"Look," Chibenashi said, putting aside his discomfort and confusion at this revelation about Meoquanee, "we won't ask you to talk about anything you don't want. I know what you're going through. You know my mother was murdered too." Sakima looked away. "What makes a huge difference to me, and always has, is that we know who did it. It's given me closure. It's given my sister closure. We can sleep at night knowing what happened and knowing that the person who did it is locked away forever." That was a lie, but it served its purpose. "Can you say the same?"

Sakima still would not meet Chibenashi's eye. A cloud passed over the sun, momentarily dimming the light. The shadow crossed Sakima's face. He looked tired. Worn out. Like he didn't have the energy within him to continue the fight.

Chibenashi saw his chance. He explained the situation regarding the DNA evidence.

"Would you give us a sample?"

Sakima stared out the small window that was no larger than a dinner plate. It was greasy. The images outside of it were blurry, distorted. Chibenashi figured that whatever was on the other side was not a view worth keeping, if the grease was preferable. Sakima did not respond.

"Without your help, we can't create a profile for her, and without that we cannot figure out who killed your mother," Chibenashi said gently. "Right now we have no direction. We need to know where True East is, and we don't even have that."

Sakima continued to stare at the greasy window. There was a handprint on it. Maybe he had tried to clean it at some point, only to make it dirtier with his touch.

"No," he said finally.

That brought Chibenashi up short again.

"No?" asked Takumwah. He'd clearly yielded the interrogation to Chibenashi, hoping to exploit the shared background, but now was back in the action.

"No."

"Why won't you give it to us?" Takumwah demanded.

"Because," Sakima replied, "I have my closure. I don't need any more answers. I don't have any questions. I haven't for a long time."

"You don't want to know who killed your mother?" Takumwah was incredulous.

"It's nothing to do with me. She has been out of my life for a long time, and her being murdered has not changed that. I'm sorry she is gone. I really am. But there is no need for my continued involvement."

"Where were you on the first night of Manoomin?" Takumwah asked.

Sakima took another swig from his beer. "Here."

"Did you go to the festival at the waterfront?"

"No."

"Did you go to any ceremony or festival anywhere else?"

"No."

"Were you just here, in your apartment?"

"Yes."

"Anyone with you?"

"No."

"Anyone who can confirm you were actually here?"

Sakima shrugged. "Probably not."

"You don't seem concerned about that," Takumwah said.

"Why would I be? Like I said, her death is nothing to do with me."

"What time do you start fishing each day?" Chibenashi asked.

"Before dawn."

"And were you on your boat the day after Manoomin?" Takumwah asked.

"Yes."

"Anyone be able to vouch for you being there?"

"Wouldn't know."

Chibenashi sighed. It was time to cut bait on this.

"Look," he said, "I hope you'll change your mind." He grabbed one of the napkins on the counter and asked Takumwah for a pen, which he provided. "If you do, I'll be in town for a few days. And after that, you can still reach me on my mobile." He scribbled his mobile phone and lodging information on the napkin and handed it to Sakima, who at least had the grace to accept it. "I hope I'll hear from you."

Takumwah handed Sakima a printed business card—the sort of thing they had no need for back in Baawitigong, where everybody knew how to reach everybody else, usually by showing up at their wigwam unannounced. "You be sure to let me know if you are going to be out of town anytime soon, yeah?" Sakima did not take the card, so Takumwah dropped it on the counter between them. It landed facedown. Sakima did not turn it over. Takumwah waited a long time before finally capitulating and doing it himself.

◆ ◆ ◆

The door slammed behind them. Chibenashi considered the doodem again. He guessed it really had been deliberate. Meoquanee was no longer part of their family. All his life, Chibenashi had known and loved Meoquanee, and he was left more puzzled than ever. Sakima couldn't possibly have been right about an affair. Could he? Chibenashi had heard rumors about such things, of course. In both directions. People had quietly and not so quietly assumed that Ishkode had killed his wife because she'd had an affair, while others in the village were equally certain that he had killed her because of his own affair so that he could be with the other woman. And Chibenashi had dismissed all of it as gossip meant to entertain people in a small village with very little to do. Just about everyone in Baawitigong had been mentioned as the potential other woman or man at one point or another.

Hearing that Meoquanee had had an affair, and from her own son . . . that was a different story. They would have to hear more from her ex-husband.

"So now what? We didn't get his DNA," Chibenashi said.

"Yes we did," Takumwah said calmly.

"And we probably could have," Chibenashi continued, ignoring the comment and hoisting his luggage over his shoulder. "Why did you go so aggressively toward him? That's not how we do things in Baawitigong."

"You're a long way from Baawitigong, friend."

We're not friends.

They walked toward the stairs, Chibenashi's luggage slapping loudly on each step. His shoulders hunched more and more in defeat with every step. They'd failed to get the DNA sample. Sakima wouldn't even talk to them. They hadn't even gotten to talk about things like Sakima's father. He would be going back to Baawitigong in defeat.

"What do we do now?" Chibenashi asked, not really asking Takumwah, as they stomped down the stairs.

"We run a DNA test," Takumwah said simply.

"With the sample we didn't get?"

"You mean the sample we *did* get." Takumwah stopped and triumphantly held up an evidence bag, inside of which was one of the used wooden utensils that had been scattered across Sakima's kitchen counter.

Chibenashi missed a step and stumbled in the recovery. He snatched the bag from Takumwah's hand. "How did you get that?"

"Slipped it in while you two were busy playing your staring contest. It was clear from the get-go that he was not going to tell us anything. He's hiding something, that's for sure. Probably worth checking on his whereabouts on the night of the murder. We have ways of doing that. Anyway, we'll take this to the lab, drop off your luggage; then I'm getting you a drink and something to eat. No arguments. It's been a long day for me and especially for you. Plus, since we'll be working together, I'm going to need to get your whole life story."

Chibenashi stood silent, his mouth agape.

"I'm kidding." He clapped Chibenashi on the shoulder in a way that suggested he wasn't kidding. "Man, I've never felt shoulder muscles so tense. You need to relax more. We're getting you two drinks."

"I don't drink."

"Never said it had to be alcohol, friend." Takumwah trotted down a few steps before Chibenashi plodded behind him.

"Is that legal?"

"Hm?" Takumwah stopped in his tracks and turned back up toward Chibenashi, who was nearly a flight behind him.

"Taking the utensil without him knowing. Using it to run a test. Can we even do that?"

"Plain sight rule."

"Never heard of it."

"Really? It's a thing."

"A thing written into law?"

"I suspect that, by the end of this, that won't matter anyway. People have a way of confessing to these things once you've got them pinned in with the DNA. I've gotten this into evidence before. Dakaasin is good at what she does."

"How do we even know it's his? Someone else could have used it."

"Did you even look at that place? I bet we're the first people to visit that apartment in years. Maybe ever."

"I didn't know you could do that—just take something."

"Like I said, friend," Takumwah said, flashing a smile at Chibenashi. "You're a long way from Baawitigong."

Blood sample and wooden utensil duly dropped off, tagged, and cataloged for priority testing at the laboratory thanks to Dakaasin's flowery signature; lodgings checked into; luggage safely deposited; showered and changed to get the feel of travel and an unfamiliar city out of his pores, Chibenashi decided to assuage his conscience. He retrieved his mobile phone and brought up his sister's contact information. He initiated a video chat.

Ashwiyaa was in the dark. He could barely see her face. He thought she might be under a blanket, head and all, with nothing but his own face on the phone to light her. This was not good.

Since their mother's death, he'd never spent a night away from her. Even though he'd just left that morning, it felt strange knowing he wouldn't be coming home to her. He could only imagine how it was affecting her.

A wave of tenderness swelled within him at the sight. "Boozhoo," he whispered.

A sniffle through the phone.

"What's wrong?" he asked. The light from the phone reflected in her eyes.

She did not answer.

"Ashwiyaa, please. Tell me what's wrong."

A long pause. When she finally did respond, her voice sounded like she was twelve years old again.

"When are you coming home?"

"Soon, nishiime; I promise."

"How soon?"

Chibenashi sighed, wanting to reassure her but also not wanting to lie to her. "Probably a few days," he admitted.

Her keening cry ripped him open.

"Please don't be sad. I'll be back before you know it."

"No you won't."

"The blood sample is with forensics," he said. "And I spoke to Sakima. Remember him? He looks terrible, by the way. So I'm making really good progress."

Ashwiyaa huffed a little breath. "Did you get what you needed?"

"A DNA sample?"

"Yeah."

"I hope so."

"Me too."

They sat there in silence for a little longer; Chibenashi bathed in artificial light, Ashwiyaa robed in darkness. It was familiar. Safe, even.

A knock at the door pulled Chibenashi out of the reverie.

"That'll be the Peacekeeper from Shikaakwa who's helping me," he said. "Want to meet him?"

"No."

"Then I'd better get going."

Ashwiyaa's voice wavered. "Okay."

"Sleep well, nishiime. I love you."

Ashwiyaa ended the call, but not before Chibenashi could hear the beginnings of a sob. He called her back, but she did not pick up.

Takumwah knocked again, this time more insistently. Chibenashi fired off a quick apology text, pleading with her to call him back and that he would drop what he was doing to take the call, then answered the door.

"You clean up well," Takumwah exclaimed. "Let's go. You haven't seen anything until you've seen Shikaakwa at night."

Chapter Eleven

The freezing air pierced Chibenashi as quickly and painfully as a snakebite. Yet another way in which Shikaakwa sank its fangs into him and ripped him open. *You're not in Baawitigong anymore,* it said. *Pay attention to me.*

"Cold," he remarked.

The wind whistled. They pulled their heavy coats, biiskaawaaganan, closer around them. Chibenashi biiskaawaaganan had Animikii Binesi stitched across the back. Takumwah's was as bejeweled and beaded as the vest he'd worn during the day. His headband was impervious to the wind.

"Shikaakwa's greatest lover is the cold. She's possessive over it. Never lets it go, especially at night," Takumwah said, sounding like he was quoting a poem or a song or a common saying, but Chibenashi was relatively certain he'd come up with that himself. He wouldn't know and, honestly, didn't really care.

They walked down the street. Large communal bonfires were set up throughout the sidewalks, and families, couples, and groups gathered around them. Many were handing out drinks and tobacco while others played music or told stories. Laughter warmed the air. It might have been a night in Baawitigong. Above them, the lights of the buildings faded out so that the glow of the moon and the stars could shine upon the city. The natural light reflected off the snow and special reflective panels on the windows of skyscrapers, which absorbed sunlight during the day and illuminated the city at night without forsaking the view of the stars. Chibenashi could make out the familiar seven stars of Bagonagiizhi, Ojiig, the Fisher whose tail would soon sweep down and paint the fall colors on the leaves, and Mishi-bizhiw, the Great Lynx. Farther down the road, he saw the silhouettes of a herd of deer scamper from behind one group of buildings and disappear behind another. An owl hooted from the top of one of the trees.

Takumwah led Chibenashi a couple of blocks down to a black door with no sign. It opened with a jingle from an unseen bell. The warmth from inside was inviting, safe, like a hug from a friend. Any reservations Chibenashi might have had about going in evaporated. He needed to be out of the cold.

"I know it isn't the fanciest," Takumwah said, "but it's the best Mongolian food you'll get anywhere in the city."

Chibenashi did not even know what was in Mongolian food, let alone whether this place was the best. There had been Mongolian tourists in Baawitigong over the years, but no Mongolian restaurants. Being a tourist town, Baawitigong emphasized its traditional roots, yet there was a smattering of restaurants with other cuisines, like Spanish or Abyssinian or Incan, so the tourists would feel more at home. But this was new. New was bad. He had dealt with enough *new* today. He wanted to eat duck with manoomin and berries, or squash with beans. Comfort food. But it would have been unthinkably rude to refuse.

Some of the staff greeted Takumwah with a wave and gestured for him to sit; clearly, he was a regular here. The place was small, and most tables and booths were full. Red lanterns were strung overhead, and everything around them advertised that they were in the Year of the Rat. Several flat-screen televisions blared silent sports and news programs. The bar was in the corner, well stocked. The bartender immediately began pouring an unfamiliar brand of beer for Takumwah from a green glass bottle with a dragon emblazoned on the side. He pointed at Chibenashi, asking if he'd like one too. Chibenashi shook his head, and so the bartender filled a glass with water. A young server indicated for them to take one of the booths against the wall; the seats were well worn, exhausted from the weight of thousands of prior customers, and groaned beneath them.

The moment they sat down, Takumwah sprang back up. "Come on; we'll go get our food." Chibenashi sighed and followed him to a buffet line full of frozen meats sliced so thinly that they had curled into cylinders; specialty ones like chicken, pork, tripe, yak, and beef, as well as familiar ones like venison and adikameg; fresh vegetables both familiar (corn, onions, squash) and unfamiliar (bok choi, water chestnut, something called winter melon); and an array of sauces and spices with names he couldn't pronounce. Overhead was a sign imploring patrons to not press their food down into the bowl. When it was their turn, Chibenashi took in the spread while Takumwah helped himself to a variety, demonstrating how to layer his chosen items, top them with noodles and sauces, and then hand them to the cooks to grill on a large flat stove in billowing clouds of steam. The cooks asked if they wanted to add garlic or pineapple or cashews before grilling the food, which only took a few moments. By the time they returned to their booth, their drinks were waiting for them along with plates of steamed white rice (no manoomin here), vegetable broth, and what looked like rolled buns sprinkled with sesame seeds.

Takumwah immediately took up his chopsticks to begin eating but then stopped short. Chibenashi had raised his hands over his bowl and begun a blessing. He thanked Gichi-manidoo for the food and offered his blessings to the four directions of the earth, his ancestors, and the living things that had given their lives so that they may eat. When he was done, he saw that Takumwah was looking at him. Chibenashi felt a bit awkward; blessings before meals were common in Baawitigong, but after a cursory glance around, he found that nobody else seemed to be doing it. Spirituality suddenly seemed very unsophisticated among the people who lived in a big city. He cleared his throat and began to eat, maneuvering the chopsticks a bit awkwardly but enough to get the job done.

The food was steaming hot, and he blew on it before taking an experimental first bite. The flavor was rich, with just a hint of spice to give it a little bit of a kick. Takumwah had been right; the food was good.

"It's good," he said.

Takumwah smiled. "Knew you'd like it."

They spent a few moments in blissful silence enjoying their food before Takumwah ruined everything.

"You follow baaga'adowewin?" Takumwah asked. He gestured at one of the widescreen televisions along the wall where two teams—one wearing white, the other red, which meant Shikaakwa was playing Ganatsekwyagon—played as if the fate of the world were on the line. The field was covered with players wielding long sticks with nets at the end, running from the other team's players as if they were predators and prey, passing and catching a ball as they made their way toward the netted goals at each end of the field.

Chibenashi shook his head. "Not anymore," he said. He'd played it in the summers, lived and breathed it for a long time, like most kids. Before *it* happened. Like so many other things that had once been important to him, it had come to seem so meaningless.

"Too bad," Takumwah said. "Shikaakwa could go all the way this year." He became absorbed in the game for a few moments, letting out a small whoop—along with the rest of the patrons—when his team scored. He high-fived one of the men in the booth behind them, who Takumwah probably didn't even know. Shikaakwa's team was huddled together in a war dance to celebrate the goal. Takumwah tore himself away from the game to return his attention to Chibenashi.

"Your sport must be tooadiwin, then?" Takumwah asked. "Popular up north, with all that ice you get. Bet you can skate faster than you can run up there. Baawitigong even has a team, yeah?"

Not one worth mentioning or following. "No."

Takumwah hummed as he searched for another topic of conversation. "Must be a change, being in a big city like this."

Chibenashi shrugged. "It's fine."

"You like what you see?"

Chibenashi shrugged again. "It's unfamiliar yet familiar. You see the same trees, we speak the same language, but I feel like a mayagi-anishinaabe. Like I don't quite belong. Just a visitor to someone else's home."

"I know that feeling," Takumwah said with a sigh.

"What do you mean? You said you were from here."

"I am. My people are. Look around you. It's all Anishinaabe. I'm T'wah T'wah. This land was once all our land. Now it isn't. Our language no longer exists. Everyone speaks Anishinaabemowin. We are still here. But we've been all but erased since you took our land."

Chibenashi was puzzled. "The Myaamia joined up with the Anishinaabe and other nations to form Mino-Aki peacefully."

Takumwah snorted. "So first of all, it's T'wah T'wah. *Myaamia* is your word, not ours. And second, that may be what they taught you, but that's not what happened."

"What do you mean?"

Takumwah waved a hand. "Forget it."

"You haven't been erased, though. You have representation in the government. We learn about you in school. And your clothing is so distinctive."

Takumwah gave him a look that was less than friendly. Chibenashi sensed that somehow he'd said something offensive. After a strained moment, Takumwah spoke again.

"A token representation. We aren't a majority and aren't taken seriously. There aren't enough of us to effect real change."

"What would you change?"

Takumwah shrugged. "I guess I just would want the acknowledgment that the Anishinaabe aren't the only ones who live here and that this land wasn't theirs to begin with. They wanted the Ininwewi-gichigami, so they took all the land around the lakes to make sure they controlled all the access." Clearly ready to change the subject away from politics, he considered Chibenashi carefully. "Something happen after you got to your lodging? You seem more tired than you did earlier."

Chibenashi shrugged. "Long day. Travel. Sakima."

"Seems like there's something else going on," Takumwah said. He slurped up a noodle.

Chibenashi took a large bite of food and took his time chewing and swallowing. "It's complicated."

"I've got all night."

Chibenashi resisted. Takumwah pushed. After several awkward silences, a few false starts, Shikaakwa winning the game of baaga'ad-owewin, and another bowl of food, Chibenashi was finally ready to talk.

Takumwah had gotten Chibenashi to reveal his favorite color (blue); hobby (he didn't have one); no really, what did he do for fun (walking, if he had to pick something that wasn't either work or caregiving); and food (manoomin baked with apples) before he got him to reveal his real passion: Dakaasin.

"We grew up together," Chibenashi said. "Our families knew each other. Our wigwams were close enough to easily walk between them. My sister looked up to Dakaasin as if she were her own big sister, and Dakaasin—who had no siblings—looked at Ashwiyaa as if she were her own little sister. We both loved walks through Baawitigong—down by the port with the tourists, in the town, and through the woods.

"You said you'd never been to Baawitigong, yeah?" he asked. Takumwah shook his head. "You take just a few steps into those woods, you feel like you're a million kilometers from anywhere. Like you're in a land that has never been touched by development." He talked about how the forests had been curated over generations, with edible plants right along the pathways, feeding any traveler. It was like entering a time warp. It could be five hundred years ago. The rat-a-tat-tat of memes echoes all around; the whisper of the wind through the needles of the pine trees and the leaves of the birches; the smell of woodsy, earthy dampness with each step taken off the paths. Wild animals that were only scarcely seen in cities roamed freely there. When it came to nature and to Dakaasin, once he started talking, it was difficult to stop. "We could talk for a long time. About anything. It made me feel safe.

"After my mother died . . . she was there for me. And for Ashwiyaa. Our father was gone; we had no family left. I took care of my sister. I have done so ever since. She was so damaged that she couldn't handle being around many people, so the community didn't help the way it might have. But Meoquanee was there. And so was Dakaasin. She was more than a friend to us. She was our family.

"And then we became . . ." Chibenashi hesitated. "Something more."

Takumwah smiled. The bell by the door jingled.

"She was my rock, the light, and I was able to feel love again after I'd lost everything else in my life. For a couple of too-short years, life was good again."

And then she left.

"I'm glad to hear that," Takumwah said. He turned toward the door and waved. "Over here!" Several heads turned at Takumwah's shout, which was loud even in the crowded restaurant.

Chibenashi choked on the pepper he'd just eaten. He coughed furiously to clear his windpipe. Dakaasin's face betrayed no shock or fear or anger, but tension radiated off her all the same. Nevertheless, she walked in like she owned the place.

"I hope you don't mind my inviting her," Takumwah said.

Chibenashi, still catching his breath, made no response.

"It's good to see you both," Dakaasin said, briefly debating which side of the booth to sit on before sliding next to Takumwah and facing Chibenashi, who would not meet her eye. "Did you get everything sorted with the DNA?"

Chibenashi nodded, still trying to suppress a cough.

"Thanks again for signing the form," Takumwah said.

"Of course," said Dakaasin. Without saying more, she excused herself to go to the line and fill up her bowl of food.

Chibenashi thought about asking Takumwah what he had been thinking. Why had he invited Dakaasin? Why hadn't he asked? What purpose did she serve by being here? Was Takumwah trying to torture him? Hadn't the incessant talking been enough?

Before he could sort out what to say, Dakaasin had returned with a steaming bowl of food. She asked a passing waiter for a glass of water. Chibenashi smiled despite himself.

They had fallen in love after both she and Meoquanee had spent the year helping him and Ashwiyaa rebuild their lives. Ashwiyaa had been especially difficult to handle in those days, since she and Chibenashi had never been particularly close and hadn't spent much time alone together. Chibenashi—still a child himself, who was both motherless and fatherless—had been at his wits' end. Ashwiyaa's instability had pushed everyone else away. What Meoquanee had provided as a surrogate mother, Dakaasin had provided as a partner. Where Meoquanee had provided food and guidance and that indefinable quality of motherness that all kids—all people—needed, Dakaasin had provided Chibenashi with comfort, love, and support. Between the two of them, he'd gotten through those first few terrible years.

Everything had changed the year he and Dakaasin had turned twenty-one.

Ashwiyaa had been only sixteen, and Chibenashi had known that he would have to stay close to her, that she needed care and support from him. She trusted no one else and looked to her brother for solace, comfort, and support, as she still did to this day. Chibenashi had known that this meant he and Ashwiyaa would always be a matched set—to be with him would mean taking on her. Dakaasin had understood and accepted that. She was in it for the long haul with him, and if that meant being in it for the long haul with Ashwiyaa as well, she was there. She'd told Chibenashi as much one night as they lay in bed together. "You and Ashwiyaa, you're my family now," she had said. "If you'll have me."

"I'll always have you," he'd responded. His eyes had brimmed with tears. She'd understood.

And then her ambition got the best of her.

Inspired by what his family had gone through, and seeing how the imperfect system of restitution had affected them, Dakaasin had declared that she wanted to be an Advocate, preferably on the Victims' side, in Mediations. She'd wanted to be the one to help those who had been wronged by others. Just as she'd found value in seeing how gaping the Neebin-shaped-and-size hole in their lives had been, she wanted to do that for others: find out what had been taken, damaged, or destroyed and help figure out what it would take to be able to replace what had been lost. And, in situations where something or someone had been lost forever, to figure out what would allow them to heal and move on. Short of a time machine, she would help them rebuild. The idea of mino-bimaadiziwin was a powerful motivator, and society was largely self-policing in that regard. If one person harmed another, it was not the fault of just that person. It was the fault of the whole community. They had failed the perpetrator as well as the victim. That's what had made, to her, crime so egregious. It wasn't just about one person harming another—the direct perpetrators and direct victims of the crime. Every violation left a crack in the foundation of their society, no matter how small. Those small cracks could add up to large ones and eventually shatter. They saw what other parts of the world were like, where mino-bimaadiziwin was not the way of life. Where external punitive measures had to be taken to keep people in line and where external incentives had to be used to bribe them to behave. She thought those were wrong, unnecessary. Helping Victims advocate for what would make them whole allowed for a system of peacekeeping and restitution that did not rely on such matters.

To be an Advocate, Dakaasin could not stay in Baawitigong. All such hearings were held in Shikaakwa, and the university that would train Dakaasin in advocacy was also in Shikaakwa.

Chibenashi was no stranger to people in his life leaving for university once they'd finished school in Baawitigong. Had the wheel spun differently, he would have gone himself, and so would Ashwiyaa. Both their parents had valued and impressed on them the importance of education—how it made people better citizens, family members, and people. But life hadn't turned out that way. And university had been absolutely out of the question for Ashwiyaa.

"I thought that we were your family now," Chibenashi had told Dakaasin after she had announced her decision.

"You are," she had said. "Come with me. Both of you. It would be a fresh start, a new city, a place to wash off the trauma and darkness of what happened to you and start life anew."

It wasn't that Chibenashi hadn't wanted to go with Dakaasin. He had, more than anything. But he couldn't move Ashwiyaa with him. She'd been through enough trauma. Even the healers and counselors with whom they had worked over the years had been in agreement: moving her to a new environment would destabilize her further. So Ashwiyaa would stay in Baawitigong, even though she had pushed the community away, and Chibenashi would stay with Ashwiyaa, and that was the way it would be.

Not only that, Chibenashi had no desire to ever be in the same city as his father again. And Ishkode had been safely ensconced away in Shikaakwa since the murder.

Deep down, he knew that Dakaasin had to have known all of this, that she had been asking the impossible of him by asking him to move. Shikaakwa was out of the question for Ashwiyaa, and so it was out of the question for him. Always had been. Always would be.

It was the place where Dakaasin's dreams lived. It was the place where Chibenashi's nightmares haunted.

And he loved her too much to ask her to stay. He couldn't have asked her to put her own dreams and ambitions on hold the way he had his own. He'd shrunk his down to fit inside Baawitigong. Hers couldn't. He'd found happiness there, and she hadn't tried to do the same. So they weren't family anymore. And they were no longer lovers. Dakaasin had devoted many years of her life to help Chibenashi and Ashwiyaa through the worst pain and trauma anyone could suffer. Now she wanted to put that to good use for others. He wasn't mad at her, truly. He had been so glad that she would help others.

But it still didn't change the fact that Dakaasin had broken his heart by leaving.

Now, as he sat with her again after so many years, the air choked with tension. They had not parted on bad terms, but they had still parted. Chibenashi was self-conscious of his hair (still styled the same), his clothes (serviceable but not stylish), and his education. He was an uneducated Peacekeeper in the presence of a trained Advocate. After seeing her in action, he could see that Dakaasin had done well. She could command attention. Her cadence of speaking was different now, very much in control, her voice and tone even but imperious. Even now—sitting in the booth, visibly nervous—she exuded confidence. Chibenashi was, in spite of himself, impressed with her.

He wondered if the fact that she was joining them for dinner and drinks on such short notice suggested she was not involved with anyone. He gave her a look. Sure enough, she had no necklace around her neck, no ring on her finger, nothing to suggest that she was married. It was the sort of news that would have made its way through Baawitigong like wildfire had it happened, but he was still grateful for the visual confirmation.

She was still as beautiful and vibrant at thirty-seven as she had been at twenty-one.

Takumwah and Dakaasin chatted amiably about work with the ease of people who had known each other and worked together for a very long time. He tried not to be jealous of their interactions. It occurred to Chibenashi that she had lived away from Baawitigong almost as long as she had been alive at the time of their decision. A whole lifetime here. A whole life built here. He could see how far Dakaasin had come. He was keenly aware of just how much he had stayed in the same place.

"You didn't come to Meoquanee's burial," he blurted out. Dakaasin and Takumwah both stopped talking in an instant. A piece of food fell out of the chopsticks Dakaasin was holding. A long pause followed.

"You're right," she said. "I wish I had. I couldn't get away for it. Work."

Chibenashi knew that wasn't true. He debated whether to belabor the point, but he decided against it.

"So," Takumwah said, steering the conversation back to Shikaakwa, "tell us about that hearing today."

Dakaasin shrugged. "It's sadly a fairly common tale around here—or anywhere, I guess. Love drives someone too far and causes harm to someone else. It makes my job difficult. I'm basically arguing against their feelings and their love, an emotion and feeling that is the driving force behind good. I'm seeing its corruption, the way it hurts people, how it can be weaponized for fear and control and violence."

"Which do you think is the biggest and more dangerous motivator?" Takumwah asked. "Love or hate?"

"Neither," she replied quickly, as if this great philosophical question was one easily answered. Which, for her, it apparently was. "The greatest motivator is indifference. Someone moves on, or moves away, and appears to have forgotten. That can sting worse than any amount of hate or love. Hate requires energy. Love requires attention. But, if you're asking me to decide between the two emotions alone, I suppose I would have to go with love."

"Why is that?" Chibenashi asked. He'd never heard someone speak of emotions so clinically. As if what drove someone to hurt or kill someone else weren't a violation of the natural order.

"Because people who are motivated by love are completely convinced that what they are doing is right. They aren't rationalizing something bad. They're feeding something good, or so they think. There is no check on their behavior, no little voice in their head telling them that what they are doing is wrong. The conscience will not save them because their conscience is telling them to do the thing that will land them in a Mediation. It corrodes and rusts without the person feeling a thing. I think it numbs them to reality. The Accused said as much today: love can justify just about any action, no matter how horrible."

Takumwah chuckled. "That's a depressing take."

"I've seen it too many times to think otherwise," Dakaasin said. "Not that I don't believe in love or don't think it's worthy. It can be the most beautiful and worthwhile thing in the world. It has motivated countless good deeds. But it has also formed the fuel behind other, bad ones. And I see firsthand the pain it can cause."

Chibenashi shrugged. None of them were here today because of love. Whatever had motivated someone to kill Meoquanee, it wasn't love. Love could never motivate someone to stab through a body with so much rage that it carved a hole in the floor beneath them.

Though two of Chibenashi's suspects were men who had once loved Meoquanee, even unconditionally.

Dakaasin ventured forth bravely in the conversation, asking Chibenashi about his sister, his work, and Baawitigong itself—how it looked, if everyone was ready for the winter. Her parents had left Baawitigong some years after she had, so she had no cause to visit for events like Manoomin. He gave short responses that conveyed the necessary information but did not invite follow-up questions. What did she care about Baawitigong? She'd left it—and them—behind.

Eventually, finally, *mercifully*, the night was over.

"It's really good to see you, Chibenashi," Dakaasin said as she wrapped herself in her coat and hat. The night could only have gotten colder since they'd all come here. Takumwah was settling up with the restaurant. He'd had a great night and was chatting happily with the proprietor. Whether deliberately or otherwise, he was taking a long time to do so. Chibenashi and Dakaasin were left to awkwardly wait for him by the door. To avoid her gaze, he studied what Takumwah was doing. No one really used money in Baawitigong unless they dealt directly with tourists. Otherwise, everything was covered through their universal basic income, which was funded primarily by taxes paid by international visitors or foreign trade partners, then distributed among all citizens of Mino-Aki. As a result, no one had to pay for necessities. Or at least, shouldn't have; the beggars he had seen earlier still stuck with him. The places by the port usually gave him his food as a gift, though occasionally he had to pay. But while Chibenashi knew how to use money, he'd never seen it used like this. He watched Takumwah sign something and press his thumbprint to a tablet held up by the proprietor. The process seemed like it shouldn't require as much time or talking as it was taking.

"How long are you in town?" Dakaasin asked.

"I'm going back to Baawitigong as soon as possible," Chibenashi replied, still watching Takumwah. He wasn't quite ready to look at her yet when they were alone. "Ashwiyaa is there, and I can't leave her for long."

He felt her gaze on him. "I'm sorry to hear that," she said. "Maybe we could share dinner again before you leave."

He focused on his makizinan, his toes warm inside. He wanted to see her, wanted to talk to her. Wanted to *understand*. "I doubt I'll have the time."

"Well," she said, taking a card out from a hidden pocket in her coat, "if you do find yourself with some spare time, please come see me. Or give me a call. It would be nice to talk to you—really talk, alone."

Chibenashi took the card without looking at it or her and said nothing. He stuffed it in his pocket, feeling it crinkle within his clenching fist.

"At the very least, call me when the DNA results come in. It can help me prepare for the eventual hearing."

Takumwah finally came over. "I'll walk Chibenashi to his lodging. Dakaasin, how are you getting home?"

"The Sky Snake goes right to my building," she said, pointing upward. "I can catch it here. Thank you for dinner, Takumwah. Chibenashi, I'll see you soon." She put a fox-fur hat on her head and opened the door, braving the whistling cold outside.

"Well," Takumwah said as they made their way back up the block, "that was fun, wasn't it?"

Chibenashi grunted and wrapped his coat more tightly around himself. Even though it was both late and dark, the light from the windows all around him reflected off the snow and lit up the city as much as if it were the middle of the day.

"Dakaasin is something, isn't she? So deep in how she looks at the world. Was she like that when she was younger? You never did finish your story about her. We could grab a drink at your room, and you could finish it."

"We have an early morning," Chibenashi reminded him. "I've had a long day. And I don't drink." He'd woken up in Baawitigong, talked with Peezhickee, and traveled hundreds of kilometers to an unfamiliar city. He'd been confronted three times by the past. He was ready to collapse and sleep for days, if not weeks. Long enough to forget. Forget about her, at least. The way she'd looked at him. The unmistakable pity in her eyes. She'd gone on to accomplish so much. And him? He was exactly where she had left him so many years ago: still in Baawitigong, still taking care of Ashwiyaa.

"Oh, come on," Takumwah said. He pushed Chibenashi playfully on the shoulder. Chibenashi stopped walking. Takumwah, ignorant of his feelings, rapped Chibenashi on the shoulder again. Chibenashi clenched his jaw, forced himself to hold still. He was exhausted. Angry. Hanging on by a thread.

"I bet you've got some interesting stories to tell about her!"

Something inside Chibenashi finally snapped. He turned around and pushed Takumwah back, harder than he'd meant or expected he could.

"Stop."

Inexplicably, Takumwah laughed.

"What's wrong? Mad you let her get away?"

Chibenashi shoved Takumwah so hard that he crashed into the window on the wall of the building behind them. It didn't shatter, but did bounce. The streets were empty, shiny with precipitation. It was too cold for any normal or intelligent person to be outside longer than necessary. No one to hear the crack of bones against glass.

"Oh, I'll take that as a yes."

Chibenashi pushed Takumwah into the wall again. "Stop that!"

"No way." Takumwah flashed that toothy grin again, the one that was now inspiring more rage in Chibenashi than he thought possible.

Takumwah pushed back. "Let's see what you got."

Before he knew what he was doing, Chibenashi was fighting for the first time in his life.

Physical fights, violence—that was neither how Chibenashi was raised nor in keeping with his temperament. He took things in, considered, acted reasonably. It was how he was raised. Take good care of each other, be good to each other, and good would happen to you.

But that was in Baawitigong. Here, in Shikaakwa? He could fight someone. And people would barely look away from their conversations or phones as he did.

A flailing of limbs. Chibenashi did not know how to punch, and it showed. Every time he tried to throw one, it missed its target. Or Takumwah dodged it or blocked it with minimal effort. Takumwah, on the other hand, clearly did know what he was doing, landing a few well-placed blows to Chibenashi's body, but not his face. He appeared to not be overexerted by it. Like he was toying with Chibenashi, two boys wrestling on the playground, rather than fighting. Chibenashi was panting, cringing, grunting, swinging, trying to best his opponent. Why he was trying so hard to fight him, even Chibenashi was not sure.

Takumwah, by contrast, was laughing, enjoying this. It was as if he was playing a game, like the baaga'adowewin he'd been so invested in watching earlier.

Finally, it ended. Takumwah had successfully pinned Chibenashi on the cold ground, their breath echoing off the buildings in the still-vacant street.

"Good," Takumwah said as Chibenashi lay panting on the ground—a turtle on its back, unable to right himself. Takumwah stood, dusted himself off. "You needed to let some of you out. You're trapped in there. Maybe you're trapped in Baawitigong, maybe you're not. I don't know. You won't tell me. You don't need to tell me. But if you keep yourself so bottled up, so distant, you'll never get anywhere.

"Besides," Takumwah continued, offering his hand to Chibenashi, who hesitated before accepting, "you apparently need to learn a couple of lessons. First lesson: never start a fight that you're not prepared to finish. And the second is that you have no business fighting because you're so terrible at it. Don't fight if you can't win, and you clearly can't win." He winked at Chibenashi. "Which isn't a bad thing."

Chapter Twelve

Chibenashi woke up to a rapping on the door. He rolled over onto his back with a groan. He was still sore from the fight, from both the punches and being thrown to the ground. He was still bone-tired from the travel and investigation and seeing Dakaasin, despite having gone to bed long ago. The bed was comfortable but unfamiliar. Bigger than he was used to and placed differently in the room. The pillows were the wrong level of firmness from the kind he was used to. The sliver of sunlight through the curtain was hitting him at the wrong angle. The table was too far from the bed. He didn't like it.

Despite sleeping long, he hadn't slept well. He didn't know if it was the unfamiliar room, the different bed, the travel, or the constant noise from outside in a city that never seemed to switch off. Whatever it was, he had woken up throughout the night, something that never happened to him in the tranquility of Baawitigong.

He stomped to the door to find Takumwah holding two cups of coffee and a smile that was far too broad for both the time and the day.

Chibenashi snatched one of the cups and slammed the door in Takumwah's face. It was too damn early, and he had things to do before he was ready to deal with that human ray of sunshine outside his door who'd kicked his ass last night.

Before he did anything else, he had to call Ashwiyaa.

He unplugged his phone from the charger and thumbed her contact information. Once the phone began to ring, he took the first sip of coffee. It was good—better than anything he could get in Baawitigong, though he would never admit that.

The call went unanswered. Chibenashi frowned. He called her again. Again, she failed to answer. Ashwiyaa had never bothered to record her own greeting; the automated voice just confirmed he'd called the right person and invited him to leave a message.

This was not normal. Ashwiyaa never ignored his calls. Something was wrong.

He called Kichewaishke.

"Boozhoo!" His best friend answered with a voice of cheerful exhaustion that was common to all parents of newborns.

"Where's Ashwiyaa?" Chibenashi said in greeting. His heart was racing. They were supposed to take care of her. It had only been one day.

"You want me to get her?"

"Is she there?"

"Yeah, she's in the kitchen with Okimaskew and the girls."

That brought Chibenashi up short. Ashwiyaa had not socialized with anyone in years.

"You want me to get her?" Kichewaishke asked.

"No, no, that's okay. I just wanted to make sure she was all right." And she was. Which made her ignoring his calls hurt more than learning that something happened to her. Dakaasin was right: indifference is always the worst. "I called her a moment ago, and she didn't answer."

"She might not have her phone with her."

That had never occurred to Chibenashi. Ever. He was so used to her being dependent on him that the idea of letting go of her one tie to him while he was gone both upset and thrilled him.

"Well . . . I guess tell her to call me later. If she's up for it."

"How are things going?"

Chibenashi thought of everything he could tell Kichewaishke: the Arrow Train, how big and cold and overwhelming Shikaakwa was, Sakima and how he'd let himself go, seeing Dakaasin, and the fight with Takumwah—and how spectacularly annoying he was.

"Fine."

"Good."

Chibenashi had never appreciated Kichewaishke so much in his life. This was why they were friends.

"I'll see you soon."

They got off the phone. Chibenashi showered. He dressed. He savored that spectacular coffee.

Long after he'd slammed the door, he opened it again.

Takumwah was standing there, playing on his phone. He looked up at Chibenashi and grinned.

"Ready?"

This day was only going to go downhill from the coffee.

Shikaakwa Gabe-Gikendaasoowigamig was, in a word, beautiful. Three hundred years old, it was the university that many young people in Mino-Aki and around the world aspired to attend. Its original building, a pyramid, was still the university's beating heart. Over the centuries, it had grown out of and into the earth itself and was now the largest earthen mound in the nation. Like much of the architecture in Shikaakwa, it was a living building; the mound was covered by various trees and shrubs indigenous to the area. Windows had been carved into the mound, the lights inside like little winking eyes between the trees and shrubs. Birds of all species made their homes there, and the twittering could be heard all around them. Over time, the university had outgrown the pyramid as it expanded the number of students and subjects it taught. Satellite buildings lined up next to the original structure to create a large circle of lodges, wigwams, labs, and libraries, with a clearing of grass and trees in the middle. Sprinkled throughout this clearing were archipelagoes of students huddling in the cold, reading and listening to music.

Chibenashi swallowed as he briefly allowed himself to wonder, as he had countless times before, how different his life would have been if he had followed Dakaasin here. Then he shook his head, extinguishing the thought. It had never been an option. No need to entertain it.

Meoquanee's ex-husband, Wiishkobak, taught here. He'd been Chibenashi's teacher in Baawitigong, and Ashwiyaa and Dakaasin's. The school in Baawitigong was small, reflective of the relatively small permanent population. Occasionally, Chibenashi and Ashwiyaa had been in the same classroom, despite their age difference. There were some years when Chibenashi had been one of only a handful in his class. Once, it had been only him and Dakaasin.

Chibenashi could not lie: it felt weird to be approaching him as a potential suspect.

Wiishkobak taught economics, and his office was in one of the satellite buildings. They walked past the main building and its woodsy, earthy smell and toward a wooden structure that looked like a log cabin. Inside was a long hallway that smelled of cedar. Doors on either side, lined up like soldiers in a row, led to offices within. The doors had been decorated with various documents, cartoons, and pictures. Most—if they were Anishinaabe—included the professor's doodem. The one outside Wiishkobak's door was a bear, just like Sakima's.

Takumwah gave the door three short raps with his knuckles; no answer. A poster in the hallway advertised that Wiishkobak was teaching a class right now. Takumwah led the way, with Chibenashi following behind.

Wiishkobak was lecturing in a room in the pyramid. It was full of students sitting in concentric circles not unlike those in a Mediation; some were taking notes on tablets, but more were just listening. He was older and thinner than Chibenashi remembered, but it was still unmistakably him. He was tall but fully built, with long graying hair tied back. He wore half-moon glasses and a leather vest and jacket, which must have been stifling in the room already warm with so many bodies. He walked around as he spoke, his voice carrying out over the dozens and dozens of heads that turned to follow him as he wandered, with only the occasional person chatting or surreptitiously watching videos on their phone. One student at the very back of the class was asleep, with a hat pulled over his eyes as he leaned his head against the wall. Chibenashi bristled at this; how could someone be given the opportunity to become educated, then waste it by sleeping through the classes?

"Many do not realize this," Wiishkobak was saying, "but our society is far unlike any other in the world. In some parts of the world, you have the capitalists, who believe that everything has its price and people can be broken down into units of money and profit. It is exploitative and damaging. It turns society into haves and have-nots. There is prosperity but no equality."

Chibenashi had not the slightest interest in economics, but something about Wiishkobak's voice carried, and just as he had been as a child, he was drawn in to the lesson.

"Then you have, in other parts of the world, the communists, the reaction to capitalists, who believe that profit should not exist and that people cannot be boiled down into profits. The problem with that system, of course, is that it forces people to act against their own nature, to make everyone act in the most egalitarian manner. But as I am sure each of us can think of someone who we may feel does not deserve as much as we do, that makes it a system that is difficult to enforce. Moreover, everywhere it has been tried, it has ended up being forced on people. Communism cannot participate in global trade, so it leads to chronic shortages. There is equality but not prosperity.

"But here, among us? We have something better. We give. We give and we give and we give. We give each other the benefit of the doubt.

We give each other what we have in surplus. We give each other what we cannot spare, because someone else is in greater need. This is, of course, the essence of economics—to provide your surpluses to others in exchange for their surpluses, which is far more efficient than trying to provide everything for yourself at any given time. It's impossible, and why so many communist societies have failed. They try to provide all things for themselves, which has never worked in the history of humankind."

Chibenashi thought back to the beggars on the street.

"Unlike capitalists, however, we do not put a price on people. We do not give in the expectation of receiving something in return. We give because it is the source of mino-bimaadiziwin. We give because it is right. And because we give without such expectation of receipt, our lives are better for it. We receive more than we give, at no greater cost than what we are able to provide. We've figured out what the capitalists have not, what the communists cannot."

This went on for a while, until finally the lesson ended and students began pouring out into the hall. The din of chitchat and laughter, people making lunch plans, and burrowing back into their phones reached a crescendo before dying down. Wiishkobak packed up his things and looked up, startled for a moment at the presence of two nonstudents in his midst. He eyed first Chibenashi and then Takumwah.

"Boozhoo!" he cried warmly, eyes on Takumwah as he greeted Chibenashi. "What a wonderful surprise. It's so good to see you, Chibenashi. You've grown so much."

This struck Chibenashi as odd. Wiishkobak had been so different on the phone, had refused to attend the burial of the mother of his son and had spat out such poisonous words. Wiishkobak then acknowledged Takumwah, telling him that he had known Chibenashi since he was a baby and had known both of his parents well. He was particularly effusive in his praise of Neebin, which Chibenashi found strange. It was like he was going out of his way to avoid any mention of Meoquanee.

"Please, sit." He gestured to the first ring of circles in the lecture hall. Chibenashi and Takumwah took their seats while Wiishkobak leaned against the lectern before them, the power structure clearly and fully established.

Before they could get to the substance of their visit, Wiishkobak made an attempt to engage in more pleasantries by asking after Ashwiyaa, but Takumwah held up a hand to stop him. "This is not a social visit," he explained. "We are here to discuss something of grave seriousness."

Wiishkobak nodded. The lightness in his expression went out, and it was as if a shadow had come to rest over him. When he spoke, his voice was an octave lower. "Of course. Chibenashi, I know you are a Peacekeeper in Baawitigong. I gather you are here to discuss Meoquanee?"

"Yes," Chibenashi said. He felt himself sink along with Wiishkobak's mood.

"It was terrible, when we heard the news," Wiishkobak said softly, his voice quivering just a little. Again, not what he had told Chibenashi earlier. "It had been many years since our marriage ended, but she is the mother of my son. We were married. We promised each other the rest of our lives. It never quite leaves you, a history like that."

"But you left," Chibenashi pointed out. "You moved here."

Wiishkobak looked away. "It was the right decision," he said softly. "It needed to happen."

"Why didn't you light the fires? Why didn't you come back for the burial?" Chibenashi had meant to build up to this subject, but it was too bizarre, and Sakima had been too angry. This show of grieving his ex-wife needed to be stopped, even if it risked making Wiishkobak clam up. There were ways to make men talk and speak the truth. They always did.

Wiishkobak's gaze snapped back to Chibenashi. He looked surprised by the question, and the two men from Baawitigong stared at each other for a long time. A gaggle of students outside passed the door, laughing uproariously about something. Chibenashi envied them and their freedom, their carefree nature, though he knew neither them nor what they were laughing about. Takumwah was a silent statue in the chair next to him.

"I couldn't," he said finally.

"Why not? I got here on the Arrow Train in a single afternoon."

"No, not that." Wiishkobak removed his glasses and pinched the bridge of his nose. He sighed. "The way our marriage ended, and why . . . it was too much to go back and see her again. Even in death."

Chibenashi nodded. "The affair," he said, testing the waters. Maybe Wiishkobak could finally shine some light on this.

Wiishkobak looked shocked for a moment. "I suppose so, yes." He sounded confused.

"So it's true, then," Chibenashi said, forming words around the sawdust in his mouth. "Meoquanee did have one?"

Wiishkobak closed his eyes and took a deep breath, like he was trying to calm himself down. "Why do you want to talk about this?"

"She's been murdered. We have to exhaust every possible avenue of investigation," Takumwah said, finally joining the interrogation.

"I doubt that will make much of a difference to this matter," Wiishkobak said.

"We'll be the judge of that," said Takumwah. "Do you know who it was with?"

"Of course I do," Wiishkobak said.

"Who is he?" Chibenashi asked, his voice no more than a whisper. He unconsciously leaned forward.

Wiishkobak opened his eyes, looked straight at Chibenashi. "He died a long time ago."

Chibenashi sank back, feeling deflated.

"We still need the name," Takumwah said.

"I assure you, you do not." After a beat, he said, "I am of course willing to entertain any other questions you may have and to cooperate in any way that I can."

Takumwah shifted in his seat, and asked the question that Chibenashi had not been able to bring himself to ask. "What was your relationship with Meoquanee like after you moved away?"

"I have not spoken with Meoquanee for nearly twenty years. I am afraid I have no insight as to her life in the interim."

"You may know more than you realize," Takumwah said. "Things you may have heard about her."

"I've left Baawitigong behind in every way," he said.

"Where were you on the night of her murder?" Takumwah asked.

"When was that?"

Chibenashi told him.

"Here, in Shikaakwa. I gave a lecture on the unique nature of the economy in Mino-Aki and how it is better than that of any other society on earth. Not dissimilar to the lecture I gave today."

"Held on Manoomin? The biggest holiday and travel day of the year?" Chibenashi was dubious.

"It is also the time of the largest conference on economics and society in Mino-Aki," Wiishkobak replied. "It's an honor to be included. Even if it does mean that you must forgo the traditional festivities one year. Worth the price of admission, in that sense."

"No doubt," Chibenashi murmured.

"Do you have anything from that—say, video or a program or materials—to verify the date and time?" Takumwah asked.

"I believe I can provide that," Wiishkobak said.

"Did you harbor any resentment about the affair?" Takumwah asked. Chibenashi knew that abruptly changing topics was a tool used by some Peacekeepers, but he had never used it.

"Me? Never."

"That doesn't sound possible," Takumwah said, challenging him.

"Anything is possible," Wiishkobak said, "except that which is completely impossible. But the full spectrum of human emotions, and our reactions to them, remain possible for every person at any given time. It's like flipping through a stack of papers: It's in there, but we may not select it. Or we may bypass it, not believing it to be an option."

◆ ◆ ◆

"I don't know that I believe him," Takumwah said as they walked through the clearing. Though they were in the middle of the largest city in Mino-Aki, the grounds of the university were as silent and quiet as the most remote parts of the woods in Baawitigong. They might as well be hundreds of kilometers away. "He didn't come to the burial. He doesn't seem to be mourning her."

"He yelled at me when I suggested it," Chibenashi said. "When I invited him to attend."

"Doesn't make him a murderer, I guess, but something major must have happened to make him skip the burial. I'm not sure I've ever heard of that before—not going to the burial of a member of your own family. If you were able. Even if you were that angry."

"I don't know what I believe about anything," Chibenashi said.

"Maybe Peezhickee can give some insight," Takumwah said.

It wasn't a bad idea, though Chibenashi would not admit that out loud. He would text Peezhickee this morning.

"And the wife," Takumwah said. "I dated a girl once who had been cheated on by her last boyfriend. Never stopped talking about it. So I heard all about the betrayal and lies and what happened. The wife would have heard that from the professor. We should talk to her, see what she says. At the very least, she could give us a better idea of whether this really was water under the bridge or whether he still holds any resentment."

Resentment that could lead to murder.

"Also," Takumwah added, "this morning, before I came over, I asked our guys to run a check on Sakima's background. The kind of place he was living in, not good enough for a fisherman. Living in a shithole like that begs questions about his past. So we may get some interesting news."

Chibenashi hummed to indicate interest while wondering how Takumwah had possibly had time to complete all of that so early in the morning.

"I'm a morning person," Takumwah said as if he had read Chibenashi's thoughts. "I like to get up while it's still dark, go for a run, then get to the dakoniwewigamig nice and early, get a few things out of the way before the real day begins."

That sounded like a nightmare to Chibenashi.

"Here," Takumwah said, indicating a street to his left. "I pulled the address this morning. We'll head over to Wiishkobak's house now. It's not far, and it's a nice walk. We can knock this out quickly. And who knows, maybe we'll even have our DNA results this afternoon."

That sounded like wishful thinking, but Chibenashi had to defer to Takumwah on that.

"Lead on."

Chapter Thirteen

Shikaakwa was not just a cluster of skyscrapers, houses of worship, government operations, stadiums, and community centers—it was also home to single-family wigwams that were not unlike those in Baawitigong, particularly in the older and more outlying districts. The wigwam Chibenashi and Takumwah were standing in front of, however, was far larger and nicer than anything that could be found in Baawitigong.

"They call this Educators' Row," Takumwah explained. "Home to most of the university educators. There's a similar row for Healers, too, and Fire Men."

"Nice to see them get this respect," Chibenashi said.

"We may live in a city, but we aren't monsters."

Chibenashi thought of the beggars on the street and how Sakima lived, but said nothing.

Kishkedee answered the door within a few moments of their knocking. Like the door in Wiishkobak's office and Sakima's apartment, their bear doodem was proudly displayed next to it. Chibenashi was still struck by the different doodem.

He got his second shock when he saw Kishkedee. She could have passed for Meoquanee's twin: small, thin, delicate, with a long waterfall of black hair down her back that was so straight it could have been ironed. She even appeared to be Meoquanee's age—over fifty but youthful and energetic. Her eyes widened in surprise just as Meoquanee's had so many times over the years with Chibenashi. But there were differences, naturally. The biggest one was that where Meoquanee was very natural and authentic in her dress and grooming, Kishkedee was made up and polished as if she were being photographed for a magazine spread. Her clothes were finely made, with delicate beadwork over her dress and white leggings. Her makizinan were some of the softest leather Chibenashi had ever seen. She had not known they were coming, so she must look this put together all the time.

Chibenashi was so struck by the similarity that it took him a moment to remember himself and why he was there. Takumwah helpfully jumped in. Before they knew it, they were sitting in the living room on overstuffed chairs while Kishkedee prepared a plate of food and a pot of coffee. Three interviews with this family, and only now was someone observing the niceties. The interview proceeded normally; Kishkedee was friendly and appeared relaxed, and she twittered away in response to their questions just like the bird for which she was named. They got her background quickly and easily: She was a lifelong resident of Shikaakwa, had met Wiishkobak and his son shortly after he had begun teaching at the university. Prior to the marriage, she had worked in politics but had resigned in order to be a mother to Sakima, with whom she had been very close. They had never visited Baawitigong as a family.

"And yet Sakima does not live with you?"

Kishkedee averted her eyes slightly. "I said we were close. It was true. Then."

"You're not anymore?" Takumwah asked.

She shook her head. "No."

"Why not?"

Kishkedee looked genuinely sad. "He had so much potential. So many opportunities. And he squandered them all."

Takumwah seemed confused. "Why would that affect your closeness?"

"His father is so accomplished. He could have had a very different life had he tried but a little more. Since he does not, over time there was less and less to talk about."

"You seem sad about that," Takumwah said.

"Of course I am," she said. "I raised him as my son. I wish we were still as close as we once had been. But Wiishkobak . . ."

Chibenashi leaned forward, gestured for her to continue.

"Wiishkobak made his decision about his son, and I must respect that."

"He is estranged from the two of you and was also estranged from Meoquanee?" Takumwah asked.

"He is not estranged from us. We see him, just not often."

"Did you like Meoquanee?"

Kishkedee took a long sip of her coffee. Long enough for Chibenashi to notice how well manicured her nails were. They were immaculate and painted the color of the late-autumn sky. "I never met her," she said.

"But you know about her."

Kishkedee nodded.

"What do you know?"

"She's the mother of his son," Kishkedee said simply. There was a sadness in her eyes. Like she wanted to be the mother of Wiishkobak's son, and she wasn't. Chibenashi wondered what that kind of want would do to a person over the course of so many years.

"Is that all?" Takumwah asked.

"It's all that matters."

"How is your marriage?" Takumwah asked.

"Lasting," she said. "We are content."

"Do you know what his marriage with Meoquanee was like?"

A shadow fell over Kishkedee's face. "Heartbreak that was completely avoidable. But one in which everyone eventually healed and moved on. Like any tragedy, I suppose. There's always that shard of glass in there. But it heals over, you learn to live with it, and eventually you don't even feel it anymore."

Or you get so used to the pain that you don't even notice it anymore, Chibenashi thought. *You would only notice its absence.*

"Your husband told us," Chibenashi said gently. "About the affair. During his marriage with Meoquanee."

Kishkedee smiled sadly. "I see."

"Has he spoken of it with you?"

She nodded. "Oh yes. Quite a lot."

"That must have been hard for him, to have to move on after his wife was unfaithful like that."

Now Kishkedee looked puzzled. "Meoquanee had an affair as well?"

"As well?"

"You didn't know about . . ."

Chibenashi and Takumwah leaned in.

"Wiishkobak's affair?" Kishkedee continued.

Chibenashi and Takumwah stared at her for a long time before Takumwah finally broke the silence.

"No."

"I'm surprised. It was why he and Meoquanee divorced. He had an affair."

Chibenashi was thrown by this. He'd begun to doubt Meoquanee. Now perhaps she had been unfairly maligned all along?

"With whom?" Takumwah asked.

"With Meoquanee's best friend."

Neebin. Chibenashi's mother.

The floor fell from beneath him. Takumwah, oblivious to what this meant to Chibenashi, continued listening intently.

"H-how long did it last?" Chibenashi's mouth was full of dried leaves. "The affair?"

Kishkedee shook her head. "I don't know. I never asked for details. All I know is that it was with her best friend and that the lady died shortly thereafter. Perhaps that explains why he did it—retaliation for what she had done to him. I appreciate him sharing that with me. I felt it demonstrates honesty, to freely admit the times you have been deceptive. And that it fosters trust to know when you have betrayed someone else. He and Sakima were very open about the effect that it had on them and the relationship."

"Sakima seems very angry with Meoquanee," Takumwah ventured. "Does he believe that she had an affair?"

"I have never heard him speak of it. But he believes in his father," Kishkedee said with warmth in her voice. "He is angry about many things in his life, and she is one of them."

"Did Meoquanee initiate the divorce?"

"No."

Chibenashi sat, stewing in the information he had just received, not listening to anything else coming from the interview. He had spent so many years thinking of his mother as a blameless victim that she hadn't been a three-dimensional person to him since she died. Like most of those who were gone, she'd been deified, preserved in amber as righteous without regard for the actual truth.

Kishkedee didn't know who he was. She had no reason to lie to him. She almost certainly had no idea what relationship he had to the person she only knew as "his wife's best friend."

Was Sakima mistaken, then? Had he created this belief of his mother's affair, or had he believed a lie his father told him?

Chibenashi tried to think back to the last time he'd seen his parents together. They had seemed happy. So had Wiishkobak and Meoquanee. They'd spent that last Manoomin together. He remembered how happy and close everyone had been. He knew his parents had argued the night of the murder. It had gotten so bad that Ashwiyaa had fled to the woods, where she had huddled under a tree through the cold damp of that night. She was found shivering the next morning. Had his parents argued about this? Had Meoquanee known? Why would she have continued to care for her friend's children if the victim had destroyed her marriage? Was this widely known? And why had nobody said a word over the years—least of all Meoquanee?

He let the questions turn over in his head for a long time.

Takumwah confirmed Wiishkobak's alibi of giving an economics lecture at the approximate time of the murder. Kishkedee had photographs from the event as well as a program highlighting him as the keynote speaker. She had attended with him; an attendee had snapped a photo of them with another speaker and posted it to social media contemporaneously. It was on Manoomin, just as Wiishkobak had said.

"What about Sakima? Do you know where he was that night?"

"I wish I did. We invited him to the lecture, but he declined. We thought he might have been upset that we were not going to observe Manoomin this year, but when we saw him the next day, he did not mention it."

"What time was that?"

"Just before midday."

"How did he seem?"

"At peace."

"This doesn't make sense," Takumwah said as they walked down Educators' Row.

Chibenashi said nothing. Takumwah took it as an invitation to continue talking, which had not been Chibenashi's intention.

"Someone's not telling the truth, and I don't like it." Takumwah was thinking out loud, gesturing with his hands wildly as he worked through the information. "But since Kishkedee has no reason to lie to us, and Sakima does, I'm inclined to believe her. Which makes this all the more confusing. Why would you lie about your wife having an affair like that? And why would the son be so upset with the mother when it was the father who was cheating? Why divorce your wife years after the affair partner died?"

"I never knew."

Takumwah stopped in his tracks at Chibenashi's words. He turned back to find Chibenashi four or five paces behind him. Chibenashi was shell-shocked and hollow, standing in the middle of the busy block, people walking around him without a care in the way all big-city people do: acknowledging your presence while respecting your privacy in close quarters.

"You never knew what?"

"Why he did it."

"Why who did what?"

"My father. Why he killed my mother. My mother was Meoquanee's best friend. She was the one having an affair with Wiishkobak."

Takumwah stood still as the surface of a frozen pond, for once in his life lost for words. Chibenashi, on the other hand, could not stop the words from spilling out. He stared forward, at nothing and everything all at once. His voice, like the rest of him, was hollowed out like a dead tree.

"He was found the next morning covered in my mother's blood. They had argued. He confessed immediately. We held a Mediation just for purposes of sorting out restitution. He asked for a prison sentence, and he received it. Life. I didn't object. It felt safest. He had already killed our mother; he could have hurt my sister too. No one asked him why, and he never told. We just discussed what would happen to him. So he's been in prison—here, actually, in Shikaakwa—for twenty years now. But I never knew or understood why. Why kill her, what had triggered it. They had seemed so happy. We had all been happy. And then he took her away. So that's why, I guess. She'd been having an affair. With her best friend's husband."

It had always been a missing piece in his life—the why. He had assumed that if he ever knew, it might fill in something for him. But at the same time, he'd been too afraid to find out, too afraid to revisit that pain. It wasn't worth whatever closure it might give him. So he had not asked. And his father had not told.

And now that the answer had been slotted in its place, he thought of his mother, whom he'd idolized all these years after her death. How could she have betrayed her best friend like that? And had Meoquanee known? Would she still have cared for him and Ashwiyaa if she had? Was it easier to imagine that she had not known? Was it worse? He couldn't decide.

He thought back to the box of photographs and papers, and Meoquanee chasing after Neebin. What had that betrayal done to her? The person she'd idolized had been the one to harm her? And she had still devoted her life to Neebin's children? Nothing made sense.

"She could be lying," Takumwah offered.

Chibenashi shook his head. "As you said, she has no reason to lie. But Sakima and Wiishkobak? They do."

Takumwah nodded. "My friend, I'm so sorry."

Chibenashi shook his head. "You didn't know." *I didn't know.*

"And I should have." Takumwah sounded angry. Chibenashi met his gaze and saw that Takumwah's jaw was clenched and his eyes were sharp. "I should have been told about the greater background to this case. You should have too. You should never have had to find out from her."

"How could anyone have known this? Wiishkobak never told and neither did Meoquanee. My father never spoke about it. No one spoke to anyone about it, as far as I know. So many rumors flew around, it was easy to ignore them, but there was nothing to suggest they were anything more than that. If someone like Meoquanee had ever spoken of it, I would have believed it. Without that, I had no reason to.

"Baawitigong didn't keep the file. It was sent to Shikaakwa following the Mediation. And he never spoke. I don't even know if he was asked." If anyone should have told him this, Meoquanee should have. Perhaps she was doing what she had always done: protected him, cared for him, managed his feelings. So she'd kept this dark secret locked in her heart—the betrayal by both her husband and best friend. And she'd spent the next two decades caring for her best friend's children while the relationship with her own blood son had withered away.

How much else of Meoquanee's life had he not known? How much of his mother and father had been a mystery to him? How much more pain had she hidden from him?

How had he failed to notice it? For twenty years? He was a Peacekeeper. Noticing things was part of his job.

"What about your sister?" Takumwah asked.

Chibenashi's head snapped up. "What about her?"

"Did she see or hear anything? Know about this?"

Chibenashi shook his head. Kicked a loose stone from the ground. "No. Our parents argued. She didn't hear what it was about, but it was bad enough that she ran away during the argument. She wasn't found until the next morning."

"How old was she?"

"Twelve."

"She might have heard something."

"If this was news to me, it would be news to her. And I don't want her to know about it. She doesn't handle bad news well."

"Even if it would help us solve this?"

"I'm not ruining her memories of our mother," Chibenashi snapped. "It's bad enough that mine were."

Takumwah looked as if he was debating with himself. Finally reaching a conclusion, he said, "I hate to even raise this issue, but what about your father?"

"What about him?" Chibenashi bristled.

"Could we ask him?"

Chibenashi's insides turned as icy as the air around them. "No."

"But you said he was imprisoned here. We could speak to him. Probably even today."

"I am *not*," Chibenashi said, seething, "going to speak to my father." He had not spoken to him since the murder. Never would.

Takumwah stared at Chibenashi for a long time, while Chibenashi refused to look at him again. He'd said all he wanted to say on the matter. No amount of pressure was going to get him to discuss this further.

"This morning, before I came to get you, I asked our guys down at the station to run Sakima's criminal history," Takumwah finally said, mercifully changing the subject. "I imagine they've pulled everything by now. Let's head over there and see what they've found. Maybe even our DNA results will be ready."

Chibenashi exhaled. "I'd like that."

Chapter Fourteen

Chibenashi's phone pinged with a text as they entered the dakoni-wewigamig. Peacekeepers, crime victims, suspects, and members of the public swarmed in and out of the building all around him, fading to nothing as he focused on his phone. He read the message; the number was unknown, but somehow he knew it was from Dakaasin.

How are you feeling today?

He was both happy and perturbed to receive it. Happy that Dakaasin had reached out, perturbed that she had somehow obtained his contact information (from Takumwah, there was no other way) and reached out before he'd had the chance. She'd only given him her information the night before. But that was so like her—unwilling to wait. He was amazed she was able to effectively work as an Advocate. From what he had heard, patience was a necessary part of the job.

She'd seemed so different, so evolved from when they were young, that he took comfort in seeing that some things had not changed. The True East he could cling to.

◆　◆　◆

While Chibenashi was distracted by the text Dakaasin had sent at his request, Takumwah vanished into a side office with his phone.

"Boozhoo," Peezhickee said, sounding frustratingly mellow. Takumwah could hear waves crashing in the background. Could feel the warmth of the Panzacola sunlight through his phone.

"Enjoying your vacation?"

"Very much," Peezhickee said. "Winters off is the best perk of working my way to the top."

For a three-person dakoniwewigamig, that was hardly impressive and likely a function of simply having been there for a long time, but Takumwah moved past that feeling. He quickly filled Peezhickee in on what Kishkedee had told them.

"What struck me," Takumwah said after finishing his summary, "is that Chibenashi had no idea of the connection between Wiishkobak and his own mother. And I have to believe that when his mother's murder was investigated, something like that would have come up, that it was somewhere in the record of the case. He never should have had to learn about it this way."

Peezhickee sucked in a breath. "No, he shouldn't have."

"So what happened?"

"This is the first I'm hearing of it."

"What do you mean? This never came up in the investigation into his mother's murder?"

"There was no investigation," Peezhickee said.

"I don't understand."

"Ishkode confessed. Immediately."

"You didn't ask him why?"

"Of course we did." Peezhickee sounded offended. "Repeatedly and in multiple ways. But he would never say. He just said that he was the one who did it. I wish I had known; it always bothered me, this case. It appeared to come out of nowhere. He and Neebin had seemed so happy. But I guess you never can know what happens in another man's wigwam."

"But if he didn't say, why didn't you try to find out by other means?" Takumwah pressed him as if he were interrogating a suspect. "Interview others? Look at his computer or phone? Something to corroborate the confession? If for no other reason than to give the family closure. Surely their Advocate wanted it."

"Takumwah," Peezhickee said with great patience, "Baawitigong is not Shikaakwa."

"I'm aware of that."

"Our dakoniwewigamig is three people strong. The most serious crime we will usually investigate in any given year is petty theft. Chibenashi spends most of his time retrieving lost property. Lost, not stolen. Someone will occasionally wander into the woods and go missing, but they always come out. It's not treated as an urgent situation unless it has been a long period of time. His beat is mostly walking through the town and occasionally chatting with people—and as I'm sure you've noticed, he doesn't like to chat with people. We've had two murders in the entire time I've been a Peacekeeper. That's thirty years now. The first murder we had during my tenure was Chibenashi's mother, Neebin. The second was Meoquanee.

"We have no crime lab, no forensic facilities, and one pathologist who rarely handles criminal work. There's a reason Chibenashi is in Shikaakwa—potential suspects are there, and the necessary equipment is there. A lot of our annual resources are being spent on Chibenashi's sojourn up there. And we are spending them because we have no other choice. We can't afford not to investigate this one because we have no leads, no suspects, and no evidence that we can process in-house. With Neebin, frankly, we could not afford to investigate. We had a suspect who confessed immediately and without prompting. He described what happened in sufficient detail that matched up with what our local pathologist could determine.

"We had limited experience in such investigations. The murder was resolved. So many women are murdered by their husbands; statistically, it was the most likely outcome anyway. We accepted it and shipped the whole case file—blood tests, fibers, everything we collected, and all notes taken—to the archives in Shikaakwa. The Victim's family accepted it. The Accused accepted it. The Mediator accepted it. We had two children whose mother was killed, and we were handed an explanation. That is what we strive for, anyway—for the person to take responsibility for the harm to the Victim and the harm to the community. We do not look closer when that happens. Wouldn't you do the same if you had the opportunity?"

Takumwah was aware of the problems many rural dakoniwewigamigoon had with limited resources and expertise. Murder was rare in Shikaakwa, as it was everywhere else, but it still happened there more frequently than it did in most other cities or towns. Contrast that with Baawitigong, which had two murders in as many decades.

"I regret it," Peezhickee continued. "An investigation should have happened. We owed Chibenashi and Ashwiyaa as much. We owed Neebin as much. But most of the time, the most obvious and convenient result is the right result. And there has been no suggestion that Ishkode was not responsible. Now we have the motive. It has all slotted into place."

"It just would have been best for Chibenashi not to have learned like this," Takumwah said faintly.

"I agree. I was hesitant to have him work this matter, but between the limited resources and the fact that it is virtually impossible to be in an arm's-length relationship with anyone in Baawitigong, we manage however we can."

Once Takumwah was off the phone with Peezhickee, a young man tapped him on the shoulder. "We have the information you asked for," he said. "Perhaps I can walk you through what we found?"

◆ ◆ ◆

Chibenashi decided to further put off any decision as to what to say to Dakaasin, or whether to respond at all, by reaching out to Ashwiyaa again. He dreaded it; news like this would be even harder on her. He wished he could tell her in person, soften the blow by being present. But he knew that he could not wait. It wasn't fair to her. He knew; now she deserved to.

He stared at the phone for a long time.

His thumb hovered over her contact information.

He knew he had to tell her.

Instead, he put the phone in his pocket.

He couldn't do it. Not yet.

He needed to be there with her. A secret like this had to be shared in person. He hoped those damn DNA results would be in soon. He'd already interviewed everyone in Shikaakwa; the existing persons of interest had pointed to no new ones. He could take the results by phone from Baawitigong as easily as he could here. With any luck, he may even be able to catch the Arrow Train home tonight.

Takumwah appeared out of nowhere and interrupted Chibenashi's thoughts. "We have Sakima's background results in," he said. "And some insights on his whereabouts on the day of the murder. You should come look at them."

Takumwah led Chibenashi to a conference room with a long table in the middle made from planks of reclaimed wood and scattered mismatched chairs all around it. The smell of the wood from the table took Chibenashi back to Baawitigong. He hadn't realized until now just how many smells a city didn't have—ones that reminded him of home. Smoke and cold in the winter. The wetness of wood and dirt in the spring. Fruit and flowers in the summer. Pine cones and rain in the fall. The table took up most of the space in the long, narrow room. A board had various papers, photographs, and maps pinned to it, some tied together with red string as if tracing a train of thought. Whether from current or past cases, Chibenashi could not say. In Baawitigong, they never had cases with sufficient complexity to justify something like that. Behind him, at the end of the table, hung a large video screen that took up most of the wall, with the surveillance video already cued up.

Surveillance videos were controversial; Baawitigong did not have any. There was no need in a town that small—the people were the surveillance system. No one could go anywhere or do anything without someone knowing about it. It was well known among the teenagers that you could not get into any sort of real trouble because your parents' friends would catch you and report back long before you could do anything. It was an effective system, refined to perfection over generations of practice. But Shikaakwa compensated for the lack of an intimate community with an electronic surveillance program, for which it was now infamous. Just as in all cities, people lived close together but did not know each other. People who lived just meters apart for decades would never learn each other's names. Some people in Baawitigong said that the average person was photographed or videoed upward of one hundred times per day in Shikaakwa, with others arguing it was more like five hundred, *and* they scanned your retinas and took your fingerprints, too, and sometimes even your blood. He hadn't been able to bring himself to ask Takumwah if any of this was true. Chibenashi didn't know how it could be; he never saw the cameras. It made him feel both relieved and alarmed to know that he was repeatedly being recorded, but it was by nameless, faceless strangers. Video went into some black box somewhere or dissipated into the cloud. All that data, everywhere and nowhere at the same time.

Takumwah led Chibenashi to the video screen. He gave it a sharp tap, and it blinked awake.

"We pulled the surveillance footage of Sakima, Wiishkobak, and Kishkedee from the night of the murder," he began. "Our guys walked me through it already, so I thought I'd walk you through it too."

"All of it?"

Takumwah nodded.

"How could you possibly sift through so many people to isolate just three in a city the size of Shikaakwa?"

"Facial recognition technology. We simply upload the photographs of the people we want into the system, and it allows us to isolate and track a person though their time in the city. We can track them from the time they leave their homes in the morning to the time they return at night."

So the rumors must be true. "And you can do all of this without their permission?"

Takumwah nodded. "Provided that it's related to the investigation of a crime or a crime in progress."

Chibenashi stood there, stunned. No one could reasonably expect privacy under those circumstances. If you wanted to meet with someone secretly or privately, or even be alone, it would be impossible. At the same time, he had to concede that it had its uses. If they'd had it in Baawitigong, they would almost certainly have found Meoquanee's murderer by now. It was clear that with greater population came greater resources. Baawitigong always had everything people needed—sufficient food, medical care, shelter for both its residents and guests—but very little of what they wanted.

Takumwah tapped the screen, and a series of video clips began playing. "The footage shows that Wiishkobak and Kishkedee were telling the truth about their whereabouts." The video clips followed Takumwah's narration, timed perfectly. "They were at the speaking engagement that night and then went to a reception. Lots of photographs, talking, drinking, eating. They seem to have had someone accompanying them the whole time—colleagues, attendees, others. Popular guests. The conference on Manoomin is a big deal, just like he said. He must have done well—just about everyone there wanted a photograph with him, and they did not return home until a short time before sunrise. They were captured on camera the whole time. There doesn't seem to be a single gap for the entire night."

Takumwah tapped through the touch screen a bit more and pulled up another set of video clips. Sakima's swollen face filled the large screen. The quality of the film was grainy; this was zoomed in from a wider shot. He was menacing as he stared directly into the camera he most likely hadn't seen. Chibenashi unconsciously took a step back.

"Wiishkobak's son, on the other hand, is far more interesting. Cameras in the apartment building catch him leaving before dawn and follow him down to his fishing boat." Again, the video clips changed in time with Takumwah's narration. "He returns shortly after midday. He and his fellow crew members unload the fish onto the dock. You'll see now that most of the others head toward the bar close to the dock, but Sakima doesn't join them. Instead, he goes in the opposite direction." Takumwah stopped narrating as the string of camera shots captured Sakima walking through the streets of Shikaakwa. He kept his head down, his gait steady but not commanding. He had a well-made but well-worn gashkibidaagan slung over his shoulder. The messenger bag looked like it was full of something.

"Where's he going—home?" Chibenashi wasn't familiar with Shikaakwa's geography but recalled the fetid apartment building being far closer to the docks than where Sakima appeared to be walking.

Takumwah shook his head. "No," he said through gritted teeth. On cue, the video cut to Sakima entering the train station.

Chibenashi stepped closer.

"Where's he going?"

Takumwah handed Chibenashi a slip of paper as Sakima took his ticket on the screen. Chibenashi looked down—it was a printout of the record of Sakima's ticket.

"He went to Baawitigong that day?"

Takumwah nodded.

Chibenashi gripped the paper so hard his hands began to shake.

"He arrived in the late afternoon, after catching the express to Baawitigong." The video clips skipped through Sakima's journey—boarding the train, then his time on the train (he slept), then exiting the train with a large throng of people. It was Manoomin, and between the locals, the families arriving late to the harvest, and the tourists who tripled Baawitigong's population during that time of year, Sakima melted into the crowd. Once he disembarked, it was difficult to continue to track him.

At that point, the video stopped.

"We can't follow him past the train station," Takumwah said solemnly.

Chibenashi nodded. "We don't have cameras in Baawitigong the way you do here."

"That's unfortunate."

"It is."

"We don't pick him up again until he returns to the train station later that night."

Chibenashi peered closer to the screen, which was playing video of Sakima entering the now mostly empty train station and obtaining a ticket. He boarded a nearly deserted train back to Shikaakwa (sleeping, again), where he disembarked and returned to his apartment building.

"What time did he return?"

"Nearly dawn."

Chibenashi studied the last image of Sakima as he entered his apartment. "Can we pull up a shot of him when he leaves the train station?" Takumwah did so. He brought the images side by side for Chibenashi to review.

Chibenashi jabbed his finger at the screen, causing the image to wobble. "He changed his clothes."

Takumwah moved closer and studied the two images. "He did."

"And he isn't carrying the bag he had with him when he left."

"What do you think was in there?" Takumwah asked.

Chibenashi shook his head. "I searched her wigwam myself. There was nothing unusual in there. Nothing appeared to be added. Nothing of value missing. Certainly no bag that he's carrying there."

"Did anyone else search it?"

"No."

"Why not?"

Chibenashi turned to Takumwah. "Why would they?"

"Among other reasons, you are personally known to the victim. You are emotionally affected. It's easy to miss things. Even if that weren't the case, you always have two people search. More if possible, but at least two sets of eyes. Fewer things are missed."

Takumwah's implication that he was incompetent chafed Chibenashi, but he had to admit that they hadn't thought about a lot of this. They should have asked for help from the beginning. Hopefully it wasn't too late now to make up for it. "I'll reach out to Ziigwan and Peezhickee," he offered. "Hopefully Ziigwan can start canvassing soon so that she can see if anyone saw or talked to Sakima. Once I get back, I'll join her."

"Not much of a point now; it's been such a long time," Takumwah said. "Witnesses' memories fade with time. People forget things. People create their own false memories based on what they have heard about a case rather than what they actually heard and saw. And the wigwam. After all this time, is it even still vacant?"

Chibenashi shook his head. "No," he conceded. "It's been completely cleaned out. Everything in it was taken to the recyclers to be redistributed."

"You allowed it to be cleaned out before the case was solved? That's still a crime scene! Do you realize what a problem this is?" Takumwah's tone was sharp. His normally excited eyes narrowed in anger and frustration. "We can't put Sakima in the wigwam even if we want to. We have him coming and going from Baawitigong, but that's it. We can't reach a resolution if all we can do is place him in the town."

Chibenashi made to protest but kept his mouth shut. He couldn't defend himself with the truth, which was that he simply hadn't known any better. "What about the DNA?" he asked.

"Assuming we can get a match, maybe. But it would be so easy for him to argue that of course his DNA would be in her house somewhere—he was her son."

Takumwah rubbed his hand over his face. "I'm calling Dakaasin," he said. "See if she has any ideas of what to do."

"We are not calling Dakaasin." Chibenashi couldn't stand her knowing his incompetence. He scrubbed at his own face. "What about the background results?"

"Ah." Takumwah tapped the screen again. He opened his mouth to continue speaking, but they were interrupted by a young Peacekeeper entering the room, looking both nervous and embarrassed at having done so.

"I'm sorry," she said, eyes darting nervously between the two men. "Someone from forensics is here with DNA for a case in Baawitigong."

Chapter Fifteen

Chibenashi followed the young Peacekeeper through a maze of corridors, elevators, and rooms. Takumwah trailed a few steps behind, tapping on his phone. He seemed to be able to follow them without looking; given that Takumwah worked here, Chibenashi supposed that he should not be surprised by that. His mind was still reeling from all he had seen in the video clips and what he'd learned from his conversations with Wiishkobak, Kishkedee, and Sakima. They had Sakima's motive and his opportunity, and the means had been found in Meoquanee's wigwam. He'd heard of Peacekeepers doing more with less.

At some point, they had moved from the dakoniwewigamig to a lab. Peacekeepers no longer roamed the halls; instead, there were laboratory technicians in sterile clothes, face masks, and disposable paper makizinan. They seemed to pay no mind to Chibenashi and the others, who were clearly invaders in their space.

After what felt like many long moments of walking and a lot of distance covered, they arrived at a more secure room than the one they had left. The door had to be unlocked by the Peacekeeper pressing her thumbprint to a panel. The heavy door swung open to reveal a windowless room that was all white—white chairs, white square table, white walls, white computer monitor on one wall. Seated in one of the chairs was a middle-aged woman with hair tucked into a white cap and wearing the same paper uniform as the others they'd seen in the halls. A scientist or technician. She stood as Chibenashi and Takumwah entered the room. The Peacekeeper shut and locked the door behind them.

"Boozhoo," said the woman, introducing herself as Mizhakwan. She explained that she had completed the DNA analysis on the blood samples that Chibenashi had brought all the way from Baawitigong. She held in her hand a packet of papers. "I'll review the results shortly, but I understand there is one more joining us?"

"On her way," Takumwah said, and just as Chibenashi began to feel the dread overcome him, the heavy door swung open once more and Dakaasin entered, looking flushed.

"I apologize," she said, looking each of them in the eye and lingering on Chibenashi a moment longer than the others. "I hope I haven't kept you waiting."

"Not at all," Takumwah said, gesturing for her to sit. He turned to Chibenashi. "I felt her expertise would be helpful, so she is here to hear the results with us. We can brainstorm the next steps."

Dakaasin took the seat in front of her, and Takumwah took the one next to hers. Not sure which was the least-bad option, Chibenashi opted for Takumwah's other side—close enough where he could hear everything while still as far away as he could be from Dakaasin without being rude. Mizhakwan stood before them, next to the video screen. After a few taps, she cued up a series of lab results. Chibenashi knew of these and what they meant but could not decipher what they held in store.

"We took the blood samples you provided," Mizhakwan began. "Based on the amount of deterioration and quality of the samples—they were in storage for some time before testing—we were only able to perform what is known as mitochondrial DNA testing. This testing is based on the mitochondria, which generates all the cell's energy. This mitochondrial DNA passes down from mother to child in a long chain stretching back along the matrilineal line through the generations past. We were able to identify this strand of mitochondrial DNA in the victim, Meoquanee." The screen showed a sequence of DNA and patterned results. All that had made Meoquanee who and what she had been was there in black and white, reduced to a series of dots and dashes on a screen.

"When we tested the sample you provided for Sakima, we isolated the mitochondrial DNA and compared the two. This confirmed that we had the DNA for the right person." Another series of dots and dashes appeared on the screen and were overlaid with Meoquanee's. They lined up perfectly. Confirmed: mother and son. They now had Meoquanee's DNA to work with.

"Now," Mizhakwan continued, "we ran this sample against the one found at the murder scene, the blood samples you provided. We would expect that we would only find one set of mitochondrial DNA at the murder scene if indeed Sakima were the culprit; he and his mother would have the same mitochondrial DNA, as would any sibling of Sakima's. But that is not what we found."

A graphic on the screen illustrated this. The DNA pattern for Meoquanee and Sakima appeared next to a wholly different set of DNA markers. When overlaid, there were dots and dashes that clashed with each other.

"So that means—" Chibenashi began.

"Sakima didn't do it," Takumwah finished.

"Not necessarily," Mizhakwan said. "What this means is that we cannot *exclude* him as a suspect. As I said, his mitochondrial DNA and his mother's are the same, due to the matrilineal relationship. His DNA and hers could both be in here, and we would not be able to tell. What this does mean is that if he did commit the crime, he didn't do it alone."

She cleared her throat.

"But that's not the most interesting thing we found. We continued testing."

Chibenashi, Takumwah, and Dakaasin all instinctively leaned forward in their chairs, hanging on every word.

"As is customary in these cases, we ran this other mitochondrial DNA sample through our archive of samples to see if it matched with anything else. The DNA from anyone previously in the system, such as those found responsible for a crime in the past, would be in here. We run these comparisons as a matter of course; it doesn't take very long."

She took a deep breath. "When we did that, we got a hit."

Takumwah actually jumped out of his chair while Chibenashi stayed glued to his seat, paralyzed. "Who?"

Mizhakwan tapped on the screen again. It showed the mystery mitochondrial DNA values overlaid with the DNA pulled from a prior case. They overlapped perfectly. They were a match.

"Miine . . . ," Takumwah said.

"This is from a prior murder case in Baawitigong," she said. "From twenty years ago."

Chapter Sixteen

Chibenashi couldn't breathe. The air was gone.

He was looking at the floor between his knees. Someone was gasping for air. Him. Someone steadied his shoulders. Someone else rubbed his back. He heard voices, but they were far away—garbled, like he was listening to them underwater. Was he underwater? Was that why he couldn't breathe? He saw the planks of wood that made up the floor of the secure room. Felt the chair he was sitting in. Rubbed his feet against the smooth floor. No, not underwater. Not literally, anyway.

The implications of this result were unmistakable.

If the person who murdered his mother also murdered Meoquanee, that meant only one thing: his father hadn't done it.

It was impossible. He was in prison, here in Shikaakwa, at the time Meoquanee was killed. His DNA would have been different from the DNA of the murderer. It wasn't.

His father had confessed to a crime he had not committed.

His father had been in prison for twenty years—had requested to go—without so much as a visit from either of his children. And he hadn't done the thing he had been accused of.

Was this another one of Meoquanee's secrets that she'd taken with her?

Had Peezhickee known? Had he investigated? Had this knowledge hung in the background of every interaction between them over the years?

Innocent people weren't supposed to be held responsible for these things.

The phone buzzed in Chibenashi's pocket. He ignored it.

Was his father protecting someone else? Sakima? Or someone they did not know about? Was he doing it to protect Ashwiyaa from someone? Protect him?

Why would he confess?

Chibenashi was still struggling to breathe.

He heard a door open, close; footsteps, then silence.

And then he felt the first tear fall.

◆ ◆ ◆

Dakaasin was transported back to a familiar role she'd played for too many years of her life: comforting Chibenashi. It was a role she'd gone all the way to Shikaakwa to escape.

"Breathe," she murmured as she rubbed Chibenashi's back. Mizhakwan had mercifully left once Chibenashi had begun panicking but Takumwah hadn't. Dakaasin had worked with Takumwah for years and had come to know him well. She'd never seen him this way. He looked angry, and like he was hurting just as much as Chibenashi.

Sitting here in the secure room, rubbing his back, helping him down from a panic attack, Dakaasin was back in that time long ago, when she had been Chibenashi's rock. And despite this, he'd been the one to drag her down.

The room had, eventually, stopped spinning. But Chibenashi still felt off-kilter.

He didn't want to do it. He'd been avoiding it for twenty years. He wanted to avoid it even more now. But now he had no choice.

"Where is the gibaakwa'odiiwigamig?" he rasped, still trying to calm himself.

The soothing hand on his back stopped. "You want to see your father?" Dakaasin asked in disbelief.

Chibenashi nodded, grateful she had said it out loud so that he would not have to. "How do I arrange that?"

Takumwah cast a worried look over Chibenashi's shoulder, which he guessed was matched by one on Dakaasin's face.

"These things often take time to arrange . . ." Takumwah began.

"Now. Today," Chibenashi spat out. He scrubbed his hands over his face. "You know why. Please. It's important. And it can't wait."

"Take some time," Dakaasin suggested. "Absorb this before you go there."

Chibenashi shook his head. "I can't. If I wait, I'll go crazy. I've waited long enough to hear the truth. I don't want to wait any longer." *I've wasted so much time already.*

"Have you . . . have you seen him? Since it happened?" Dakaasin asked.

Chibenashi shook his head.

"Then maybe we should . . ."

"Please." His voice cracked on this one word. Chibenashi hadn't paid his father a visit, hadn't written him a letter, hadn't initiated or responded to any contact with the man since that day he'd knelt in his mother's blood, seeing his father with the same blood on his hands and holding a shaking Ashwiyaa. He'd seen him across the room at the Mediation, and that was it. His father had worn the same expressionless mask on his face both times. A far cry from the man Chibenashi had known, who had always been so affectionate, so expressive.

In the span of a day, he'd gone from ignorance to learning about his father's supposed motive to finding out he had apparently been innocent all along.

Dakaasin was right—that alone was enough revelation for a day, a month, a year, a lifetime. A visit would only add to the load he was carrying. Might crush him completely. No matter. He had to be strong enough to carry that information. Had to see his father, hear his story, and find out who and what he was protecting with that lie.

None of that could wait another day. He and his father had had the last twenty years stolen from them. He was an orphan who'd just learned that one of his parents was still alive, still wanted him, and could see him.

While Chibenashi was lost in his thoughts, some silent conversation had been held between Dakaasin and Takumwah over his head. They'd reached an accord at last.

"Let's go," Takumwah said, offering his hand.

Chapter Seventeen

A father in prison is an impossible weight for his children to carry. He, of course, is the one who is responsible for harm committed against another person. He is the one whom the system singled out and whose presence in that cage was negotiated and agreed upon by the Victims. In Ishkode's case, his children were the only living victims. His wife was the only one who hadn't survived the crime.

In Ishkode's mind, his crime had not been the murder. It had been his failure to prevent it. Neebin's death was, and always had been, on his hands. And for that he deserved to be where he was.

Society depended upon all people working toward that greater common goal—loving and taking care of each other, helping those in need, and never hurting someone else intentionally. If an injury was inflicted, it must be righted as soon as possible. Immediately, if it could. And in his case, as with so many others, the way to right the injury was to lock him away.

But his children? They were out there in the world, bearing the scar of what he had done. They were the survivors not only of the crime but also the punishment. They were the ones who had to look people in the eye, bravely face the world while announcing, "My father is a criminal." Mino-bimaadiziwin dictated that people should never judge others without walking in their makizinan, should never hold children responsible for the actions of their parents, and should support children who had been hurt by their parents' actions. But people were only human, and it happened. When Ishkode's children weren't the subject of gossip, they were the object of pity: for having lost their mother, and having lost their father, and having to deal with the insult and injury of the crime that had taken both their parents away. His children had grown up with people briefly burying a reaction behind a polite or even welcoming expression.

No Mediator could take everything into account and dictate that the children be treated as if none of this had ever happened. For it *had* happened, and nothing could change that.

Ishkode's children had borne that branding for twenty years. Ishkode had risen every day in his cell, feeling that his children, not him, had been the ones serving a life sentence.

The best and easiest way for Chibenashi to deal with his father being in prison all these years had been to ignore it. Never talk about it. Never draw attention to it. The stain is already on you; the guilt by association is there. Add to that the victimhood by association and, well, it created a shadow from which you could never truly escape.

The trauma of losing his mother had been stifling. The trauma of what had come after had been suffocating.

Chibenashi had not simply been allowed to raise Ashwiyaa after it happened. Peezhickee had taken him and Ashwiyaa away from their home and father so that they would not see him being arrested. They took them to a group-care home in Wiikwedong while everything was sorted out. He and Ashwiyaa had been placed in two large rooms—one for boys, one for girls—where children slept on stiff rope beds with thin blankets that did little to keep out the chill. He couldn't sleep all night, kept awake by the soft sobbing of the children around him. He saw one boy give his little brother a pillow so that it would be more like the comfort they had had in their home. They were gone by the next afternoon. Chibenashi never knew what became of them. He remembered that about the three days he was there: kids would appear, then disappear, just like that. Ghosts who materialized in and out of existence and memory.

It had been twenty years, and Chibenashi could still feel the coldness, the emptiness of the place. How scared he was that he might be left there forever, where forgotten, abandoned, and victimized children were sent away until they could be dealt with. He hadn't been told anything: why they were there, how long it would be, or where they would go. It was the not knowing that was the hardest part. Being kept in the dark just made an already difficult and confusing situation even worse. He and Ashwiyaa had been among the lucky ones. They were out quickly, and with a family friend.

Meoquanee had come for them. She'd taken them back to their home, stayed with them that night and every night until it had been agreed that he was both old enough and responsible enough to care for his sister. Meoquanee had pledged to keep an eye on them. And she had, every day, until she had died. Whatever her motivations had been, she'd been there when no one else had. After they returned home—which had been cleaned, arranged, and made welcoming for them—people came. People cooked and brought prepared food. People came to talk to him, to Ashwiyaa, to Meoquanee. People told stories about what their mother had been like as a child, a teenager, trying to supplant the bad memories with better ones. Trying to fill the gap. But no one had stayed as long or gotten as close as Meoquanee. Ashwiyaa wouldn't respond well to anyone but her or Chibenashi. Screaming, crying, refusing to speak. Throwing out insults. Throwing things. Trying to hurt herself. People were understanding, persistent. But eventually, one by one, they all stopped coming, leaving him and Ashwiyaa alone.

Not Meoquanee. She'd stayed.

From then on, he and everyone else in Baawitigong operated on an unspoken agreement: they would not mention it, and neither would he. Everyone would outwardly pretend that it had never even happened, though the truth screamed out in the silence. When Chibenashi met new people, he omitted it from his background. When asked about his parents, he always said they were dead. It was easier and, in many ways, true. Chibenashi had even stayed out of Shikaakwa. Between Dakaasin and his father, there were too many ugly memories here, too many ghosts to fight.

Now he was in Shikaakwa. Dakaasin was back. His father was back. It was time.

Chibenashi had always felt that he could never forgive his father. The question now was whether his father could forgive him.

The gibaakwa'odiiwigamig was so empty that Chibenashi's thoughts echoed off the walls. The soft *swish-swish* of makizinan on hard floor could be heard up and down the corridor leading to the housing area where the inmates spent their days. Imprisonment was the result of negotiations that had completely broken down between a Mediator and an Advocate who could not reach a resolution that fully satisfied the Victims. Locking someone away did not bring anyone back from the dead, uninjure someone, or repair or replace property. It was punitive, and punitive actions did nothing but reinforce bad feelings. The goal of Mediation was to make people whole, not avenge them. It was to make the perpetrators atone for what they had done, not punish them for it.

Chibenashi had wanted to come alone. But this was an investigation into two murders now, and there was another potential suspect at large. They needed answers. And Ishkode, the only one who presumably knew what had happened, could give them. So, reluctantly (after they'd left him no choice), he'd consented to Dakaasin and Takumwah joining him. Takumwah wanted to know whether Sakima could have done it. He had asked Chibenashi if a fourteen-year-old could really have committed the crime. Chibenashi doubted someone so young could have done so. He remembered how small Sakima had been at the time. Maybe that's why Wiishkobak had been so disappointed in him.

Dakaasin saw him first. Ishkode sat cross-legged on a woven rug on the floor of his cell, meditating. He was dressed in the simple brown tunic and pants given to prisoners. His makizinan—well worn—were neatly placed on the ground next to the rug. The door was open so that the sound of the wind and water off the lake could be heard. The few other prisoners were equally quiet as they spent their time in either their individual cells or the common area. All cell doors were open, and people could wander in and out as they pleased. One man painted a landscape scene from memory. One gently beat a drum with his hands, humming a song or prayer (too softly for any of them to make out the words). A fire burned in the large fireplace against a wall in the common area, warming the room. In the summer, they might be outside in the courtyard.

Chibenashi saw his father as if for the first time. Somehow, in his mind, his father had never aged in the intervening two decades. Chibenashi had grown; he had begun a career, had fallen in and then out of love. Meoquanee had gotten divorced. Her husband and son had moved away. Her ex-husband had remarried. Kichewaishke and Okimaskew had married and become parents twice over. Peezhickee and Wakwi had grown old. The port had grown larger, as had the crowds. The world had changed. Three wars in two decades overseas. The reemergence and dissipation of tensions between the Anishinaabe and the Lakota to the west. A ship bearing an international crew had traveled to Mars.

But, in Chibenashi's mind, Ishkode had been a forever constant. Still as he was twenty years ago: early forties, long hair, dark skin, well-defined muscles from all the running he did. He was imprisoned and always would be. He would never change because Chibenashi would never see him again. He was forever petrified in Chibenashi's mind as a murderer.

Now, seeing him in the flesh for the first time in decades, Chibenashi found that Ishkode had changed as the rest of the world had. He was in his sixties; his hair was an iron gray and cut short, the lines on his face cut deeper, his skin more pale from not being in the sun. He obviously couldn't run several kilometers a day as he had before, but he had the lithe body of someone who practiced yoga daily. And he had just been definitively excluded as the murderer he had confessed to being.

No one paid the visitors much mind as they entered, likely out of respect for the privacy of whomever they were visiting. Chibenashi led the way to the cell and stood at the doorway.

Ishkode's eyes were still closed. His breathing and mind were still deep in meditation. No one had advised him that he was having visitors today. According to what Takumwah had learned when they arranged for the visit, Chibenashi's suspicions had been correct: no one had ever visited Ishkode. Who would, other than his children? And yet, despite all of this, when Ishkode opened his eyes, he did not seem the least bit surprised to see him. Nor did he seem to be surprised at the changes in Chibenashi.

"Ningwis," he said, greeting Chibenashi with a title that no one had called him in twenty years: *my son*. His expression did not change. He seemed neither happy nor sad to see his only son.

"Boozhoo, noos."

Neither man said anything for a long time. Takumwah and Dakaasin faded away into the background as much as possible, taking seats at a table across the common area, giving the two their privacy.

"You've grown," Ishkode said at long last. "A Peacekeeper."

"You can tell just by looking?"

Ishkode shrugged. "One hears things, even in here. I confess I would not have expected you to go that route."

"What did you expect?"

"Something safer."

He gestured for Chibenashi to sit with him on the floor, which he did. Chibenashi discovered, once they were both seated, that he was taller than his father.

For all his emotion and insistence on coming, Chibenashi had not planned on what to say upon meeting his father. He opened and closed his mouth a few times, like a fish, straining for the right words. There was so much to say, so much lost time; how could he begin? He felt it may be important to begin gently. But as they so often did, clever words failed him, and he blurted out: "I know you didn't kill ngashi."

A shadow fell across Ishkode's face.

"Of course I did," he said in a low, even voice octaves below his normal tone.

Chibenashi shook his head. "No, noos. I know you didn't. I know it for a fact."

"I said," he repeated in a sharper, louder voice, "that I did."

Chibenashi blinked rapidly in disbelief. "I don't understand."

"There is nothing to understand. I accept responsibility for the crime. I am doing what everyone, including me, agreed was the way to make you and your sister whole again following my wrongdoing. If you must understand something, understand that."

Chibenashi leaned back, looked at the ceiling. There was a water stain in the wood. "Meoquanee is dead."

Ishkode did not respond, so Chibenashi tilted his head forward to look at him. His father looked truly astonished in a way he had not when his only son had wandered into his prison cell unannounced after two decades of silence.

"I am sorry to hear it," he said after several long moments.

"She was murdered."

"I am especially sorry to hear that. By whom?" Ishkode spoke with such casualness, he might have been asking about the weather.

"That's the problem," Chibenashi said. "We're still figuring that out. *I'm* still figuring that out."

Chibenashi's phone buzzed. He ignored it.

"I am certain that you will," Ishkode said. "Is that what brings you to Shikaakwa?"

"Yes. It did." He brought his fingertips together, considered what to say next. He had to be careful, not just in this tightrope conversation with his father but also to keep the integrity of the investigation intact. He'd already made so many mistakes. "We ran DNA on her blood samples. We found something. But it wasn't what we were expecting. The test results related back to ngashi's murder. Whoever killed her also killed Meoquanee." He took a deep breath. "Which means that it could not have been you."

Ishkode set his jaw. "I have said what happened."

"But it's not true. That you did it."

"It is true. It does not matter what your DNA analysis says. I know what happened. I have said it."

"Tell me, then." Chibenashi raised his voice now. Behind him, Takumwah and Dakaasin snapped their heads to attention. The other inmates were pretending not to be listening in. Chibenashi's companions began making their way over to the cell. "Tell me what happened that night, if you say it happened."

"I have already said it," Ishkode said. "My story has not changed. You may read it in the case file that you no doubt have access to."

He didn't have access to it, and he didn't want to read about it in a case file. He needed to hear it from his father. "But things have changed, and I need to know—"

"Nothing has changed." Ishkode's voice was firm, a father reprimanding his son. "Is that clear? Nothing."

"Everything has changed." Chibenashi was pleading now. And he was no longer just talking about the case. "Nothing is the same."

"The constant in life may be change, but when it comes to this matter, I am afraid nothing has changed, and nothing will change." Ishkode stood up, stared down at his son. His face was silhouetted against the window, making him appear dark and intimidating. "I thank you for your visit, but now it is time for you to go."

Chibenashi scrambled to his feet. He was taller than his father now, by several centimeters. Still, he felt smaller. He was a teenager again, and his father was still an authority figure. Nothing had changed in the intervening decades, just like in his mind. "But we've only just started talking."

"And now I regret that our talking must end."

Chibenashi rocked back a bit on his heels. After all he'd lost, he'd just regained his father and was about to lose him again.

"Why are you sending me away?"

Ishkode looked down.

"What aren't you telling me?"

He reached out to take his father's hand, but Ishkode stepped out of reach, leaving Chibenashi grasping at nothing but air. He felt just how empty his hand was. His father was less than a meter away, and yet it was the greatest distance they'd ever been from one another.

"Noos," he implored, "don't you want to get out of here?"

Ishkode turned his back on his son and faced the window. A bird twittered outside in the bleak, white cold. Chibenashi waited for him to turn around, to say more, to even dismiss him, but he realized that this had been dismissal enough. Their relationship was like a piece of pottery that had been shattered, and when he finally had tried to put it back together, so many pieces were missing that it would never be whole again. The weight on Chibenashi's shoulders had not lifted. It had doubled.

"I'll come back," Chibenashi said, half promising, half threatening.

"If you must."

Seizing his courage, Chibenashi strode forward to stand next to his father but stopped short of touching him.

"I don't understand what's happening," Chibenashi said. "And I don't know what you're afraid of or who you're trying to protect. But we have a chance to fix this now and to regain what we've lost. You could be home with us again—with me and Ashwiyaa. And I'm not giving up on that without a fight."

His father looked forward resolutely.

"I'll get you out of here, noos. Even if you refuse to help me."

Ishkode closed his eyes, swallowed, and continued to say nothing.

"I'll see you soon," Chibenashi said.

Chapter Eighteen

Wakwi loved walking through the woods just before dawn, when the sky held the purple-gray promise of a new day ahead. Wrapped in her thick blanket to ward off the cold and humming to herself, she shuffled along with a gait that belied her speed. No one could walk over snow and ice as deftly as Wakwi. And as she did so, she considered how blessed she was to live in this place, at this time, with these people.

So many people in the world had to construct temples, churches, ashrams, mosques, shrines—artificial houses for their spirituality. But the Anishinaabe lived and breathed their spirituality. They ate it. Inhaled it. Drank it. Bathed their faces in it in the rain. Listened to it in the song of the crickets and loons at nightfall and saw it blink in the lights of the fireflies. It slipped through their fingers, whispered through their hair, crackled in their fire. It was everywhere and everything, all and nothing at once. This, the earth and its creatures, was their spirituality. Their daily lives, their prayers. And Wakwi was blessed to see it all.

In this predawn time, she would walk and listen for the artificial sounds of the world waking up. A few lights would go on in wigwams, and she would hear music or morning television. The jingle and buzz of phone alarms. None of this would drown out nature, however. How could anything?

Wakwi usually walked a preferred route, but occasionally, on days such as today, she felt like living dangerously and would vary her route.

This one would accommodate the shorter days by positioning her in just the right direction to see the sunrise. Even now, she could see the first few threads of pink stitch across the sky, paving the way for the sun.

And that's when she saw it.

She stopped, frozen, and stared at the crouched shadow darting through and between wigwams. She couldn't make out who it was, but it was clear the person didn't want to be seen. They moved furtively, paranoid, eager to get out of the way.

The silhouette was not one Wakwi recognized. She may be getting older, and the predawn light was dim, but she had prided herself on being able to recognize just about everyone in Baawitigong. The locals, at least. And the tourists had long since cleared out for the year. Whoever this was, it was not some lost soul from a cruise ship nor some hunter with a permit. It had to be someone else.

And the person had been running from Meoquanee's old wigwam.

Chapter Nineteen

The next morning, Chibenashi wasn't quite sure if he could say he woke up, for he had never gone to sleep. He'd tossed and turned all night, the revelations of the day churning over and over in his mind. Everything he'd ever known and believed and understood about himself, his father, and his mother had been ripped apart. Meoquanee may have had an affair. His mother may have had an affair. His father had definitively not killed his mother yet continued to insist that he had despite DNA evidence excluding him.

The noise outside the window had been welcome as he lay in bed. If he could focus on that noise, he could ignore the turning over and over of information in his head. He'd had half a mind to take something—anything—for it, but he had decided against it. He hadn't gotten drunk since the night of his mother's murder. Had he stayed sober that night, he might have seen something, or stopped something.

The morning began with a series of increasingly upset and desperate texts from Ashwiyaa, which just made him feel worse. He'd left her to twist in the wind. She'd called him several times while they were in the gibaakwa'odiiwigamig. He hadn't responded to a single one until late in the evening, when he'd told her he would call her later with news. It was a lie. All of this had to be told to her in person.

He switched off his phone.

Chibenashi somehow hauled himself out of his room and down to the lobby. Takumwah had not come to meet him at his room today, wisely giving him his space. He bought a cup of lukewarm coffee and an overpriced croissant in the café. He winced at the bitterness of the coffee, but it was better than nothing. He would need extra caffeine today if he was going to stay both awake and one step ahead of the pain in his head.

He had to push through the exhaustion and confusion and anger. Whoever did this to their mother and to Meoquanee, they were still out there. Targeting the women in his life. Which meant the only one left, Ashwiyaa, was in danger. And if nothing else in his life was that True East, it was her safety. He had to solve this.

Takumwah greeted him from where he'd been loitering in the doorway. He declined to comment on Chibenashi's sleepless eyes, unshaven face, and wrinkled clothes. Some days, just getting out of bed was a victory. "Ready?" he asked.

Chibenashi nodded. Time to face the day.

"I thought I might take the lead with Sakima today," Takumwah said.

"I can handle it," Chibenashi said.

"I know you can," Takumwah said, though it was clear in his expression he didn't really think that. "But sometimes aggressive is the way to go, and I think that'll be the case today. You'll need to let me handle that part. It'll throw him off."

Chibenashi was too tired to argue.

Sakima trudged up the damp stairs to his apartment, gashkibidaagan wrapped across his chest. He was caught by surprise when Takumwah clasped him hard on the shoulder.

"Sakima!" Takumwah said heartily. "We meet again."

Sakima jerked away. "What do you want?"

"Let's go for a walk," Takumwah said, roughly leading him back down the stairs.

They escorted him to the dakoniwewigamig and the same conference room where Chibenashi and Takumwah had reviewed the video footage the day before. It already seemed like a lifetime ago.

Takumwah relieved Sakima of his gashkibidaagan. It was faded and frayed. Some beads were missing, causing the designs to disappear halfway through—and there was a bloodstain on the side. "Nice bag. What have you got in there?"

"None of your business," Sakima said, trying to snatch it back. Takumwah pulled it out of reach.

"We've seen this bag before," Takumwah said. "In some interesting video footage of you the day of your mother's murder. The Manoomin that you claimed not to have attended in Baawitigong. Remember telling us that?"

Sakima defiantly crossed his arms despite the confusion on his face. Clearly he was not expecting this side of Takumwah. Neither, for that matter, was Chibenashi. He was reluctantly impressed with Takumwah's skill in adapting his interrogation style to meet the moment.

Takumwah touched the screen on the wall, cued up the video montage of Sakima's movements that day, and began playing it. Sakima's face flushed as he watched his movements on the day his mother had died. When the image of Sakima leaving the train in Baawitigong ended, Takumwah and Chibenashi both turned to him.

"I also have your background results, Sakima," Takumwah said. "Some minor skirmishes over the years. Bar fights and such. Seems like violence is how you resolve disputes. Maybe that's what you did here. So . . . care to revise your story?"

"Okay, fine. So I went back to Baawitigong that day."

"Why?"

"I didn't kill my mother."

"Did you see her?"

Sakima turned his head to look out a window that wasn't there.

Takumwah charged over and slammed his fist on the table, shocking Sakima out of his reverie. "I asked you a question. Did you see your mother?"

Sakima shuddered, then nodded. "Yes," he whispered.

"Pleasant visit, was it?"

Sakima did not answer. Takumwah grabbed his face and jerked it toward him. "What kind of visit was it?"

"N-not good," Sakima stuttered.

"What was 'not good' about it?" Takumwah jerked his face again. "Start talking. Or perhaps we can take this to the gibaakwa'odiiwigamig, where you can meditate on your options for a while."

"I didn't go there to kill her," Sakima said urgently. "And I didn't kill her. I swear."

"Convince me," Takumwah said.

So Sakima tried.

Sakima blamed his mother for the breakdown of his parents' marriage and his forced relocation from Baawitigong to Shikaakwa, a difference that, Chibenashi could attest, was like moving from the earth to the moon. When Sakima asked his father why they were moving, he always had the same answer: "Your mother." For years it had boiled inside him like acid.

Sakima had not adjusted well to life in Shikaakwa. He sank into a deep depression. He'd not wanted to become a fisherman; he had ended up a fisherman. Unlike in Baawitigong, where people revered and admired those who fed the community, the same was not true in Shikaakwa. They paid lip service to their contributions but in practice gave them the worst housing, down by the docks to make sure they could get in and out of their boats quickly. No one really knew that about Shikaakwa. They let people believe that they had committed some sort of wrong to get such crappy housing. So not only was he doing the necessary work to feed the community but he was also branded some sort of miscreant by virtue of where he lived. The hypocrisy strangled him.

Over the years, he thought about his mother and how it was her fault that he was here and that his life had turned out this way. He was thirty-four years old. No education. No girlfriend. No prospects of improving his life. No real friends. Not even a family. Just more of the same. Wake before dawn. Trudge down to the boat. Spend all day in a stinking vessel doing backbreaking labor. Return to his small rotting apartment inside of a larger rotting building. Spend his evening alone. Repeat.

He was alone when Manoomin dawned, and feeling lonely. His father—who had no scruples about sharing his disappointment in how his son had turned out—would be giving a lecture on economics and personal responsibility with his perfect wife at his side. Wiishkobak spent his Manoomin forgetting that he had a son, that he had ever had a family back in Baawitigong.

His small apartment had not much in it, but it did contain the few mementos from Baawitigong that he had allowed himself to keep. Feeling alone and resentful, Sakima decided that he didn't want any more reminders of the woman who he decided had ruined his life. He went to the closet and pulled out a round birchbark box that was battered and stained, the sinews holding it together coming apart at the seams. Inside were a few old photographs of him and his mother, and some letters and cards she had sent to him in those first few years. Fighting tears, he'd stuffed them all in his gashkibidaagan. He'd taken it on the boat with him, having half a mind to throw it into Ininwewi-gichigami. He would revel in watching it all sink to the bottom. But, as the day passed, he had decided against it. He would take it to the woman. Throw the photographs at her feet. Tell her to her face exactly what she had done to him, exactly what he thought of her for having done so. That would be far more satisfying than simply flinging it into the lake. He wanted to see her face when she realized how she had ruined his life—and his father's life. He would relish it.

And that's precisely what he did. Walked straight from the boat to the pier to the street to the train station. Boarded the first Arrow Train to Baawitigong. It was crowded, and he was lucky to get a spot. The agent at the station had taken pity on him—Manoomin and no way of getting home. She'd ensured that he would get on that train. He'd spent the trip pressed against the window, his hair leaving a grease spot, thinking about just what he would say.

He'd gotten to Baawitigong in the late afternoon, still as light as midday at that time of year, and made his way to his mother's wigwam, where he'd spent the first fourteen years of his life. She'd been both shocked and delighted to see him, throwing her arms around him without a care of the years that had passed. She was warmer and smaller than he had remembered. She was like a twig that could snap in half at the smallest amount of pressure. It had almost seemed impossible that someone so small, who looked so frail, could be responsible for so much destruction.

It had infuriated him.

While everyone was getting ready for Manoomin, he and Meoquanee had stayed in her wigwam. She'd tried to feed him; he'd refused. He had simply handed over the gashkibidaagan and told her to look inside. Her face had lit up when he had done so; she had made the bag for him when he was a child, and it apparently touched her that he still used it. When she saw what was in it, her face had fallen. She'd understood what was happening, why he was there.

Her stricken face catalyzed him to say everything he'd ever wanted. Every resentment, every anger, every wrong turn in his life came pouring out of him. He lashed out, blaming her for everything from the move to his apartment and lack of a girlfriend. It was her fault, all her fault. Tears had run down his face in steady tracks. He was screaming so hard at her he was spitting. And Meoquanee stood there, taking it all.

She said nothing in her own defense. Accepted the gashkibidaagan and everything inside. Accepted his anger, his rage, his blame. Accepted it all. Unconditionally. Embraced it.

The last words she'd said to him were, "I love you."

His response: "Never speak to me again."

And he'd walked into the night, to catch the last Arrow Train back to Shikaakwa, for the lonely ride home back to his lonely life.

"If I hadn't left," he said in closing, "maybe I could have stopped it."

Sakima was panting, sweating, from recounting the story. Once he was finished, he bent his head forward in his hands. He began shaking silently.

Takumwah opened his mouth to question him further, but Chibenashi's hand on his shoulder stayed him. "Come on," he murmured, and led Takumwah out of the room into the corridor. As the door closed, they heard a strained sob.

They stood there, face-to-face, for a long time. Neither man had come from that room unaffected by what they had heard.

"I believe him," Chibenashi said finally.

Takumwah blew out a breath. "I hate to say it," he said, "but I do too. I've questioned a lot of suspects in my time. And when it's like that . . ."

"You can't fake that," Chibenashi agreed.

They stood again in silence for a few moments.

"We should still talk to him more," Takumwah said. "Find out what he saw in Baawitigong. He sounds like he was so single-minded he probably had tunnel vision. Still, he might have seen something. Anything can help at this point."

"Agreed."

"No one you spoke with in Baawitigong saw him?"

Chibenashi shook his head. "It was a holiday; everyone was at the harvest and then the sacred fire. No one was home. They were the only ones." He thought of how Meoquanee had betrayed none of this when he last saw her at the sacred fire. How tortured had she been? And why had she felt that she could not share her pain with him?

They both sighed, defeated.

"Wait a moment," Chibenashi said, a memory flashing to mind.

"What?"

"His gashkibidaagan. He had it with him when he went to Baawitigong but did not have it when he returned. Now he has it again."

"Damn it." Takumwah flung the door open, where Sakima sat, still sobbing, with his head buried in his crossed arms. "The bag," he said.

Sakima wiped his arm across his snotty nose, caught his breath. "What bag?"

"This." Takumwah held the gashkibidaagan up in front of Sakima's face and shook it for effect. A few beads flew off a loose thread and clattered on the floor. "You didn't have it with you when you returned from Baawitigong. Now you have it. How did you get it?"

Sakima shuddered a breath. "My father brought it for me. Said he got it from whoever was cleaning out her wigwam."

Chibenashi huffed a breath.

He had searched that wigwam personally. Reviewed the catalog of belongings over and over before it had been cleaned out.

That bag had not been there.

Chapter Twenty

Ziigwan didn't pick up until the third ring, which, in Chibenashi's experience, was late for her.

"Can you find out if Sakima has been back to Baawitigong recently?" Chibenashi had ducked into a corner of the hallway after their interview with Sakima ended.

"And boozhoo to you, too, Chibenashi. Things are fine here. How is Shikaakwa?"

"I'm sorry." Chibenashi expressed more shame than he felt. "I don't mean to be rude."

"Sakima, huh? Sounds like things are getting narrowed down."

"Possibly," Chibenashi said. "We saw that he was there on the night of Manoomin. We need to know if anyone else saw him there. Where. Who he talked to."

Ziigwan made small noises of assent; it sounded like she was making notes. "Anything else?"

Chibenashi considered for a moment. "The official inventory for Meoquanee's wigwam."

"I can send that to your phone now."

"Would it say who cleaned it out and where the things inside went?"

"Not sure. But I'll send it right over."

Chibenashi opened the information as soon as his phone pinged. He went back to the room with the video screen and held up his phone. The file transferred to the large screen. He tapped the screen and, using fluid movements, enlarged and reformatted it so he could fit the entire inventory on the screen. Everything he remembered being in the wigwam was there, including the photographs. He remembered pulling them from the circular birchbark box with the porcupine-quill designs. The photographs of Meoquanee and Sakima that he'd never seen before. The ones that Sakima must have delivered to her. Those were in the wigwam.

He ran word searches for *gashkibidaagan*, *bag*, *satchel*, *beaded*, anything he could think of to associate with it. Nothing came up.

He blew out a breath. His memory on this was accurate, which comforted him. Chibenashi was so unmoored by the events of the last few days that he was worried he might be compromising the investigation. Like most people, he preferred his own memory and the conversations he had with others. But written records like this were good at jogging memories about what was said and when.

He then scanned the document for information about cleaning out the wigwam—who had done it and when. There didn't seem to be anything special about it: The recyclers from Baawitigong appeared to have taken the lead. Everything had been accounted for. Most possessions had been appropriately recycled, refurnished, or redistributed based on need. Everything else had been given to family or friends. There was no record of a bag having been delivered to anyone. The people now living in the wigwam had no connection to Meoquanee or her family.

So it hadn't been the recyclers who had returned or retrieved the gashkibidaagan. It had already been gone by the time the place was inventoried.

Where had it gone?

◆   ◆   ◆

Chibenashi stood behind Takumwah as he pounded on the door of Wiishkobak's wigwam on Educators' Row. He was unyielding in doing so until, finally, a disheveled Wiishkobak, clothes haphazardly thrown on, flung open the door.

Takumwah and Chibenashi had brainstormed various theories as to what had happened to the gashkibidaagan on the way over. Perhaps the bag had been sent to Wiishkobak by some sympathetic person in Baawitigong.

Or, maybe, Wiishkobak had been behind the murder all along but had arranged for someone else to perform the act itself.

Takumwah grabbed Wiishkobak by the arm. "You're coming with us," he said in greeting.

Wiishkobak jerked his arm away, adjusted the glasses on his face. "What is the meaning of this?"

He got his answer once he was in the same room in the dakoni-wewigamig as Sakima, who was no longer crying but was still upset.

"Noos," Sakima whispered. His eyes widened in fear.

Wiishkobak walked straight over to his son and smacked him across the face with the back of his hand.

"You worthless thing," he hissed. "What have you done now?"

Sakima shrank from his father, not answering him.

"Speak!"

"Nothing!" Sakima cried. "I swear!"

Wiishkobak rounded on Takumwah and Chibenashi. "Tell me. What has he done?"

"That's what we hope to find out," Takumwah said, kicking out a chair and gesturing for Wiishkobak to sit. Wiishkobak chose a different seat. He resolutely did not look at his son.

"We're hoping to clear the air a bit regarding the family history." Takumwah held up the gashkibidaagan. "We need an answer as to how you came to have this."

Wiishkobak shook his head. "Sakima has had that bag forever. His mother made it for him. Explains the poor quality."

"When were you last in Baawitigong?" Chibenashi asked.

"When my marriage ended."

"Yes, about that," Takumwah said. He stood and walked over to the door. "We've heard some conflicting stories about who was unfaithful to whom in that marriage. We understand from you and your son that it was Meoquanee. We understand from your wife that it was you."

Wiishkobak's and Sakima's heads snapped up. They looked at each other in confusion.

"You two have much to discuss," Takumwah said. He got up. "We'll be outside."

Chibenashi jumped up and followed Takumwah out of the room. He looked back at them as they walked out. Sakima's lower lip was quivering, and Wiishkobak's face was carved wood.

"What was that for?" Chibenashi hissed.

"If they trust each other, they will not tell us the truth. We need one to flip on the other."

"Shouldn't we put them in separate rooms?"

Takumwah shook his head. "We have to break their trust with each other first. Otherwise, they have every incentive to stay silent to protect the other."

The two men stood in the hallway for a long time. For several long moments, there was nothing but silence on the other side of the door. Then, voices grew louder and louder. Shouting. Finally, the door swung open, and Wiishkobak stormed out. His face was rigid with rage.

"Ready to talk with us?" Takumwah asked with mock friendliness.

"I'm not speaking with you," Wiishkobak practically spat.

"That is, of course, your right." Takumwah was as calm as Wiishkobak was enraged. With Wiishkobak's temper aroused, there was no need for him to play the role of angry investigative Peacekeeper anymore. "However, we could hold you for three days if you refuse."

"I can have an Advocate here with one phone call."

"And your Advocate can wait for three days for all I care," Takumwah said. He was the same smiling fool who had met Chibenashi at the door of his lodgings with coffee. "I may feel more generous if you were to give me something in return."

Wiishkobak's eyes narrowed. "Such as?"

"A DNA sample?"

Wiishkobak scoffed. "I'm not giving you one."

"It would help us to exclude you as a suspect."

"My whereabouts on that night are well documented and airtight, and you know they are. You're not taking my DNA. Not today. Not ever." He made to leave, but Chibenashi held up a hand.

"Please don't leave like this," he said.

"If you think I'm responsible, go ahead—detain me. I am innocent of anything sordid you may be accusing me of. And that boy in there"—he pointed to the door that had just slammed shut—"is nothing but a liar."

Then he turned on his heel and stomped down the hallway, daring Takumwah to chase after him as people parted before him to clear the way.

Takumwah and Chibenashi watched him leave. "I'm satisfied," Takumwah said.

"What if he leaves?"

"Then he leaves."

"But wouldn't you want to hold him, just to be safe?" This was all so far outside of Chibenashi's experience, he was torn. But wouldn't they want to keep a potential suspect from fleeing or destroying evidence?

"The cameras will follow him every step he takes," Takumwah said. "So he's not sneaking away in the night. If he tries, we have another Peacekeeper tasked with following him and keeping him here. I'm not going through the trouble of detaining him now, with Sakima here." He threw open the door to the room to find Sakima still seated in the chair.

Chibenashi was going to follow him but then decided to chase down Wiishkobak.

"So your wife is a liar, then?" Chibenashi asked. "Meoquanee had the affair, not you?"

Wiishkobak's face turned to granite as his expression hardened.

191

"We still need to talk," Chibenashi said, "about the truth of your marriage to Meoquanee. About who had an affair."

"You don't want to pursue this," Wiishkobak said gravely.

"If it means finding Meoquanee's murderer, of course I do."

"You know it's not me," he said, his expression and voice gentle. "You know that." Chibenashi did not react. "Whether or not you can admit it, we both know it's true. So trust me when I say you don't want to go down this road. It won't shine a light on anything."

"If you've lied to me, of course I'm going to pursue it."

"I told you the truth," he said to Chibenashi. "With one exception."

"Which is?"

"I said that the man who Meoquanee had an affair with has been dead for many years," he said. "He's still alive."

❖ ❖ ❖

Chibenashi stood in the hallway for a long time after Wiishkobak left. More confused than ever, he went to the room where Takumwah was interrogating Sakima.

"Have you been back to Baawitigong since your last visit?" Takumwah asked.

Sakima sighed, then nodded his head.

"Have you been there since we talked to you at your apartment?"

Sakima hesitated, then nodded.

"You went back within the last two days?"

Sakima nodded again.

"When?"

"Last night," Sakima whispered.

"What were you doing there?"

"I got a call that some of her things were going to be destroyed."

"Why did you care about that? You said you'd returned everything to her. You didn't care anymore."

"Why do you think? I saw her the day she was murdered, I didn't go back for the burial or the days before, you started poking around . . ."

"Did you get the bag?" Takumwah asked.

"Yes," he whispered. "That's what I came back for."

"So you lied when you said your father got it for you?"

"Yes."

"Why?"

"I knew how it would look."

"You're right," Takumwah said. "It doesn't look good."

"But it is why I decided to go now. I got a call from the recyclers; the bag was going to be burned for energy. I thought that I didn't want it anymore, but I couldn't let it be destroyed." He shrugged. "Hard to explain."

"We know that isn't true," Takumwah said. "They never had it."

"I'm telling the truth."

Takumwah looked pensive for a moment. Chibenashi couldn't figure out what he was thinking. Finally, Takumwah spoke.

"Explain how the blood got on it."

Sakima shook his head. "I can't. There wasn't any blood when I last had it."

"We're having it tested."

"Good."

"We'll be keeping you here for now."

Sakima looked at Takumwah with shock.

"What do you mean?" he asked.

"We have reasonable suspicion that you may have been involved with your mother's murder. You were there on the day she was killed. You argued. You have lied to us. You returned to Baawitigong after you spoke with us. You could very easily and quickly leave town again. And, most crucially, the DNA testing cannot exclude you as a suspect. And there is blood on your bag. Therefore, we must hold you." Takumwah looked grave. Clearly he thought Sakima was worth the effort of keeping him here.

Chibenashi's stomach sank. He couldn't argue with anything Takumwah had said. The reasoning was solid. Sakima was the closest thing they had to a suspect. Wiishkobak was overreacting, which was suspicious but not completely out of line for someone who was connected to a murder victim. And Wiishkobak was correct in that they had absolutely no grounds for suspecting his involvement.

Despite all of this, he felt this was not the answer. Or at least, not the complete one.

◆　◆　◆

Once Sakima had been processed into a holding room—different from the cells in the gibaakwa'odiiwigamig, this one was meant to be temporary and had none of the comforts of a cell that was used for long-term occupation—Takumwah led Chibenashi down the stairs, out the door, and to a small café across the street. It was late evening now. The sun was gone, the sky was grayed out by a thick layer of clouds, and the cold bit at every patch of exposed skin. The café was not inviting, but it was warm. There was a table available. Against the far wall opposite the door, a band was playing soft music: drums and flutes, neither sad nor happy. The melody was steady, enough to keep conversations going and drinks flowing, but not so powerful that it would overwhelm. Takumwah ordered two coffees and frybread. Once it was delivered, Chibenashi slathered his in maple syrup. He needed this comfort food right now. They sat in silence for a long time, letting the music fill the empty space between them.

"What do you think about Wiishkobak?" Chibenashi asked.

"I don't like him."

Chibenashi waited for Takumwah to elaborate, but he didn't.

They didn't speak again until the coffees were mostly consumed and what dregs were left in the bottoms of their cups had gone cold. Takumwah seemed to be steeling himself for something, and so it did not surprise Chibenashi when he finally spoke.

"I think we need to speak with your father again."

Chibenashi tensed but nodded.

"We know that it was not him who killed your mother. I think he can offer us more insight into who actually did do it—and possibly clear up the matter of who had an affair with whom."

There was no doubt in Chibenashi's mind that his father could offer insight. There was also no doubt that he would refuse to do so. He told Takumwah the same.

"Look," Takumwah said, leaning forward, "I won't pretend to know how difficult this is for you. I can't possibly. I don't know if I'd have half the strength you've displayed if I were in your makizinan. I know today was hard for you. I know yesterday was even harder. To ask you to speak with your father again is the worst thing I could possibly ask of you."

Chibenashi held up his hand to stop Takumwah's speech.

"I'm a Peacekeeper," Chibenashi said. "I get it."

And, if he was being honest with himself, he wanted to go back. Wanted to try again with his father. When he'd talked to him yesterday, it had all gone wrong. He had visited too soon. Dakaasin and Takumwah had been right. He had been too raw from the revelations, too wound up. He had come on too strongly. But he would try again. Tomorrow. He would rest up—perhaps he would even get a half-decent night's sleep tonight. He would think carefully about how to approach him. It wouldn't be about either case. They would put those aside. Instead, Chibenashi would come to him as a son looking to reconnect—connect, really—with his father. He hadn't realized until yesterday just how much he'd missed that relationship. Like a limb had been amputated all this time, and he'd been limping along without realizing it. He had a chance to make this whole, make it right. Get the relationship to the point where he could not only speak with his father like family but also bring Ashwiyaa with him. She'd lost a father too. Perhaps it could help heal the wounds deep inside her—the ones Chibenashi thought he was putting a bandage over at best. Once trust was established, he could get his father to share what really happened to his mother. Solve her murder, and Meoquanee's, all in one fell swoop.

The easy answers he'd accepted for the last two decades were gone. He was ready to ask the real questions. Accept what were almost certainly the most complicated answers.

But he really just wanted to talk to his father again.

Chibenashi returned to his lodgings that night, full of hope that they would start taking those first tender steps toward reconciliation and resolution. Two families might receive closure when he was done. With that full heart, he checked in with Ashwiyaa, parrying her questions about where he was and who he had talked to and when he would be home. Soon enough, he reassured her. He left out the parts about their father and mother. He would do that in person.

Much as he wanted out of Shikaakwa, he couldn't possibly leave now. There was so much to know. So much that had been destroyed. So much to re-create: Trust. Understanding. His father was a stranger. There were twenty years of gaps to fill. Twenty years of answers to questions he hadn't even formed yet. Twenty years of heartbreak and sacrifice and roads not taken to tell his father about, to get his advice on whether the choices he'd made were really the right ones or if he'd just surrendered. He'd failed at so much; he just had to succeed at this. He would lay the foundation for the relationship. He would make it right, all of it. As he drifted off to sleep, he felt the creeping of a hopeful smile across his face.

And then his phone rang.

Chapter Twenty-One

When Chibenashi was thirteen, his father had given him a bow and taken him shooting for the first time. They trudged out in the early-summer sun to the clearing in the middle of the woods that was home to the unofficial shooting range of Baawitigong.

It had been an awkward year for Chibenashi. He had shot up half a meter in height, and everything about him was overgrown. His limbs were thin and gangly, like birch twigs sticking out; his feet were three sizes too big for his body. His hair was so greasy that he could have bottled the oil. His voice squeaked and creaked with every attempt to speak, rising and falling an octave with the cadence of his speech, making each statement sound like an uncertain question, and he had become so embarrassed by it that he began speaking no more than necessary. Ashwiyaa was considered such a handful that their mother rarely left Chibenashi alone with her. Ishkode, one of the Fire Men who managed and curated the forests with controlled burns, was so busy in summers that Chibenashi hardly saw him at all. But on this beautiful morning, just when the fire season was beginning, Ishkode had roused Chibenashi from his sleep and taken him out for target practice, just the two of them.

Neither one had spoken during the walk through the forest. Chibenashi had been in the woods many times before with his father, starting from when he was very small. He knew the way through, though no path had ever been cleared and the trees, shrubs, and fallen logs used as landmarks changed over time. Ishkode walked a few paces ahead of his son, not looking back, trusting him to keep up and not get lost. People often told them that their stride was similar and that from behind, it was clear they were related. Anyone watching them that day in the woods would have agreed.

Ishkode carried the bows and had a quiver of arrows slung across his back. His own bow was worn with use; Chibenashi's gleamed with new oil and stain, its bowstring taut, the curve of the bow unyielding. The arrows were mismatched, purchased or made at different times in Ishkode's life, all thrown together in the quiver. Some arrows were new and shiny, others old and taped together. Some were missing the feathers from their fletching, while others were fully intact.

The clearing was still wet with morning dew when they'd taken their places. It was empty that day. Several targets were attached to birch trees at the end of the clearing. Chibenashi had watched his father slip on his glove and take a few test pulls of the bow. Ishkode then handed the new bow—just as large as his own—to his son. It was heavier than it looked. When Chibenashi had pulled at the bowstring, his overstrung and thin arm muscles failed to hold it in place.

Throughout the course of the morning and into the early afternoon, Ishkode had patiently instructed Chibenashi: How to aim. How much strength was needed. How not to overdraw the bowstring. The proper stance. How to angle his body. To not just point and shoot but rather aim it, pull the bowstring taut, and then simply let go. That, for Chibenashi, had been the hardest part—to use all his strength and exhaust his already-weak triceps to pull the string just the right amount, only to just let go after all that effort. He kept jerking the arrow back every time he released it, causing it to go wildly off course.

"Forcing it won't work," Ishkode had finally said. "It's natural to want to control all aspects of it. It's hard work setting it up. But you have to trust that you set it up and aimed it correctly. It's time to let go and let the arrow go where you've directed it. By helping it along, you're actually hurting it."

Chibenashi's ego had been bruised more than once that morning, and he bristled at this advice. "I know," he'd snapped, angry that he kept getting it wrong and that his father made it look so easy.

Ishkode had wisely noted his son's frustration and let him take a few more misfired shots.

"Letting go is the hardest thing you'll ever have to do," Ishkode had said. "Not just in shooting—when you have to trust everything you've done to prepare the shot—but in life as well. You can spend your entire life planning out what you're going to do, to do everything right. At the end of the day, however, you have to accept the circumstances and just let go. Sometimes the arrow hits the right spot. Sometimes it doesn't."

Chibenashi had rolled his eyes at this wisdom and concentrated on aiming his next arrow.

"Whether the arrow goes astray or hits its mark," Ishkode continued, ignoring his son's indifference, "you can't dwell on what led it to happen. Did you pull too hard, or misaim, or have the wrong stance. It's fired. So all you can do is try to set up the next one better."

Chibenashi had fired another arrow. It got closer to the mark this time. A flock of birds cried out and scattered away from where the arrow had hit, peppering the clear blue sky.

"Well done," Ishkode had said. "You got closer that time. Setting up the next shot is far easier and more accurate if you were able to let go of the last one—from just removing your hands upon firing to ignoring any frustration about where the arrow landed."

Chibenashi had trudged forward and retrieved the arrows that were scattered among the trees and targets. Ishkode's targets had more arrows stuck in them than Chibenashi's did. He did his best to search and managed to retrieve all but one of the arrows.

When he got back and dumped the arrows in the quiver, his father had patted his back and given him an approving look. "You're going to be great at this one day, I can tell," he'd said. His eyes crinkled with pride. "Trying is half the battle. The more you practice letting go, the easier it will be."

◆　◆　◆

It had been quiet in the gibaakwa'odiiwigamig when Chibenashi had visited the day before. Today, it was silent, as if the entire building and all its inhabitants were collectively holding their breath. He could feel eyes watching him, even though he was alone. He knew why he was here. Everyone else knew why he was here. But no one said it out loud. Chibenashi himself refused to believe it. The words had echoed in his mind as he'd ended the call and walked straight from his lodgings to the gibaakwa'odiiwigamig without stopping. He was not even sure how long he had been walking or if he'd gotten lost on the way. His legs had carried him from there to here, and he'd been in a haze the whole way. His makizinan were dirty and damp from the streets. The cold had whipped his face into numbness; he only felt it tingling now that he was inside, little pinpricks across his nose and cheeks. The sort of pain that reminded you that you were still alive.

He was taken not to the cells or the common area where he had met with his father previously—he was led past it. Inside, the prisoners were forlorn; some were crying. Chibenashi could hear one man tell another that there was nothing he could have done. A large bowl of overflowing food had been placed at the entrance to one cell, which sat empty. The smell of tobacco wafted through the cool air.

Chibenashi knew what he would find once they led him to the inner room of the gibaakwa'odiiwigamig. He still wasn't prepared to see the body of his father lying flat, a blanket draped over him from the shoulders down, the ligature marks on his neck still visible from where he'd hanged himself after Chibenashi's visit.

He knelt before his father's body. Just as it had been in life, his face was severe, emotionless. Unlike most bodies, there was little difference between the dead man's face and the live one's. Chibenashi imagined that his father had died that day, too, upon seeing his mother's body. He'd taken responsibility for it, and what had been left of his soul had clearly already left him. He'd been dead for years. Chibenashi had not known because he had not seen him. Had not wanted to see him. Had not believed in him.

Just yesterday, Chibenashi had been offered an impossible gift. And his father had cruelly and selfishly yanked it back from him before he could claim it. He had grasped at air when he'd expected something tangible.

All that lost time.

They would never get it back.

He'd set up his shot. He'd misfired. This time, there was no second chance.

A draft from an open window blew a few strands of his father's hair across his forehead. Without thinking, Chibenashi reached out to brush it back into place. It occurred to him that this was the first time he'd touched his father in twenty years, and it would probably be the last time. He froze, then slowly withdrew his hand, wanting to draw out the moment as long as he could, before finally removing his fingertips from the cold, lifeless forehead.

He closed his eyes and tried to forget everything he knew to be true: The truth that he'd never seen past his own hatred and resentment, never seen past his own selfish needs and refusal to go to Shikaakwa. The truth that his father had never once asked him to. The truth that he never once reached out in twenty years, never expected it or asked for it. The truth that Chibenashi had looked into his father's eyes yesterday and saw that he truly did not want Chibenashi there. The truth that after all that squandered time, once Chibenashi had finally come and vowed to free his father, Ishkode had rejected it and rejected him. Gone where Chibenashi could not chase after him, could not make up for lost time, could not ask *why*.

A Peacekeeper's worst nightmare in an investigation is the death of a crucial witness before he can be interviewed. A son's worst nightmare is the death of a parent before being given the opportunity to set right all wrongs from the past, express true gratitude for the time that had been given, and state the love he felt. Chibenashi was hit on both ends. He closed his eyes.

"Was there any warning?" he asked the Custodian who stood next to him.

According to the Custodian, no. Ishkode, always a model prisoner, had not deviated from his normal routine, though he did seem more reserved and quiet than usual. Had there been warning, he would never have been left in his cell alone, free to access the items in the common area. Never would have been able to unstring the sinews from the drum that he had used to asphyxiate himself. He had done so in total silence, at least according to other prisoners. No struggle, no fighting—just silent acceptance. He had not even left a note of explanation or farewell. Given that Ishkode had spent twenty years in here and formed relationships with other residents, that was particularly jarring. Though choking in his own grief, Chibenashi heard the true sadness in the Custodian's voice as he described what happened and the reaction of others. Clearly, Chibenashi was not the only one mourning today.

"It's so late," the Custodian said. "You must be so tired. Perhaps you could get some rest, and in the morning, once you have had some respite, we can discuss next steps."

Chibenashi shook his head.

"If I may," the Custodian offered, "I would be honored to light the fires for him. I have spent twelve years working here. Your father has been here the entire time. He and I spoke often. I would like to be able to do this for him." Heartened and stung that his father had formed close relationships with others in the decades he spent away from his children locked up for a crime he didn't commit, Chibenashi nodded.

"Is there anyone I can call for you?" the Custodian asked.

He couldn't tell the Custodian to call the only person he really wanted to—Meoquanee. She could have told him what to say, and sat there with Ashwiyaa as he broke the news over the phone, and stayed with her until he could come back to face her. She could have hugged him and told him the sweet lie he desperately needed to hear—that it wasn't his fault. She could have told him what to say and how to say it. She would have held his hand through this, figuratively and literally, and it would have been okay because she would know how to navigate through the tangled thorns of this mess without drawing blood.

His father's fault. Had he told the truth, Meoquanee wouldn't have been killed.

In the end, he simply shook his head, thanked the Custodian for his kindness, and declined his offer of a ride back to his lodgings. He would prefer to walk, he said. Lose himself in the sounds and scents of the city at night. No, he would not be too cold. Yes, he knew the way. Yes, he would be fine on his own. Would prefer it, even. It would let him process everything.

The Custodian held up his hand to signal Chibenashi to wait a moment. He dashed into the cell where Ishkode had lived. He brought out the drum, missing its sinews, and offered it wordlessly to Chibenashi. He stared at it for a long time, debating, then decided he wanted it and accepted it with a nod.

On the long walk back, he thought about everything that would now never happen between him and his father. Things that he had never known he had wanted until he knew for certain he would never have them—and only after learning too late that he could have: The apologies Ishkode would never be able to refuse. The forgiveness Chibenashi would never beg for but would always crave. No tentative reconciliation, fragile and thin as the first sheen of ice on the water, which they would both carefully tiptoe around. The truths they would never speak to each other. It wasn't about what they would do or wouldn't do. It was the lost opportunity. The years weighed heavily on his shoulders. All the opportunities he had had to make things right, all the years he had allowed to pass by in a haze. He'd always said he had no desire to get to know his father better. That when his father died, he would not mourn. You couldn't mourn what you'd never known; there was no sense of loss there. Any and all mourning had happened at the time of the death of his mother. Her murder had killed both parents and his relationship with them. He'd never known that he would mourn the loss of the next twenty years, that it was possible to grieve for what might have been rather than what had been.

He looked up and down the street; it was empty. The beggars he'd seen during the day were gone. He hoped that meant they had somewhere to go. He needed to believe that something in this city was good.

As he shuffled along on the pavement outside, kicking what little icy bits of dirt the ground would let go, he thought about what Wakwi had told him, about how life was about creation, destruction, and re-creation. How he'd created his own narrative about his past and his family and how it had been destroyed in several ways over the course of a single day—and how he couldn't possibly fathom the re-creation that was supposedly to come. How could you begin again after all that had happened?

Wandering the mostly empty streets, he was suddenly struck by a need. No, not a need. A pull. There was only one person he wanted to see, who could give him what he needed and welcome him with open arms. He had to go now. There would be no waiting until morning. He fumbled around through his pockets and found the wrinkled card with Dakaasin's neat handwriting on it. Rubbing his gloved thumb over it, he took in the address and pulled out his phone's guidance app. Maybe he could catch her before she fell asleep. Maybe, if he knocked on her door, she would answer. Maybe it wasn't too late.

Chapter Twenty-Two

When Dakaasin opened the door, her eyes were rimmed red and she was huffing for breath. Her hair was in a messy braid that drooped to one side. She was the disheveled Dakaasin who looked and acted less than perfect—the side of her that no one ever got to see.

But Chibenashi did.

"What's wrong?" He momentarily forgot his own agony in the face of hers.

"He killed her."

"Who?"

She sniffed. "That Mediation you attended the other day? The man who was ordered away from his ex-lover? He reinstalled the tracking software. He figured out the Victim's new passwords. He listened to her calls, heard what she said about him, discovered where she was and who she was with. And he killed her. I just got the call."

Chibenashi opened and closed his mouth a few times, trying for a response. "I don't understand," he said lamely.

Dakaasin gestured for him to enter. She led him past the otter doodem and through her apartment—small but homey, not unlike how her family's wigwam had been in Baawitigong—and to the fireplace next to the patio, where a fire burned. Despite the cold and the fact they were in the middle of the city, her apartment carried the sweet and calming smell of sweetgrass. Sure enough, he saw some braided strands of it coiled in a basket on the mantel and smelled the smoke from where some had been burned earlier. It was too cold to go out, but through the glass doors and windows, Chibenashi could see several tall trees on her balcony, as befit the living skyscraper they were in. Though they were at least thirty stories in the air, the presence of the birch and fir trees covered in a light dusting of snow made him feel as if they might have been in Baawitigong. Despite the anonymity of the city that Peezhickee had warned him about, Shikaakwa had managed to cultivate community. On his way in, he'd passed a communal firepit on the ground floor of the building, and a group was sitting around it, laughing and telling stories the way people frequently did in Baawitigong.

Since Dakaasin hadn't responded to his earlier comment, Chibenashi tried again, grateful to have someone else's death to talk about. "I thought he was being kept away from her."

Dakaasin shrugged. "Technology like that can be exploited, even from afar. All you need is a weak spot. I guess here, it was knowing what her passwords might be. Others can apparently do it directly if you leave your device lying around. And there's ways to remotely turn on microphones, cameras, access the data within them, you name it. Look, it doesn't matter how he did it."

"You're right. I'm sorry."

Dakaasin went to the kitchen to put together a plate of something, and Chibenashi jumped up to join her. Manners be damned, she was suffering, too, and he wasn't about to ask her to serve him food and drink now. He put his hands on hers and silently implored her to stop. She did. She led him back to the fireplace, where they took seats upon the floor. Framed above the fireplace was a photograph of the Binesi outlined in lightning, captured at just the right moment on a stormy night. It was a well-known and well-loved picture among families in Baawitigong and surrounding areas, having been captured by a local photographer. A bottle of wine was already open on the table with a single glass next to it that was nearly empty. Dakaasin topped up her glass and Chibenashi took a deep drink straight from the bottle. They settled next to each other and stared into the fire for a long time.

Dakaasin broke the silence. "The cases, they all blur together after a while, you know? One resolution bleeds into the next, and so many are unremarkable. But the failures? Those stay with you every time."

"Isn't every case a failure in some way?"

Dakaasin snorted. "I prefer to believe that isn't true."

"There's no real restitution, is there?"

"You mean, can we ever really make things whole again for victims of crime?"

Chibenashi nodded.

Dakaasin huffed a laugh. "I wonder."

"Me too."

"I mean," she said, "it's a negotiated system, right? Everyone agrees on what the value of the injury was and what actions the person responsible can do to make it right. And, look, we are fortunate here, okay? Crime rates are far higher in other parts of the world where people are more individualistic and community is less important. Mino-bimaadiziwin is just not a thing in other places. We are fortunate to have that as our guiding light. And more often than not, people claim responsibility and take the restitution seriously. Prison is a last resort. In too many places, it's the first resort.

"But you can't heal every wound, can you? Half my job is convincing people to accept less than it would take to really make them whole, just to end the whole thing. It's asking them to compromise on the most uncompromisable things in life. Things that can't be undone and nothing can fix what happened. We listen to them and ask them what they want, but then we turn around and ask them to minimize their losses and accept the gap between what they want and what they can receive."

She laughed darkly. "And that's only the beginning! Then we have to get the other side to agree. They agree to take responsibility, but in their hearts, so many of them do not feel that they've done anything wrong. Getting these sides to agree? And to take that agreement seriously? It's often nothing short of a miracle.

"Then, finally, we have to get the Mediator's buy-in. Which they almost always do, since it means they don't have to do any actual work. So bad deals get approved all the time." She took a gulp of her wine.

"What could you have done differently?" Chibenashi asked.

Dakaasin thought for a long time. The fire flickered off her dark eyes. "I don't know," she said finally. "I asked for him to be monitored. I asked for him to be banned from using his devices. I argued for it." Her voice caught in her throat as she turned to him and said, "And it wasn't enough." She took a drink.

"You tried your best."

"And it still wasn't enough. I failed. I don't like to fail." She shook her head. "You more than anyone know how much this system fails. Look at your father."

He shrugged, not quite ready to talk about it. "Not sure what else they were supposed to do."

"Check. Not just accept his word. People admit to things they have never done all the time, for reasons that we both do and do not understand. Some do it for no reason at all. That's why good Advocates seek additional information to support a confession and why the good Mediators require it. To a certain extent, whoever accepts responsibility is helping with the healing, which is the goal. But no innocent person should be given that responsibility when it involves incarceration. Not when we've reached the resolution of last resort."

"It was a long time ago."

"You all deserved better."

"Yeah," he said. "We did."

They sat in silence for a while longer before Dakaasin turned to Chibenashi and asked, "What are you doing here?"

Now it was Chibenashi's turn to stare into the fire, not meeting his ex-girlfriend's eye. "My father is dead."

Dakaasin sat up straight, eyes blown black. Some wine sloshed out of her glass from the speed of her movement. She ignored the red stain on the floor. "What?"

"He hanged himself." He was surprised at how clinical he sounded.

"Oh, Chibenashi." She reached to touch him but pulled back as if he might bite. He did not move to indicate she could or should. He stared resolutely ahead into the flames, unfocusing his gaze and hoping they might hypnotize him. He didn't want to see the pity in her eyes, the regret he knew would be there. He knew that she was thinking what he was thinking: *If only I had done more, and if only I had done it sooner. If only she hadn't left,* he thought. That wound would never close.

"Somehow, this was the only place I could think to come." He turned his head slightly toward hers and gave a weak smile. "Thank you for letting me in. I know it's late."

Dakaasin reached out for Chibenashi's hand, confident this time. He took it. A familiar warmth bled from her hand to his.

"Our visit triggered it, didn't it?"

Many moments passed while Chibenashi did not deny it. Dakaasin said nothing either. Chibenashi couldn't blame her. What could she say to that? What could anyone say?

"I'm glad you got to see him," she said finally.

"I'm not."

"Why not?"

"If I hadn't, he might still be alive."

"And he might not." This was the Dakaasin that Chibenashi remembered—always open to possibilities, refusing to let Chibenashi stay in his own head too long, debating every unknown. She'd been destined to be an Advocate. Baawitigong would never have been able to hold her. Like many caged animals, she had found a way out.

"Would you rather have never seen him again?"

Chibenashi considered her question. "Hard to say. He never should have been there in the first place. But I never questioned it."

"It's not your fault that he was in there."

"I could have said something at the Mediation."

Dakaasin shook her head. "You were a child. You were in shock. You'd just lost your mother. He had confessed. No one investigated anything. The case file was locked up—still is locked up. You bear no blame for this. None whatsoever."

"How can you be so sure?"

"Chibenashi, I've seen it. Trust me when I say that it wasn't your fault."

"Then why do I feel like it is?" Tears sprang to his eyes.

"Because you've always carried the weight of the world on your shoulders." Dakaasin gave him a knowing smile. He dared meet her eyes. "You've raised your sister most of your life, and I know how seriously you take that responsibility." Left unsaid was how that responsibility had cost them their relationship. He'd loved Dakaasin; he'd loved Ashwiyaa more. "You still carry it, long after many would have tried to move on. You'll carry it for the rest of your life. Maybe even the rest of hers. I know you. You felt responsible for your mother's death, like you could have prevented it had you been awake that night. You feel responsible for Meoquanee's death, like she'd still be here if you hadn't sent her to see Ashwiyaa. And now your father's, like he would still be alive if you had not gone to visit him. Do you see a pattern? Whether through action or inaction, you believe bad things are your fault. And they are not. They are not your fault."

Chibenashi wanted to believe her so badly it hurt.

He let go of her and hung his head in his hands, hiding like a child. This case had already been more challenging and more personal than any other he had worked in his career. Now that it had cost him his father, it was hard to see a path forward in both this case and in his own life. Untying that knot felt impossible on this night, at this late time, and in this place. Here, he could ignore all that was waiting for him out there. Here, he could indulge.

"I've missed you," he whispered.

Dakaasin closed her eyes, seemed to steel herself for what she said next. "I've missed you too," she said.

"You broke my heart, you know, when you left me."

She opened her eyes. They were shining in the dim light. "And you broke mine when you wouldn't leave with me."

They left those confessions hanging in the air.

"Do you want me to leave?" he asked her.

She sighed. "I don't know."

"What do you want?"

"From you?"

"From me. From anyone. From life."

"I want . . . I want to be . . . just to be . . ." She trailed off. She seemed a bit lost for words, as if she had not contemplated the end of the sentence when she began it. She looked to the fire for help but, receiving none, sat in silence. After a few more moments, she smiled a bit and said, "That. Just that. Just to be."

Just to be. He could fill in the rest of that sentiment: Just to be normal, just to be content, just to be free of the pain and free of the loss. Just to be responsible for himself and not anyone else. Just to be able to do what *he* wanted for a change. Just to be able to relax all his muscles rather than stay coiled like a spring at all times, ready to react. Just to be able to exhale.

What he wouldn't give just to *be*.

"How do we get from here to there?" Chibenashi asked. "To just be."

Dakaasin laughed harshly. "If you figure that one out, let me know. I feel like I've been running nonstop for so long I don't know how to stop. Always the next achievement to reach. Setting up the next goal before I've finished savoring the last one."

She chuckled. "If you're always moving, you don't have time to think about what you've left behind." She downed the rest of her wine.

Faced him. She was vulnerable yet determined. "I wouldn't mind trying it. To just be for one night." Her eyes glistened.

He shuddered. Closed his eyes. "Neither would I."

"And I don't want to be alone."

"Neither do I."

Dakaasin grasped his hand. He grasped it back. They threaded their fingers together. She pulled him close. He closed his eyes and fell forward, knowing Dakaasin would be there to catch him, as she had done for so long before she'd dropped him and left him behind without a second look. She flooded his senses. Her taste, her smell—it was home. He seized her closer. Oh, he'd missed this. It had been so long since he'd felt someone's skin beneath his lips he'd almost forgotten what it was like. But never fully. Dakaasin in his arms was something he would never forget. The storm that had been swirling around him abruptly stopped, and he clutched her tight to stay in the eye of the hurricane. She pulled him even closer, and he felt himself firmly planted on the ground, instantly transported back to a time before his future had been stolen away from him.

Dakaasin broke away. Her pupils were dilated, and she was breathing heavily. "I've missed this," she said, echoing his thoughts. That had used to happen too. Before she'd started dreaming of a world with no place for him.

Chibenashi shuddered again.

"Come here," Dakaasin said.

He turned off his phone and tossed it onto the couch, out of reach. Ashwiyaa, Takumwah, this case—they could all wait until the cruel light of morning. He would deal with consequences then. But tonight? This was for him. And for her. This was the eye of the storm, and nothing was pulling him away from this moment of peace. He let himself believe it was real and drank as deeply from Dakaasin's lips as he had from the wine.

Chapter Twenty-Three

The watery purple light of early dawn seeped into the room. Dakaasin was asleep on the floor under a thick blanket. Her hair spilled over one of the couch cushions they had sleepily grabbed in the night. Their clothes were piled next to them. A squirrel scurried along one of the barren trees on Dakaasin's balcony. The fire from the night before was now a pile of ash. And Chibenashi was on Dakaasin's computer.

He hadn't lied. It had been difficult for Chibenashi to see a path forward.

But not impossible.

Dakaasin's computer was that path forward. The only one he could think of.

Neebin's case file had been locked away for twenty years. He, a Peacekeeper, could not access it without special permission that often took weeks or months to receive. Closed files were considered private, not accessible to most people, including Peacekeepers or Victims' families. Reopening them, even reading them, was considered harmful and detrimental to the idea of making people whole. So access was strictly guarded, requiring multiple layers of permission.

But certain people did have access, right from their laptops. Like an Advocate. Like Dakaasin.

He had dismissed the need for his mother's file. Hadn't wanted to revisit it, hadn't seen a need to. But now, in light of everything? With the DNA and his father's death? It was the only option left.

So he hadn't lied to her out loud. Everything he'd said to her that night was true.

He had just kept a few things to himself. The greater good demanded it.

He had gone to Dakaasin's place feeling vulnerable, wanting and needing the comfort of someone who would understand, and in Shikaakwa she was the only one who would or could. That hadn't been a lie. He was glad to think that maybe he'd even provided her with some comfort too. He'd needed her, but he'd needed something from her too. And he hadn't lost sight of that.

It wasn't really optional, he'd rationalized to himself. Someone had killed both his mother and Meoquanee. Whatever had happened, whoever that was, his father would rather die than reveal it. Things did not add up with Sakima and Wiishkobak, but it was a far cry from a resolution. And all the while, Ashwiyaa was in Baawitigong, vulnerable and exposed.

He knew Dakaasin had access. She'd admitted it to him freely. The confirmation was the final permission he needed.

He still cared about her, had never stopped. But he still cared about Ashwiyaa more.

So he'd waited for Dakaasin to fall asleep. Gone to her laptop. Played around with a few passwords he knew she favored until he'd found the right one. Discreetly searched until he found what he was looking for. Quietly transferred the file to an encrypted cloud site only accessible to him so that he could review it later. Given her involvement in this matter, it should raise no eyebrows or special attention that she had accessed the file. And as for Dakaasin? She never needed to know what happened. Being a rule follower, she would never do this herself.

Strictly speaking, she did not need it, and it was up to him to obtain the necessary permission.

But some things were bigger than seeking restitution in a Mediation. Dakaasin had been right—some things couldn't be made whole again. They were destined to be forever broken. So permission and bureaucracy and process were meaningless. But knowledge? Closure? That was something greater, not something to wait for when you had the opportunity to obtain it. He had a sister to protect. He had monsters to slay.

Chibenashi's life had turned upside down. His family was at risk. He couldn't wait for permission. He only had to hope for forgiveness, and Dakaasin would have to forgive him. Would understand. Had to understand. He kept telling himself that over and over, as many times as necessary.

Once it was done, and there was no going back, he closed his eyes and blew out a sigh. He had it. He would look at it when he got back to Baawitigong. Now that he had a burial to attend—his second this year—he would be going home soon. There was nothing left to do in Shikaakwa. At least not now. Sakima and Wiishkobak? Takumwah could handle them. He had to get out of the city. Get home, reflect on everything. Tell his sister what had happened. Bury his father. Broadcast his innocence. Reconcile all of what he'd learned with what he'd always known. He could perhaps face Shikaakwa again another day.

It was a good plan, he'd decided. A solid plan.

He opened his eyes.

Dakaasin was standing over him. The blanket was wrapped around her. Her eyes were daggers. Her face fell.

And he knew, in an instant, two things.

The first was that she knew what he had done.

The second was that there was absolutely no forgiveness to be had.

Chapter Twenty-Four

"Tell me this isn't what it looks like."

Dakaasin's tone was almost pleading. He knew that she was, after what had happened between them the night before. Not just the physical intimacy but the emotional vulnerability. Both of them reopening old wounds and hoping they would heal over cleanly—not leaving the jagged scars that had been there before.

Chibenashi didn't want to lie to her. He simply closed the laptop, stood up, and began gathering his things.

"Chibenashi."

He couldn't look at her. He stuffed his phone deep into his pocket, as far as it would go.

"Chibenashi!"

Dakaasin crossed the room in several swift strides and grabbed his arms. "What were you doing on my computer?"

She knew. He knew she knew. There was no point in confirming it out loud.

Her eyes searched his face, despair and betrayal creeping into every single crevice of her skin, right into the shallow crow's-feet crinkling around the corners of her tear-filled eyes. The longer she stared, the more slackened her grip became, until she dropped her hands from him altogether.

"Was that why you came here?" Dakaasin asked. Her words were icicles, cold and sharp. "Is that why you slept with me? After all these years? Did you use me for this?"

"Of course not."

"Then why?"

How could he even begin to explain the complicated motivations and feelings he had about this? Yes, he'd wanted the access, but he'd also needed to be in the arms of someone who understood. Only someone from Baawitigong could possibly comprehend the enormity of the discovery of Ishkode's innocence coupled with his death. Only someone who knew and had once loved Chibenashi could understand the depths of his despair. Dakaasin was the only person who knew and understood the regret and guilt he carried from it and would carry for the rest of his life. And no other person would have left herself so vulnerable to Chibenashi that, with her guard down, he could steal from her.

Somehow, she knew all that.

"You're despicable," she hissed.

He nodded. "You're right."

"You're a liar."

"It's hard to explain."

"You realize that you have now compromised your investigation so much that it would be virtually impossible to bring this before a Mediator? No Advocate would let their client admit to this, and no Mediator would accept your evidence."

He knew what this was going to cost Meoquanee, that her family might never receive the peace of resolution. He'd strayed so far from where he was supposed to be. "This is bigger than that."

"Nothing is bigger than that."

"You said so yourself," he threw back at her, "just last night. This system fails over and over. It failed my mother. It failed my father. It's failed me twice already. It would have failed me a third time."

"You have lost any chance of actually putting that person in a position to accept that responsibility."

"Do you think I care about that anymore? I need to know, now, who it is. Not in a week. Not in three moons when I may have access to files. Now. I have to protect myself and my sister."

Dakaasin shook her head.

"I can't risk that third failure. I'd never forgive myself."

"What do you propose to do now? Pursue your own vigilante justice? Are you insane?"

"It's how our ancestors did it."

"That was five hundred years ago. Things have changed a bit since then."

"To a system that will undoubtedly fail me yet again. I'd rather know and take my chances on what happens next. I deserve that much at least, don't I? To know for certain? Without delay? To have all the information so I can put the pieces together myself? I'm the one who is to be made whole by this. This is how I'm made whole again: to solve this once and for all. Who is targeting the people I love and why? Don't I deserve to know who to keep at a distance? Who to save my sister from? Because she's next, isn't she? The only person I have left. Everyone else in my life has been picked off, one by one by one."

The fury and betrayal in Dakaasin's eyes turned to confusion and concern. "You don't sound like yourself."

"You don't know what I sound like. You know what I used to sound like, sixteen years ago. Back before you left us."

Dakaasin glared at him, looking as if she had been slapped.

Without another word, and without another look at Dakaasin, he swept out the door. He did not look back. He knew that he would never see her again. She would never allow it. It was a dear price to pay for his sister's safety and his own knowledge. But at this point, he had no choice. He had to absorb the cost, and he found he was willing to pay it.

Chibenashi was walking through the lobby of his lodgings when Takumwah appeared out of nowhere at his side.

"I was going to tell you about the blood results from Sakima's bag, but I just heard," he said, eyes wide and full of compassion. Chibenashi couldn't stand it. "About your father. Where have you been? I've been trying to reach you."

His phone was still off from the night before. He hadn't even checked it. Panicked, he patted his pockets and snatched it out. He switched it on; in the few heartbeats it took to fully turn on, his stomach writhed in agony. What if Ashwiyaa had had a crisis the night before? He hadn't been available to her.

One good-morning text from his sister, nothing more. Sent only a few moments ago. She hadn't panicked and sent him more. He breathed out a sigh of relief. She hadn't even tried to call. He texted her back.

He had forgotten Takumwah was there until he finally looked away from the phone.

"Anyone ever tell you that you have an addiction to that thing?"

Many people.

"So what did the blood results say?"

"Same as what was found at the crime scene," Takumwah said. "Nothing new, unfortunately." He grasped Chibenashi's arm in support. "But never mind that. Your father, Chibenashi. I'm so sorry."

Chibenashi nodded. What could he say at this point?

Takumwah looked him over. "These are the same clothes you wore yesterday. I'm worried about you. Did you sleep at all?"

Chibenashi shrugged. "Not enough."

"Here, let's get you to bed." He led Chibenashi toward the elevators, but Chibenashi shrugged him off.

"I can find my own way."

"Let me help you. You don't have to put on the brave face here."

Chibenashi didn't deserve help. Didn't need it either. He'd helped himself. For once.

"I'm not taking no for an answer."

Chibenashi whirled around on him, his temperature rising with his anger. "We are not friends. I don't need your help. I don't want your help. Leave me alone."

Takumwah just grinned stubbornly. What would it take to get this person out of his life?

"Been there, my friend. Been there." He still walked Chibenashi to the elevators but did not touch him. "I won't force myself where I'm not wanted. I understand the need for space, though I always seem to need people around me when things get tough. You're not alone. I don't want you to worry about a thing on this case, today or any other day. I've been in touch already with Ziigwan; she's handling things out there. Says she hasn't uncovered anything new but is working on it. Reviewed everything in your notes and hers. No one saw where Meoquanee went after Manoomin. I'll speak with Sakima again. If you need to get in touch with anyone to prepare your father's body and transport him back to Baawitigong, you let me know. This may be the big city, but we take care of our people here. Especially in times like this. And even though you're from Baawitigong and you're Anishinaabe, you're my people. Nobody's perfect, after all, right?" They reached the elevators. Takumwah pushed the call button for Chibenashi, clearly desperate to do anything, no matter how small, to ease his burdens today. Apparently running out of things to say, he began repeating himself, the way all people do when confronted with someone else's grief. "Definitely my people, especially in times like this. Like I said, I've been there, brother. I've been there. It is dark in that place. But you won't have to go through it alone. Even if you need your space. You're not alone."

Chibenashi prayed to Gichi-manidoo, the Sky Woman, and the gods that lived in all the temples and churches and synagogues throughout Shikaakwa and the world—anyone who was listening—to please make the elevator come faster. Someone answered. The doors pinged open and people, dressed and washed and starched for the day, spilled out. Once it was mercifully empty, he entered.

"Thank you for your kindness," he said.

Takumwah beamed. "Don't worry about a thing today," he said, still repeating himself. "Not a thing."

Chibenashi nodded and rapidly pressed the button for his floor. Takumwah's smile was the last thing he saw before the doors closed. Somehow, he knew that it would be the last time he would ever see it.

Safely behind three locked doors, Chibenashi stood in the shower and let the water rush over him. He never took long showers—didn't have time, didn't have the inclination. But he was shivering. It must be the relentless cold of Shikaakwa. The kind that gets in your marrow and can only be cured by long periods spent in steam. He knew what he really needed—a sweat lodge—but he wasn't about to go out into the world and find one. He didn't want some unfamiliar midew to lead him through this. Sweats involved trust. He needed prayers but was not ready to seek them out, especially ones from strangers. Baawitigong was too far, physically and spiritually. So this would have to do.

He remembered his first sweat. It was the same summer that Dakaasin had left. He'd been so lost. He'd lost so much. Wakwi had suggested it. He'd entered the oval-shaped lodge at sundown. There were three other men there, men Chibenashi knew by name and reputation but not personally. They had nodded at him in greeting, pity in their eyes. Everyone knew him and his family, what had happened. Even in there, that safe space, he could never escape that. He'd always been, always would be, the victim's son. The murderer's son. The prisoner's son. That label always followed him among the locals. Chibenashi the Victim. Chibenashi the Son of a Killer. Chibenashi the Son of a Prisoner. Chibenashi the Orphan.

At least in the sweat lodge, they didn't gossip in hushed whispers that he could still hear.

The tourists poured into Baawitigong like invading ants over left-behind crumbs. But the sweat lodge remained just for locals. Their oasis.

They'd all laid back as the midew, who had long since left Baawitigong and whose name Chibenashi had forgotten, began chanting prayers and beating a drum in time. Tobacco was passed, just like in the old days. Very little of the ceremony had changed throughout the centuries. Tobacco was smoked for recreation in much of the world, until it wasn't, but it was still an integral part of the sweat. As the night drew on and the haze of smoke and steam and sweat grew thicker, he had felt his lungs grow heavy and then lighter and more open than ever before. His stress had trickled out of his pores, bit by bit. He felt as if he'd exhaled every care in the world, everything for which he had ever felt responsible. The offerings to the Sky Woman and Gichi-manidoo were made. Creation. Destruction. Here, in the sweat, the Re-creation could happen. He'd left that night under a starry sky, so clear he could see the northern lights dancing above them in a river of green and gold. Every single corner of his lungs crackled with the sweet fresh air, like he'd never breathed before. He felt like he was glowing brighter than anything in the sky. Surely he himself could be seen from space.

He hadn't exorcised every demon that night. Far from it. But for a short period of time afterward, he felt at peace. And he craved that same feeling now.

It was safe in the steam. The outside world wouldn't intrude. He couldn't even see it in here; the haze of the steam clouded and softened it like a dream. He could ignore the ramifications that awaited him. He could ignore the weight of the information he was going to absorb. He could inoculate himself against the pain of the past he was about to revisit for the first time ever—really revisit it, seen with new eyes from twenty years in the future.

When he emerged, he was not sure how much time had passed. It was not yet evening; it was probably not yet even afternoon. He could check the time on his phone but was afraid to look at it. He didn't feel the same refreshment he'd felt after his first sweat, his second, or any of the dozens in between. He was now just standing in humidity, towel around his waist, still breathing the same air he had been before.

He couldn't deal with his grief for his father or Dakaasin. But he could hunker down and read the file he'd taken. Before anyone could stop him. He reached for his phone. It buzzed.

Ashwiyaa.

She started sobbing the moment he answered, before he even had a chance to greet her.

"What's wrong?"

"How could you?" she shrieked.

"What happened?"

"Why? Why? Why didn't you tell me that our father was dead?"

His lungs closed. His heart stopped.

"What do you mean?"

"It's true, then?"

Chibenashi stammered in reply.

"How could you not tell me?" She sobbed uncontrollably. He was hundreds of kilometers away. Powerless to help her or protect her.

"I had to tell you in person."

She bawled. He heard a clatter, almost like she'd dropped the phone. Or thrown it. He sighed heavily, tears coming to his own eyes. He scrubbed his hands over his unshaven face, his blotchy eyes. He choked on the steam that still lingered in the room. You couldn't open the windows in this place.

"Chibenashi?"

Kichewaishke.

"I'm so sorry," Chibenashi said. He could hear Ashwiyaa wailing in the background. He could only imagine what the scene was there.

"You need to come home." His voice was flat. Chibenashi had never heard it so sterile and emotionless before.

"I'm coming as soon as I can."

"Today."

"I don't know if I—"

"Today. You have to. Chibenashi, I've never seen anyone so upset."

Chibenashi nodded. "Yes. Of course."

"You could have told me."

Chibenashi had no good explanation for that.

"Look," Kichewaishke said, "I'm really sorry about your father. We'll talk about it when you get here. We're here for you. I hate to put anything else on you in the face of what's just happened. But we can't handle this alone. We tried. She's inconsolable. It has to be you."

He shuddered. "I understand."

"Hurry home."

He packed up swiftly. Threw things into his bag. Didn't bother to fold clothes or put toiletries into a case. Just threw it all in the bag as fast as he could without regard for anything but speed. He would take Takumwah up on his offer to handle the case from here. All of that could wait.

After giving his room an extremely cursory glance, he flung open the door. Takumwah's furious face greeted him. Chibenashi stumbled and screeched to a stop so as not to run into him.

"You're understandably in a very difficult place right now," Takumwah said, "but did you stop and think for a moment about the repercussions of what you've done?"

Chibenashi swallowed. He had to get to the train station. There was no time for this.

"How long have you been waiting here?"

"As long as I needed to."

"I have to go," Chibenashi muttered. He brushed past, and Takumwah followed, hot on his heels.

"Everything—*everything*—we have worked for is now thrown away."

"I can't handle this right now."

"It was always toeing the line, letting you work on this given your close association with the victim. Being both an investigator and a witness. And when the connection to your own history came up, we absolutely should have pulled you off. But against my better judgment, we proceeded. Dakaasin vouched for you. Peezhickee spoke so highly of you. I helped you navigate this, even though in nearly any other situation, I would have said no, taken you off of this, handed it back to Baawitigong and said, 'Give me someone else.' I liked you and trusted you and saw how much this was costing you. I believed in you."

"Nothing changes anything we've found." Chibenashi smashed the elevator button as hard as he could.

"No, but it completely compromises the integrity of the investigation. We were getting somewhere with Sakima. But you took a shortcut. What other ones have you taken? The chain of custody for the blood samples? Interrogations of Sakima and Wiishkobak? The problems in the initial investigation back in Baawitigong—failing to interview all witnesses, failing to interview your own sister, who was a witness and supposedly the last person to see the victim alive? No Mediator will accept this evidence, and no competent Advocate would allow them to accept responsibility for something that could easily be a setup by a Peacekeeper who is too closely tied to the outcome and who needed a resolution, regardless of whether it was fair."

Chibenashi swallowed. "I know." He paused. He couldn't say the truth: that he had decided that none of this was as important as protecting his sister. So he didn't. "I have to go," he said again. This time it was an apology, not an attempt at escape. He did have to go. Yet another thing he'd done wrong. Another harm he'd caused.

The elevator doors mercifully opened, and Chibenashi stepped inside. Unlike earlier, Takumwah followed him in.

"I need you to give it to me," Takumwah said.

He couldn't hand over what had cost him so much. "I don't know what you're talking about."

"Don't make this harder than it already is."

"I don't know what you're talking about."

"I spoke with Dakaasin. They can track uploads of these records."

"If Dakaasin uploaded something she should not have, then that is a shame." His stomach burned with acid at the lie. But he was in too deep now to go back. He wasn't giving this information up.

Takumwah stared at Chibenashi, gaping at him in horror. Like he'd never seen him before. Chibenashi remained defiant and felt a little justified in doing so. No one else could have told his sister about this, and Dakaasin knew better than most that the best way to hurt him was to hurt Ashwiyaa.

"My father's death stalled this investigation. I am doing what I can to unstall it."

Takumwah shook his head. "You know, I thought everyone was vouching for your character. Now I see it was just pity. Maybe some guilt for having failed you so long ago. And definitely incompetence. Small villages like yours? We're always cleaning up your messes. Peacekeepers aren't the best and brightest there like they are here; they're just the ones who aren't good enough to leave. Whose imaginations and ambitions fit inside a small village. Everybody knows everybody, so you can't be objective, can't solve a crime half a meter in front of your face because you're too blinded by your past, your relationships, and your prejudices. You might be okay with that in Baawitigong and any other backwater. But we aren't okay with that here."

The doors opened.

"Then it is for the best that I am leaving."

Chibenashi practically limped out of the elevator.

Takumwah grabbed his arm.

"Whatever character you have," he hissed, "don't throw it away. Don't betray Dakaasin like this. She'll face consequences for letting the information fall into your hands. She let her guard down, and she will pay dearly for it. Think of all she's worked for, how much this means to her." The pace of his breathing picked up. "For the last time: give it to me."

Chibenashi looked away. He could stop now. He could turn to Takumwah, apologize, and hand the information over. He could end this right now. He looked at Takumwah, then looked toward the exit. He thought about what Wakwi said about creation, destruction, and re-creation. Thought about Ashwiyaa's voice over the phone and what risk there was to her. If building a new and better future required destroying everything, then there was really no choice at all. He'd been stuck at the bottom of the circle for too long. It was time to complete the destruction so that he could get to the re-creation.

"I have a train to catch."

He pulled his arm from Takumwah's grip.

Takumwah seized it again.

"I told you once before," Takumwah said, seething. "Don't start a fight that you can't win. You have no business fighting."

"Then fight me," Chibenashi dared him. "Here, in front of all these people. Throw the first punch. Subdue me. Take what you think I have. Right here, right now, with this audience." The taste of blood, the rawness of flesh, the tenderness of fresh bruises—that was pain Chibenashi could handle right now. Anything was preferable to this.

Takumwah and Chibenashi stared at one another for a long time. Chibenashi could physically feel something break between them, a bond he hadn't noticed growing in the first place—one only noticeable by its sudden absence.

Long moments passed. Chibenashi knew that Takumwah would not do it. One ill turn deserving another was not the man's style. The more he believed Chibenashi had crossed the line, the more Takumwah would now follow it. He had to shut this down. He was wasting valuable time here, and he needed this one last obstacle out of his way.

"Dakaasin betrayed me back," Chibenashi said. "My sister heard what happened to our father. From someone other than me. It should have been me. It *needed* to be me. She is unstable, and Dakaasin knows it. Dakaasin is the only person who could have done it. She hit me right where she knew it would hurt, the one place that could never fully heal." The more he said it, the more plausible it sounded. He thought of Ashwiyaa's broken voice on the phone and continued. "She broke my heart once over Ashwiyaa. She's now done it twice. Maybe she even thought this was the fatal blow. When you go back to her, you tell her that she succeeded. And that I hope it was worth it."

Takumwah shook his head. "She wouldn't do that."

"There is no one else who could have done it. She knew what I know. She knows how to contact my sister. And she knew it would hurt me the most."

Straightening out his leather jacket and bracing himself for the cold outside, he repeated, "I have a train to catch."

Without looking back at Takumwah, he strode out the doors and into the blistering cold.

Later, on the train, he refused to look out the windows the way he had on the way in. He shut his eyes against the blur of the city as it passed. He was done with Shikaakwa. Before tossing him back to the village, it had wrung everything it could from him. Including his integrity.

Chapter Twenty-Five

Chibenashi wrapped his coat tightly around himself as he disembarked the Arrow Train. The wind and cold whipped around him so hard it felt like it was trying to push him back onto the train, back to Shikaakwa to do the right thing. He pressed on.

He'd only been gone a few days, but a lifetime had passed. The gravity of it all had come crashing down around him. He'd said before that he would never go to Shikaakwa. Now, he knew he could never go back, even if he wanted to.

Not that the situation in Baawitigong was any better. The lake was too frozen over for any ships to dock; only the occasional icebreaker would make its way through for essential ships. The village became geographically isolated in the dead of winter. It was all locals now, hunkered down for the winter, the only ones strong enough, hardy enough, and crazy enough to live in one of the coldest places on earth. There was no hiding from each other. No secrets to be kept in this frigid landscape. Only in summer could people retreat to the woods without leaving footprints, slip into crowds with anonymous faces, and dive under the water.

He could swear that every face in town that he passed was staring at him. Every step felt like it was taken in lead makizinan. He knew what awaited him at Kichewaishke's wigwam, and he resisted going, while duty dragged him every step of the way toward the inevitable.

Knowing that he would likely have his hands full for days—if not weeks—upon his return to Baawitigong, Chibenashi had spent the entire train ride reviewing the file. He'd found a part of the train with several rows of empty seats. Secreting himself by the window in the last row, he had pulled out his tablet for the first time since the train ride to Shikaakwa, when he'd taken it out but not used it. He had accessed his encrypted cloud site and pulled up the file he'd purloined from Dakaasin that morning. The sun had set, and the last blood-red threads of the day crisscrossed the sky as the Arrow Train raced along the horizon. Nothing to look at out the window anymore anyway.

He had steeled himself against what he might find in this file. Whatever was in there required some attention to detail. Things that were missed because they were too small and the weight of his father's confession so big.

What he had seen in the file surprised him.

There was virtually nothing there.

No witness interviews recorded anywhere. Chibenashi had never been interviewed, but he had assumed that was because he had not witnessed any crime, being passed-out drunk all night. But Ashwiyaa hadn't been interviewed either. Neither had any neighbors, friends, or anyone else who had crossed paths with his mother that day. There had been no search of the wigwam. The murder weapon was never tested forensically to ensure that it really was the weapon. His father's confession was recorded, but it was minimal at best. There had been no interrogation of him about how or why he had done it. He watched the grainy video of the old interview, and it was clear even to Chibenashi across the decades that his father was hiding something. His throat constricted at this; they had obviously taken his father's confession at face value and, pleased to be able to put away such a violent crime so quickly, done the bare minimum required in order to close it out. Even the DNA testing, taken from the blood found at the crime scene, was done as a matter of course, with the test run and results obtained weeks after the murder, long after his father's confession and even after the Mediation had been completed. Things took longer in those days, particularly cases from far-flung villages like Baawitigong when no one locally or in Shikaakwa was pressing for the results. And it was clear that, once obtained, no one had even bothered to look at them.

DNA testing had been far more rudimentary back then. It required larger blood samples than were required today, and they were run more slowly. They had taken quite a bit of blood and compared it with the DNA found in his mother's hairbrush. He swallowed thickly. He remembered that brush: made of polished wood, gleaming in the reflection of the light as his mother had used it to brush her long, thick hair every night and every morning. He'd never seen the brush again after her murder. He supposed this had been why. Until this moment, he'd forgotten about it and was briefly sad as he wondered what else about his mother had been swept away by the intervening years.

They had also taken DNA from her toothbrush to ensure they had the right source to compare the blood results to. The testing had run both regular (autosomal) and mitochondrial DNA. Twenty years ago, mitochondrial had been considered the most reliable.

He read through the results slowly, since there was no analyst there to walk him through it. When he was done, he sucked in a breath, choked back a sob, and willed his tears inside.

It had returned nothing more than his own mother's DNA—nothing showing a link to his father. And his father's DNA had been all over that house. As had his, and as had Ashwiyaa's. There was a more recent annotation in the file about the results that looked autogenerated. He first read straight past it, then looked more closely. It didn't make any sense. He made a mental note to ask Peezhickee about it. He couldn't ask anyone in Shikaakwa.

Had someone bothered to even read this, his father could have been set free decades ago. Perhaps he would even be alive today.

Chibenashi didn't understand. Why would his father have not pressed for the very evidence—that was available and sitting in the records database all along—to be reviewed? Why would he have taken his own life when that possibility had been raised?

Chibenashi churned these thoughts over and over in his head as he trudged through the village. Snow was beginning to pile up on either side of the roads, which were clear and wet due to both government and locals plowing. You had to stay on top of the snow here in Baawitigong; it was not uncommon to get a meter of snow in a few days, and you could easily get buried in it. An older couple, bundled up but recognizable to Chibenashi, waved at him as they snowshoed across what was ordinarily grazing land in the summer. He gave a cursory wave back. He could feel their eyes on the back of his head.

He was surprised when he reached his neighborhood. Had Baawitigong always been this small? Was the walk from the station always this brief? It seemed impossible that he had fit his entire life in this place. No wonder Dakaasin had bolted for a place where she could live high enough to touch the stars.

He turned toward Kichewaishke's wigwam but thought it would probably be better to drop his stuff off at his own wigwam first. Start a fire and get some tea ready for Ashwiyaa. Maybe he could change his clothes. The ones he had on, while clean, felt dirtied by everything that had occurred back in Shikaakwa. So he would pop in, get the wigwam ready, and put away everything from Shikaakwa (literally and figuratively) before getting his sister. It made sense.

He got to the door and was surprised to find it unlocked. He knew he had locked it before leaving for Shikaakwa. As far as he knew, Ashwiyaa had not been home since he had been gone. He pushed open the door carefully. The wigwam had the dusty, abandoned feel of a home that had not been lived in for some time. Which was ridiculous, he felt. It had only been a few days. Curious how such a short trip could feel so long.

He swept the wigwam carefully, feeling like even though everything was just as he'd left it, something about it was off as well. He checked every room and corner; he peeked behind every door and within every closet, opened and closed drawers and threw back shower curtains. Lifted up cushions. Looking for what, he could not say.

Until he found it.

On a piece of paper that could be from anywhere, taped to the refrigerator, was written:

STAY AWAY

He stepped back a few paces involuntarily until he hit the counter. He picked up his phone and called Ziigwan, who was not surprised to hear he was back, as news of his return had already spread through the village like wildfire. She said she would get the wigwam dusted for fingerprints. She warned him that kitchens were difficult, since they were often the most-used room in the home and therefore typically covered with fingerprints from the people who lived there, which often diluted the prints from strangers. Moreover, kitchen surfaces tended to be wiped down more often than other parts of the house, so it was equally as common to find no fingerprints at all. Chibenashi knew all of this but understood she had to tell him anyway. He thanked her and, now not being able to touch the wigwam again until this work had been completed, set down his bags and steeled himself for Kichewaishke's wigwam.

◆ ◆ ◆

Kichewaishke seemed both relieved and pained to see Chibenashi.

"Boozhoo, my friend," he said, pulling Chibenashi into a hug. Chibenashi tensed up at first but relaxed far sooner than he usually did when someone hugged him. He supposed his time in Shikaakwa had worn him down on this, as it had in so many other ways. "Have you eaten?"

Chibenashi nodded, hoping his friend would truly take this as a no and not trouble with feeding him.

"I'm glad you're home," Kichewaishke said. "We all are. How are you?"

Chibenashi shrugged, and Kichewaishke nodded. "I know." He stepped aside to allow Chibenashi into the wigwam. It was warm in here, heated by both fire and bodies. The baby, Megis, was sleeping in a cot near the fire. Okimaskew walked out from the kitchen, wiping her hands on a towel as she approached Chibenashi and enveloped him in a hug. "I'm so sorry," she told him. He hugged her back, finding comfort in the literal embraces of his old friends. "Tell us everything," she said.

He demurred. "How is Ashwiyaa?"

Okimaskew wrinkled her face before answering honestly, "Not well. Especially today, after everything. She's been pretty withdrawn since you've been gone, not really leaving the room she's been staying in. Eating okay, but very anxious. We haven't been able to get much out of her. She waits by the phone and tries to get a hold of you. That's how we know if she has or not—the only time she talks is when she's talking to you. That first day or so, she was fine, but I think the longer you were gone, the harder it was."

"I appreciate you taking care of her," Chibenashi said. "Especially given everything you have to begin with." He gestured at the baby.

"Think nothing of it," Okimaskew said. "Do you want to go see her? She was sleeping a little while ago, but I bet she'll be happy to see you."

Chibenashi doubted that very much, given the call earlier. "I'll let her sleep," he said.

"You must be famished," Kichewaishke said. "Let us feed you. No, don't argue. We're going to."

"Absolutely," Okimaskew said in agreement. She made for the kitchen, but Megis started wailing. "Looks like you're not the only one who needs to eat."

"You feed her; I'll grab Chibenashi some food," Kichewaishke said. Okimaskew disappeared with the baby into their bedroom while Kichewaishke dashed into the kitchen. Chibenashi, alone in the room, settled into the couch. He stared at the fire dancing in the fireplace, allowing himself to get lost in it. Neither thinking nor feeling, just watching.

He didn't notice he had company.

"You're back," chirped a small voice. Chibenashi smiled at little Biidaaban, who had joined him.

"I am," Chibenashi agreed. "Thank you for letting my sister stay with you. I know it can't be easy having someone new in your home."

"I don't like her."

Chibenashi laughed, knowing that Biidaaban's parents would have scolded her for her brutal honesty had they been there. Personally, it was one of the things he loved best about Biidaaban, and it was refreshing to be around it again after everything he'd been through in Shikaakwa. He didn't blame the girl. He knew Ashwiyaa could be a lot to handle, particularly when you were little and didn't understand the situation. "It's okay," he said. "I know she's sad all the time."

"No she isn't."

"Of course she is."

"No. She isn't." Biidaaban was insistent.

"What makes you say that?"

"She's not sad. She doesn't cry when she's by herself. She's quiet. She's serious. She doesn't sleep."

Chibenashi smiled. He knew how Ashwiyaa's catatonic states could come across to a small child like Biidaaban. "Well, I'm sure it's confusing to see her. What might seem like anger or fear is sadness. We're all sad right now." Biidaaban looked at him quizzically but didn't respond. "It was so good of you to take care of her. It really helped me out."

Biidaaban shrugged and scampered off.

Kichewaishke appeared with frybread and maple syrup as soon as his daughter had vanished. "Some comfort food, eh?" They sat together in silence, Chibenashi munching on the food out of politeness more than anything else.

"If you want to go home, we can call you once Ashwiyaa's up."

Chibenashi shook his head. "Am I in your way here?"

"Of course not."

"Then I'd rather stay, if it's all the same to you." He told Kichewaishke what he had found at home and how the forensics team was likely there now, combing over the place.

"I'm so sorry," he said. "Man, what a few days this has been for you, eh?"

Kichewaishke didn't even know the half of it.

"Yeah."

Kichewaishke and his family had long since gone to bed, leaving Chibenashi alone with the dying embers. Footsteps snapped him out of his thoughts. Ashwiyaa didn't walk into the sitting room—she staggered. Hair messy and sticking out, like a bird's nest. Glasses perched precariously atop her nose. Face blotchy and eyes rimmed in red. She looked how he felt. He was up in a heartbeat to help steady her, but she pushed him away.

"Ashwiyaa, please."

Her eyes clenched shut for the length of several ragged breaths. When they reopened, they were pleading. *Make it stop.* He put his arms around her, and this time she did not resist. She fell into him, and he caught her just in time. The weight of both their grief was too much for him to bear in that moment, and they collapsed together to the floor. Her shaking triggered his until he found he was shivering uncontrollably with sobs that he'd held back for so long, through it all. He had meant to be strong for her, and yet here, with her, he broke down completely. Everything he'd been feeling, everything he'd tamped down, was now clawing its way out of him, and he could no more stop it than he could a wolverine from shredding through a paper cage. All the monsters came out: The guilt of leaving her behind. The shame of not telling her about their father's death himself. The fact that by not telling her what he'd learned about their father's innocence as soon as he had learned it himself, he'd denied her a chance at reconciliation with him. She perhaps needed it even more than he did. He had been nearly a grown man when their mother was murdered; she had still been a child of twelve. Chibenashi had at least had a childhood. Ashwiyaa was still scarred from her lack of one.

Once he calmed down and stopped sobbing, he took a now-catatonic Ashwiyaa back to the couch, then retrieved her belongings from Biidaaban's bedroom, where she had been staying. Closing the door softly behind them, he led her back to their wigwam. He hoped the team was finished, and he was relieved to find that they were. Upon entering, he saw they had done an unusually good job of cleaning up after themselves. They'd even heated the wigwam for him. Usually, they left traces behind, like fingerprint powder or footprints from where their people had come in and out of the house. The speed and precision showed that word had gotten out about what had happened, and they were being extra respectful. Chibenashi felt very appreciative, especially since he did not believe he deserved such a courtesy.

He got Ashwiyaa to her bed, then made his way back to the kitchen. The threatening note was gone. He felt dehydrated from all the crying. His head throbbed. He rummaged through the refrigerator, hoping for something, anything, to drink. He needed—wanted—more than water. With disproportionate relief, he found some iced tea in the fridge. He poured a cup and gulped it down like he was dousing weeks of thirst. He poured a second cup and swallowed it as fast as the first one.

He lit the fires for his father in silence.

He glanced at the clock. It was so late, and the exhaustion finally hit him. All day he'd been steeling himself for his sister, and traveling, and living the consequences of his actions. He stumbled to his bed and face-planted into the familiar, if cold, sheets. The exhaustion overcame him like a tsunami. For the first time in days, he fell into a deep sleep.

Chapter Twenty-Six

A grief hangover was apparently far worse than an alcohol-induced one. Chibenashi woke up with a pounding headache and dry throat, despite having had his best night of sleep in nearly a week. He sat on the edge of his bed, cradling his head in his hands, willing the pain to go away. He had to beat this back. If he was doing this poorly, his sister had to be in even worse shape.

He couldn't deal with his phone at the moment. So many broken promises would be called out in there. Instead, he fumbled for his tablet. He wanted to review the file in the privacy of his bedroom before facing the day. Wrap his mind around the DNA evidence. See what was missing, and from that, see if anything could be salvaged. Compare that with whatever they'd found last night.

He unlocked it with his thumbprint and went to his encrypted cloud site.

The file was gone.

He closed the site and reopened it. Rebooted his tablet. Went through the site folder by folder. It was unmistakable—it was gone.

Chibenashi's stomach dropped past his feet.

This was not good. Very not good. And it was also very confusing. No one but him had access to this site. It was personal, not related to work. No one else was authenticated as a user. He was the only one allowed. And this tablet—the only device from which he had ever accessed the site—had not left his control.

Now he had no choice but to face his phone. He deliberately ignored any notifications and directly called Ziigwan.

"You'd best come in," she greeted him. "Peezhickee is here."

"I thought he was in Panzacola?"

He could practically hear the shrug. "He's back now."

"I really . . ." He trailed off. "I really can't leave Ashwiyaa. And given what happened with my father . . ."

Ziigwan sighed. "Look, I worked through the night on this one. Makade even came in all the way here to help me. Nothing in the database. Only the prints you'd expect to be in the wigwam: you and your sister's. Nothing suspicious except that Wakwi thought she might have seen someone near Meoquanee's wigwam the other day."

Chibenashi leaned forward as if Ziigwan were right in front of him. "When was that?"

"Day before yesterday. Very early in the morning."

He sat there, considering.

"I have her statement, if you want it."

"No thanks," he said. "I'll talk to her myself. I think I can spare the time. It's about our safety here, after all."

"Should I come over?"

"No thanks. I'll handle it."

He hung up the phone. It was all falling into place. Sakima's whereabouts two nights ago. He'd been in Baawitigong. No one had been here. He had to have been the one to leave the note. Chibenashi was sure of it. Sakima was their person after all.

Now to deal with the file.

Takumwah's phone rang, and he grimaced at the name. He wanted nothing more than for it to go to voice mail. He'd wasted enough time on this. But duty and pity won out, and he took the call.

"Yes?" Takumwah's voice was short, clipped.

"Did you do it?" Chibenashi's voice was confused, not accusatory.

"Do what?"

"Or have a hand in it?"

"A hand in what?"

Chibenashi ground his teeth so loudly that Takumwah heard it over the phone.

"You know what."

"I have work to do."

"The . . . thing you thought I had. I don't seem to have it."

"Then I suppose you were telling the truth."

"Anymore."

Silence.

"I'm listening," Takumwah said finally.

"What capabilities do you people have to go to an encrypted file site and retrieve a document?"

Takumwah considered this for a long moment. "Is that what happened here?"

"You tell me."

"I have not had anything to do with you or your case since you left here yesterday."

"You swear?"

Takumwah could hear rising panic and concern in Chibenashi's voice.

"Are you suggesting that you have been hacked and the file is now missing?"

"Without admitting anything—"

"You sound like an Advocate."

"Without admitting anything, let's just say that I want to know if you or your team or Dakaasin's have accessed a private, encrypted file site that I have access to and which is not part of my work or any dakoniwewigamig."

Takumwah's mind began to race. This was far, far worse. Not only had Chibenashi obviously stolen the file but he hadn't even kept it secure.

"Like I said," Takumwah repeated, "I have had nothing to do with you or your case since you left here yesterday. And neither has Dakaasin." They'd both washed their hands of him. The betrayal had carved deep.

Chibenashi remained silent for so long that Takumwah wondered if the connection had been lost.

"What about the gashkibidaagan that Sakima had with him, that held all the stuff he brought back to Meoquanee?" Chibenashi asked.

"This case is over," Takumwah said, voice rising. "Because of you."

"Could you tell how Sakima got it back?"

"It's like he said," Takumwah said. "He got off the train, retrieved the gashkibidaagan from someone standing in the station, then turned around and got right back on the same train for the return trip to Shikaakwa. He wasn't in Baawitigong long enough to do anything."

"But who gave it to him?" Chibenashi asked. "We know it wasn't the recyclers. They never had it."

"We looked at his phone records—the call came from the recyclers in Baawtitigong. Your inventory was wrong, which doesn't surprise me in the least. It's over." Takumwah spoke with finality. "Now, is there anything else?"

Chibenashi sat silent for a moment. "I guess not."

Takumwah hung up the phone.

Then he picked it up again. Selected the appropriate contact information.

"Boozhoo."

"Boozhoo, Dakaasin," he said. "Listen, did Chibenashi call you?"

"I've blocked his number."

"Smart move. Well, I just got the weirdest call from him . . ."

For the first time in memory, Wakwi looked surprised to see Chibenashi. The wiigwaasi-mashkikigamig was where many came when they felt they could not receive welcome anywhere else, when even their own homes and beds and minds were hostile to them. "Boozhoo," she said. It was warm and full of the smell of cedar and smoke. A welcome respite from the cold.

All of this applied to Chibenashi, but it wasn't why he was here. He had a burial to plan and sins to atone for, but he had to get this pressing business off his chest first.

"Tell me about what you saw," he said without preamble, knowing she would understand what he was asking about.

Wakwi bristled. "This is not the place for such talk. This is a holy place."

"Every place on earth is holy," Chibenashi retorted. He gestured around. It was empty, save for the two of them and the howl of the wind outside. "It is the only place we can talk about it." He gave her a pleading look. "Please. I'd like to get home before my sister wakes up."

Wakwi looked puzzled and then shook her head. "Such a shame, that one." She gestured for him to sit near her and the fire. With a pair of metal tongs in her shaking, birdlike hands, she removed five stones and placed them in a bowl before them. She took a jug of water from the other side of her and poured it in, engulfing them both in steam.

"There is no such thing as a hurry when matters of the soul are at stake," Wakwi said. "You carry much regret with you."

"Doesn't everybody?"

"You especially."

There was no arguing with that.

"Remember what we spoke of when this horrible crime first occurred," Wakwi said. "Creation. Destruction. Re-creation."

"I remember."

"This applies to beliefs as well. Beliefs we have about ourselves. Beliefs you had about your parents. Beliefs you had about Meoquanee. Beliefs you have about others. Friends. Lovers. Family. We create a myth about them, based on fact or fiction. That belief about who they are sustains us. We act upon it. Then something happens—and it happens in every relationship—and the myth we built up and created is shattered. Real life, real problems, appear. And it destroys whatever we thought we believed about them. They are no longer gods—they are human. And humans are broken, broken things. We used to listen to the animals to guide us. Now we largely ignore them. We don't take to heart what they still have to tell us. We used to listen to the earth more. Now we don't. It was different in the old days, when things were wild everywhere. But now we are broken, broken creatures. Facing that reality is jarring and difficult. So many fail to do so.

"It is in the re-creation when you fully understand who someone is and what you thought you knew and accept that knowledge. This creates the strongest of bonds. To accept who someone really is. To embrace the destruction and participate in the re-creation." Her eyes studied his closely. "It is one of the hardest things one could ever do."

Chibenashi's mouth went dry. How had she known about him and what he had done?

"It applies to the self, too, doesn't it?" he asked.

Wakwi nodded gravely. "We create myths about ourselves as well. What we have done to others and why."

His own myths about who he was and what he was capable of had indeed been shattered. He didn't know how he could face himself.

He nodded. "What I've done to her."

"To who?"

"My sister."

"She is restless. Very restless."

That wasn't what he was expecting her to say. That wasn't the word people usually used to talk about Ashwiyaa. "What do you mean?"

"All night, walking around, that one. I doubt she ever sleeps."

"My sister?"

"Yes."

This was getting uncomfortable.

"I'm here to talk about what you saw the other day," Chibenashi said. "It could help us solve Meoquanee's murder."

"Always walking around, lost in that head of hers."

"And my mother's murder," he said. It was the first time he'd said it out loud since it all fell apart. He added some information he shouldn't: "The two may be related. Connected."

He expected greater surprise from Wakwi, but she just sat there, shaking her head. "I tried offering her ceremony. The sacred medicines. I never stopped trying. Your friend, the mashkikiwinini, I know he tried. Very sad, when one's heart is closed to healing. The body cannot heal without the spirit."

Chibenashi didn't want to ignore what she was saying, but this wasn't anything he didn't know already. They'd tried everything. Ashwiyaa had pushed everyone else away. Meoquanee was gone. That left him. He couldn't fail her now.

"Please," he asked Wakwi again, desperation creeping into his voice. "What did you see by Meoquanee's wigwam?"

She held his gaze. "My boy," she said. "I believe I already told you."

◆　◆　◆

Chibenashi blew in with the cold wind and snow at the dakoniwewiga-mig. He'd just hung up the phone on a call with Kichewaishke. He'd called the dakoniwewigamig in Shikaakwa before that but was careful not to ask for Takumwah.

There was much to sort out.

He was close. He could taste it.

It was like dancing the rice, putting together the pieces of a crime you were investigating. It was making intricate moves while the ground was ever shifting beneath your feet. Unstable, slippery. Constantly moving. Always taking much longer than you think. Requiring you to approach it from all angles, leave no kernel untouched or unconsidered. Over time, the bits you don't need float away, and then you can sift through the grains. Put them through a sieve. It's all there, waiting for you. He was dancing the rice, and the husks were coming off.

Peezhickee stopped him in his tracks. He was tanned and looked far less relaxed than he should have after his time on vacation. "Come sit with me," he said by way of greeting, leading him to the table where Ziigwan was sitting. Chibenashi joined them, but before he could open his mouth to speak, Peezhickee began.

"You may be surprised to see me here," he said.

Chibenashi nodded.

"I received some distressing news from Takumwah, so I came back as soon as possible. You understand, I hope, what I am referring to."

He nodded. "I can explain," he said.

"I have no doubt that you can. Explanations, however, are irrelevant in this moment."

"I'm on the verge," Chibenashi said. "I think we can solve this."

Peezhickee put his hand on Chibenashi's shoulder. "You are a good man, Chibenashi. I have thought as much for many years. And you carry on you a strain that no person should. You have been ill served by life. By me. But it has compromised you. So I am sending you home. Bury your father. Look after your sister. We will solve this."

"But—"

"Your work is not needed on this matter," Peezhickee said. "We will have to do what we can to salvage this investigation." His normally genial face was now carved granite. "Go home."

Chibenashi looked at him, pleading with his eyes.

"We will discuss at another time. Ziigwan and I have to leave. We're going to Shikaakwa now. We have to meet in person with the dakoniwewigamig and the Advocates about your theft of the file. The Advocate from whom you stole it is facing disciplinary action for failing to secure her access."

Chibenashi's stomach dropped. It wasn't unexpected, but it still hurt to see that his actions had consequences for her. It had seemed like such a good idea at the time. Another myth he'd created.

"About that . . ." Chibenashi sighed. There was no point in denying it anymore. "I saw a note in the file about the DNA results. I realize you probably can't tell me, but—"

"I know what you're referring to," Peezhickee said.

"There's a recent annotation," Chibenashi said. "Just from the other day. It's the first update to the file in twenty years. It linked to another matter, a more recent one."

Peezhickee's expression betrayed nothing.

"The annotation references that the mitochondrial DNA matched my mother's case as well as Meoquanee's. But the annotation also references DNA results for Sakima. His paternal DNA."

Peezhickee gestured for Ziigwan to leave them. He appeared to briefly debate something with himself before saying, "This is not the right time to tell you, but you have the right to know. And not knowing has led to too much torment. Best for you to hear it now while you can ruminate without fear for your work responsibilities."

Chibenashi's throat itched, and his stomach clenched. He braced himself.

"You won't see this in any file because I did not put it in there. Your father, when he confessed to killing your mother, confessed to something else as well. I did not question his confession to the murder, and so I did not investigate further. But this other confession, I did seek out independent confirmation. Unofficially."

He hesitated, then continued, "You were not your father's only son."

Chibenashi opened his mouth to speak, but Peezhickee held up a hand to silence him. "Your father and Meoquanee had a relationship when you were very young. A fleeting one, but a relationship nonetheless. From that fleeting relationship came a child—a son. Sakima. Wiishkobak raised him as his own, never knowing the truth. But on that last Manoomin, the night your mother . . .

"Your father, Wiishkobak, and Meoquanee all told the same story. The evening started off well. Your families were celebrating together. Maybe you remember it. Everyone was having fun. And then your father and Sakima walked away to retrieve something—no one could remember what—and as they walked away, their mannerisms, stride, something about it made Wiishkobak realize that Sakima was your father's son. Even in the dark, the resemblance was uncanny."

Chibenashi thought back to all the times people had told him and his father the same thing.

"You had left by then, so they went back to your wigwam. There were accusations. Shouting. It drove your sister out into the woods, as you know. The truth eventually came out."

Peezhickee left the story there. He didn't need to say more. Chibenashi knew the rest.

Sakima was his brother. From another mother and another clan. It felt like it should have surprised him more than it did.

"So he died to protect someone he loved," Chibenashi whispered. Sakima. Who had the motive, the means, the opportunity. And the DNA sample had failed to exclude him. His name appeared in the file for his mother's case.

"And now," Peezhickee continued, "things have been so compromised that I don't know if we'll be able to get Sakima for this. Even if he confesses."

Peezhickee turned to Ziigwan, who was gesturing for them to leave. "I dislike the cold, and the sooner I resolve this, the sooner I can return to Panzacola. Your friends are in trouble, and your partner and I have much to do to clean up your mess. But our train leaves in just a short while. Please go home to your sister. We can discuss more when I return."

◆ ◆ ◆

Peezhickee's revelations were in danger of crowding out all other information. Chibenashi had to tamp it down. If he had destroyed the official case, the least he could do was solve it.

He thought about the two phone calls he'd made before he met with Peezhickee.

The first had been with the Shikaakwa Dakoniwewigamig. Sakima had been spotted on video not leaving the platform in Baawitigong. The person who delivered the gashkibidaagan was obscured. Wiishkobak's whereabouts were as well traced as ever; he had been teaching another course at the university. And, importantly, Sakima's fingerprints were not in the house anywhere with the note. It was possible he'd wiped them down, but Chibenashi had seen Sakima's apartment, the chaos in which he lived. No way someone living in that level of degradation and filth could be so meticulous otherwise. Despite the fact that the DNA seemed to implicate him, it would have been impossible for him to be in Chibenashi's wigwam to leave the note.

The second call had been with Kichewaishke. He'd asked to speak with Biidaaban.

"I'm hoping you can help me solve a mystery," he'd told her.

"Of course," she'd said solemnly.

"You said last night that Ashwiyaa never sleeps. What did you mean by that?"

"I mean she doesn't sleep."

"Does she lie in bed awake?"

"No. Every time she thinks everyone else is asleep, she leaves."

That had tripped him up. "Every time?"

"She always thought I was asleep. But I was not. The baby would cry and wake me up. And I didn't like sharing my room. So I would lie there and be so quiet. Like a mouse. She'd look at me for a long time, and then she'd open the window and climb out. Or she'd walk out to another room. I'd hear her on her phone, typing things."

"Every night?"

"Yeah."

He had considered that. "What about Waabigwan? Didn't he bark when she did that?"

"He was always asleep. And he was always very sleepy in the mornings when she was here."

"Isn't he always sleepy?"

"No. He barks at everything. But he hasn't barked at all since she came to us."

Chibenashi chewed on this as he entered the house quietly and peeked into Ashwiyaa's room. Sleeping soundly, despite what Biidaaban said. This was the Ashwiyaa he knew—sleeping when the world proved too much for her. He ventured in and watched her for some time. Even breathing, slight snoring. She was definitely asleep. He placed a hand on her shoulder, and she did not wake.

Biidaaban had observed Ashwiyaa during an unusual phase, when she was in an unfamiliar environment, and they were under extreme circumstances.

He thought about the file, what it had contained. The DNA test results. No extra DNA at his mother's crime scene. And yet there was DNA that matched it at Meoquanee's crime scene. His mother had obviously not risen from the dead to kill her best friend. So what had happened?

Chibenashi considered what his mother and Meoquanee had in common: Both had been murdered on the first night of Manoomin. Both were mothers. Both had lived in Baawitigong their whole lives. Both had been married once. Both had cared for him and his sister. Both had enjoyed running. And their relationship had been more complex than he had ever understood.

He tiptoed out to the kitchen. He poured another cup of the iced tea that had so effectively quenched his thirst the night before, but after one mouthful decided that it was too cold for that. He instead switched on the electric kettle. The pot in which they normally kept the coffee grounds was empty, so he explored the cabinet. Finding a fresh sealed bag, he cut it open and smelled the grounds. Closed his eyes and let the smell center him.

As the coffee brewed, his thoughts turned back to the DNA evidence again. He remembered something curious about the way both tests had been conducted. Both had tested mitochondrial DNA. He remembered what Makade and Mizhakwan had told him about such testing: it was less reliable because it could be taken from more degraded or smaller samples.

He could hear the buzz of his phone nearby but ignored it. He was onto something here. He was so close. He could feel it. He had to focus. He still wasn't prepared to handle what might be on the other side of a call anyway.

He spooned sugar into his cup and poured the coffee. He desultorily stirred it as he thought. It was the kind of testing done two decades before, when it was still largely in its infancy, considered less reliable than most kinds of modern testing. Then something else flashed in him. It tested the matrilineal line. Siblings who shared a mother would have the same mitochondrial DNA as each other. And so would a mother and child. It had been the necessary type to analyze since there was nothing of Meoquanee's to compare it to in her home, so they'd used her son's as a basis for it.

He sipped the coffee. It was bitter; the sugar hadn't dissipated yet. He put in another spoonful, sipped again. Still bitter.

A mother and child shared mitochondrial DNA.

He dropped the cup.

This wasn't possible.

He began to gag.

Two DNA profiles had shown up in the test from Meoquanee's murder. One of the same DNA profiles had also appeared in his mother's case file, though hidden in plain sight. There had been no separate DNA profile in his mother's case, only her own—because it had been her mitochondrial DNA. Which would be identical to any mitochondrial DNA from anyone else in her line. Sakima and Meoquanee would have the same mitochondrial DNA. And only two people living both now and then could have had that same mitochondrial DNA as his mother. Him. And Ashwiyaa.

He coughed, gagged again, gasped for breath.

Something was wrong.

It wasn't possible. It couldn't be.

Was this what Wakwi had talked about? *The destruction of what we thought we knew about the people we love.* Had she been talking about Ashwiyaa? Trying to warn him in her typically cryptic way?

Chibenashi fumbled for his phone. He grasped it. His fingers were uncoordinated. The phone clattered to the floor and out of reach.

He fell to the ground on his hands and knees. The room was spinning. His breath was heavy.

He'd been drugged.

He heard footsteps behind him. Ashwiyaa was standing there, arms crossed, wide awake. Her expression was blank. She regarded him with lazy detachment, head cocked to the side, as she watched the drug take him. Everything around him faded to black, except her.

"I was starting to think you'd never go for that sugar," she said.

Chapter Twenty-Seven

The day before his mother's murder had been one of the happiest of Chibenashi's life.

As far as Chibenashi was concerned, Manoomin was the best holiday of the year because his family, his community, and the natural world were bursting with happiness and optimism. A perfect celebration of life and community. None of it was stronger than it was on the first night. The harvest itself was largely symbolic, but the feelings that welled up inside him every time he attended were not.

He remembered the canoe in which they used to go out to the lake to begin the harvest. It had always been the same: his father steering the canoe in the back, Chibenashi using the other oar to propel it forward, his mother with the stick to hit the reeds, and his sister with the bags to collect. This year, though, had been different. His father had let him steer the canoe while he used the oar in the back. Their mother had given Ashwiyaa the stick and had held the bag herself. Steering the canoe was harder than Chibenashi had thought; it required a stronger hand on the stick, fighting the current, navigating around the delicate reeds and the path of other canoes, and working in perfect concert with his father. It was different when you were leading. Rather than simply follow the stroke of the person in front of you, you had to ensure a consistent rhythm so that the two would not be out of whack. When the chanting and the singing started, he felt like part of something greater—a single instrument in harmony with a greater orchestra.

They had danced the rice that night with Meoquanee, Wiishkobak, and Sakima. Like all kids, Chibenashi had grown up dancing the rice himself and watching the adults do it the correct way. Kids tended to slip and fall and treat it more as a game than a task. He held tight to the birch logs as he wore the well-loved family ricing makizinan, twisting his ankles just right after years of practice. His mother and Meoquanee had laughed next to him. Wiishkobak and his father passed a beer back and forth as they jokingly called out corrections and warnings. "If you break your ankle, you won't get out of it!" his father had shouted with a smile in his voice. "You'll just have to do it longer!"

Sakima and Ashwiyaa—skinny and awkward and fourteen and twelve, respectively—pointedly looked like they were not having fun, even though it was clear that they were. Chibenashi understood the feeling but was truly starting to appreciate the familial nature of the event. Their two families were one that night, happy and relaxed.

Just as the sun set on their family for the last time, his father took his mother by the hand and brought her to the sacred fire, where they began dancing with each other. Chibenashi remembered how the flames flickered off their eyes, their hair, their teeth. He remembered the wide smiles and stolen kisses between them. And then he'd left them to find his friends, Kichewaishke and others. Ashwiyaa had given him a pleading look, begging him to take her along, but he'd just smiled back at her and left her with both sets of parents and Sakima. They got into the alcohol, and the rest of the night was a black hole.

Just moments after he left, Sakima and Ishkode had walked away to get another pot for the manoomin, and Wiishkobak would see the resemblance.

There would be a fight that would cause Ashwiyaa to flee the house.

For twenty years, Chibenashi had looked back on that night and ransacked his memory for clues. What had he missed that would have suggested his father was shortly to murder his mother? He'd never seen anything to suggest what was coming. Even though he would dismiss it following the murder, there had been real love between his parents that night.

It never occurred to Chibenashi that he'd been asking the wrong questions.

It had never occurred to Chibenashi that Ashwiyaa might have come back home.

Chapter Twenty-Eight

Usually, whenever Chibenashi woke up, he could tell that some amount of time had passed. This time, it was impossible to tell how long he had been out. It could have been moments or days. It had apparently been long enough for him to be tied up where he lay on the floor, on his stomach, hands bound behind his back. His head throbbed. He felt hungover and dehydrated and like he'd been beaten with a stick. His back and chest muscles strained under where he'd been tied with . . . not rope. Duct tape? Zip ties? Something that did not bend when he strained against them. He felt cool metal: his handcuffs that he carried with him as a Peacekeeper—ones he'd never had to use in the line of duty.

He blinked. Whatever light there was in here was too bright. He was still on the floor of the kitchen. The cool wood beneath his face was beginning to hurt. No matter how he strained his head, he could not see a window or door to gauge what time it was. He wondered if Ziigwan or Peezhickee were back from Shikaakwa yet. He had no way of reaching them if they were.

Chibenashi wished he were still blacked out. Reality was too inconceivable, too frightening, and he dared not even breathe. The revelations of the past day—the past days—would all have been too much to handle on their own. But now this last one, the last puzzle piece clicking into place, revealed just how wrong he had been about everything and everyone. It had all been staring him in the face the whole time.

He lay there, recriminating, when he heard the soft sweep of footsteps walk toward him. Ashwiyaa knelt down and looked at him.

"You're awake," she said. "You didn't sleep as long as your friend's animosh usually did."

She'd changed out of the baggy clothes she usually wore. These were more formfitting, revealing a shape to her he hadn't known was there. Muscles he hadn't known she had bulged. He couldn't remember the last time he'd actually seen his sister's arms. They were . . . formidable.

"Then again, he didn't require as many drugs as you do to keep down," she said. "And he hardly had time to build up any resistance."

She gazed at him with the same disinterested look she'd given him when the drugs had first kicked in, then bent and hoisted him over her shoulders like a sack of manoomin. He groaned with the pain that came with being moved after lying on a hard surface in an uncomfortable position for a long time. She moved with ease, like he weighed nothing. He blinked and looked around. It was dark outside. Impossible to know what time it was. At this time of the year, it was dark more than it was light. It could be late afternoon or the loneliest time before dawn.

Ashwiyaa deposited him on the hard ground in front of the fire with a thud. At least there was a blanket on the floor here, though it offered minimal relief. His joints cried out in agony. His brain nearly throbbed out of its skull. He couldn't help the yelp of pain that escaped him. Ashwiyaa rolled her eyes at the sound, as if it annoyed her that he was in pain and incapacitated because of her.

Confusion overwhelmed him. Desperate as he was to reject it, DNA testing didn't lie. His sister was the one who had killed Meoquanee and had killed his mother. Since children had the same mitochondrial DNA as their mother, it had not shown up as a separate DNA profile for his mother's murder. He was lucid enough to accept that this could be the truth, but he could not yet believe it.

He tried to say, "I don't understand," but all that poured out of his mouth was a slurry of grunts and gibberish.

"Don't speak, nindawemaa," Ashwiyaa said. "You'll only hurt yourself further. And you've already hurt yourself enough."

She knelt by the fire, poked it a bit. The embers were dying. She stared at the glowing remnants of logs. They reflected in her eyes, making them look red.

"None of this had to happen, you know." She rested back on her haunches, not really looking at him. She faced the fire but stared at some point beyond it that only she could see. "I never wanted it to happen. It wasn't planned this way."

Chibenashi again tried to speak. Ashwiyaa clicked her tongue and walked out of his line of sight. When she returned, she had a roll of duct tape in her hands. She ripped off a piece and faced him.

"I said," she hissed, slapping the tape over his mouth, "don't speak."

She pressed her hand over his mouth to emphasize the point. Chibenashi stopped making any noise. He didn't recognize his sister. She spoke with a coldness and authority that he'd neither seen nor heard from her before.

"As I was saying, this wasn't planned. It's been twenty years, and I never thought I'd have to hurt you. I didn't want to hurt you. Really, I haven't ever wanted to hurt anyone. It just . . . happens. I break from myself and watch it happen. One of those out-of-body experiences. Like a vision quest but a twisted, obscene version of one. Maybe it means that I'm both twisted and obscene. I suppose I am. Twisted and obscene. But only because they made me that way.

"Our father was the first person to see what I was capable of. It was out in the woods, past the grazing areas. I was alone, or so I thought. I saw a baby apichi that had just fallen from the nest, learning to fly. Something about it was so fragile, so breakable. I had to break it. Just to see if I could. I didn't want to hurt it. I just wanted to see if I could do it. So I did. It broke. It broke so easily. I thought I'd feel bad, but instead I just felt . . . powerful. I turned around and there he was, our father, staring at me like he'd never seen me before. Maybe he never really had. He always watched me so carefully after that. Around you. Around others. Around animals. I was never alone. I thought for sure he wouldn't tell our mother, but like an idiot, he did.

"Ngashi wasn't content to just watch me—she wanted to stop me. Like I was some sort of deviant. I had only done the one thing the one time! And I probably wouldn't have done it again. I already knew what I was capable of; I didn't need to prove it again. But she was worried about me. About what I might become. So she asked Meoquanee to have a look at me. She had many looks at me. All the questions. All the assumptions. She tried to get me on pills. Tried to ask me stupid questions. Had I hurt any other animals. Had I ever started fires. Had I ever hurt a person. Had I ever thought about hurting a person. Or myself. Like I was messed up in some way. I wasn't! I was just a little girl. I hated it. They made me feel like a specimen in a jar. A wolverine in a cage.

"Noos started everything. If he had just not said anything, not overreacted to what he saw, not started this chain reaction, none of this would have happened. None of it. Everything and everyone would have been fine if he had just left well enough alone. But no. He had to run and jump to conclusions. Assume I was a threat to others, and get others involved to try to 'save' me." Her eyes flashed and her voice went shrill. "I wasn't a threat until he made me into one!"

Her screech was loud enough that Chibenashi wondered—hoped, prayed—that someone else could have heard it.

"He took my freedom away from me. So I took away from him what he loved the most."

Their mother.

"No," she snapped, as if hearing his thought. "Not her. You."

Chibenashi gave her a puzzled look, hoping the expression would not set her off again.

"He was so close to you. He loved you. He loved you so, so much. You were the good child. The one who didn't have the issues. The one who wasn't a threat. The one who would never kill a baby bird just to see if he could. Chibenashi could never hurt a baby bird. Chibenashi *was* the baby bird. It's even what part your name means—big little bird. The little bird who thinks he's so big. I think maybe that's what disturbed him about it so much—by hurting a baby bird, I could hurt you. And I did hurt you. I took both your parents away from you and left you alone with me.

"Killing ngashi wasn't so different from the baby bird. It just took a lot more planning and a lot more cunning. I couldn't crush her like I did the baby bird. But if I could get her subdued, I could cut her just in the right place. That doesn't take much. Just the ability to hold the knife and the strength and will to use it in the right place. That's all killing is, really. We all have it in us. We all can; most of us just don't. Most are too weak to do it. That's the first thing you have to kill—that weakness.

"They were so weak, the two of them. Weak in the face of commitment, weak in the face of taking responsibility, too weak to tell the truth. Ngashi was the first to figure it out, when she saw Sakima and noos at Manoomin. They walked away with the same gait, same stride. She turned to Meoquanee to say something. Meoquanee's eyes said it all. That's when ngashi realized—it wasn't the stride, like Peezhickee told you."

How did she know what Peezhickee said?

"It was Meoquanee. She as good as confessed. I know. I saw it. I figured it out that night but didn't say anything. I realized that these people who thought they were all so superior to me? They were monsters too. Noos betrayed our mother. Meoquanee, the selfless paragon that we all thought she was? She'd deceived her husband for fourteen years. She deceived her son until the very end and never admitted the truth to him. You tell me, who is the real monster?

"We left Manoomin quickly, all of us, and I was sent to bed. Sakima was sent back to their house, alone.

"Even though I was sent to bed, I heard the anger, the tears. I couldn't hear the words, but I didn't need to. I saw my chance to make things right for what they'd done to me. So I snuck out. I knew they'd be arguing for a while. So many *feelings* to sort out." Ashwiyaa didn't say the word *feelings*—she spat it out. "I left the wigwam, heard their shouting. Anyone who walked by would have heard what they were talking about. Had the night ended then, that would be all anyone in the village would have ever talked about with regard to our family." She smirked, reminiscing. "But of course, it wasn't. White Teeth is so easy to come by. I know you deal with it in your incidents that you investigate. Tourists use it on each other in bars and restaurants, use their victims, then scuttle back to their cruise ships before they can experience the consequences. Very easy to come by if you know where to go. And even though I was twelve, I knew where to go. And with so many people and tourists, no one really paid me much attention. I can be small and invisible when I want to be.

"Slipping it to you was so easy. It's always been easy. Offer you a drink, you down it without question or hesitation. I've been doing it to you for twenty years. Every night. Haven't you ever wondered why you sleep so well at home? And how well you didn't sleep in Shikaakwa? I wonder if you even can anymore without my help. But that night was my first. It was so easy; I didn't need a practice run. I just did it. You and your friends, thinking you were so cool, out at the edge of the woods, in the dark, with alcohol you weren't supposed to have. You were all well on your way to getting drunk. But I couldn't risk you coming home. You had to be out all night. So I snuck up and slipped it into your drink. It did its job. You thought you were drunk. You haven't touched the stuff since. I took that away from you too.

"When I got back, things had calmed down. They were both asleep. Ngashi was in their bed, noos was on the couch. Ngashi should have thrown him out. Might have saved him. But thankfully for me, she didn't. I stood there, watching them, for a long time—first him and then her. The last moments of peace either would ever know, and they slept through them. I don't know how long I waited there, but finally I knew I was ready. I'd overcome my weakness."

Chibenashi bit back sobs, knowing she might hurt him again if he made a sound. He didn't recognize this woman before him. This wasn't whom he had given up his life to care for.

"I woke ngashi and told her that I'd heard a noise outside that scared me. I remember how exhausted she looked—the kind of tired that's not only physical. She had so much going on, but she put that aside and did this for me. It was almost enough to make me reconsider it. Almost. But that's why killing that weakness is so important. The baby bird was sweet. Ngashi was sweet. So I did it. I led her to where I said I heard it—like an animal to slaughter. She was groggy and disoriented, and it was really easy to jump her. I wasn't too much smaller than her at the time anyway. She was so caught off guard she didn't fight back the way she should have. Fighting back would have meant hurting me, and I don't think she had it in her to do that, even at the cost of her own life.

"There was a struggle, but not a big one. I cut my finger, dripped blood. She died quickly. I tried to make it as painless as possible, but, well, there's only so much you can do. I regret it, for her sake. All she did was love, and all anyone did in return was betray her. But not for the greater sake, which was to punish noos for what he had done to me. What he had turned me into. For his hypocrisy.

"I sat there, watching the blood pool. It didn't look the way I expected it to, really. Not like in TV or movies or in books. It was sticky. It was dark. It had a smell to it. You never think something like that would have a smell. But it did. Like copper. I almost cried. I almost lost it. But I didn't.

"Then noos came out. He had to have so many regrets from that night, but I think his greatest regret was letting his guard down about me. For once, he let himself see me as the little girl I had been, not the monster he'd made me into. He came out just as ngashi breathed her last. He ran to her, cradled her body in his arms, began sobbing. I don't think he realized it was me at first. He didn't even see me. He had eyes only for her in that moment. He loved her so much. He touched the knife, held the body. It was like he came up with the idea himself. His sobs got louder and louder. It was only a matter of time before they'd wake up our neighbors. And White Teeth only lasts a short while. I knew our time was limited.

"So I told him that I had done it. That I'd do it again, to you, right then and there. That you were drugged and out there somewhere sleeping, perfectly vulnerable. That I would expose his other secret— Sakima. And kill him too. Unless he did something to save you. He had to decide, then and there, whether to confess to the crime himself. Whether he would agree to imprisonment for the crime. If he was in prison and did not speak the truth, I would leave you and Sakima alone. I would leave you alone for the rest of your pathetic lives if he confessed. If he didn't, I would scream and cry that he did it, that I saw him do it, and while it was all being sorted out, you and Sakima would be killed too. It was sort of a bluff. I don't think I could have pulled it off. We would have been taken away; someone would surely have noticed you had been drugged."

Ashwiyaa smiled like a fox. "But he agreed. He did it knowing he would lose you, lose Sakima, but doing it so he could keep you both alive. He swore to suffer the punishment and to never reveal what happened. Prison was for you two, not for him."

Chibenashi's body curled into a crescent-moon shape at this news. His stomach cramped as the force of the truth of her words squeezed him from within. What he had learned in recent days had been bad enough. And now this?

"I had to survive, of course. We never would have been left on our own unless you were responsible for me, and I couldn't show what I really felt: nothing. Satisfaction. People never would have believed noos's confession. Really, they shouldn't have. All they had to do was a little investigation. My finger was cut, and nobody ever noticed or asked about it. A little bit of forensic work would have revealed that he was not responsible. But that didn't happen. A twelve-year-old shouldn't be able to trick an entire investigative team. But I did." She sounded proud.

"You staggered home and played your part so, so perfectly. It shouldn't have gone as smoothly as it did. You believed exactly what I needed you to believe. And our father complied. He saw how you believed. He willingly went to prison so that you could stay alive, blissfully ignorant and unaware. You lived with me all those years, under my control. And he knew it. He knew that if he made any move to save himself, to clear his name, you were dead. There was no one here to protect you from me. So he protected you as best he could, from afar. It was pathetic.

"I played the role of traumatized sister. It had the desired effect. It kept you close, away from him, hating him, focused solely on me and my needs so that you wouldn't stop and think about all the holes in the case. That became even more important when you became a Peacekeeper. Don't ask me to psychoanalyze that. It was clear you felt responsible and wanted to protect me. As the years passed, I had to pretend to be more and more traumatized so that you would never put all of your focus on your work but would always keep some of it on me.

"I had to do it to keep Meoquanee fooled too. She never really suspected it was me, especially given what had happened the night of Manoomin, but I think she kept it in the back of her mind as a possibility. I think she could start to believe that what I had done to the bird was an isolated incident. And she was so awash in her own culpability, so distracted with the loss of her own family, that she reframed all of it.

She began treating me as a victim, not a criminal. Someone to approach with love and understanding, not fear and accusations. If they had only done that from the beginning, this never would have happened. It would have been so easy for them to avoid this! They had the power and they had the knowledge, and they did nothing with it."

She closed her eyes, hummed in frustration, as if trying to calm herself down.

"It was exhausting, nindawemaa. So exhausting. For twenty years I've carried this weight around with me, day after day, night after night, year after year. Two decades I've had to play the part."

Chibenashi knew better than to fight against his handcuffs in this moment or make any sound at all. She was a brittle, dried stick on a hot day. One spark was all it would take to make her ignite. He'd never heard actual victims speak this way, let alone perpetrators. Every perpetrator believes they are a victim in some way. But this was a whole different level. It was almost inhuman.

Chibenashi thought back to the story of the Wendigo, the cannibalistic monster who would stalk the community and eat the good right out of men and turn them into monsters. Wasn't that what Ashwiyaa was? Wasn't she devouring herself from the inside with this hatred and belief in her own victimization? It had plainly destroyed her. And in destroying her, she had destroyed so many others. He had never really believed in such things, dismissed it as a story to keep children in line. This, though—this was the real thing. A Wendigo in the flesh. The monster without the fangs.

"Even I couldn't carry this forever. The act, the pretending. It was too much. I had to do it in front of you and Meoquanee. I was glad to have an excuse to not see others. It took its toll, isolating you from everyone. Making sure the community stayed away. They meant so well. Maybe if I'd allowed it, things would have been different. But I didn't. I couldn't afford to let someone sway you. Meoquanee just wouldn't quit. It was exhausting, keeping everyone at bay. After so long, it does things to you. So I decided that enough was enough. I had to end it. I had to stop pretending.

"That's when I saw Sakima in Baawitigong for the first time in forever. How he's let himself go. Hardly recognizable. I knew who he was. I saw him when he went past our wigwam and into Meoquanee's. I heard the shouting. And again I had my chance. It's like it was meant to be."

She smiled. "It was appropriately symbolic, the anniversary of ngashi's death. If I were to have planned it, I probably would have picked that day anyway. It was easy to operate without having to hide much. Everyone else was at the sacred fire that night. Except for me. Meoquanee and Sakima had fought that afternoon. I knew that someone other than me had to have seen him.

"And then, Meoquanee came over to check on me! You sent her right to me."

Chibenashi wanted to interrupt her. Wanted to scream, *You told me she never came to you!*

"And like you always have, you believed me when I told you she never arrived." She smiled her predatory smile. Could she read his mind? "We were all by ourselves. The only two people in Baawitigong who were away from the festivities. I said I wasn't feeling well. She offered to stay. I declined. I said that the wigwam was hard for me to be in on the night of Manoomin, especially alone, given what happened. Could I come to hers and stay with her until you got home? It was almost too easy. She agreed immediately. I went over with her. I hadn't really decided what to do or even if I was actually going to go through with it. It had been twenty years, and things were going well. I had gotten away with it. I wondered, had I really killed that weakness that keeps us from murdering each other?

"I saw the knife. I grabbed it. She was even easier to subdue than ngashi. Even more surprised. Fought even less. She was so petite, and even though she was in great shape, she wasn't ready to fight me off. Sakima helped in a way; she was holding his gashkibidaagan. It got blood on it when I cut her. It was quick, quicker than even ngashi. You may not have been a good Peacekeeper, and you may not have solved any actual crimes, but your phone is full of protocols. I knew to wipe down everything. Remove everything from the wigwam that could provide a known sample of Meoquanee's DNA so that there would be no direct comparators. Her body wouldn't be found until late the next morning, making it next to impossible for good DNA to be obtained from her. It only took a little while. When I left, I took the bag. And it worked. No one suspected me. No leads. No suspects. The case went cold."

Then she sighed, and her eyes narrowed, and she glared at Chibenashi.

"And then you went to Shikaakwa. And you ruined everything."

She stood up, took a few frantic paces around the room to work out nervous energy, glaring at her brother the entire time.

"I wanted to give you more time. You understand? I couldn't keep faking it, but I did want to give you more time. But then you went to Shikaakwa and found out that they'd actually done DNA testing on ngashi? And it matched the DNA testing on Meoquanee? That put us on an accelerated course, I'm afraid. Especially since you actually went and talked to noos. I tried to stop you. At least the old man held up his end of the bargain. At least he had the dignity to kill himself rather than break his word. He did it to save you. Again." Her eyes narrowed, cold as black ice. "Do you have any idea what I would have given for him to love me that much?"

But he did, Chibenashi wanted to say. Couldn't she see it? Their father hadn't "made" her into anything. He'd been trying to help her too. Just as Chibenashi had never seen his father's love for what it really was, neither had Ashwiyaa. All the man had done was love and try to save his children. Chibenashi had realized it too late. Ashwiyaa would never see it. Chibenashi remembered how much his father had held himself at a distance the last time they saw each other. Was there love behind that mask she wore, a dam that had been on the verge of breaking?

"Everything could have been different."

She picked up a metal poker for the fire. Cast iron. Sturdy. Began twirling its length between her fingers, resting it against her palm.

"Everything *should* have been different."

She sat down next to Chibenashi, still holding the poker in hand, deathly calm.

"I had to get Sakima back here one more time, just to scramble things, so I snuck into the recyclers and called him. I told him that I had his stupid gashkibidaagan and asked if he wanted the bag before we destroyed it. He came for the bag; I gave it to him. He was stupid enough to start carrying it around after that. He was like a baited hook, and you swallowed it, just as I'd hoped you would."

She stared into nothingness for a few moments.

"No one at the recyclers took notice of me. No one noticed me on the platform with Sakima. No one notices me. I had known Sakima for years, yet he failed to see me, just like everyone else does. Just like you did. Just like you continue to do."

In a flash, she jumped to her feet and smashed the fireplace with the poker, damaging the river stones that surrounded it. Chibenashi curled into himself and flinched at the impact. She blew some hair out of her face and gave Chibenashi a smile. Then she sat down next to him again as if nothing had happened, placid as the surface of the lake. Chibenashi fought not to tremble.

"Don't worry; I'll stop rambling soon. But I need someone to know what I am capable of. I need someone to know. And it feels like that someone should be you. Do you understand why I'm telling you? I'm not sure if you can figure it out. You've failed to figure out anything else."

Chibenashi swallowed. He had been so engrossed in what she was saying, in discovering who his sister really was, that he had not been thinking about what this little monologue and what she had done to him actually meant for his safety. No more ambiguity. Ashwiyaa really did mean to kill him. Could do so at any moment, without provocation or warning, just as when she had smashed the fireplace. He supposed that was part of the message too. *Be afraid. Pay attention to me. Any breath could be your last. I am unpredictable. I am a force of nature. Do not underestimate me. Look what happened to the people who did.*

He was on his side, legs near the fireplace, head toward the couch. Behind him was a low table with wooden legs. He felt delicately for anything on which he could find purchase. His fingers brushed against a tiny rough splinter jutting out from the table leg. That one splinter was his only hope. His life hinged on that splinter. He very slowly, very cautiously, rubbed the handcuffs against it, trying to find a way to get the splinter into the keyhole.

Appearing not to notice his struggle, Ashwiyaa suddenly crouched before him. With the same speed and abruptness she'd demonstrated earlier, she ripped the duct tape off his mouth in one swift stroke. He cried out involuntarily.

"Now, now, if you can't use your inside voice, I'll have to tape you up again," she said.

"How?" he asked. He moved his mouth around, trying to form words, but he was still having difficulty from the drugs.

"How what? How did I learn all of this? The DNA evidence for both Meoquanee and ngashi. Going to see noos. The fact that he was dead—had killed himself. The disappearance of your mystery file. What Peezhickee told you earlier this evening?"

He nodded.

"I should have learned it from you. All of it. I bet you've been scrambling to blame others. I know you already blame Dakaasin and that guy you were working with in Shikaakwa—Takumwah, right? The Myaamia guy? Yeah, they didn't tell me."

They're called T'wah T'wah, Chibenashi thought. *Myaamia is our word.*

269

"Did you know it's possible to track someone else's movements through their phone? To clone it? It isn't that difficult. It didn't take me long. I can record all your calls. Read all your texts in real time. Download your files. Delete your files. Access your encrypted sites."

Ashwiyaa, moving even faster than she had earlier, whipped the poker in one hand across the top of Chibenashi's body to crack through the legs of the table. The poker grazed his forehead, leaving a shallow cut. It screamed with pain, like the iron from the poker had embedded itself within his skin. He froze in panic, desperately trying to control the heavy breathing that had begun. He had to stay calm. The blow to the table had cracked its legs and caused the top to collapse. The leg with the splinter had been snapped completely. He felt for it gingerly. It had a very sharp tip. He grasped it behind his back, stock-still. He didn't know what he intended to do with it. He just knew that he wanted it in his hand.

"So you see, my brother, I've always been watching. Following. I deleted ngashi's file. Cruel that you accused your friends of doing it remotely. But I suppose I can't blame you for being ignorant. Though really, you should have had your phone checked for this sort of thing. It thinks my fingerprint is also your fingerprint, that my face is also your face, that my voice is also your voice. You can trick a device into whatever you want, so long as the user has left it vulnerable. And that's exactly what you did. You left it, and yourself, vulnerable. To me."

All he'd ever wanted to do was keep her safe.

"So," she said, dragging the poker across the floor slowly, making it squeal. "Now you know it all. What do you think?"

He stared at her. She stared back. She put her hand to the cut on his head. He winced in pain.

"I asked you a question," she said. "What do you think?"

In that moment, all he could tell her was the truth. "I think I want to save you."

Her eyes glittered with rage. Chibenashi would swear they actually turned red. "Wrong answer!" She swung the poker and hit the floor, carving a large gash in the wooden planks. "Try again."

He swallowed thickly. "I'm so sorry for what we did to you."

Ashwiyaa shrieked and jumped to her feet. "Wrong!" She struck the wall. "Answer!" And the fireplace again. Panting, she turned around, eyes wild, poker gripped in two hands. "I'm going to ask you one. Last. Time." She staggered to Chibenashi and lifted the poker over her head, where she could bear down on him in an instant. "What do you think?"

Chibenashi considered the answer to the most important question he'd been asked in his life. Ashwiyaa towered over him. He felt the broken table leg in his hand. There was no way to use it to defend himself. She breathed faster and faster. Her arms twitched. He answered.

"You were right," he said. "You were right about everything. And we were wrong."

He watched Ashwiyaa's face carefully, searching for any trace of the sister he had known. Rage softened to happiness as he saw that yes, this was what she had wanted to hear. She lowered the poker.

"Thank you," she said, tears in her eyes. "You do understand. Smarter than I gave you credit for." She smiled at him.

Chibenashi smiled back. He'd done it.

Then Ashwiyaa raised the poker again.

"I'm sorry, nindawemaa," she said.

Chibenashi rolled out of the way just in time to avoid the blow from the poker as Ashwiyaa swung it down as hard as she could, carving another gash into the floor. He kept the broken leg of the table firmly grasped in his hand. He was pressed against the couch now. Nowhere else to move.

"What are you doing?" he cried.

Ashwiyaa blew a piece of hair out of the way. "You have to know how this ends. Why I've been smashing the place up. My brother came home from Shikaakwa, ashamed of his failure to solve the case of Meoquanee.

He betrayed the trust of his community and his colleagues in two cities by stealing a file he should never have been able to access. Having completely obliterated his credibility, he comes home in a rage. He sees me here, sees how I've trapped him. A fight begins. A struggle ensues. And he takes a few swings at his poor sister. Only after she somehow grabs the poker is she able to fight him off for her own safety. She takes several swings that miss, hits the fireplace, the floor, the table. Until finally she catches a lucky blow and hits him in the head. He is dead, but only because she had no choice. She's found later, injured, the sole survivor in a family of murderers and cheaters. She then can slip away, far away from this wigwam and this town that has brought her nothing but sorrow."

"But you've bound me with my own handcuffs. Come after me way too many times for that to be believable. No one will believe that I was trying to hurt you."

Ashwiyaa shrugged. "I think your dakoniwewigamig has already shown its incompetence at solving crimes."

"Someone else will piece together what I have," Chibenashi said. "They'll figure out it was you, the same as I did."

"Ah, but that's the beauty of mitochondrial DNA," Ashwiyaa said. "A brother and a sister who share a mother will have the same mitochondrial DNA. So really, it was you who was implicated by the DNA evidence, and having finally been the one to stop you, I will be lauded as a hero. I'll get the respect that I deserve. That I have always deserved. And it will be wonderful."

She raised the poker again. Chibenashi was trapped. He looked at her. His eyes begged.

"Please."

Ashwiyaa reared up and prepared to strike again in a final, fatal blow.

The door to the wigwam flew open.

Then came a voice.

"Stop!"

Chapter Twenty-Nine

Ashwiyaa jumped back, lowering her weapon. Chibenashi exhaled audibly—partly in relief and partly in shock.

In ran Kichewaishke, Peezhickee, and Ziigwan, followed improbably by Takumwah and, impossibly, Dakaasin. Kichewaishke and Dakaasin immediately went to Chibenashi, while Takumwah and Ziigwan made for Ashwiyaa. Peezhickee put his hands on his hips, surveying the scene, as he waited until the more spry and youthful Peacekeepers had successfully subdued their suspect. He was, after all, still technically on vacation.

Ashwiyaa kicked Ziigwan away and wrenched out of Takumwah's grip with a well-timed somersault. She still held the poker firmly in her hands. Brandishing it as a sword, she faced Takumwah, and they circled each other. Ziigwan staggered to her feet and approached Ashwiyaa from the side. Ashwiyaa swung at Ziigwan, who ducked just in time, and then at Takumwah, who had tried to charge at her again. She missed him too. The three studied each other warily, Ashwiyaa wildly swinging the poker.

"You can't beat all of us," Ziigwan said.

"I've been doing it for twenty years," Ashwiyaa taunted.

She swung the poker again, missing Ziigwan's head by millimeters.

Kichewaishke and Dakaasin knelt next to Chibenashi. Kichewaishke checked his injury. "Are you okay?" Dakaasin asked.

"Yes," he rasped, never more glad to see her.

"Good," she said. Dakaasin stood up and, approaching from behind, jumped on Ashwiyaa's back. She wrapped her arms around Ashwiyaa's neck and tried to choke her into submission. Ashwiyaa swung the poker over her head at Dakaasin but missed. Dakaasin squeezed harder, but Ashwiyaa bit down on her arm with enough force to draw blood. Dakaasin screamed but continued to hold on. This gave Ziigwan and Takumwah the opening to knock down Ashwiyaa, who landed with a loud cry on top of Dakaasin. Takumwah kicked away the poker while Ziigwan covered Ashwiyaa's body with her own. Dakaasin struggled out from under them with Takumwah's help. Ziigwan held Ashwiyaa down while Takumwah knelt and cuffed her hands. Panting, Ashwiyaa tried kicking, but everyone moved out of range. Dakaasin finally sat on Ashwiyaa's legs, holding them in place.

"Are you ready to stop fighting?" Ziigwan asked Ashwiyaa.

Ashwiyaa looked like she would spit venom at her if she could. "Never." She made no more attempts to fight back.

Ziigwan sighed. "Better bind her feet too," she told Takumwah.

"With pleasure," he said, grabbing the duct tape off the kitchen counter and wrapping Ashwiyaa's legs.

Kichewaishke was now checking Chibenashi for other injuries. "Did she hurt you?" he asked.

Chibenashi shook his head. "But she slipped me something." He paused a moment, then added, "Again."

Kichewaishke gave his friend a long look, then nodded. "We'll get you all checked out. I'll put some yarrow on that cut. Glad you're all right."

"Me too."

"I can't believe we didn't see this coming."

"Me neither."

"I guess we really didn't know every one of Baawitigong's secrets after all."

"I guess we do now."

"Good," Peezhickee said from his position in the doorway. "You're finally finished."

◆　◆　◆

Too many impossible things had happened today for Chibenashi to fully process them.

Ashwiyaa was taken away by Peezhickee to sit in the cell overnight until she could be taken to Shikaakwa for her Mediation. Kichewaishke was cleaning and treating Chibenashi's wound.

"What are you all doing here?" Chibenashi asked.

"Was that really not obvious?" Takumwah asked.

"Well, no, it isn't. Not you being here. Or you." He raised a shaky hand toward Dakaasin. "I didn't think I'd see either of you again."

"Fair assumption," Dakaasin said.

"We weren't planning to come here," Takumwah acknowledged. "But it was your phone calls that changed everything.

"When you asked me whether Dakaasin had deleted the file, I was concerned and immediately thought to contact your dakoniwewiga-mig. But first I called Dakaasin to ask if she had done so. She hadn't. We were both very concerned. But then Dakaasin remembered that she'd dealt with a similar issue in a recent hearing. The one we both attended, remember? In that case, the victim's phone had been cloned and accessed remotely by her stalker. It occurred to us that if your files were being stolen, perhaps your phone had been compromised at some point.

"We were all in the meeting together in Shikaakwa; we had just wrapped up. We were walking Peezhickee and Ziigwan back to the train station. We mentioned your phone call and what you had said. And we were all brainstorming what it could have meant. Then we connected the dots about who could have had access to your phone. We also thought of who would have benefited. And finally, we considered who would have not only had access to your phone and benefited from stealing from you but also could have been implicated by the DNA evidence. By the time we arrived at the train station, we all realized something was wrong. So we all got on the train. Even me and Dakaasin. Without luggage or anything."

"We tried calling you from the train, but we got no response," Ziigwan said. "We tried over and over. By the time we arrived, we put together that you might be in trouble."

"So we literally ran over here as fast as we could," Takumwah said. "And we made it just in time."

"Then what about you?" Chibenashi asked Kichewaishke.

"Ziigwan called me to see if I'd seen or heard from you," he said. "And asked about Ashwiyaa. I told her I wasn't concerned. But later, I was telling Okimaskew about it, and Biidaaban overheard. She told us what she'd told you about Ashwiyaa—things we hadn't noticed but Biidaaban had. So I tried calling you, too, and when I couldn't reach you, I came over. Looks like I was just in time for the party."

Chibenashi huffed out a laugh, wincing with pain as he did so. He looked around at his colleagues, friends, and former friends. He sobered. "I can't begin to thank you for saving me," he said. "What you all did to get here in time." He addressed Takumwah and Dakaasin. "I broke your trust and stole from you." Looked at Ziigwan. "I tarnished our dakoniwewigamig's reputation and created so much more work for you." At Kichewaishke. "You've already done so much for me."

Takumwah shrugged. "We all take care of each other, whether we deserve it or not. Mino-bimaadiziwin." Everyone nodded.

"And I'm glad we did," Dakaasin said. "Any life is worth saving. Even yours."

Chibenashi laughed. "Thanks for the compliment."

"Well, none of this erases what you've done."

He nodded. "I understand." He knew what she was really saying: nothing he had done, nothing that had been done to him, and nothing he could ever do would ever erase the betrayal of her trust. Mino-bimaadiziwin didn't change that. It was hard, but he had to accept it. He had considered the price when he'd made his decision.

"And it hasn't changed your standing in the dakoniwewigamig," Ziigwan warned him. "That meeting was long for a reason. Yes, we caught the person who murdered two people. We saved you, her intended third victim. Who knows what she would have gone on to do? But the end doesn't justify the means on this."

"It could affect what happens at Mediation," Dakaasin pointed out. "We may only be able to get her for her attempt on your life, not what she did to Meoquanee or Neebin."

Chibenashi agreed, though he didn't want to.

"We'll do what we can," she said. "But I need you to be prepared for that."

"I understand," he said. He limped over to the kitchen and pulled his phone from where it had rolled under the counter. He picked it up, flipped through a few things, and then handed it to Dakaasin. "Perhaps this will help?"

She took the phone, confused. "What is that?"

"Ashwiyaa's confession."

"What do you mean?"

"I captured it. All of it. I tried calling Ziigwan, but it was too hard. The drugs were already in my system. So just before I dropped the phone, I was able to open up the voice-recording app. I managed to hit 'Record' just before it fell. I just turned it off now. It should have captured everything."

Chapter Thirty

Time passed. Chibenashi healed. Takumwah and Dakaasin returned to Shikaakwa. Peezhickee finished his vacation. Ziigwan continued her work. The Blooming Moon rose. And Ashwiyaa refused to confess to anything.

Chibenashi had survived the attack, and there had been witnesses to her attempt on his life. She had also assaulted both Takumwah and Ziigwan. Those matters were going forward. But as for Meoquanee's and Neebin's murders, things were more complicated. The recording was not of good quality, and it was difficult to hear much of what Ashwiyaa had said. Even after forensics managed to clean it up, her voice was too far in the background to be of much use. Not only that, Chibenashi's theft of the file had decimated his credibility. Therefore, his testimony about what Ashwiyaa had told him about those prior cases was out. And even if others could connect the dots, it was all too circumstantial without something—anything—of proof to tie them together. As Ashwiyaa had correctly pointed out, the mitochondrial DNA evidence could apply to him as much as to her, and he never had an alibi for the night of Neebin's murder.

In trying to solve their murders, he had made it impossible to get resolution.

Sakima had not been pleased with him. He didn't say it in words. He said it in a punch to the face that Chibenashi conceded he probably deserved.

"I don't care what your fucking intentions were," Sakima panted, tears running down his face. Takumwah had restrained him before he could hit Chibenashi again. "And I don't care how estranged we were. She was my mother. I had the fucking right to be made whole. And you took that from me." Chibenashi wisely decided not to point out that Sakima had not done a thing to help make that happen, and in fact had actively helped to block it. Sakima had been living with an open wound his whole life. It had turned septic and poisoned the rest of him.

Chibenashi decided not to tell Sakima about his true parentage. Let him have that small, blissful bit of ignorance. If no one else had ever told him, what good would it do to tell him now? They were not brothers—not really. Blood was not what made a family. Wiishkobak had raised Sakima. He, imperfect as he was, was Sakima's father.

One thing that had come out since was that—contrary to what his current wife, Kishkedee, had said—Wiishkobak had never had an affair with Chibenashi's mother, Neebin. Kishkedee had wanted to point suspicion away from her husband and therefore reversed it around. What motive could he have for killing her if he was the one who had strayed?

Such was the nature of unconditional love, Chibenashi supposed. There was no lie you would not tell to protect them.

Neebin's case was not being reopened.

"The file has been compromised," Peezhickee had explained. He sat on one side of the table, Chibenashi on the other. "Moreover, there was a confession on the books which was never recanted. Therefore, the prior decision is not being disturbed."

"But my father can't be branded a murderer forever. Not when I can prove he didn't commit it."

Peezhickee had fixed Chibenashi with a look. "Yes, he can. And, based on what you have told me, in some perverse way, this seems to have actually been what he wanted."

"He saved me."

"Then I am sure he is grateful for how this has turned out. And perhaps, in a way, it would be enough for him that you know who he really was and what was really in his heart."

"I hope so," Chibenashi said. "I wish I knew for sure."

"I knew him," Peezhickee said. "I saw the kind of father he was. He had such big dreams and high hopes for you. He loved you and your sister more than anything. I know it would have satisfied him that you knew the truth, knew the real him, and why he did what he did. But saving you meant more. Even if the cost was the brand of murderer."

With those two cases officially closed, only one remained: the attack on Chibenashi.

"You're the last Victim," he was told by his Advocate, Niimi. Dakaasin had recused herself, being a witness to what had happened and knowing the Victim and the Accused personally. The sort of thing that Chibenashi should have done from the beginning. Niimi typically represented the Accused in these matters, but she had agreed to move to this end of the table as a personal favor to Dakaasin. "She's the best," Dakaasin had promised. "Far better than I could do for you." She hung up the phone before he could ask any questions.

"With you being the last Victim," Niimi said, "you are the only one who has the right to seek restitution from Ashwiyaa. Your needs and loss are paramount. You are family, and you survived the attack with minimal injuries. The threats were real, but you emerged largely intact. Therefore, the Mediator will look to what you really lost. And we will have to articulate that as clearly as we can. We'll be limited as to what we can ask for, and we have to remember that we will have to keep it just to your losses. We cannot factor in the two murders that we know she committed."

Chibenashi nodded, ashamed of what his single-minded pursuit of protecting Ashwiyaa had cost. The guilt would follow him for the rest of his life. "I understand," he said.

"At the same time," Niimi continued, "we do not have to pretend that those murders did not happen. She has wronged you in so many ways. The betrayal of what she did goes beyond that attack. She took your mother from you. You spent your life raising her. You were forever tied to Baawitigong because of her, when you might have decided to go elsewhere. You made all your life's decisions around her. Do not be afraid to ask for compensation for that, if you agree that those were losses—and losses for which she is responsible.

"The goal in this hearing, as with all Mediations, is to put you back in the position you would have been in had your sister not betrayed you. Therefore, her punishment could be light, or it could be more severe, depending upon how you view your time spent with her.

"So," Niimi said, folding her hands. "I want you to spend the time between now and the Mediation asking yourself: What did Ashwiyaa really take from you? What do you believe she owes you? And what is it that you want?"

He thanked Niimi for her guidance and pondered the questions. He thought about that for a long, long time.

For as long as he could remember, Ashwiyaa's fate and well-being had been the primary focus of his life. And now here it was again, the primary question for him to answer.

What did he want for Ashwiyaa? What did he want for himself? And did he have the right to ask for either after all he had done and after all she had done?

Chapter Thirty-One

Chibenashi arrived in Shikaakwa for the third Mediation of his life on a late spring day. In contrast to the early winter, when the city had been cold and huddled into itself, it had the air of taking a deep stretch after a long sleep. Birds chirped and flew through the air from trees up and down the living skyscrapers. The mirrored surface of Ininwewigichigami was unfrozen and crystal clear. Flowers seemed to sprout out of every available crevice. Blossoms filled the trees, and when the breeze blew, it snowed flower petals that landed on the ground below before being crushed beneath the steps of busy people running from one place to the next.

For the first time in his life, he had not been living with Ashwiyaa. For the first time in memory, he was not caring for her in some way. He was, for the first time, free. Free to come and go as he pleased without worrying who would watch after her. Free to use his phone without being surreptitiously spied on by his sister. Free to not be lied to by someone he loved. At the same time, for the first time in his life, he was completely without family. No mother, no father, no sister. No Meoquanee.

Another first: Chibenashi's days were completely free. He was no longer a Peacekeeper.

The fallout from his theft of the file had never gone away. After everything that had happened, Peezhickee had had no choice but to ask Chibenashi to resign. He had done so without argument. The theft had been an act of desperation on his part; he'd known that it could cost them a result. But knowing the truth about his family had been worth it to him. Despite being asked to leave, he had departed on good terms and still saw Ziigwan and Peezhickee regularly. They were seeking a replacement for him, but he knew it would not take long. Tourism season was about to begin again in earnest, and they would need additional hands.

Without a job or a sister to occupy his time, he was free to think. He could imagine nothing more terrifying than an endless stretch of time alone with his own thoughts. The usual lies no longer worked, and every time he let his mind wander, his thoughts were like a series of mirrors capturing every angle of himself, and he didn't like what he saw. He focused his attention on the Mediation. What, if anything, would he ask for? The answer eluded him for months. He wanted what he could never get: his family back, whole and intact. But no Mediator's decision could raise the dead. No agreement among Victim and Accused could rewind time. Nothing could give him back twenty years of forgone opportunities, self-imposed limits, roads not taken—all because he'd felt that he had to stay for her.

Were those losses? Did he deserve compensation for that? Or was that advance payment for the wrongs he would one day commit?

On the fifth day after his father's death, Chibenashi had gone to the cemetery again. Wakwi performed the Bagidinigewin. Ishkode's jiibe-gamig was placed next to Neebin's, side by side in death as they had been in life, both victims of their daughter. This time, when they called Eagle, he landed. This was the sign Chibenashi needed: though there had been a betrayal at the end, they would have knit themselves back together if they had been given more time.

But he'd also felt the loss. The wigwam was big and empty. Ashwiyaa's bedroom sat like a museum exhibit, untouched since the night she had been taken to Shikaakwa. He had still not repaired the damage she had inflicted during her attack on him. The river rocks around the fireplace bore the scars from the poker. The floor was dotted with gashes. The table was gone, having been shattered by her blows. He hadn't bothered to fix any of it. He hadn't even tried, but he couldn't exactly articulate why. A monument to his failures? A memorial to what he had lost? A reminder of what it had nearly cost him? He could not say.

He spent time with Kichewaishke and his family, as he always had. Only now he opened up to his best friend about what the last twenty years had done to him. He'd been carrying a load for so long that, once lifted, he didn't quite know what to do with himself. Grudgingly, he had to admit that Takumwah had been correct: he needed to talk more. For the first time, he shared with someone his thoughts and feelings about the case, his parents, his sister, the loss of his career, the self-inflicted wounds, and how difficult it was to untangle all of it.

Kichewaishke had also helped him cope with his withdrawal symptoms.

Ashwiyaa had been spiking his food and drinks with White Teeth for years, ever since the night she had murdered their mother. He had never noticed it. He always slept well, never had any hangovers, and slept through the night each night. His nights in Shikaakwa, away from Ashwiyaa, had been his first without some sort of drug in his system. It had caused his poor sleep and irritability in Shikaakwa, which he had attributed to the unfamiliar environment, anxiety about the case, and ambient noise from the city around him. It turned out that he was suffering from withdrawal symptoms, which had only continued in the weeks and months following Ashwiyaa's arrest. Kichewaishke had been there every step of the way, giving him clonidine and balsam fir for his headaches. Slowly, over time, the poison Ashwiyaa had been feeding him was wrung out of his system, physically and spiritually. His body became less and less dependent on it, and he grew stronger and stronger.

Where Kichewaishke helped mend his body, Wakwi helped mend his soul. Through healing circles and smudging with sweetgrass and cedar, he was recovering internally.

They had sat again in the wiigwaasi-mashkikigamig, where they discussed what had happened in the aftermath of his last visit: Ashwiyaa's attack, her confession, everything else he had lost.

"But consider also what you have gained," Wakwi said. "Remember, this is the last part of the circle." She raised her arm and pointed her finger. "Creation." She drew a half circle in the air. "Destruction," she said, labeling the bottommost point of the circle. "And then re-creation." She drew the second half of the circle and returned her finger to where she had started. "You aren't back where you started; you're at the beginning of a completely new circle. Everything you know has been destroyed but also has been re-created. In a way, you have been given a tremendous gift. The old world is gone. The new world is here. What do you plan to do in it?"

That was the question that lay before Chibenashi now at the Mediation. He sat at a table next to Niimi. Across from him was the Mediator, an older man looking at him with professional interest, hands in his lap, politely waiting for Chibenashi. At the adjacent table, staring forward without an expression on her face, was Ashwiyaa. This was the Ashwiyaa he knew: vacant, withdrawn from the world, nearly oblivious to everything around her. The act she had perfected over a lifetime. But Chibenashi knew better now. She was taking in everything, betraying nothing. That blank stare hid a cool, calculating woman who was thinking several steps ahead of everyone around her. Behind them, in the rows of chairs arranged in concentric circles, were the witnesses to the attack: Takumwah, Ziigwan, Peezhickee, Dakaasin, and Kichewaishke. Wakwi, Okimaskew, and Biidaaban were also there, as they were witnesses to Ashwiyaa's conduct in the days leading up to it.

The prehearing was first, in which the witnesses testified to what they witnessed Ashwiyaa do before and during the attack. Ashwiyaa denied everything, insisted that she had been the victim of Chibenashi's aggression and had acted in self-defense. "He was going to hurt me," she said. "I was so vulnerable, so dependent on him. And he used that to lock me away from the rest of the world. I thought he was keeping me safe, but he wasn't." She trembled, shrank down to make herself look smaller. This was also the Ashwiyaa he'd known.

She claimed that the hearing was unfair because, as a Peacekeeper, Chibenashi was able to coerce a number of witnesses to testify falsely on his behalf. She pointed to the theft of the file, which had cost him everything, as the motivating factor—he had taken it out on her. "He's always blamed me for losing her," she said. She claimed that his actions suggested he had been the true culprit in both Neebin's and Meoquanee's murders, and he was hurting her not only out of a propensity to attack his female relatives, but also because he wanted to cover his tracks even further. The parade of witnesses, plus forensic evidence proving that Ashwiyaa had been monitoring Chibenashi's phone and accessing his files, overwhelmed her claims. The Mediator found Ashwiyaa was responsible for Chibenashi's injuries. She reacted with silence. The Mediator called for a short break before the second phase.

"How are you feeling?" Niimi asked him. Chibenashi just shrugged in response.

Kichewaishke asked him the same question. He again shrugged. "Talk to me," Kichewaishke pressed.

"I don't know. Really. The outcome isn't surprising."

"Do you know what you're going to ask for?"

He just shrugged again.

Dakaasin spoke to him next.

"You could put her away for life, you know. Just based on what she did to you."

"I know."

"Or you could set her free."

Chibenashi chewed his lip for a moment before responding. "I know."

"But you won't be able to save her."

He felt panic rise in his chest. "What does that mean?"

"It means . . . it means that you should ask for what you need and want. Not what you think she needs."

It was inconceivable for him to think that way. After twenty years of denying his own wants in favor of her needs, he had no idea what they were anymore. Her needs had subsumed everything, and it was difficult to remember if his had ever even existed.

"Just . . . know what you want. And what your options are."

"Is that legal advice?"

"Just something that I wanted you to know," she said. As she walked away, Takumwah approached her. Put an arm around her waist. A kiss to her temple. This was a new consequence of Chibenashi's actions, and he forced himself to be happy about it. At least one positive had come out of this nightmare. They both deserved happiness, especially after what he'd done to them. If he'd destroyed their trust in him, the least he could do was cheer them on as they found it in each other.

After the break came the restitution phase, in which the debate would be over how Chibenashi could be made whole. He, not Ashwiyaa, would be the focus this time. It was an unusual position for them. For twenty years, Ashwiyaa's needs had dominated. Always. And Chibenashi had been willing to subordinate his wants and needs to hers.

Now that time of his life was over.

The Mediator offered Chibenashi the floor to make his request via his Advocate.

Niimi stood up. "If he may, the Victim would like to be heard directly on this," she said.

The Mediator nodded. "Very well. Chibenashi, please speak."

Chibenashi stood up, cleared his throat, and, not looking at Ashwiyaa, began.

"For as long as I can remember," Chibenashi said, "all I've ever wanted was to protect Ashwiyaa. That was more important than anything else in my entire life. I thought it was the right thing to do. I will never be able to articulate or fully understand how much that has cost me.

"Partly it was because I had no choice, and partly it was out of a sense of duty, but make no mistake: I wanted to do it. I wanted to be there for her. I felt like I had failed her in the most essential way because I had slept through the most traumatic event in either of our lives. I had failed to watch over her, and I was not going to let that happen again.

"I was so single-mindedly focused on this directive in my life that I excluded everything else that wasn't tied to it directly. I never married. Lost the one serious relationship I've ever had. I never pursued my education. I stayed in my hometown of Baawitigong—and I mean it when I say I stayed there. I never left for any reason because Ashwiyaa could not leave. I never visited my father in prison. I withdrew from the community. I had few friends. I left home to go to work, and that was it. If I wasn't working, I was home with Ashwiyaa. For twenty years, that was my life. All for her. Just the two of us against the rest of the world."

He chanced a glance at Ashwiyaa. She stared straight ahead, a blank look on her face, as if hearing nothing.

"We felt targeted. I had convinced myself that bureaucracy was too slow to protect her. It might shine a light on our case, but it might come too late to protect her.

"I had a choice to make: I could solve the murder the right way that would ensure that the perpetrator was caught, or I could solve it quickly and ensure my sister's safety. I chose Ashwiyaa. I always have. That decision cost me everything. My job. My relationships with people I care about deeply. My reputation. I knew it could happen. And I did it anyway because next to Ashwiyaa's safety, nothing could compare.

"I still believe that. Her safety is still my priority. Her protection is still what I want more than anything."

He closed his eyes and remembered. How small she was as a baby and the awe with which he'd looked at her when she'd wrapped her tiny fingers around his that first time. How his mother had told him how important it was to be careful with the baby and how his father told him that her protection was now his job. How her big eyes melted him each time and how he would have moved earth itself to see her smile.

"I love her more than anything in this world. I always have. I always will."

He cleared his throat, shuffled his feet. His makizinan made the barest scrape across the floor. "My midewikwe told me lately that we all live the creation myth in our lives. We create a myth about our lives and people we love. That's the lie we live. Often, that myth gets destroyed. If we are lucky, it gets re-created out of the ashes of the lie we once believed. And that's what I believe this is. I once believed a lie about who Ashwiyaa was: that she was a helpless, traumatized child. She's thirty-two years old, and I still saw her as the child I had failed to protect. I see now that's not who she is. That's not who she ever was. So now I am with someone who is, in so many ways, a stranger. And yet in this re-creation, all I feel for her is what I have always felt for her: unconditional love.

"Nothing can give me back the years of my life that I lost when I believed the lie. And nothing can give me back the sister I thought I had—the person who never really existed. Therefore, I ask for nothing for myself. I ask for her. I ask that you give her what it turns out I could not: protection, care, and safety. Only when she has those three things will I be made whole. I was never whole to begin with, but knowing she is safe and cared for and protected is the closest I will ever be."

He sat down, his speech over. Niimi reached over and patted his shoulder. He hadn't realized it, but he was trembling.

"Thank you," said the Mediator, who had listened intently to Chibenashi's request. "Do you have any proposals for how we are to keep her safe? Would you, say, request that we return her to your care?"

Chibenashi laughed softly and shook his head. "I think I have shown that I am incapable of providing Ashwiyaa with the care, protection, and safety she needs."

The Mediator nodded. "I agree." He turned to Ashwiyaa's Advocate. "And is there anything that the Accused wishes to say on her behalf, either on her own or through her Advocate?"

Ashwiyaa's Advocate shook his head no. Next to him, Ashwiyaa still sat, stone-faced.

"Does the Accused have any objection to the requests of the Victim?"

Ashwiyaa's Advocate whispered in her ear, and she shook her head. "We do not," her Advocate said.

"Very well," the Mediator said. "These situations are so difficult. Family members who harm others are the greatest perversion of mino-bimaadiziwin; we cannot create a good life for our community if we cannot do so within our own families. I do not countenance stories of Wendigos. However, I do not disagree that I think something very terrible has possessed this poor woman. Whatever the cause, the effect is clear and unmistakable. The risk to her brother is great. Her betrayal of their relationship is horrible. And his love in the face of that betrayal is commendable."

He cleared his throat. "I do not often recommend imprisonment. It is counterproductive in most cases. It punishes rather than rehabilitates, offers little to no restitution to the Victims, and casts a shadow over the family. All around, it is a resolution of last resort, for it typically offers nothing to Victims or Accused. I am also cognizant that the father of both the Victim and Accused spent the last twenty years in gibaak-wa'odiiwigamig, which affected both. However, imprisonment under the right circumstances can create an opportunity for an Accused to receive help for issues that are causing them to harm others. I think such imprisonment may be appropriate here."

There was a gasp as Ashwiyaa broke her silence to protest. Her Advocate clasped her shoulder and whispered to her, shaking his head.

"It would provide the Victim with what he has requested: care, safety, and protection for his sister."

"Please, this is too much—" Ashwiyaa's Advocate protested.

"We are a Victim-driven system," the Mediator reminded the Advocate in a raised voice. "The goal is to make the Victim whole. He has expressed a wish that his sister be protected and cared for. Therefore, it makes sense to house her in a facility that will treat whatever is causing this—psychology, biology, Wendigo, what have you. She will be released upon a determination by a Healer and a Counselor that she is no longer a threat to herself, her family, or anyone else. Once that determination has been reached, she will of course be returned to her family."

Ashwiyaa made to respond, but her Advocate put his hand on hers and shook his head again.

"Is that acceptable to the Victim?"

Chibenashi thought long and hard about this. He didn't want her locked away—the ultimate punishment. But he thought again. His wants. Her needs. There was never any question about which he would choose, even now.

"She will get the help she needs?" he asked.

The Mediator nodded. "We have had tremendous success with others."

"Have they ever been released?"

The Mediator kept his expression even. "Some have."

Maybe there was hope for her after all.

"The Healers and Counselors will discuss. But, if I may say so, Chibenashi: you have spent twenty years as a caretaker. And your stated goal, then and now, has been for the help that your sister needs, correct? To care for and protect her, to keep her safe?"

Chibenashi nodded.

"Then I think the way to do that is for you to let go. Let someone else carry the burden for you."

"It's not a burden. It's love."

"Whatever word you choose to use to describe this, the point remains: you can best help your sister by not helping her. Let her go someplace where she will be cared for, treated. With that help, you will be made whole. And that would be the best solution for all involved, correct?"

After a few long moments, Chibenashi nodded, a lump forming in his throat.

"Becoming whole after a loss is not painless," the Mediator said. "But I find that it is often worth the cost."

Chibenashi felt a tap on his shoulder. Dakaasin. She leaned forward and whispered, "I've had some great successes with this solution. She really will be taken care of. It's not like the place where they held your father. She'll get the help she needs. And hopefully she'll come home to you one day. You could be a real family together."

It was more than he deserved, this reassurance. Even if it was a lie, it helped. He cradled it close. He nodded and smiled, the lump in his throat too thick to allow any words out.

"Then if there is nothing further?" No one said anything. "We are resolved," the Mediator said. Everyone remained seated while he took his leave.

"This is good," Niimi said. "Isn't it?"

Chibenashi shrugged. "I hope so." He looked over to Ashwiyaa's table, where his tearful sister was being prepared to go to prison. "Can I see her before she goes?"

Niimi hesitated, then nodded.

Chibenashi walked over to Ashwiyaa's table and knelt beside her chair. He touched his hand to hers. She flinched.

"I meant what I said," he told her with conviction. "I love you. I always have. I always will."

Ashwiyaa looked at him through tear-filled eyes. "Then why are you letting them do this to me?"

"Because I love you, and I serve you best by letting you go."

"You're letting them hurt me."

He swallowed, the lump in his throat thickening. "Seeing you so tormented? That hurts me the most. I hope this will help you. And when it does, no matter how long it takes, I will be waiting. Arms open."

◆ ◆ ◆

"So now what?"

Chibenashi turned at the sound of Peezhickee's voice. The Mediation room was empty, save for the two of them. He answered honestly. "I'm not sure."

Peezhickee nodded. "Perhaps that is not a bad thing."

"That doesn't make it a good thing."

"I never said it was. Sometimes it's enough that it isn't bad."

Chibenashi nodded. "I suppose that's what I deserve, after what I did."

"You deserve happiness, Chibenashi, as all of us do. It's like I told you before: time to live a little. Perhaps that reconstruction can apply to yourself too. You destroyed your honor. Perhaps you could rebuild it with a new life. Everything that tied you down is now gone. This is an opportunity that few receive. I hope you will not squander it."

Chibenashi smiled. "I didn't think you would wish the best for me."

"It is as the Mediator said: A purely punitive approach to life accomplishes nothing. When one of us redeems himself, we are all stronger. I believe you can do it. I believe that you will reward my faith."

Chapter Thirty-Two

Anishinaabe Moon: Manoomin Giizis (Ricing Moon)
Islamic Calendar: 13 Muharram 1443
Chinese Calendar: Cycle 78, year 38, month 7, day 15 (Year of the Ox)
Hebrew Calendar: 14 Elul 5781
Mayan Calendar: 13.0.8.14.6
Gregorian Calendar: Sunday, 22 August 2021
Ethiopian Calendar: 16 Nahas 2013

The trees were full of ripe apples waiting to be eaten. The cranes glided under the scattered clouds in the blue sky. The trees swayed in the wind, the bees buzzed, and the lilacs were small fireworks of color as they reached full bloom. You could smell the raspberries no matter where you were. The town was once again overrun with tourists taking in the natural splendor. They skimmed Baawitigong's surface, but it was the life of the locals that was blossoming.

Chibenashi stood in his empty wigwam for the last time.

It was the morning of the new Ricing Moon, the first day of Manoomin. One year had passed since Meoquanee's murder. Ashwiyaa had been gone for half that time. Two moons had passed since the Mediation. Chibenashi had not visited his sister yet. Her Advocate had conveyed the message: Don't come. Not yet. Maybe not ever.

His life had changed so much from last Manoomin, and yet it was unchanged in a key respect: he still had a family member incarcerated. It had been a shameful shadow in his life—always there, lurking, attached to him physically. But now the shame was gone. Even though he was still associated with someone in prison, he felt that it did not define him in a way that it had in prior years. He'd focused all his attention on Ashwiyaa to compensate for it. Now it was just a fact of his life. A sad fact, to be sure. One that he would not wish on anyone. But it was a part of his history. Not a part of his future.

With a satisfied sigh, Chibenashi walked over to the door. He turned back for one last look. Most of his possessions were gone, taken to the recyclers or redistributed to the community. In his hand was his bag, which held the few things he wanted to keep: His mother's dream catcher. His father's drum. The photograph of Meoquanee and his mother. And, wrapped around it all, Ashwiyaa's blanket that she'd cocooned herself in for so many years. He would carry them with him as he went forward. Jangling next to them was a new phone. It was wiped clean, empty, ready for new things to be loaded: new contacts, new photographs, new communications. The bag was light, and Chibenashi was even lighter. A weight he'd never realized he'd been carrying had been left behind, and though he felt weary from the effort of carrying it all these years, its absence made him aware of his strength.

He opened the door and looked out into the open, wide world. On a day as gorgeous as today, anything seemed possible.

He stepped through the doorway. Sunlight kissed his forehead. He took the first step of many. He did not look back.

GLOSSARY OF
ANISHINAABEMOWIN TERMS

Animikii Binesi: Thunderbird, a mythical bird that has power to both punish and protect. A central figure in Anishinaabe mythology.

Animosh(ag): Dog. The use of apostrophes is not used to indicate possession in Anishinaabemowin. The use of the suffix *an* after the noun is used to indicate that it belongs to the noun before it.

Anishinaabe-Aki: Land of the Anishinaabe.

Anishinaabeg: Ojibwe, Odawa, and Potawatomi people, the people of the council of three fires, original people lowered to the earth. "Ojibwe" means "people who wear the puckered moccasins"; "Odawa" means "people who trade." "Powawatomi" or "Bodewotm" means "keepers of the fire."

Anishinaabemowin: The language of the Anishinaabe.

Anishinaabewi-gichigami: Literally "Lake of the Anishinaabe," commonly referred to as Lake Superior.

Apane: "Always."

Apichi/Apichiwag: Robin(s).

Baaga'adowewin: Stickball, a game that inspired the game that is commonly referred to as lacrosse.

Baakwaanaatig: Sumac.

Baawitigong: Literally "Land of the Rapids," commonly referred to as the cities of Sault Ste. Marie, Michigan; and Sault Ste. Marie, Ontario, Canada.

Bagidinigewin: Burial rites.

Biidaabin: Represents sunrise.

Boozhoo: A greeting similar to "Hello."

Bagonagiizhi: The constellation typically referred to as Pleiades.

Dakoniwewigamig(ong): Police station or police department.

Dibaajimowinan: Another way to say "stories"; these are said to be told during the time of Biboon (winter) also.

Doodem(ag): Clan(s), represented by animals, water, trees, and weather, and patrilineal in nature.

Emikwaan: Turtle shell.

Ganatsekwyagon: What is commonly referred to as Toronto, Canada.

Gashkibidaagan: A large shoulder bag covered in beaded floral patterns, historically made by women and worn by men.

Gibaakwa'odiiwigamig: Prison.

Gichigami(in): A sea or large lake, or multiple seas and large lakes.

Gichi-manidoo: Great Spirit.

Giiwigaabaw: Kickapoo people.

Hocągara: Ho-Chunk people.

Ininwewi-gichigami: Literally "Illinois's Sea," commonly referred to as Lake Michigan.

Jiibeygamig: Cemetery.

Jiibeygamigoons(an): Spirit house(s)—a small house built atop a grave in which offerings for the journey to the spirit world are placed.

Makizin(an): Shoe(s).

Mamaceqtaw: Minomini people.

Manoomin: Wild rice.

Mashkikiwinini: Doctor/healer.

Maskoutench: Mascouten people.

Mayagi-anishinaabe: Foreign, not of the Anishinaabe.

Meme: Pileated woodpecker.

Meshkwahkihaki: Fox people.

Midewinini/Midewikwe: Medicine Man or Woman, respectively, a spiritual leader belonging to Midewiwin.

Midewiwin: Literally "The Way of the Heart" or medicine society.

Miine!: A phrase used to emphasize surprise.

Minawaa giga-waabamin: "I'll see you again"; the closest word the Anishinaabe have for "goodbye."

Mino-Aki: Literally "The Good Land," name of the nation located in what is commonly referred to as the North American Great Lakes region.

Mino-bimaadiziwin: The "Good Life," or good living as a result of good living, similar in concept to karma.

Mishi-bizhiw: A constellation made up of the stars of the constellations typically referred to as Leo and Hydra.

Misko-bineshiinh(yag): Cardinal(s).

Miskwaadesi: Painted turtle.

Mnaadendamowin: Respect.

Myaamia/T'wah T'wah: Miami people.

Naadowewi-gichigami: Literally "Iroquois' Sea," commonly referred to as Lake Huron.

Naano-nibiimaang gichigamiin: Literally "The Five Great Lakes," or "The Five Freshwater Seas," commonly referred to as the Great Lakes.

Neshnabé: Potawatomi people.

Ngashi: "My mother."

Niibin: Represents summertime.

Nindawemaa: "My brother."

Ningwis: "My son."

Nishiime: "My little sister."

Noos: "My father."

Odawaa: Ottawa people.

Ojiig: Constellation typically referred to as the Big Dipper / Ursa Major.

Okosimaan: Pumpkin.

Omiimii(wag): Passenger pigeon(s).

Othâkîwa: Sauk people.

Panzacola: Commonly referred to as Pensacola, Florida.

Shawanwaki: Shawnee people.

Shikaakwa: Commonly referred to as Chicago, Illinois.

Shkitaaganaaboo: Bark tea.

Shkwaa Naakwe: The afternoon, midday.

Tooadijik: People who play sports similar to ice hockey.

Tooadiwin: Sport similar to ice hockey.

Wiigwaasi-mashkikigamig: Birchbark medicine lodge.

Wiikwedong: Keenaw Bay, near what is commonly referred to as Marquette, Michigan.

Wyandot: Huron people.

Zhaan: "Go."

ACKNOWLEDGMENTS

Sharing this book with the world is a dream come true, and I have so many people to thank for making it happen.

Thank you to my agent, Sara Megibow, this book's eternal champion, for plucking me from the slush pile and holding my hand through this process.

I am grateful to the wonderful team at 47North. I particularly want to thank my editors Melissa Valentine and Adrienne Procaccini, for their enthusiasm and care for this story, and Charlotte Herscher, for helping shape it into something better than I could have done on my own. Thank you to the eagle-eyed copyeditors and proofreaders who caught my errors and pointed out my inconsistencies.

Thank you to Molly von Borstel for the jaw-droppingly beautiful cover.

Miigwech to Elizabeth M. Carrick and the First Nations speakers for their Anishinaabemowin language review. Not only did they improve the Anishinaabemowin in the book, they ensured that we used the Anishinaabemowin that is closest to that which was spoken in precolonial times. Any errors or inconsistencies in the Anishinaabemowin you may find in the book are mine, not theirs.

I also want to thank Laura Wally Johnson, Stacey Parshall Jensen, Lydia Redwine, Ayesha Abdul Ghaffar, Jesslyn Chain, Leah Blanchard, and Brooks Kohler for their invaluable feedback on earlier drafts of this story.

Thank you to my Blanchard relatives for the stories they've told and Chippewa traditions and histories they've shared with me. Thank you to my uncle Edmund Blanchard for connecting me with so many resources and people, including his materials from the Newton Township Historical Society; my dad, Gerry Blanchard, for sharing his knowledge, research, and photographs; and my aunt Eirnella O'Neil, for her permission to put my late uncle James O'Neil's picture of the Binesi outlined in lightning on Dakaasin's wall—it's a real photograph, called "The Thunderbird," and it's beautiful. Thank you to my fellow Sault Tribe members for their invaluable help with finding the right resources for additional research. I'm particularly indebted to the works of Basil Johnson, Andrew Blackbird, and Frances Desnmore; information from the Saginaw Indian Tribe of Chippewa's Ziibiwing Center of Anishinaabe Culture and Lifeways; the *Historical Atlas of Native Americans* by Dr. Ian Barnes; *Atlas of Great Lakes Indian History* by Helen Hornbeck Tanner; *Eating with the Seasons: Anishinaabeg, Great Lakes Region* by Derek Nicholas; the Albany Government Law Review article "Anishinaabe Law and The Round House" by Matthew L. M. Fletcher; and the Decolonial Atlas website.

Thank you to Hayes Shair for answering my questions about architecture. The living skyscrapers and vertical forests in this book are sadly not my invention—real buildings and entire cities are already being proposed around the world, such as in the Middle East and China. There is so much wonderful, innovative, and sustainable architecture out there that is worth checking out, and I'd like to think that if history had turned out a little differently, buildings that incorporate nature would have become commonplace long ago.

Thank you to Julia Walton for your moral support and encouragement. Thank you to Daphne Landa for watching my children so I could finish the edits to this book!

And finally, thank you to my husband, Toufic, and daughters, Poppy and Lily, for everything. I love you beyond words. This is all for you.

ABOUT THE AUTHOR

B. L. Blanchard is a graduate of the UC Davis creative writing honors program and was a writing fellow at Boston University School of Law. She is a lawyer and enrolled member of the Sault Ste. Marie Tribe of Chippewa Indians. She is originally from the Upper Peninsula of Michigan but has lived in California for so long that she can no longer handle cold weather, and resides in San Diego with her husband and two daughters. *The Peacekeeper* is her debut novel. For more information, visit www.blblanchard.com or follow her on Twitter @blblanchard.